LUNCH LADY

2-FOR-1 SPECIAL

The First Helping
books 1 & 2

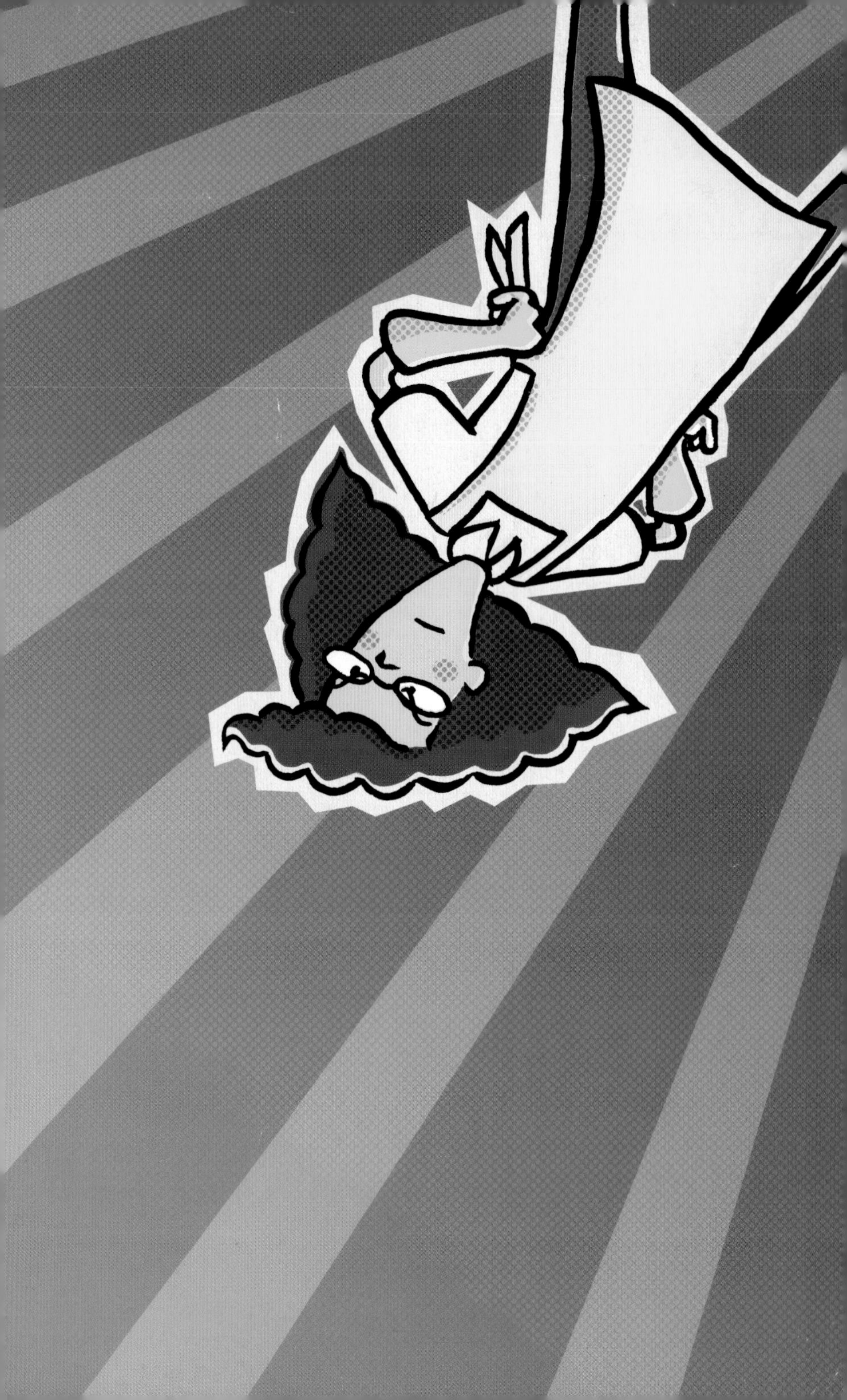

Jarrett J. Krosoczka

LUNCH LADY

2-FOR-1 SPECIAL

The First Helping
books 1 & 2

colors by
Joey Weiser

Alfred A. Knopf 🐕 New York

THIS IS A BORZOI BOOK PUBLISHED BY ALFRED A. KNOPF

 Published in the United States by Alfred A. Knopf, an imprint of Random House Children's Books, a division of Penguin Random House LLC, New York. The titles in this work were originally published separately and in paperback in the United States by Alfred A. Knopf, an imprint of Random House Children's Books, a division of Penguin Random House LLC, New York, in 2009.

Knopf, Borzoi Books, and the colophon are registered trademarks of Penguin Random House LLC.

Visit us on the Web! rhcbooks.com
Educators and librarians, for a variety of teaching tools, visit us at RHTeachersLibrarians.com

The Library of Congress has cataloged the individual books under the following Control Numbers: 2008004709 (The Cyborg Substitute), 2008043117 (The League of Librarians).

ISBN 978-0-593-37742-0 (trade)

The text of this book is written in 12-point CCHedgeBackwardsLower.
The illustrations in this book were created using ink on paper and digital coloring.

MANUFACTURED IN CHINA
November 2021
10 9 8 7 6 5 4 3 2 1

First Omnibus Edition

Random House Children's Books supports the First Amendment and celebrates the right to read.

FOR MY G AND
RALPH MACCHIO THE PUG
—J.J.K.

CONTENTS

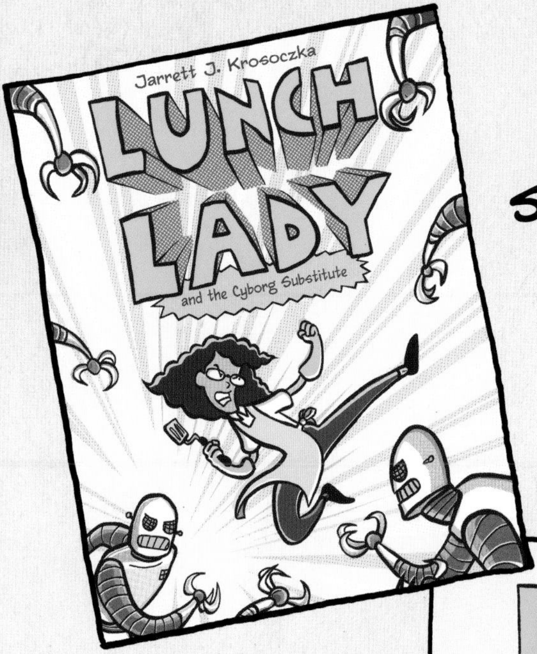
Jarrett J. Krosoczka
LUNCH LADY
and the Cyborg Substitute

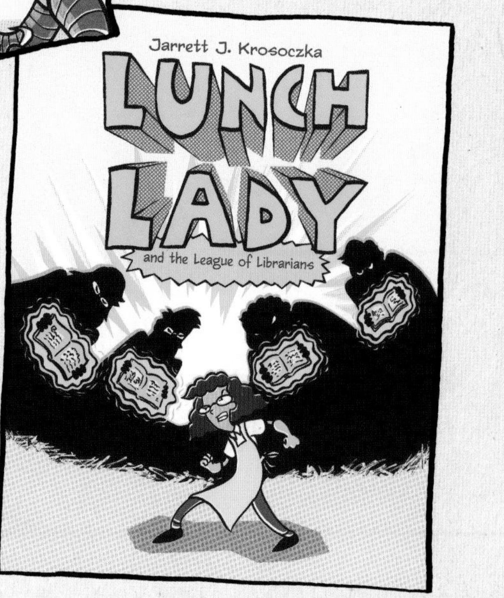
Jarrett J. Krosoczka
LUNCH LADY
and the League of Librarians

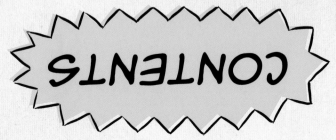

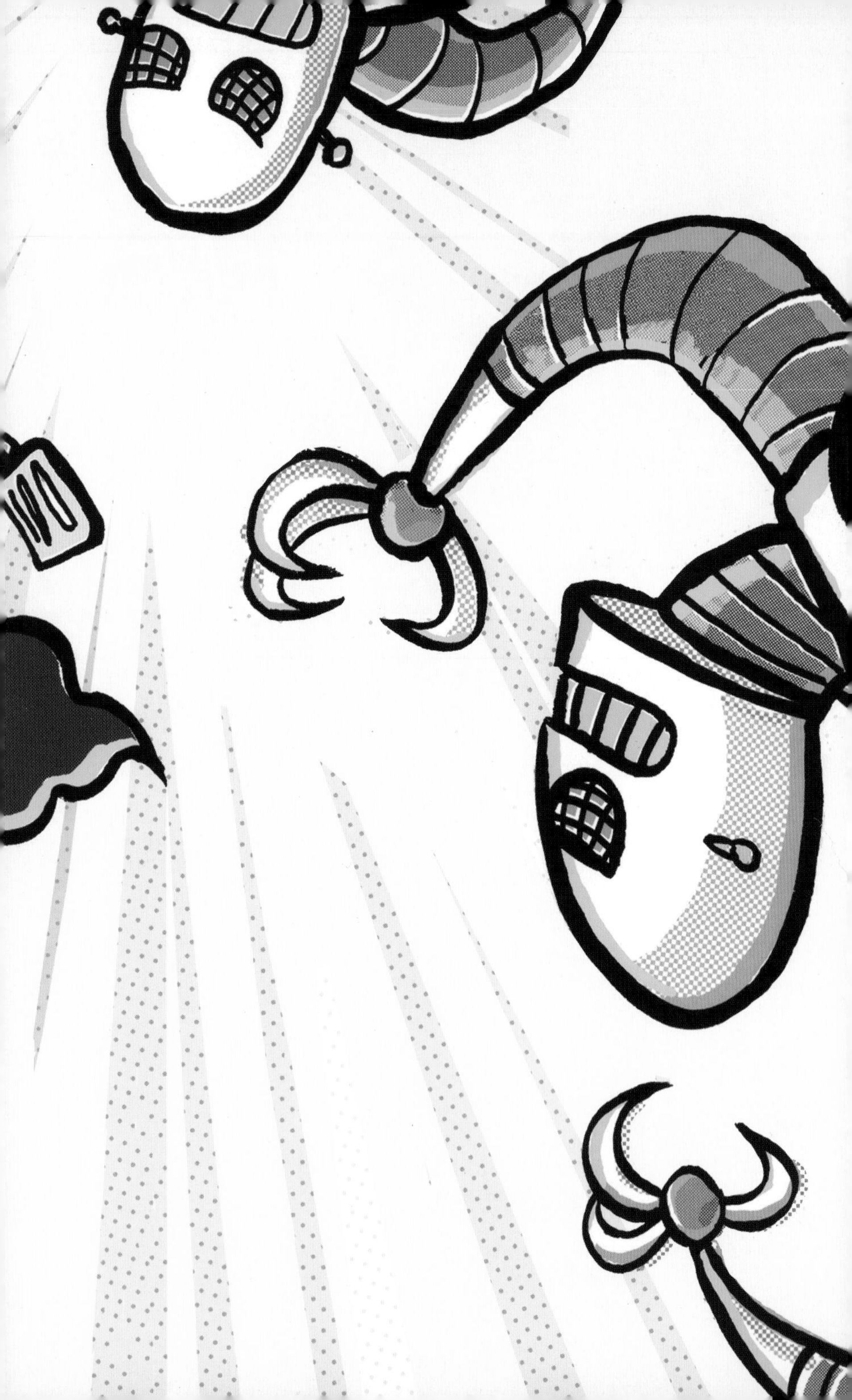

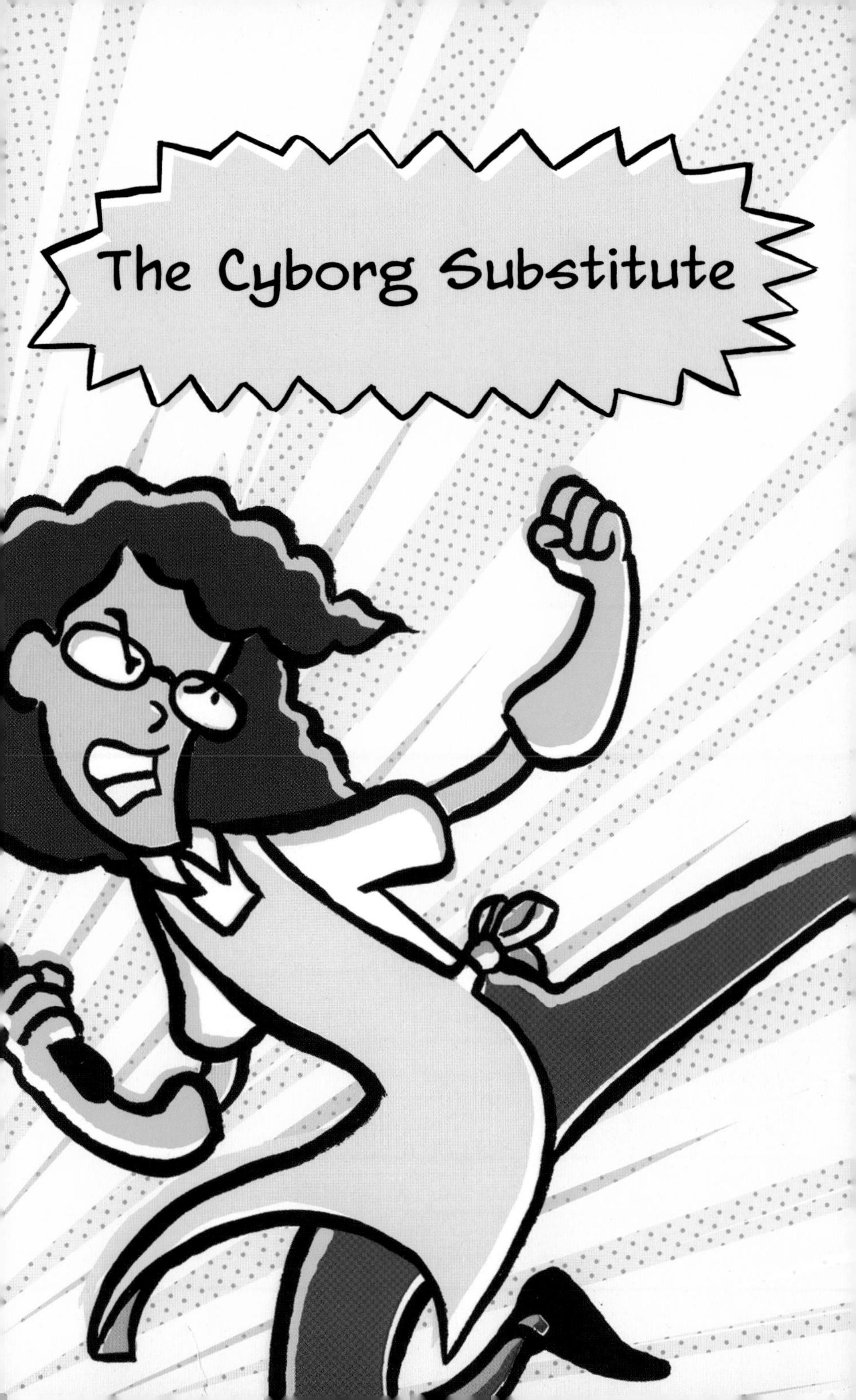
The Cyborg Substitute

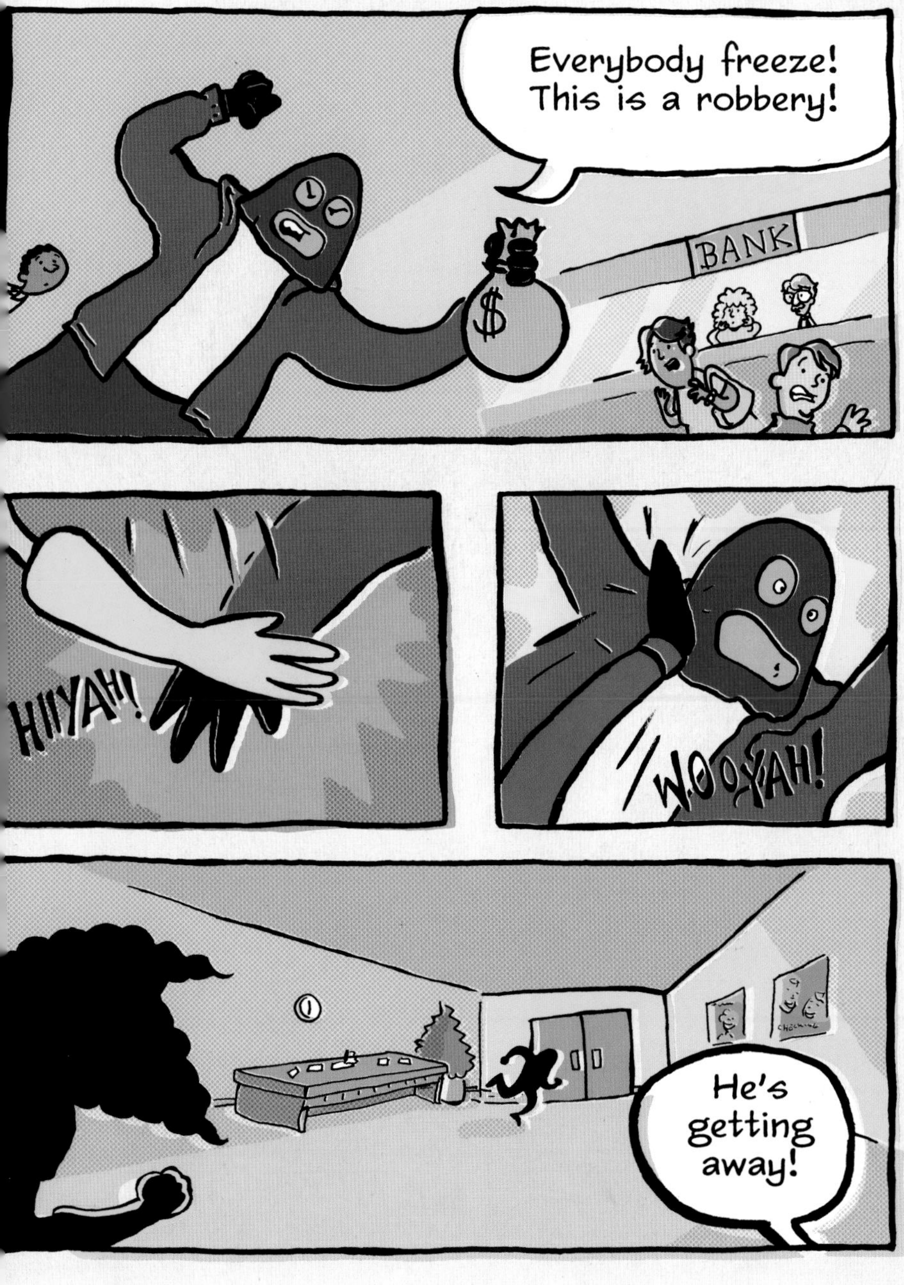
Everybody freeze! This is a robbery!
BANK
HIIYAH!
WOOYAH!
He's getting away!

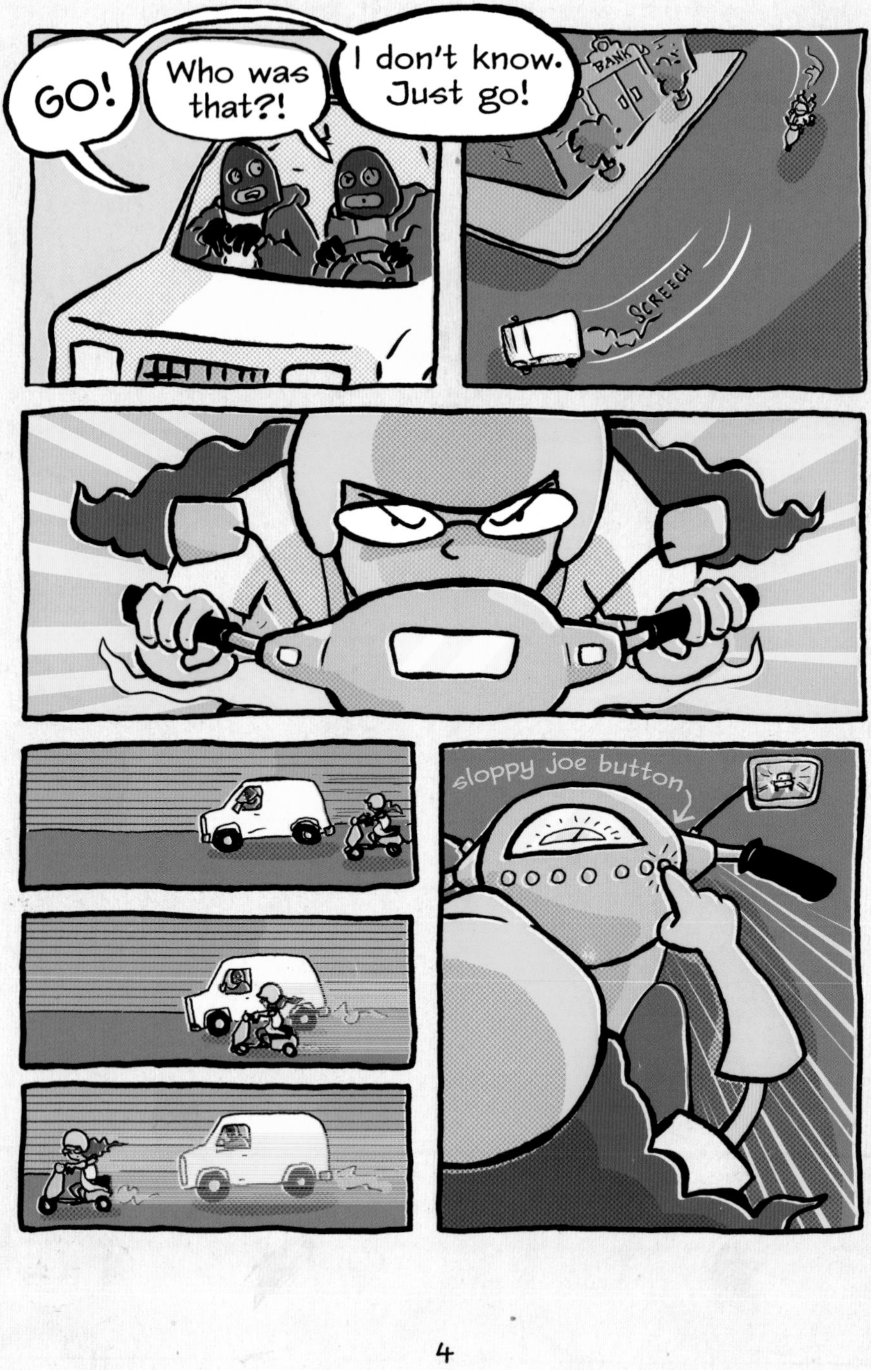
GO!
Who was that?!
I don't know. Just go!
BANK
SCREECH
sloppy joe button

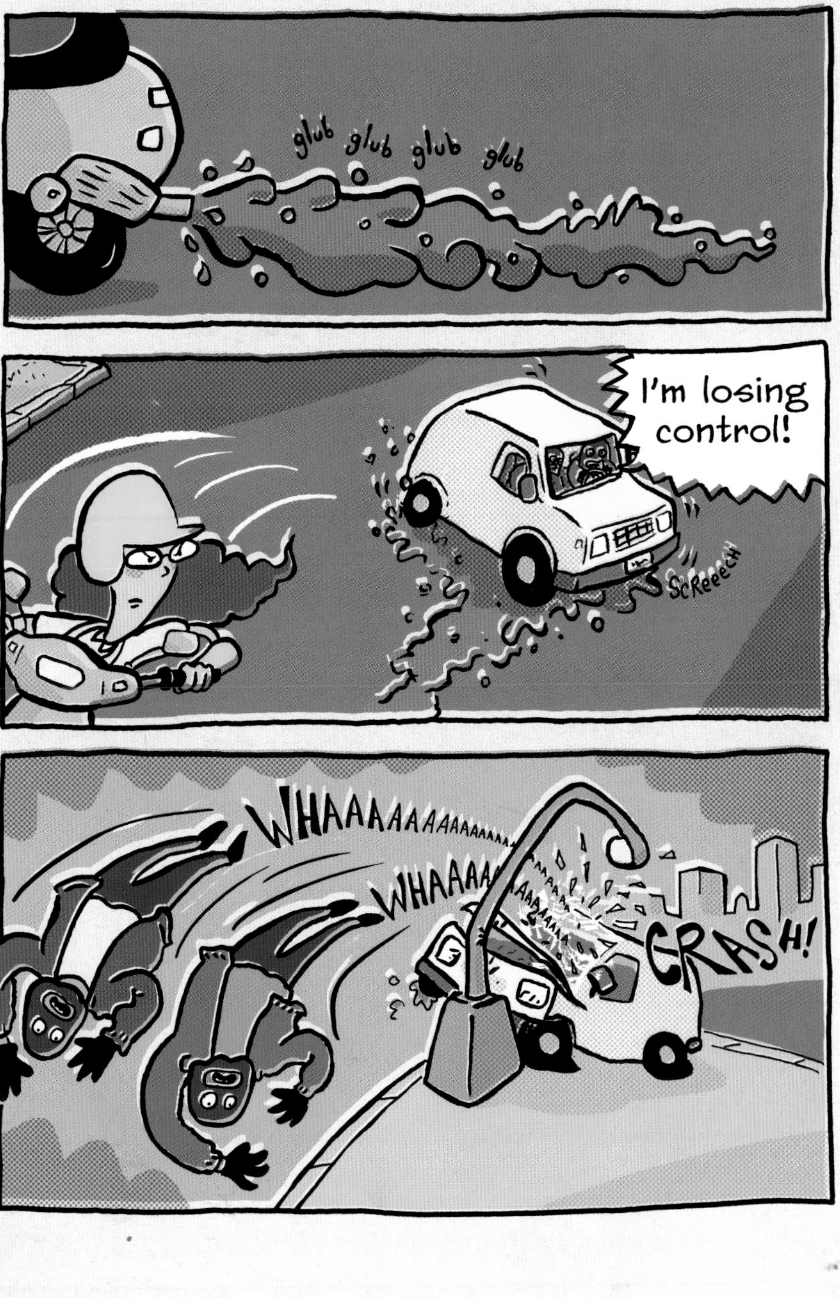
glub glub glub glub
I'm losing control!
SCREEECH
WHAAAAAAAAAAAAAAAAA
WHAAAAAAAAAAAAAA
CRASH!

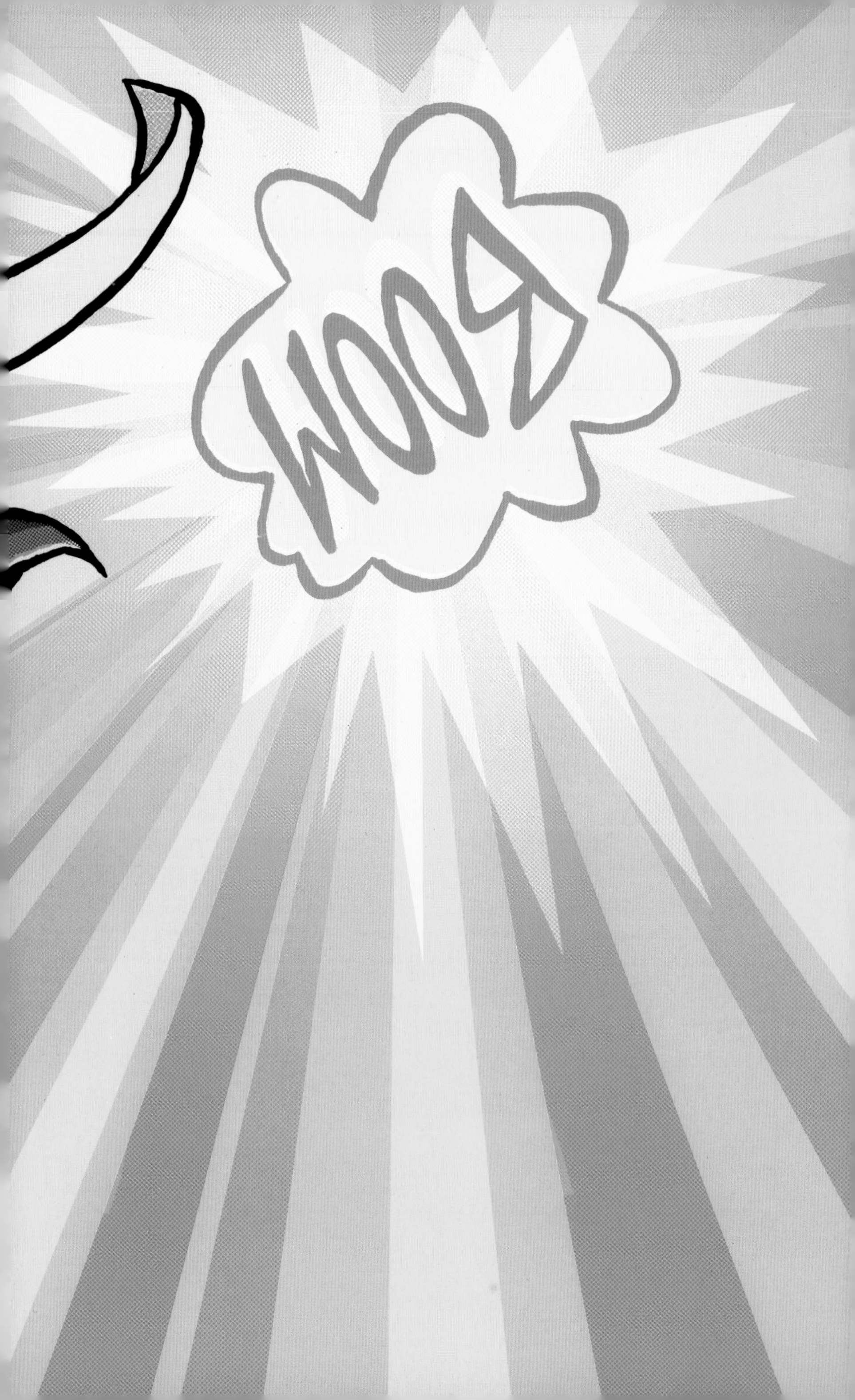
BOOM

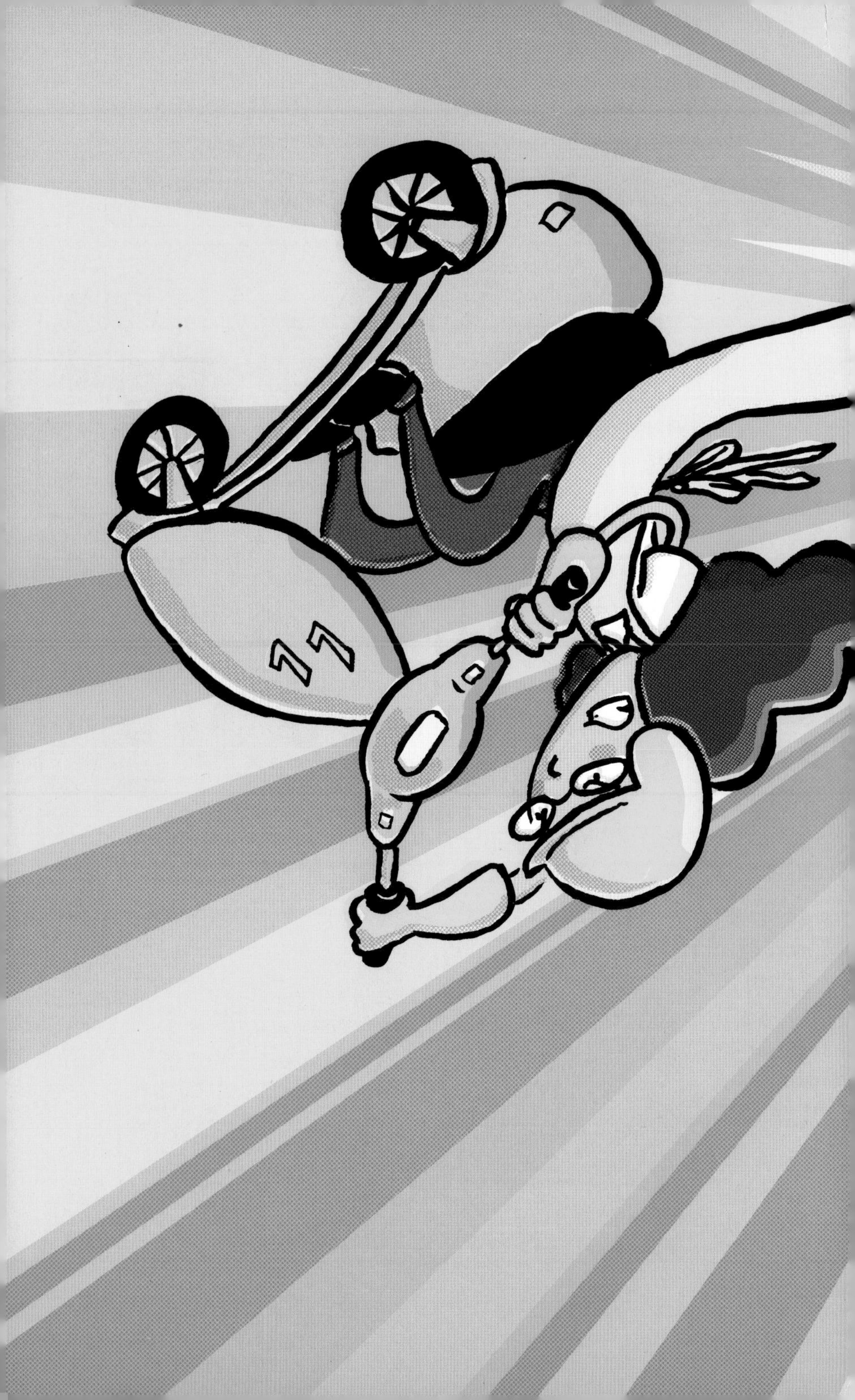

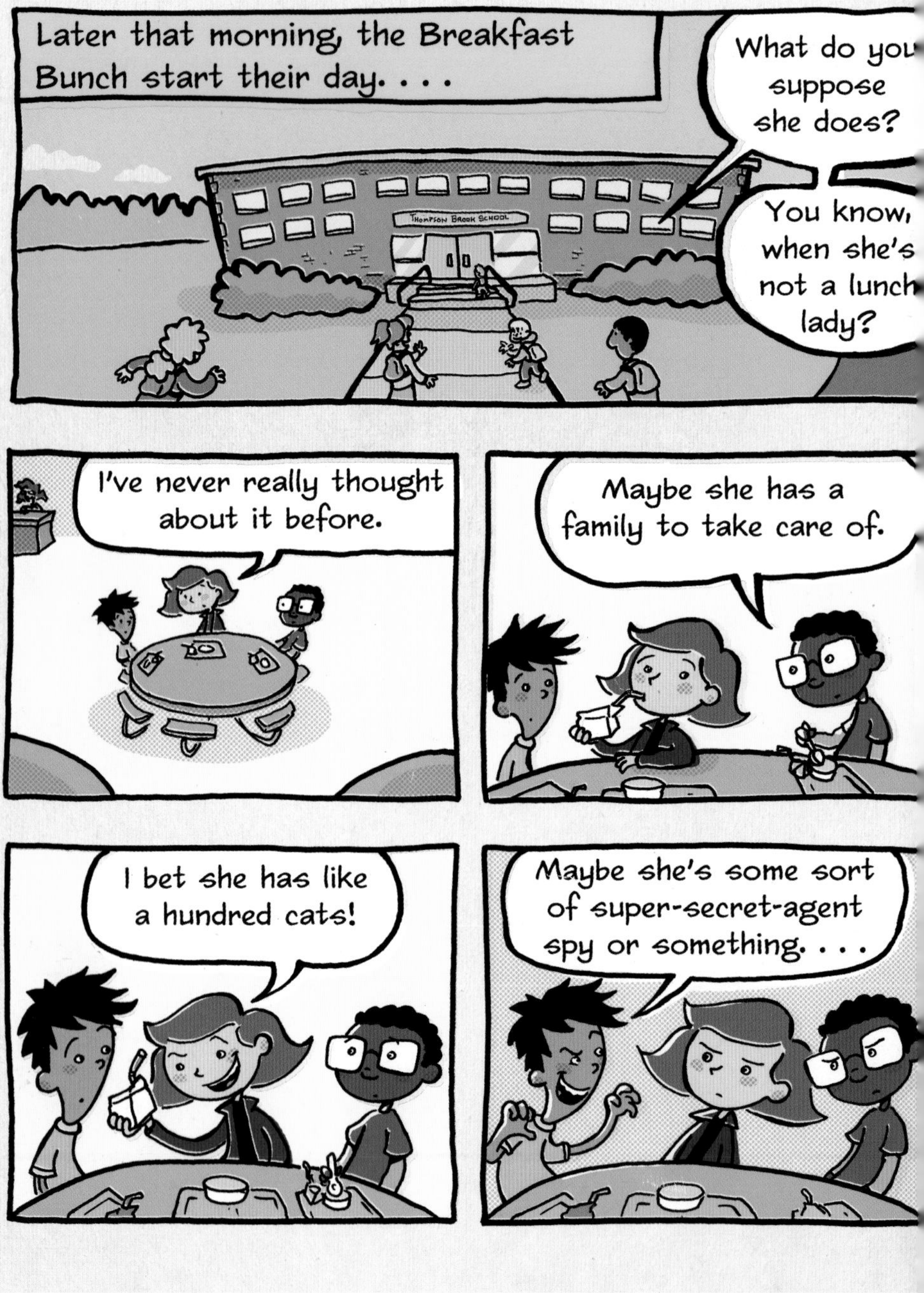
Later that morning, the Breakfast Bunch start their day. . . .
What do you suppose she does?
You know, when she's not a lunch lady?
THOMPSON BROOK SCHOOL
I've never really thought about it before.
Maybe she has a family to take care of.
I bet she has like a hundred cats!
Maybe she's some sort of super-secret-agent spy or something. . . .

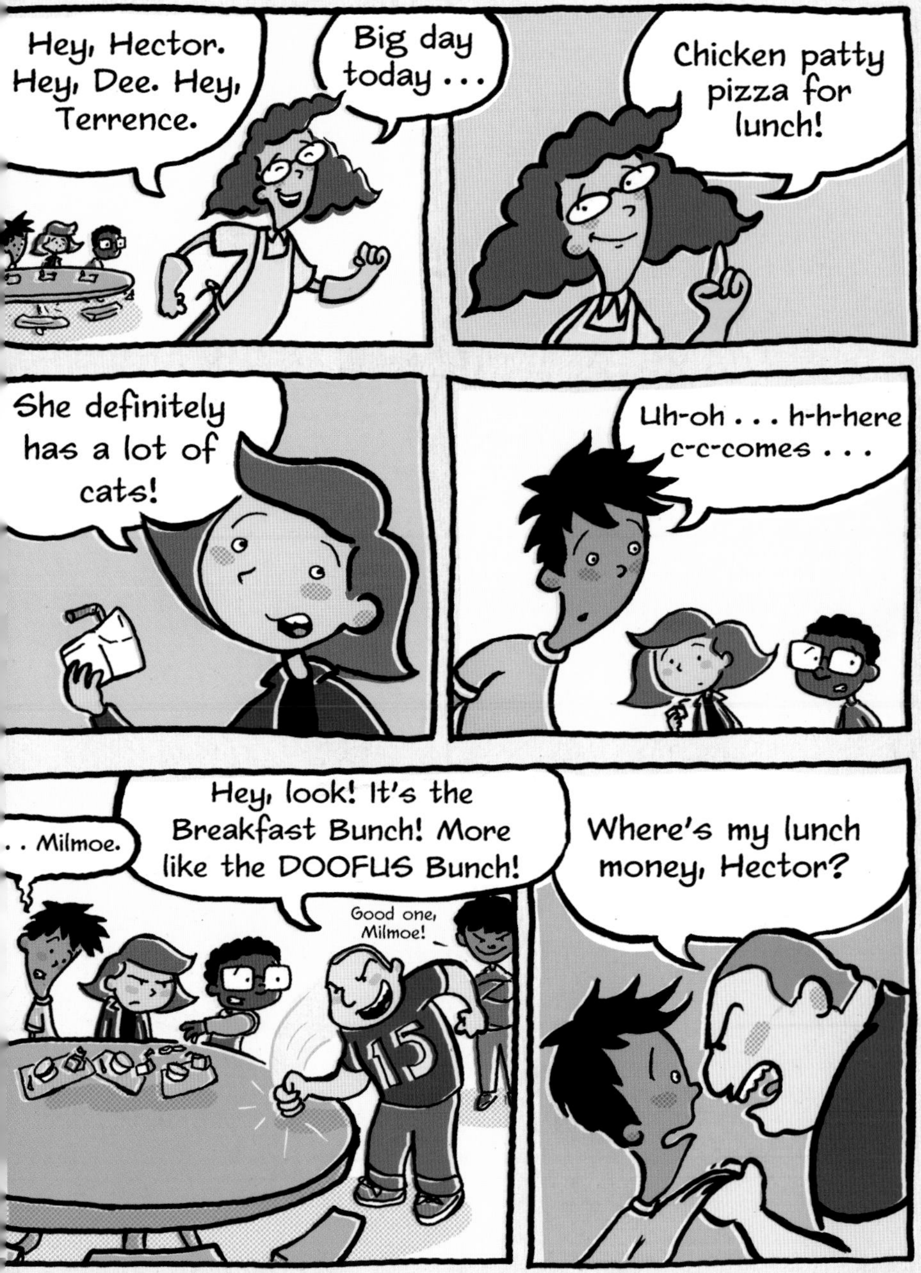
Hey, Hector. Hey, Dee. Hey, Terrence.
Big day today . . .
Chicken patty pizza for lunch!
She definitely has a lot of cats!
Uh-oh . . . h-h-here c-c-comes . . .
. . Milmoe.
Hey, look! It's the Breakfast Bunch! More like the DOOFUS Bunch!
Good one, Milmoe!
Where's my lunch money, Hector?

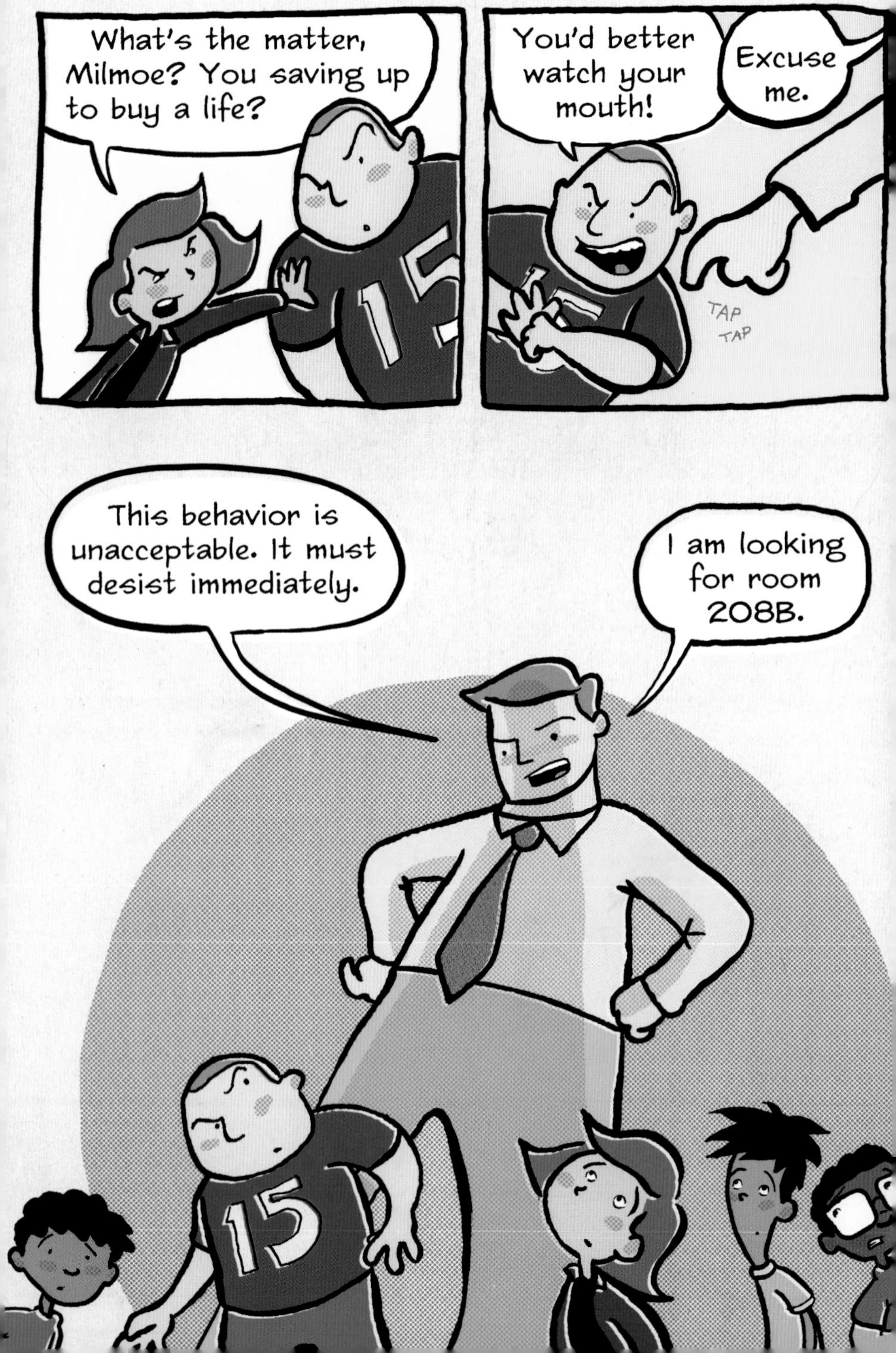
What's the matter, Milmoe? You saving up to buy a life?
You'd better watch your mouth!
Excuse me.
TAP TAP
This behavior is unacceptable. It must desist immediately.
I am looking for room 208B.

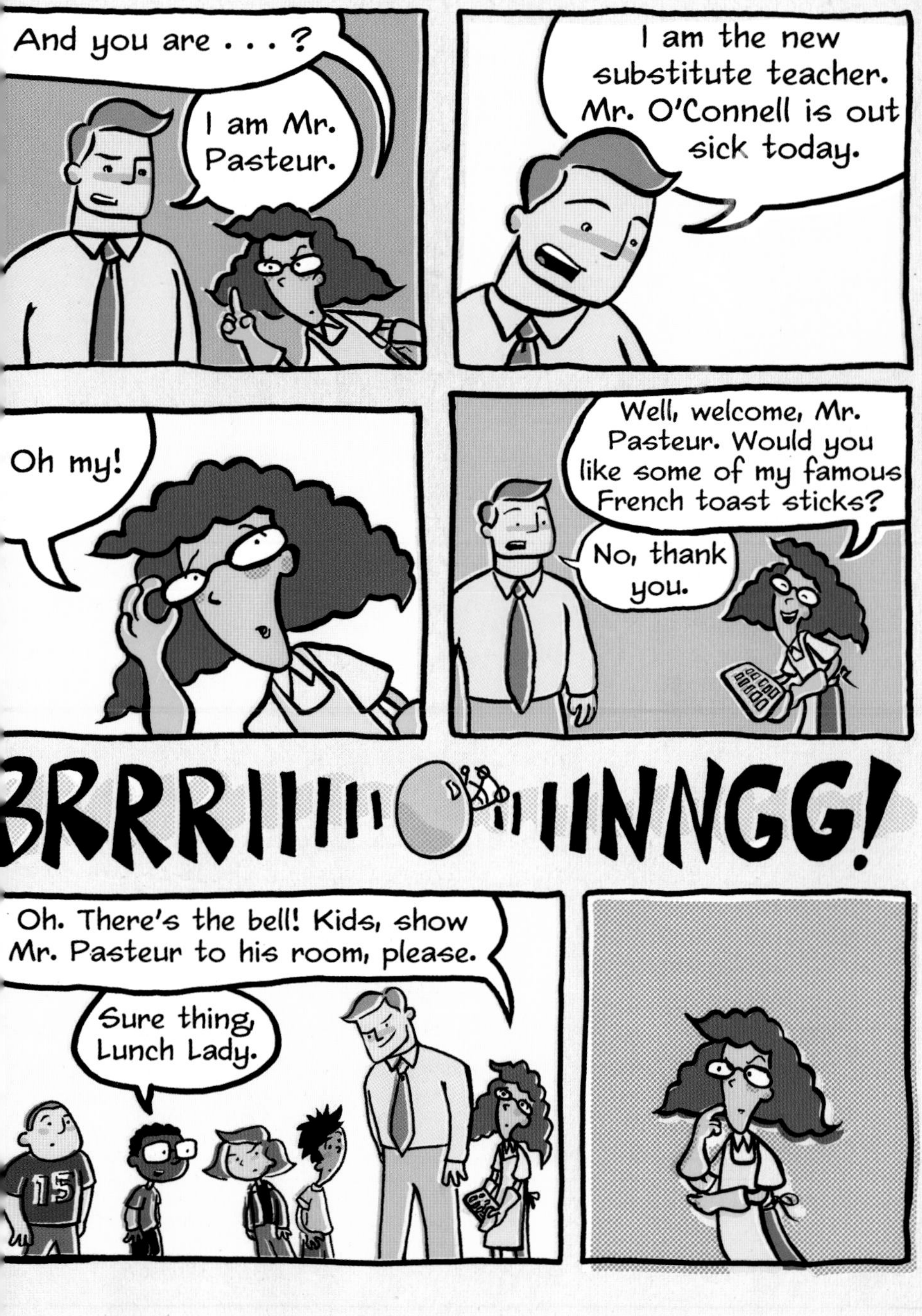
And you are . . . ?
I am Mr. Pasteur.
I am the new substitute teacher. Mr. O'Connell is out sick today.
Oh my!
Well, welcome, Mr. Pasteur. Would you like some of my famous French toast sticks?
No, thank you.
BRRRIIII IINNGG!
Oh. There's the bell! Kids, show Mr. Pasteur to his room, please.
Sure thing, Lunch Lady.
15

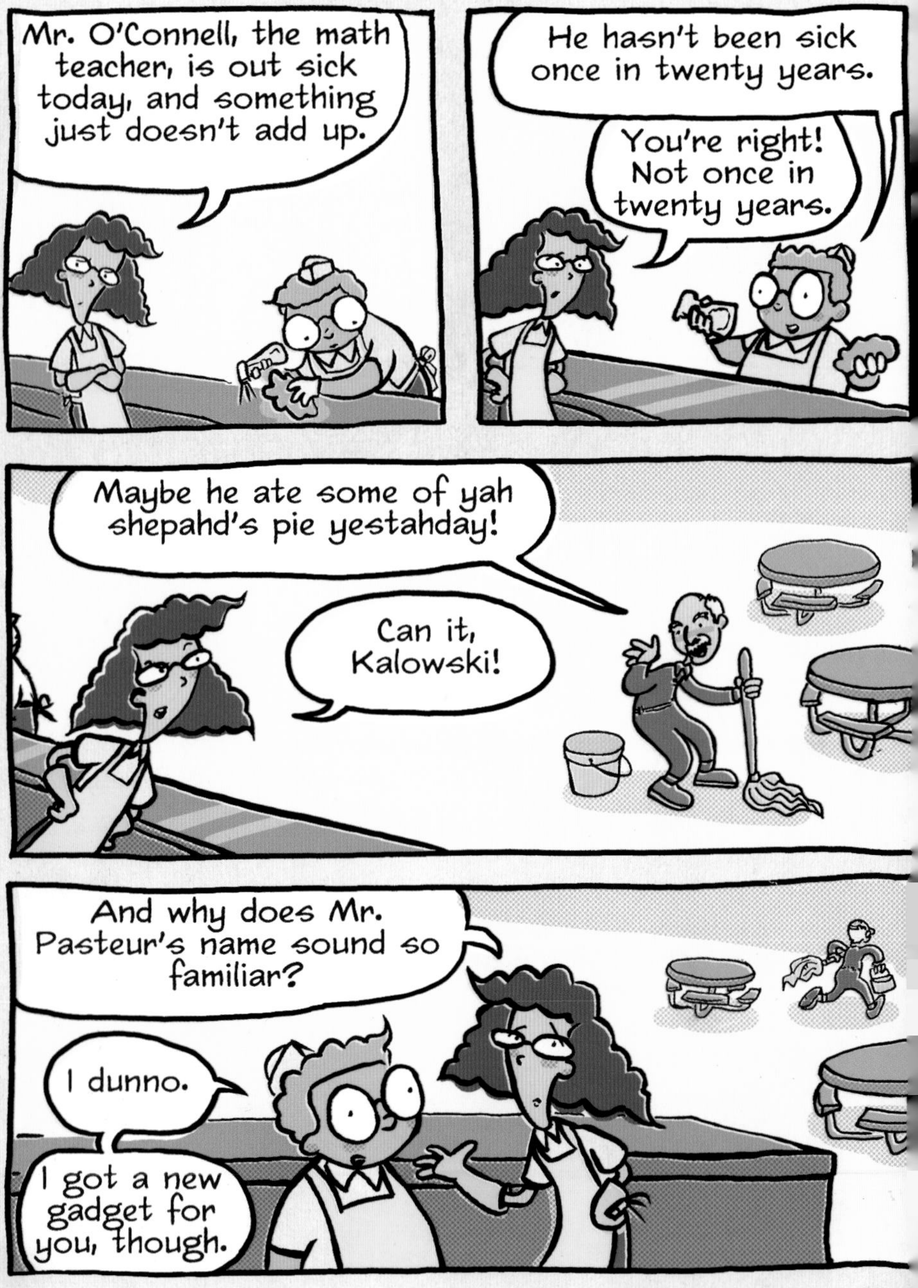
Mr. O'Connell, the math teacher, is out sick today, and something just doesn't add up.
He hasn't been sick once in twenty years.
You're right! Not once in twenty years.
Maybe he ate some of yah shepahd's pie yestahday!
Can it, Kalowski!
And why does Mr. Pasteur's name sound so familiar?
I dunno.
I got a new gadget for you, though.

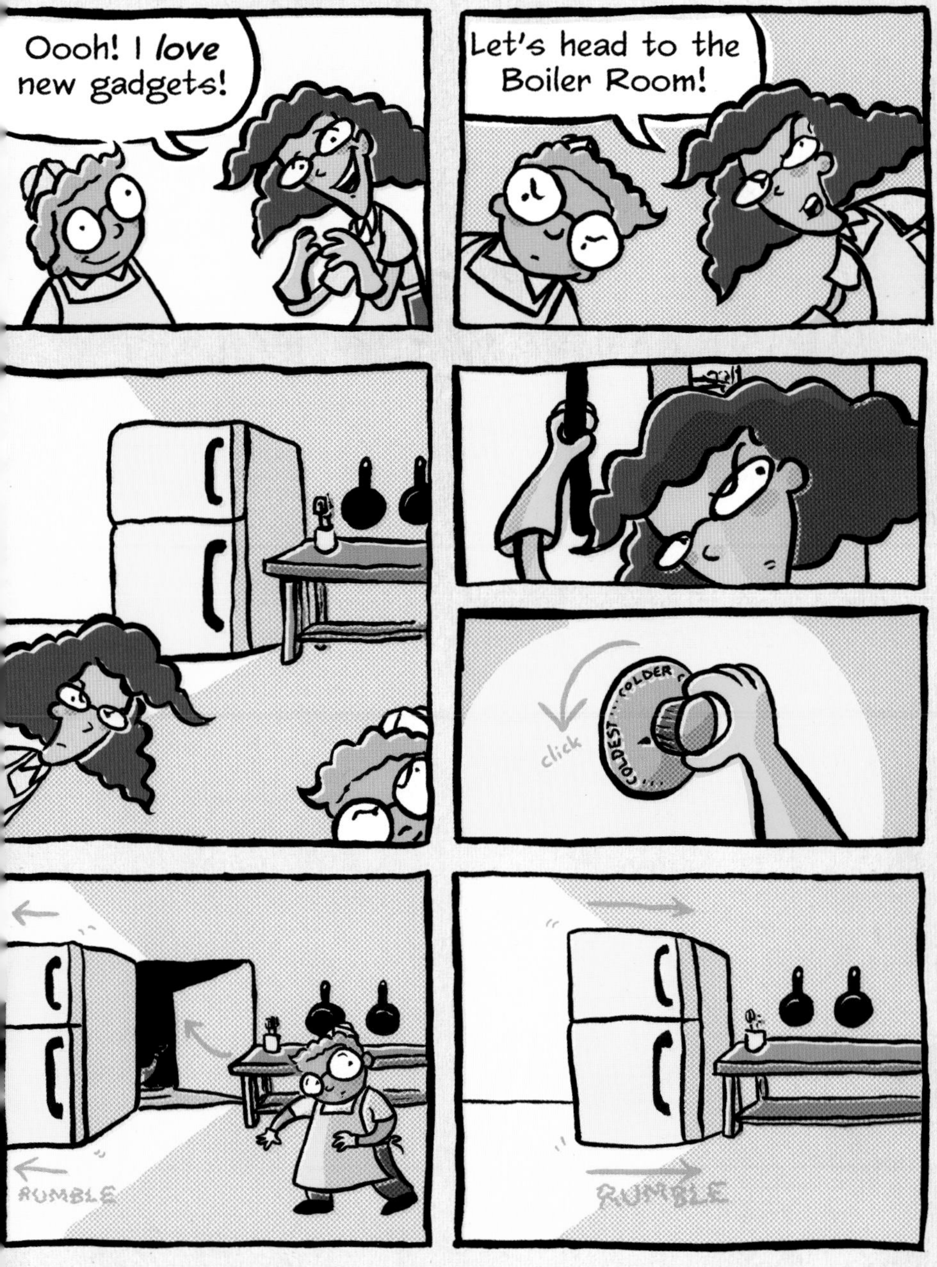
Oooh! I *love* new gadgets!
Let's head to the Boiler Room!
COLDEST ... COLDER
click
RUMBLE
RUMBLE

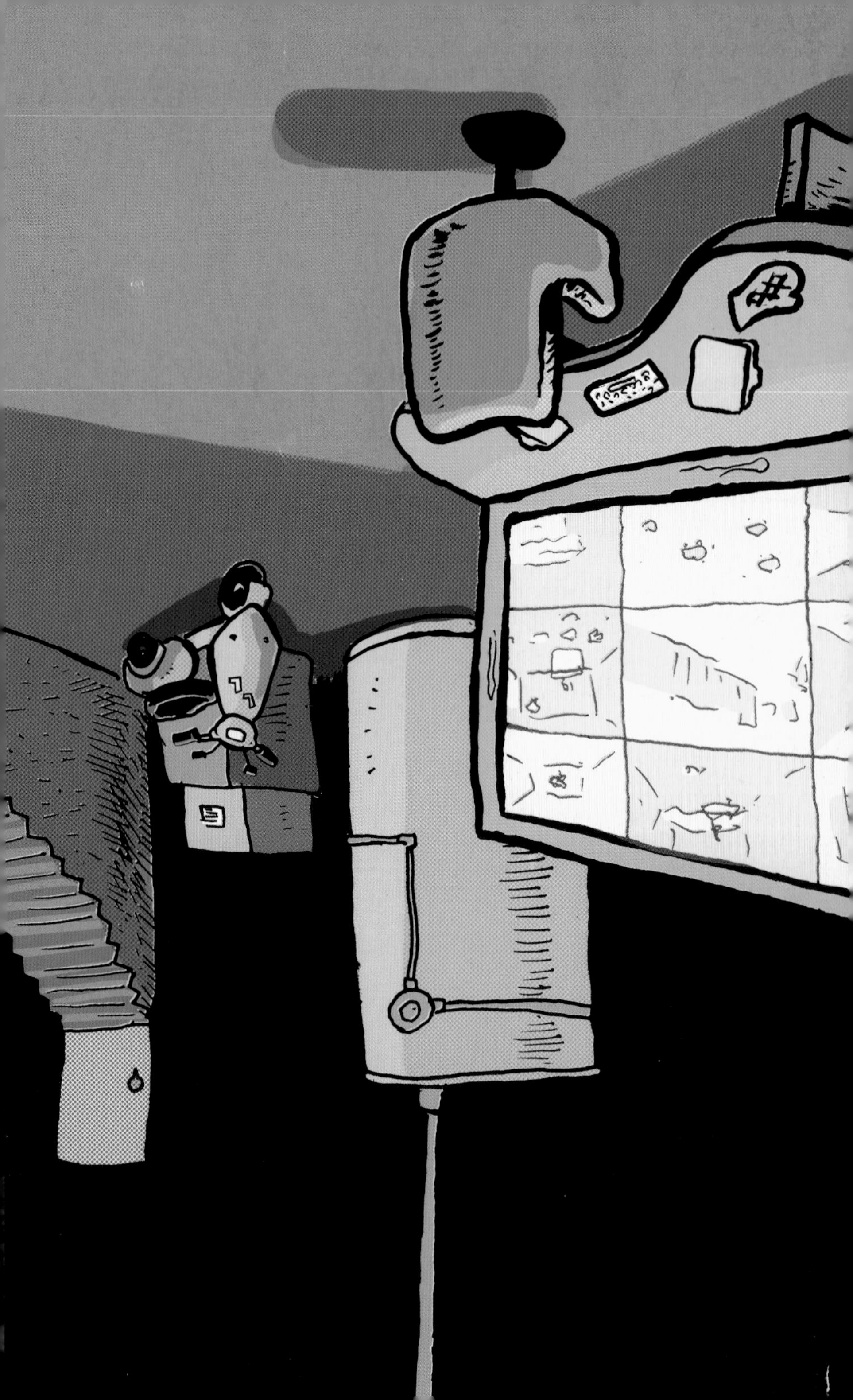

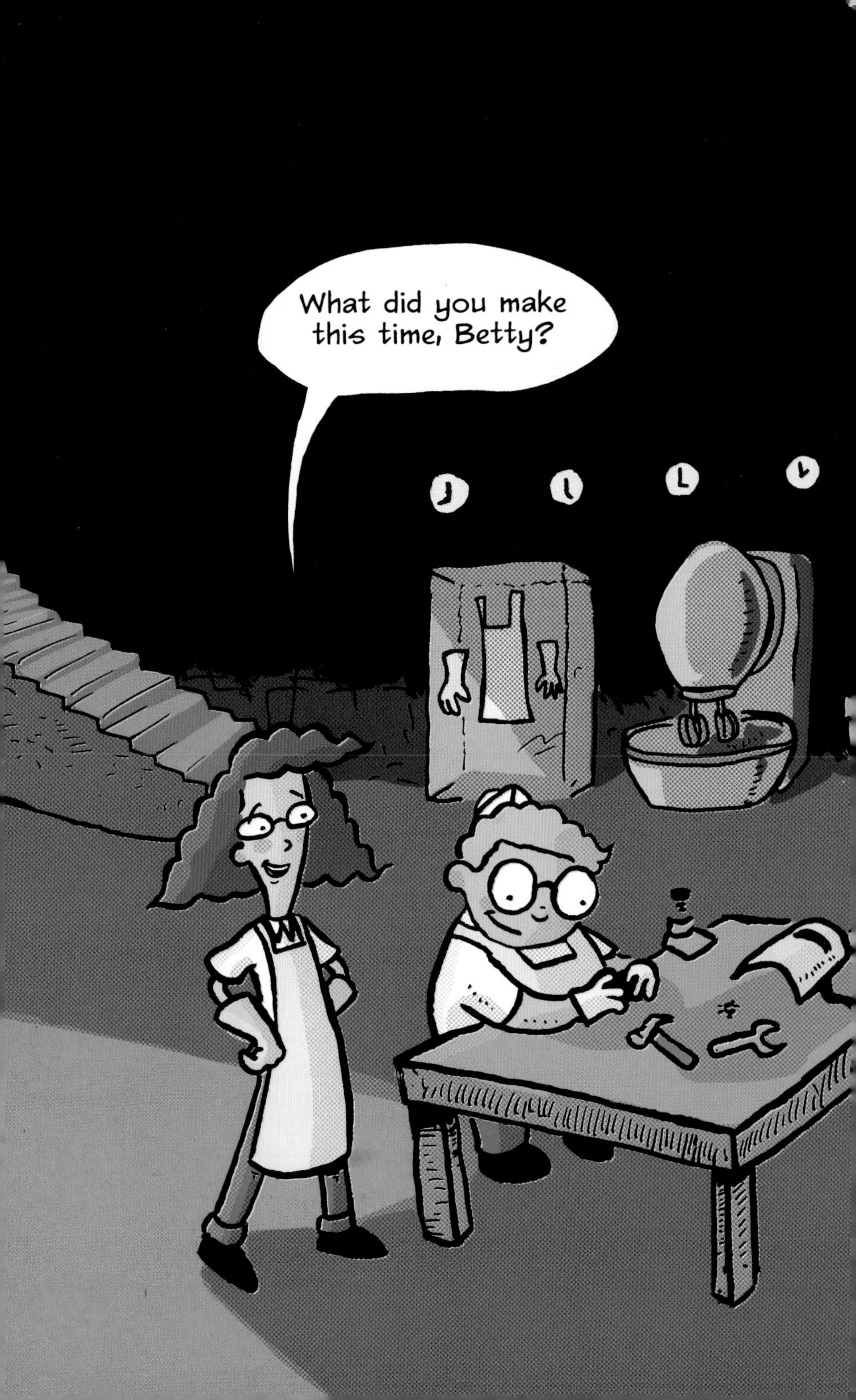
What did you make this time, Betty?

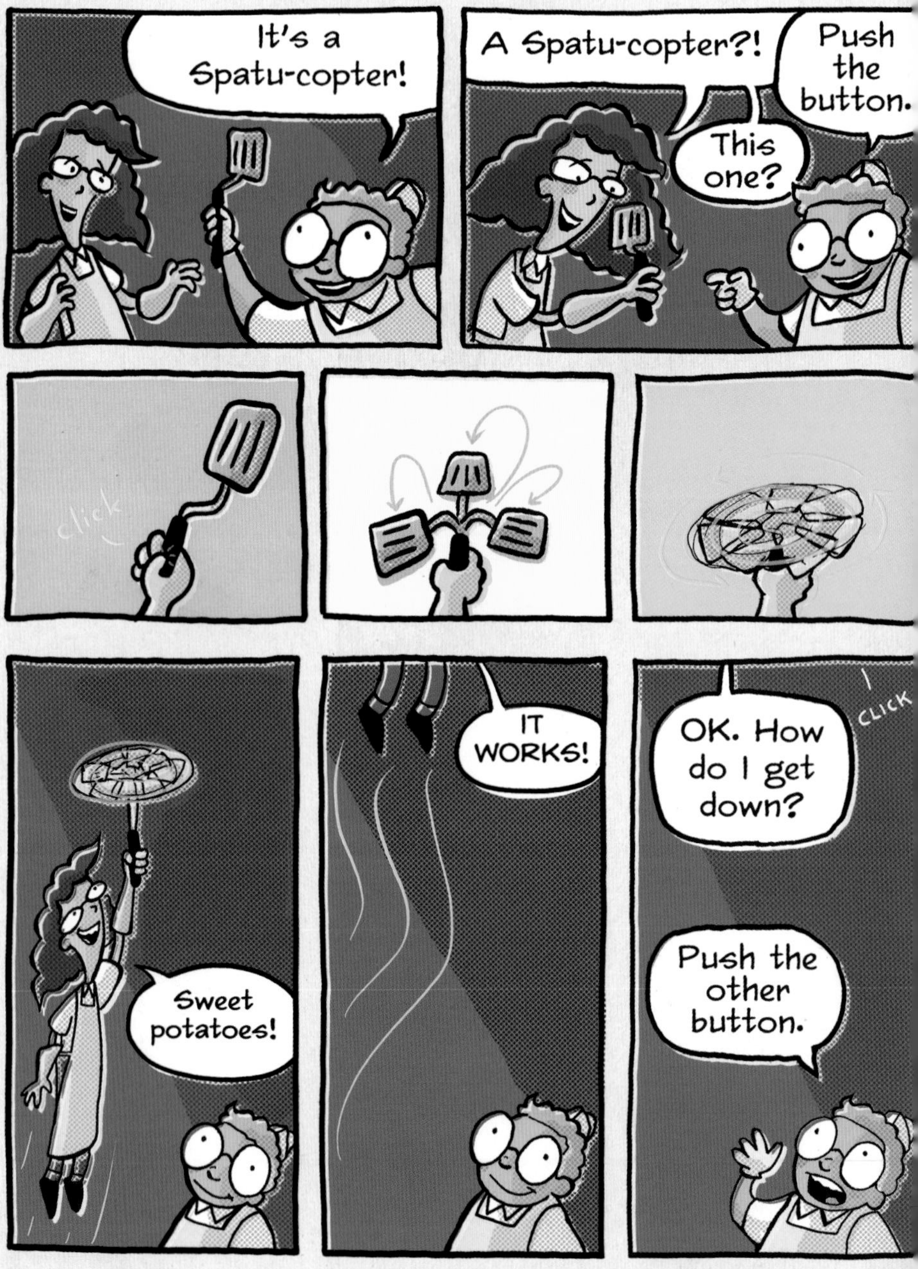
It's a Spatu-copter!
A Spatu-copter?!
Push the button.
This one?
click
Sweet potatoes!
IT WORKS!
CLICK
OK. How do I get down?
Push the other button.

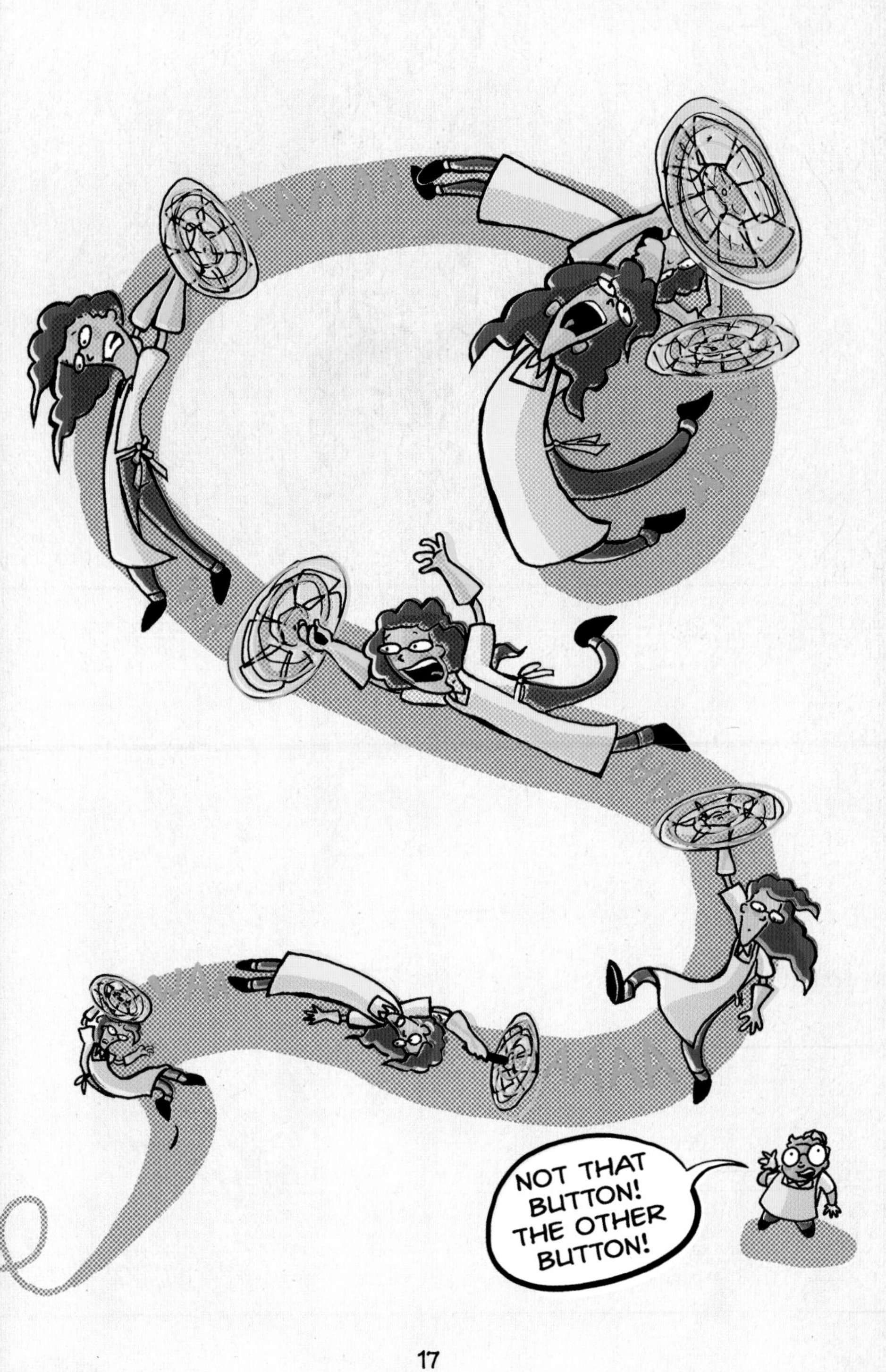
NOT THAT BUTTON! THE OTHER BUTTON!

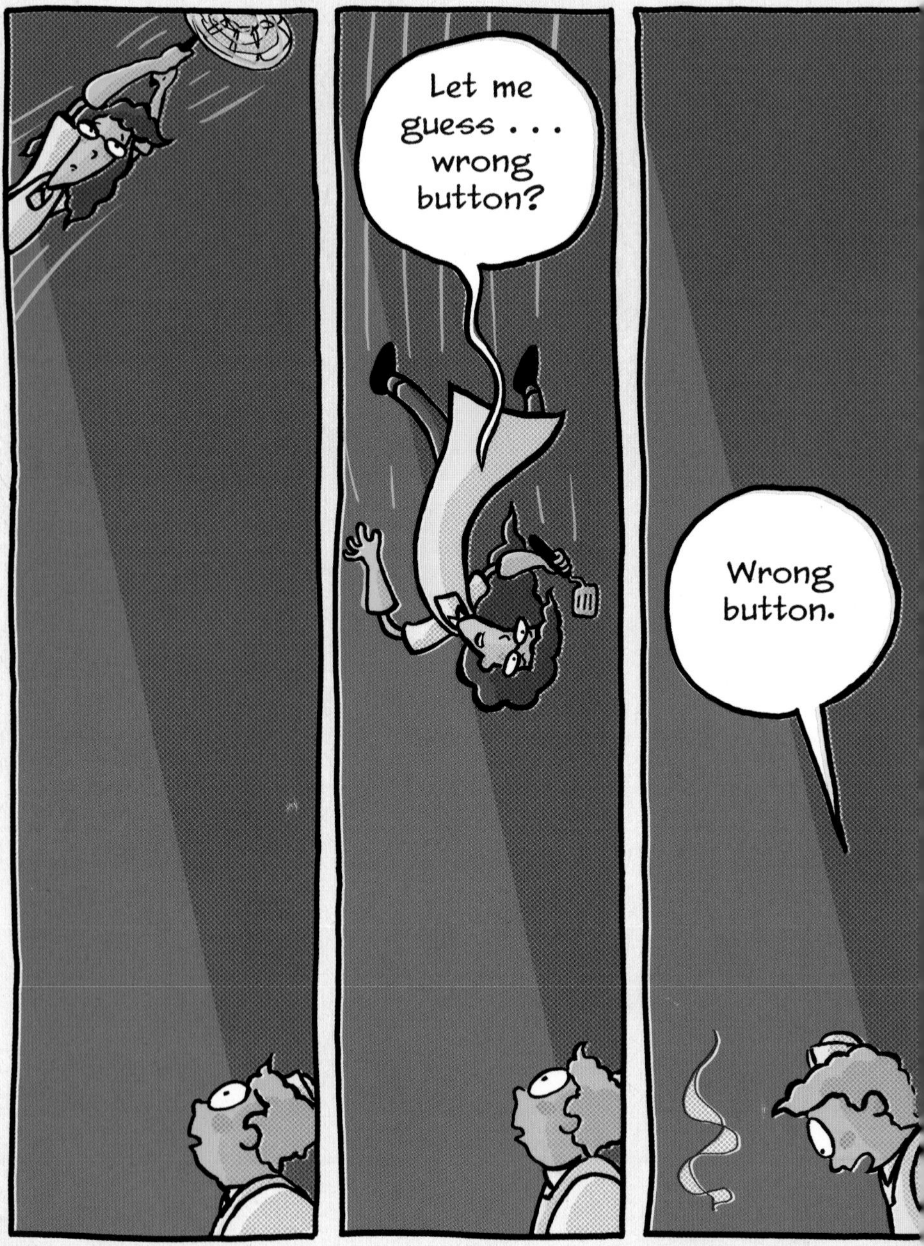
Let me guess . . . wrong button?
Wrong button.

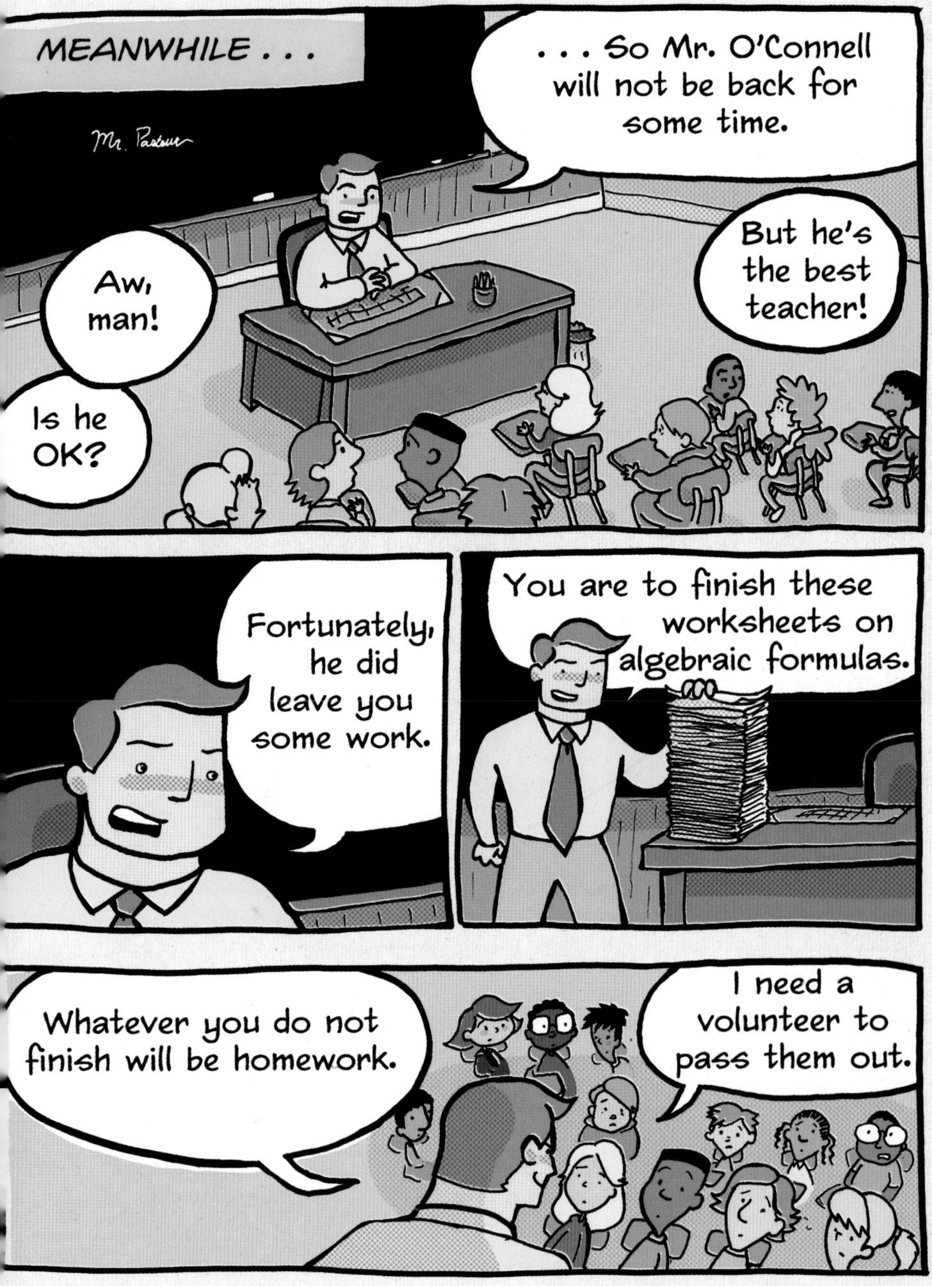
MEANWHILE . . .
. . . So Mr. O'Connell will not be back for some time.
Mr. Pasteur
Aw, man!
Is he OK?
But he's the best teacher!
Fortunately, he did leave you some work.
You are to finish these worksheets on algebraic formulas.
Whatever you do not finish will be homework.
I need a volunteer to pass them out.

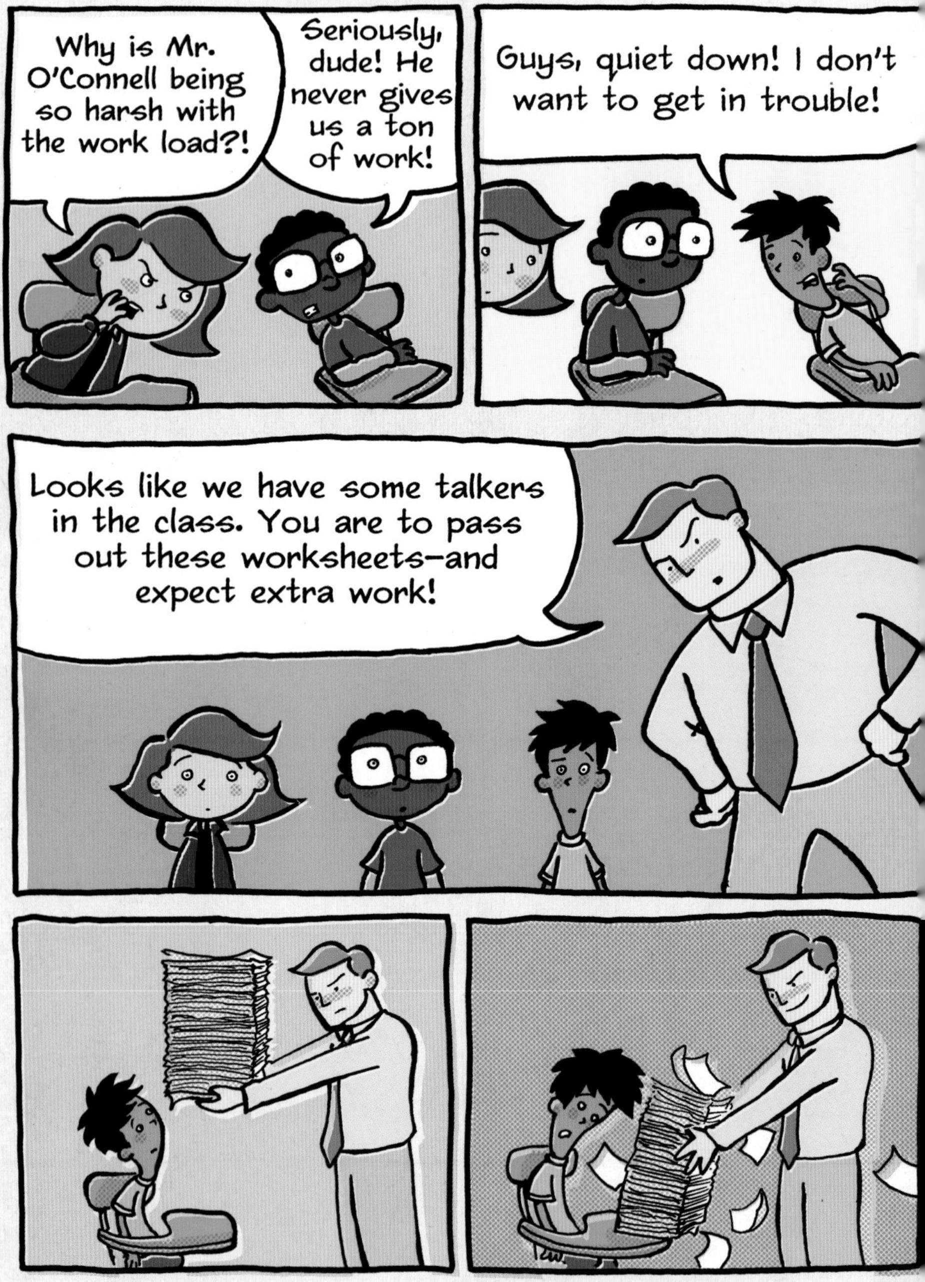
Why is Mr. O'Connell being so harsh with the work load?!
Seriously, dude! He never gives us a ton of work!
Guys, quiet down! I don't want to get in trouble!
Looks like we have some talkers in the class. You are to pass out these worksheets—and expect extra work!

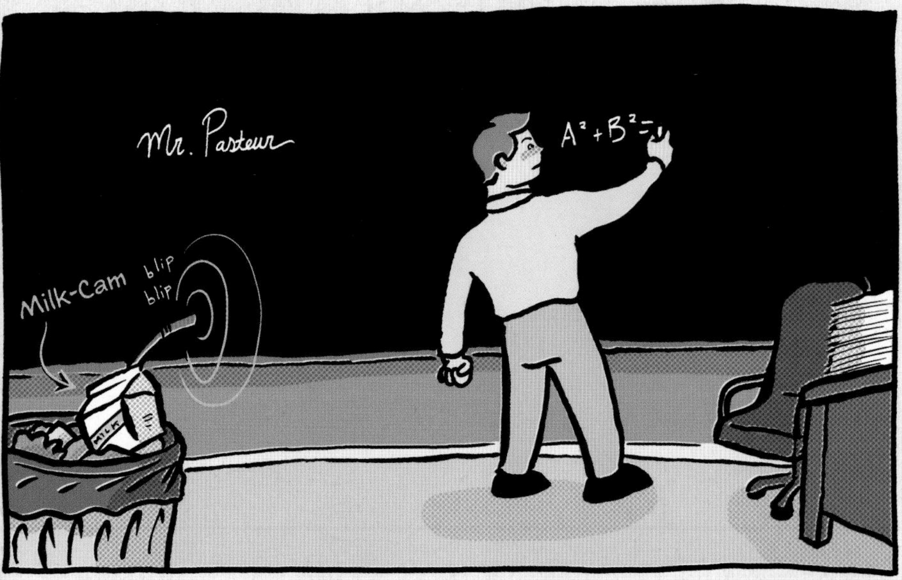
Mr. Pasteur
A² + B² =
Milk-Cam
blip
blip

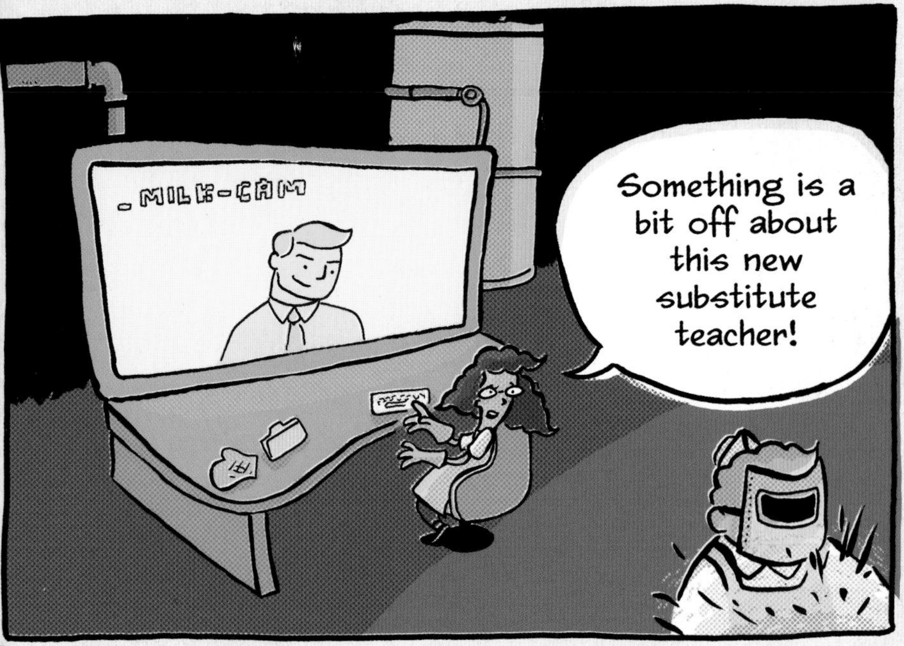
_MILK-CAM
Something is a bit off about this new substitute teacher!

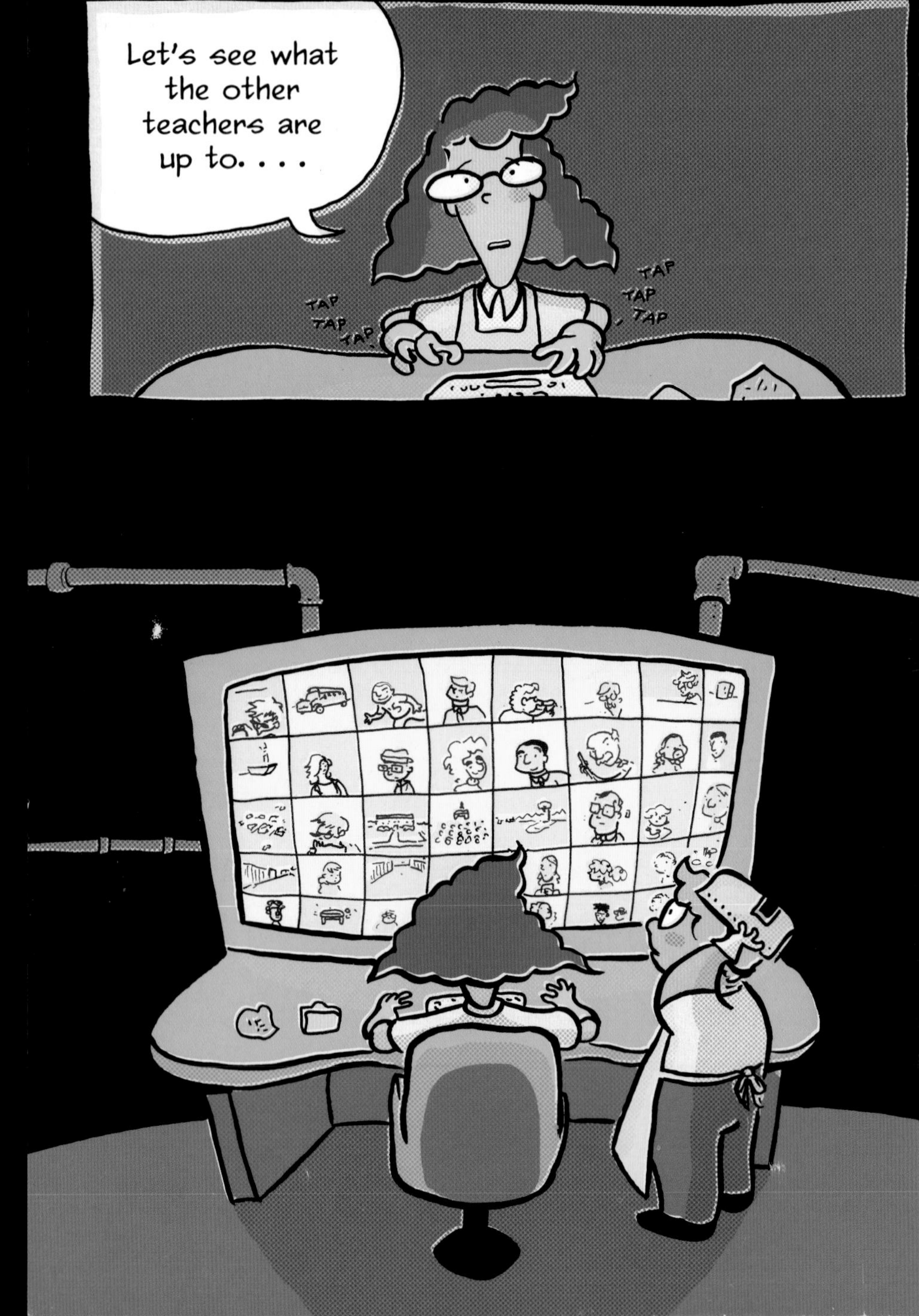
Let's see what the other teachers are up to. . . .
TAP
TAP
TAP
TAP
TAP
TAP

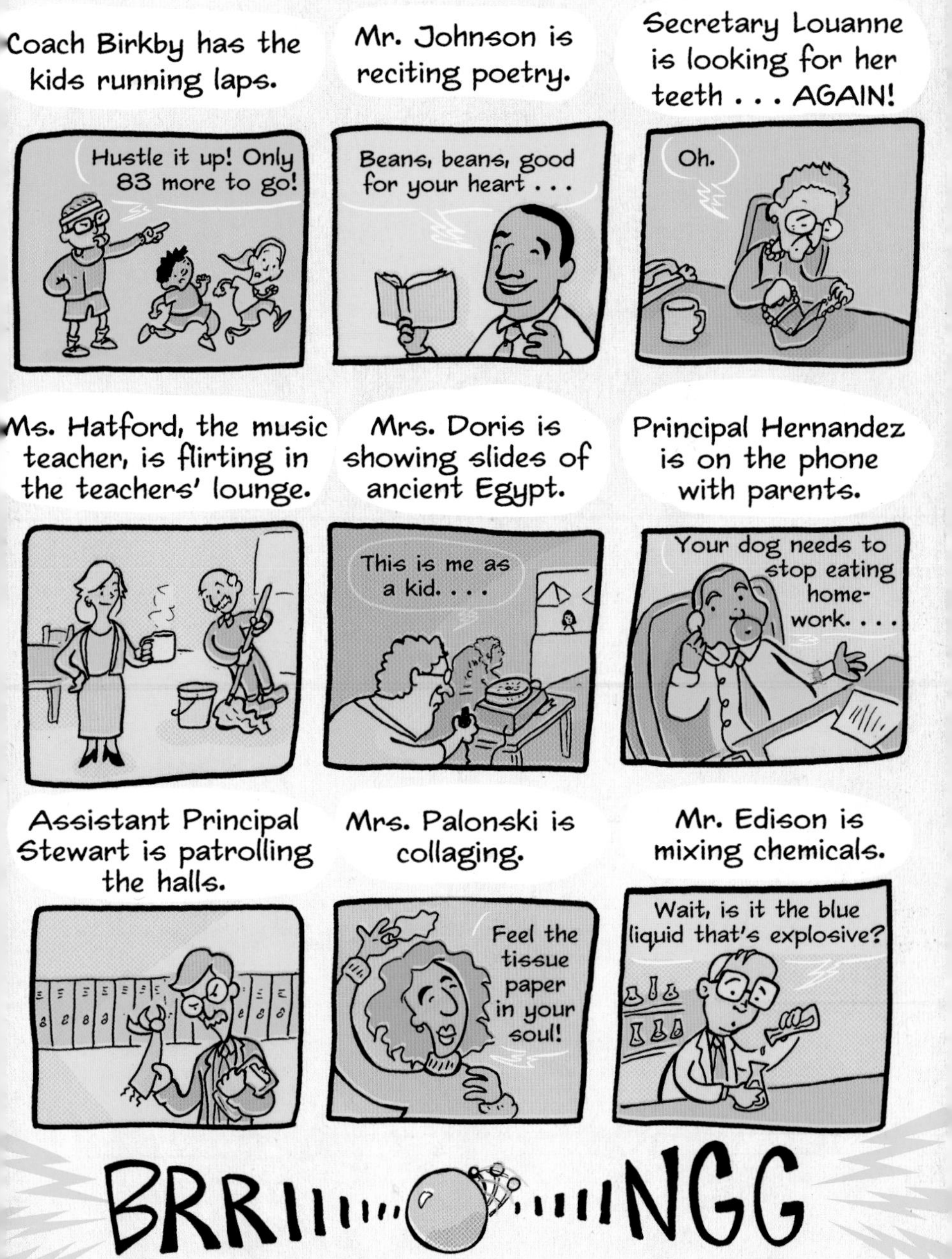
Coach Birkby has the kids running laps.
Hustle it up! Only 83 more to go!
Mr. Johnson is reciting poetry.
Beans, beans, good for your heart . . .
Secretary Louanne is looking for her teeth . . . AGAIN!
Oh.
Ms. Hatford, the music teacher, is flirting in the teachers' lounge.
Mrs. Doris is showing slides of ancient Egypt.
This is me as a kid. . . .
Principal Hernandez is on the phone with parents.
Your dog needs to stop eating home-work. . . .
Assistant Principal Stewart is patrolling the halls.
Mrs. Palonski is collaging.
Feel the tissue paper in your soul!
Mr. Edison is mixing chemicals.
Wait, is it the blue liquid that's explosive?
BRRIIIIIIIIIIIIINGG

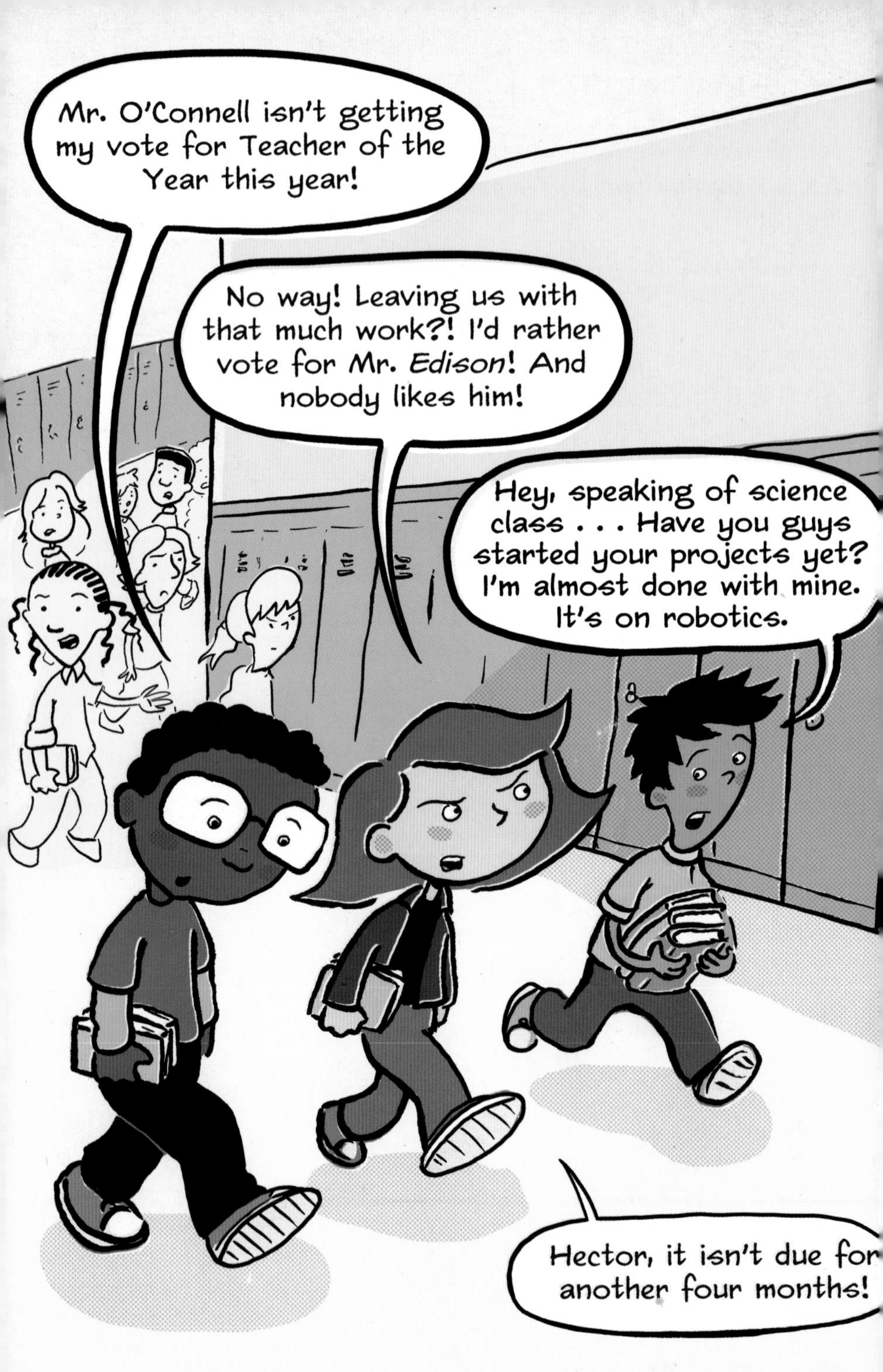
Mr. O'Connell isn't getting my vote for Teacher of the Year this year!
No way! Leaving us with that much work?! I'd rather vote for Mr. *Edison*! And nobody likes him!
Hey, speaking of science class . . . Have you guys started your projects yet? I'm almost done with mine. It's on robotics.
Hector, it isn't due for another four months!

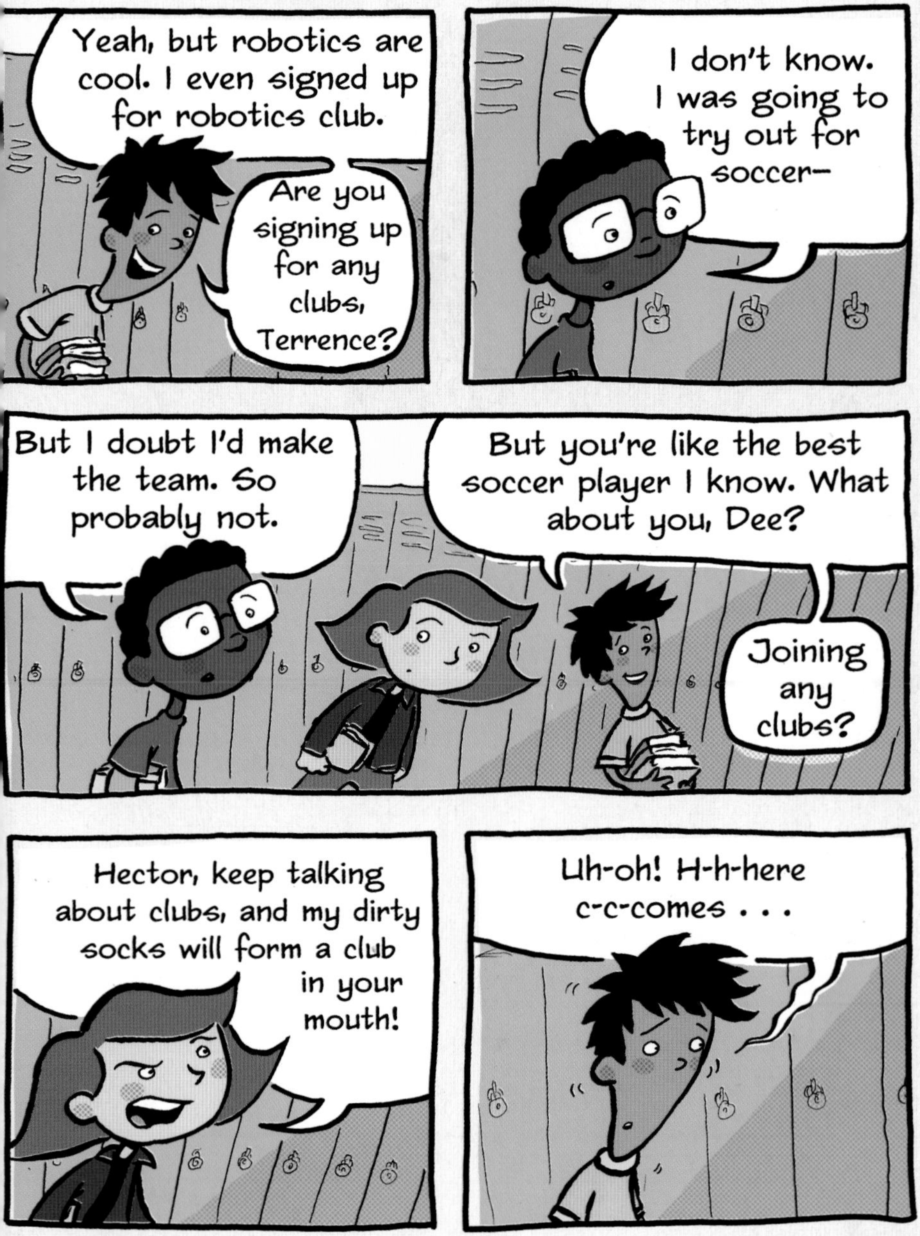
Yeah, but robotics are cool. I even signed up for robotics club.
Are you signing up for any clubs, Terrence?
I don't know. I was going to try out for soccer—
But I doubt I'd make the team. So probably not.
But you're like the best soccer player I know. What about you, Dee?
Joining any clubs?
Hector, keep talking about clubs, and my dirty socks will form a club in your mouth!
Uh-oh! H-h-here c-c-comes . . .

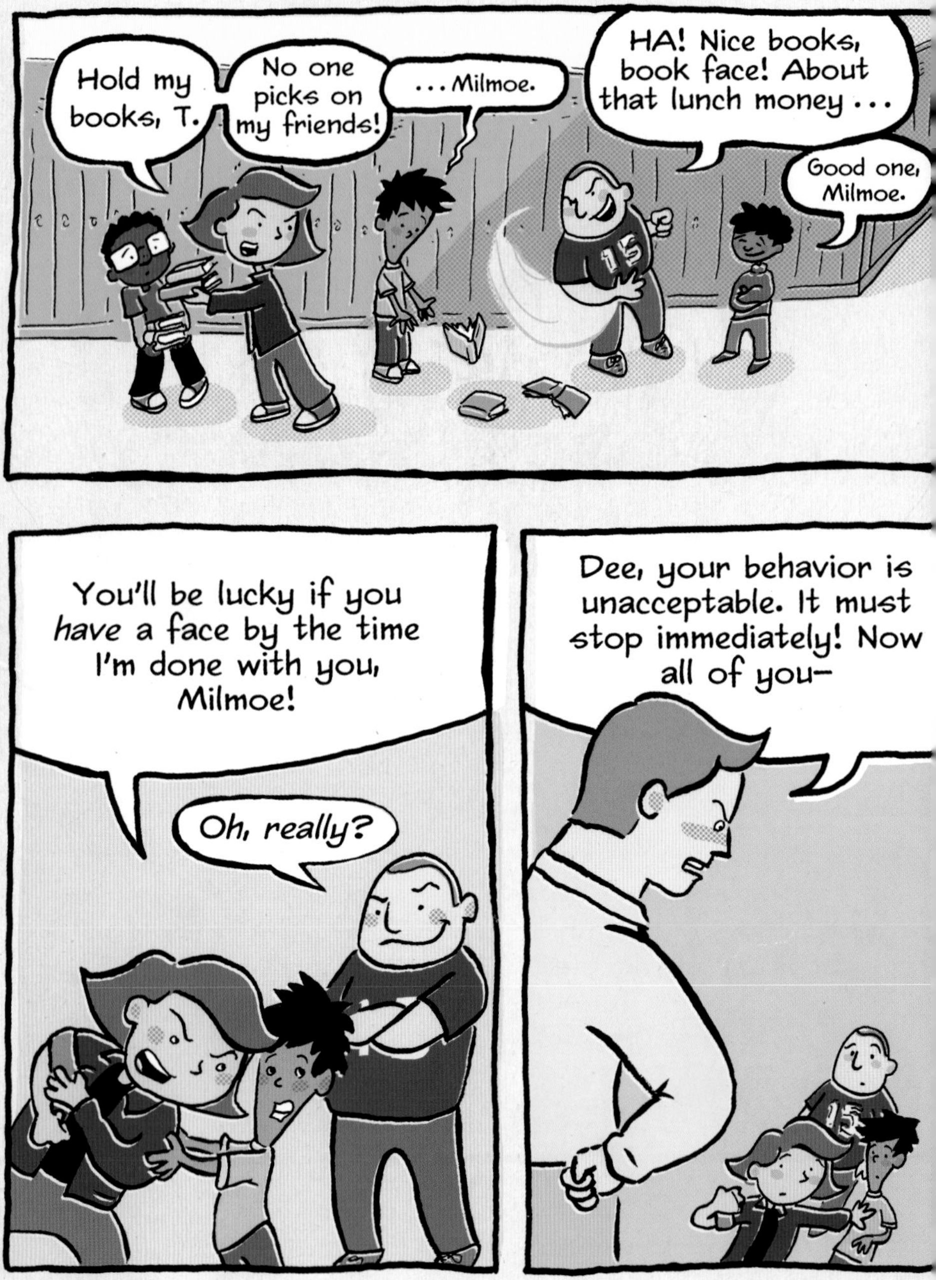
Hold my books, T.
No one picks on my friends!
. . . Milmoe.
HA! Nice books, book face! About that lunch money . . .
Good one, Milmoe.
You'll be lucky if you *have* a face by the time I'm done with you, Milmoe!
Oh, *really*?
Dee, your behavior is unacceptable. It must stop immediately! Now all of you–

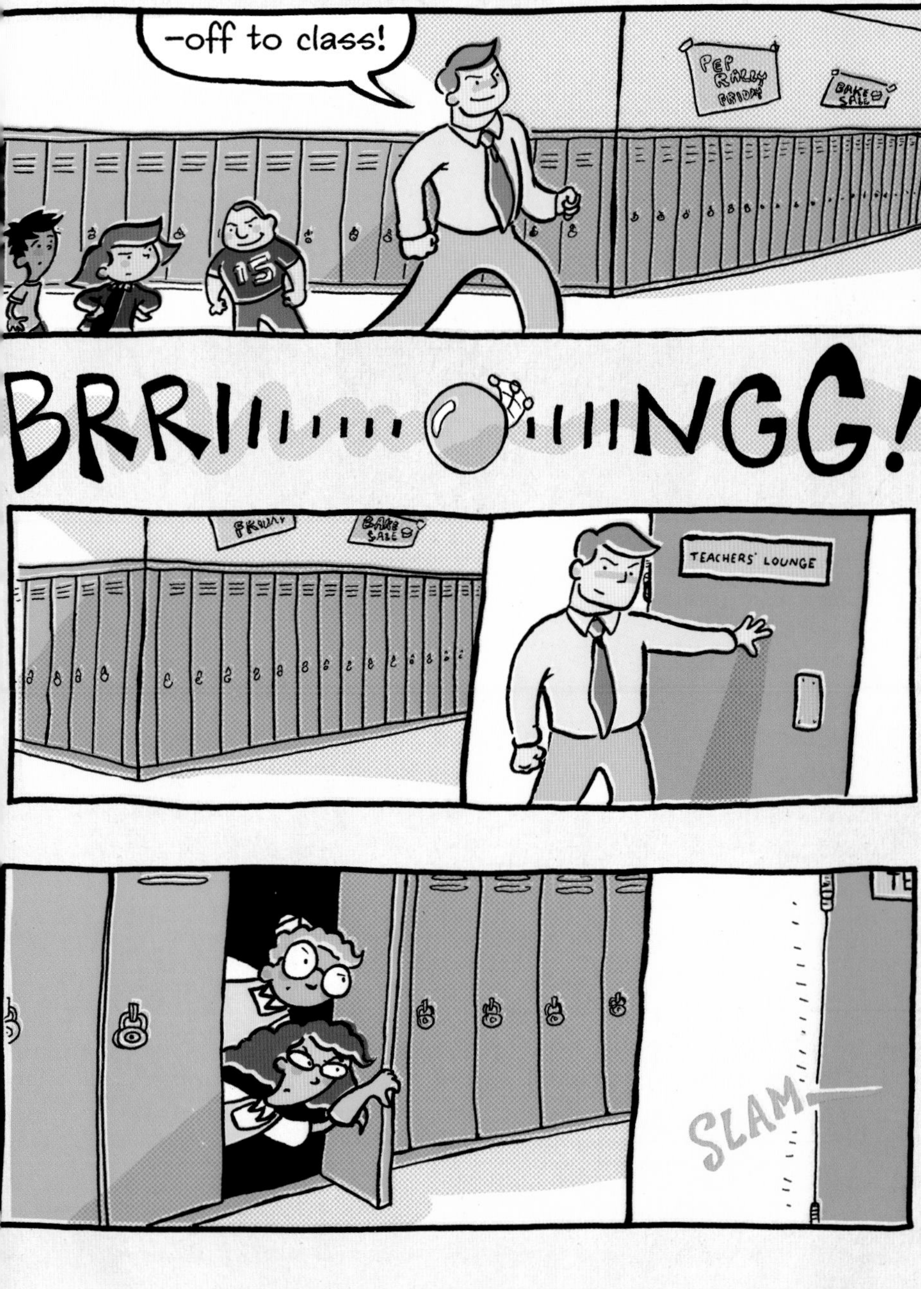
-off to class!
PEP RALLY FRIDAY
BAKE SALE
15
BRRIIIIIIIIIIIINGG!
BAKE SALE
TEACHERS' LOUNGE
SLAM

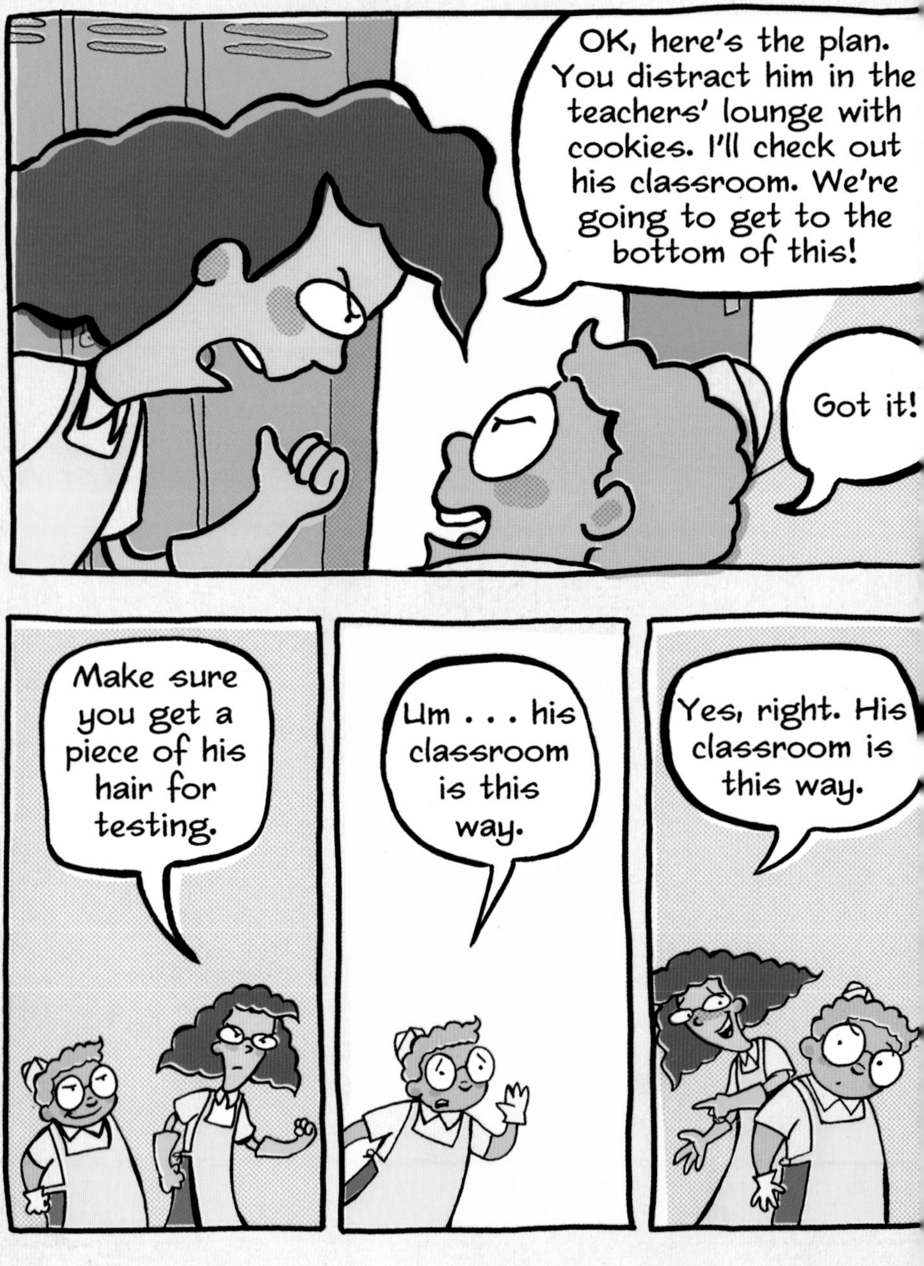
OK, here's the plan. You distract him in the teachers' lounge with cookies. I'll check out his classroom. We're going to get to the bottom of this!
Got it!
Make sure you get a piece of his hair for testing.
Um . . . his classroom is this way.
Yes, right. His classroom is this way.

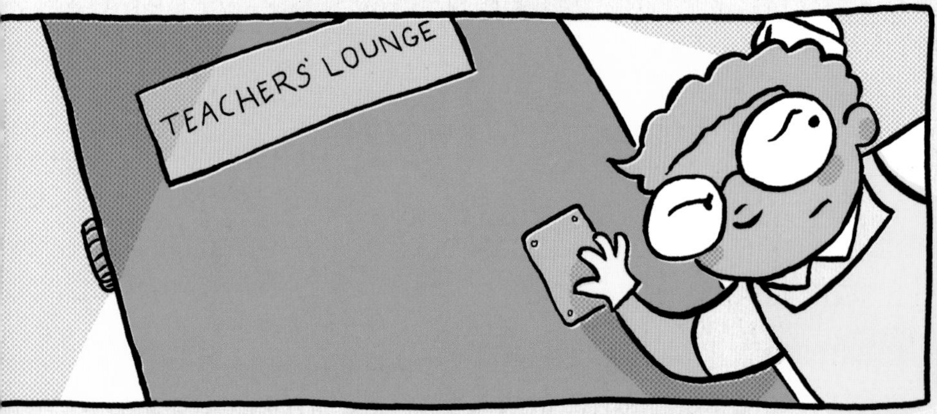
TEACHERS' LOUNGE

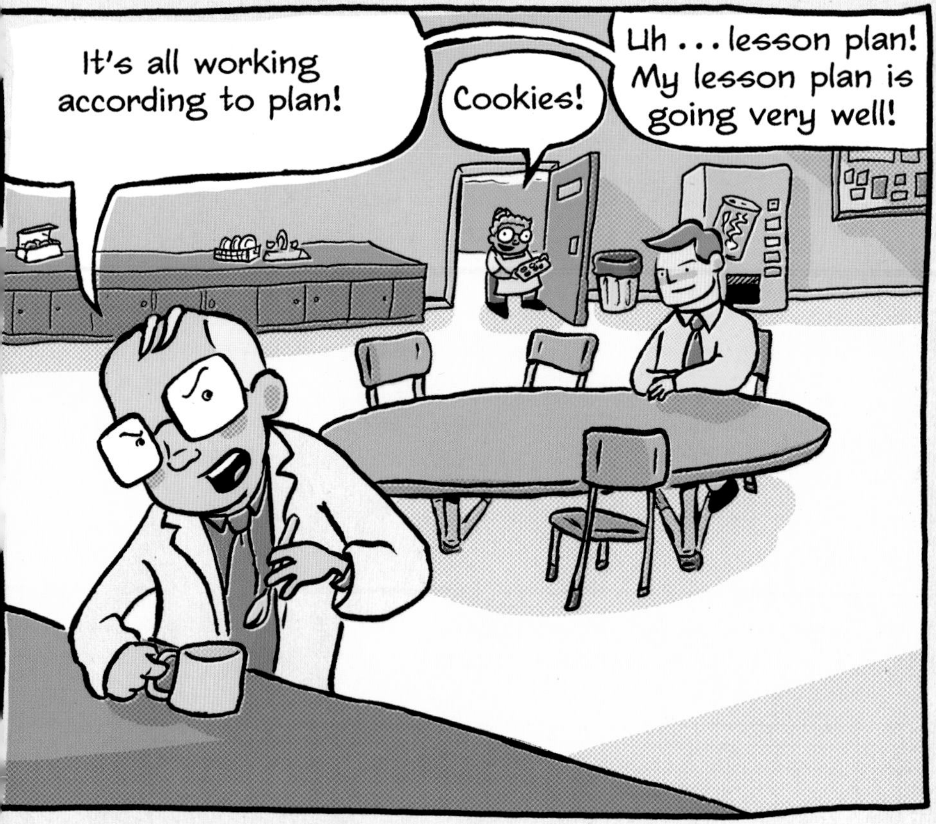
It's all working according to plan!
Cookies!
Uh . . . lesson plan! My lesson plan is going very well!

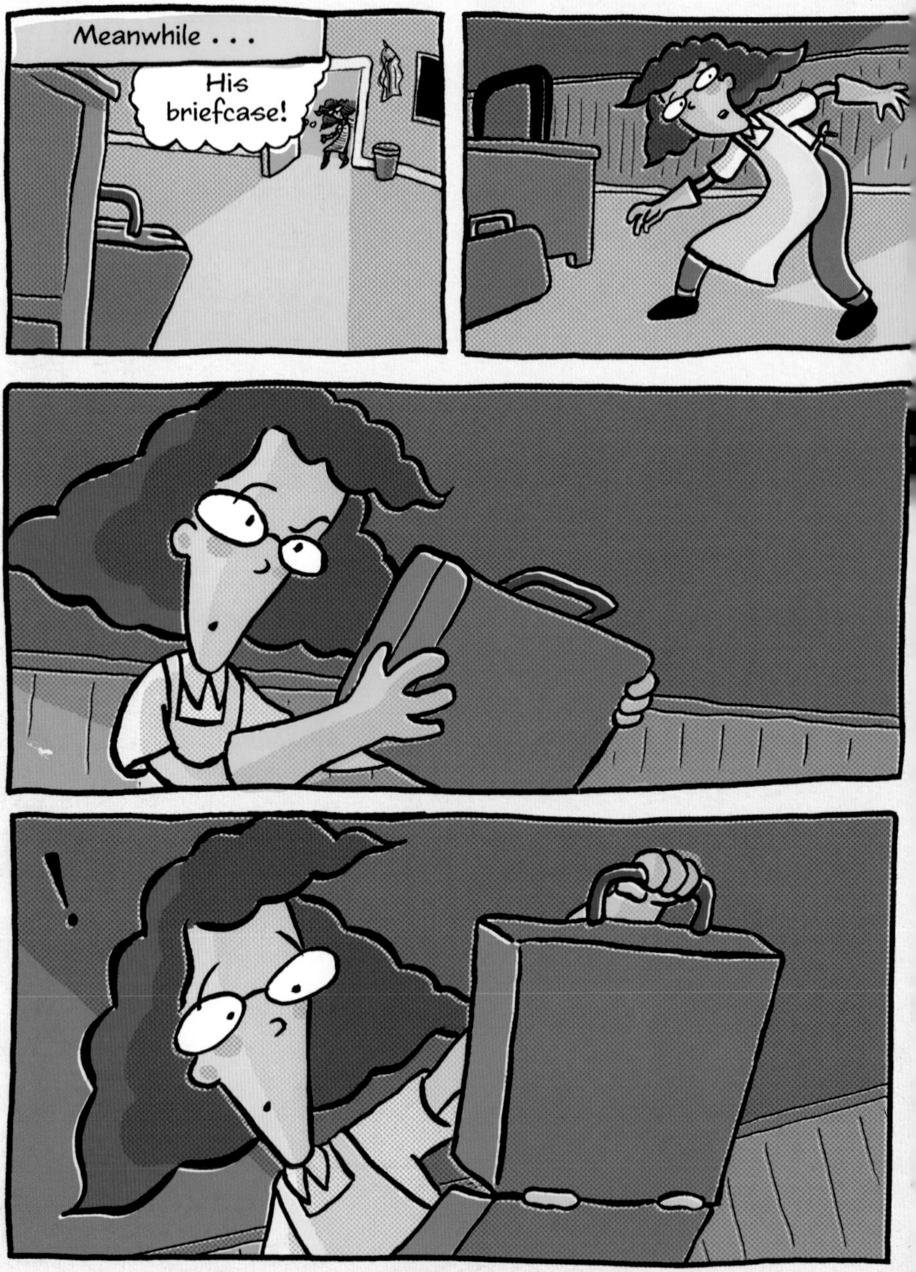
Meanwhile . . .
His briefcase!
!

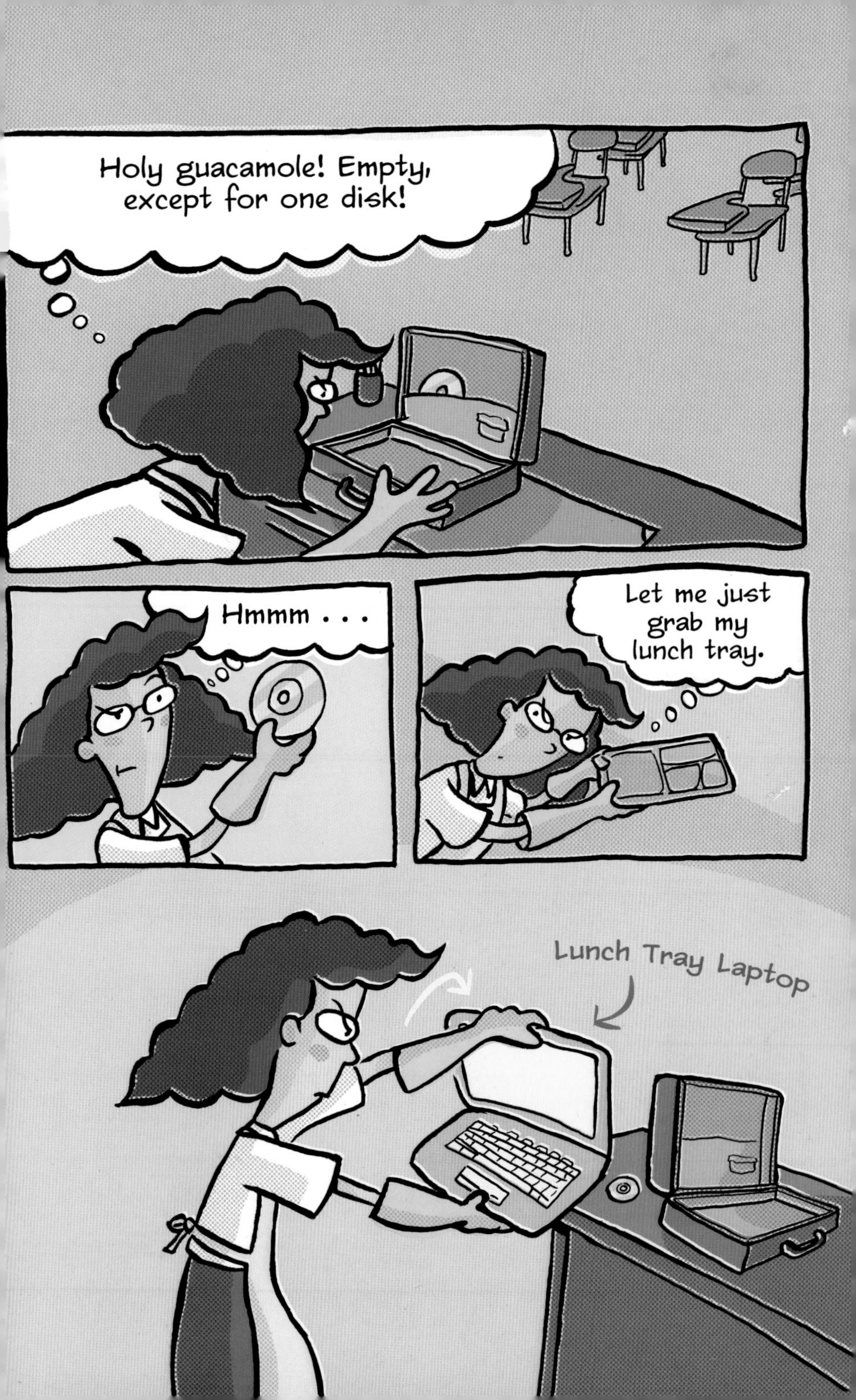
Holy guacamole! Empty, except for one disk!
Hmmm . . .
Let me just grab my lunch tray.
Lunch Tray Laptop

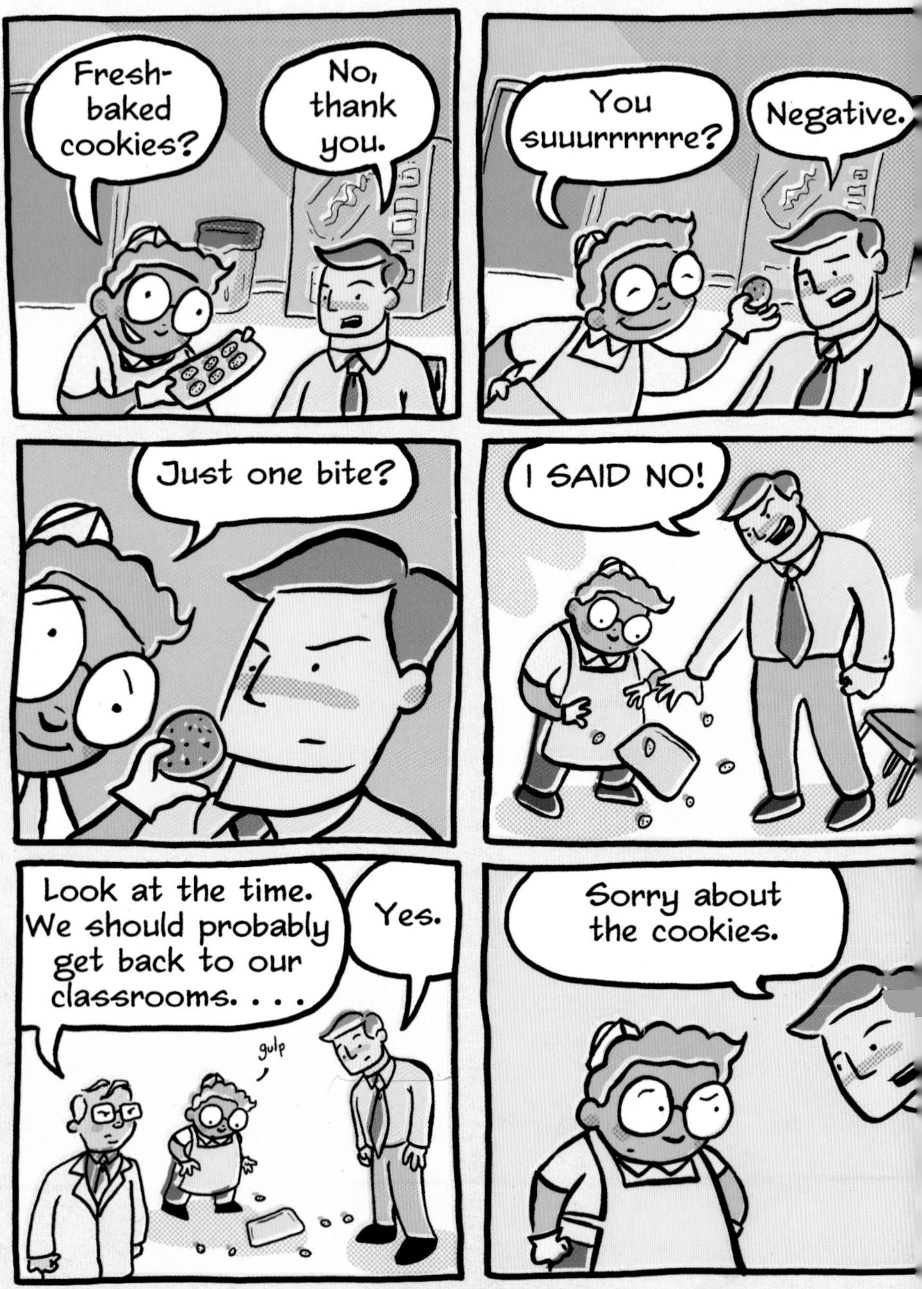
Fresh-baked cookies?
No, thank you.
You suuurrrrrre?
Negative.
Just one bite?
I SAID NO!
Look at the time. We should probably get back to our classrooms. . . .
Yes.
gulp
Sorry about the cookies.

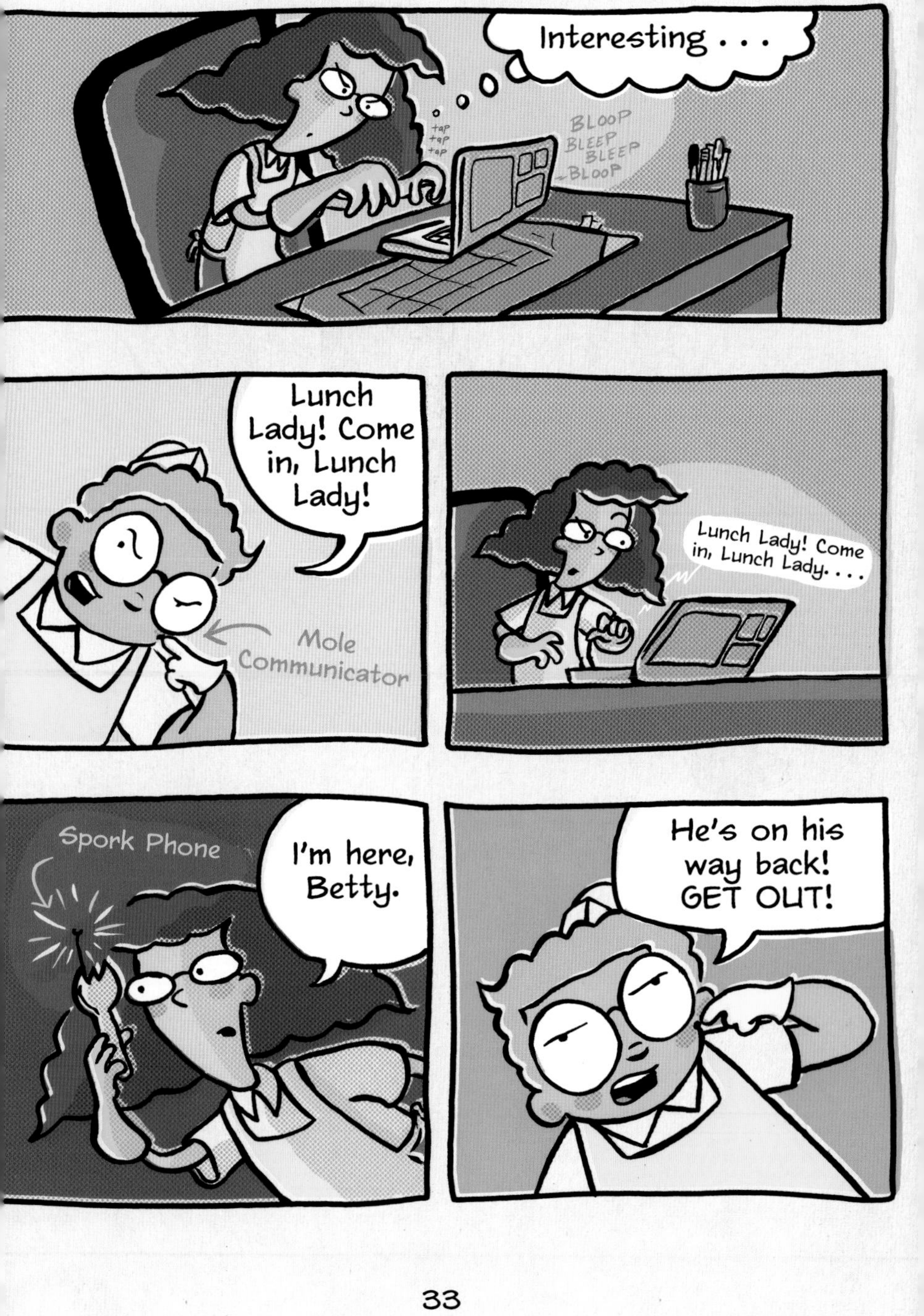

Interesting . . .
tap
tap
tap
BLOOP
BLEEP
BLEEP
BLOOP
Lunch Lady! Come in, Lunch Lady!
Mole Communicator
Lunch Lady! Come in, Lunch Lady. . . .
Spork Phone
I'm here, Betty.
He's on his way back! GET OUT!

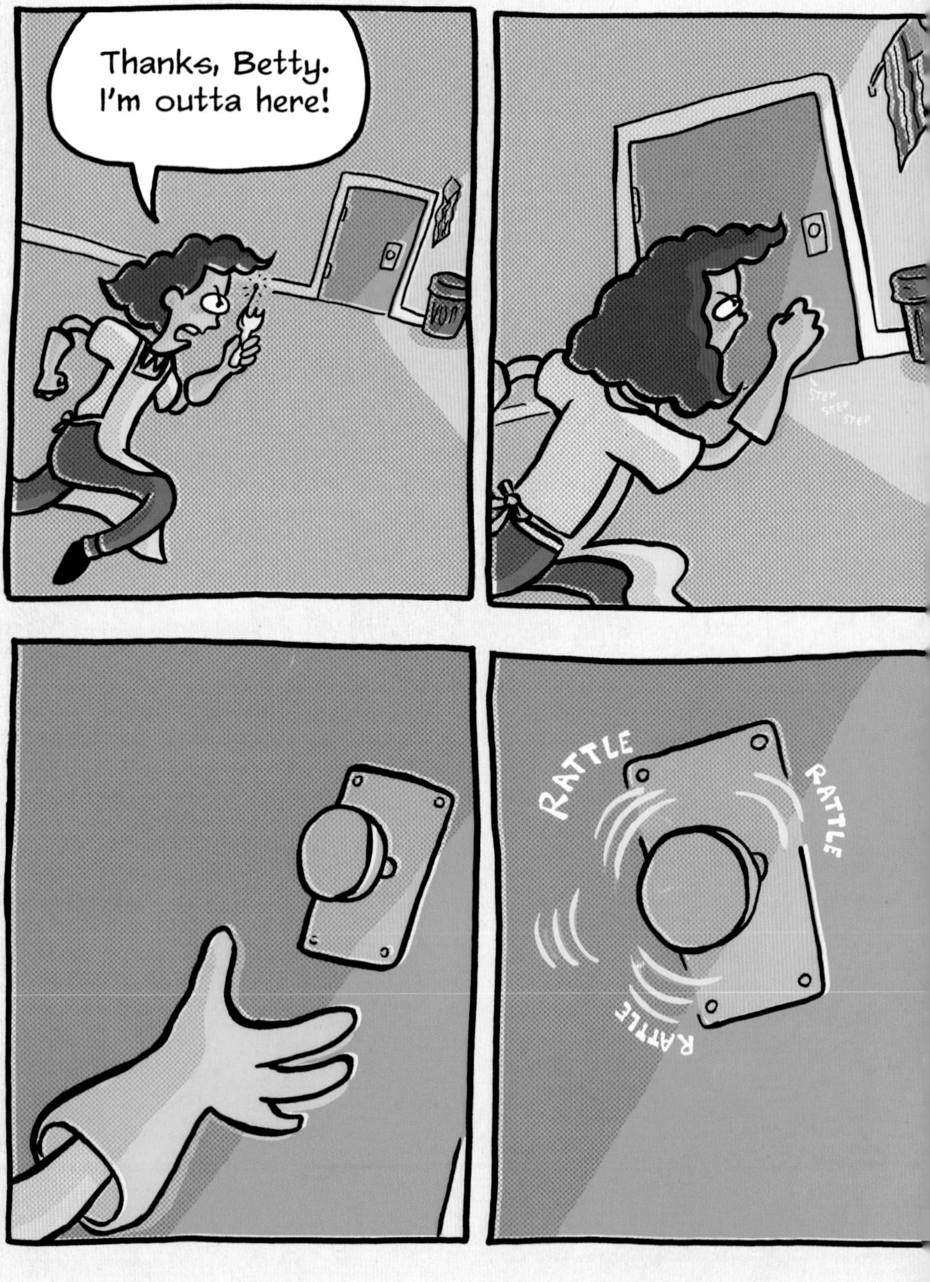
Thanks, Betty.
I'm outta here!
STEP
STEP
STEP
RATTLE
RATTLE
RATTLE

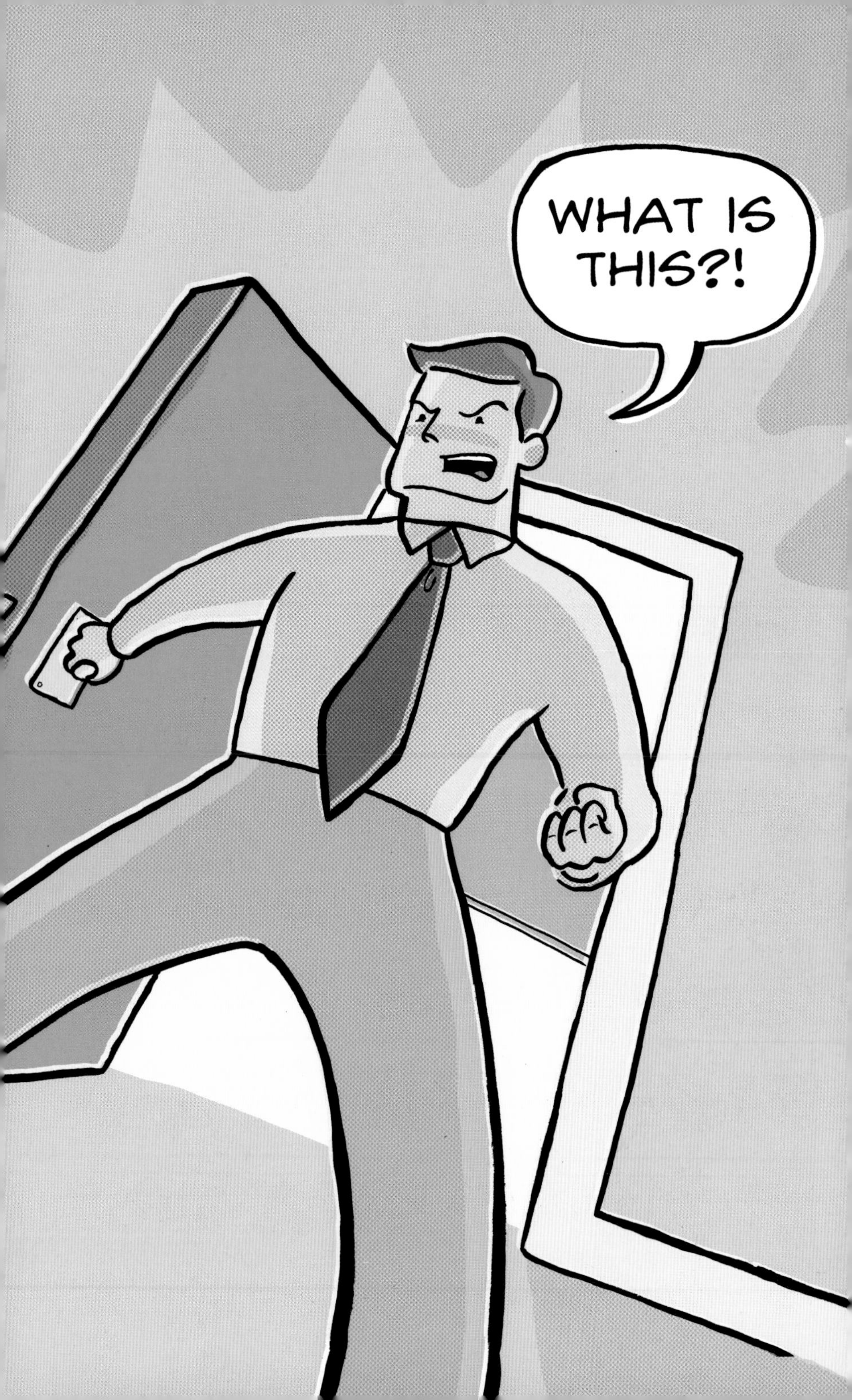
WHAT IS THIS?!

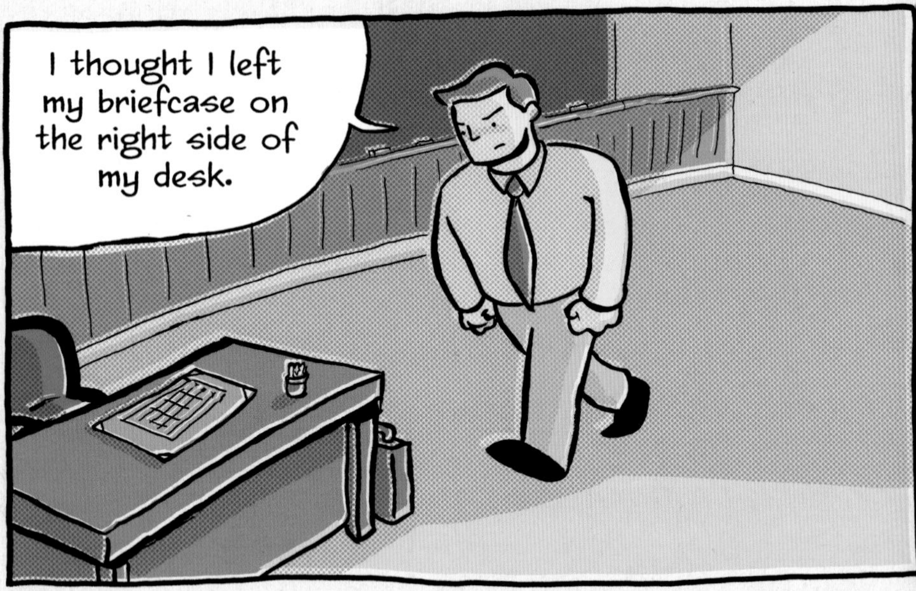
I thought I left my briefcase on the right side of my desk.

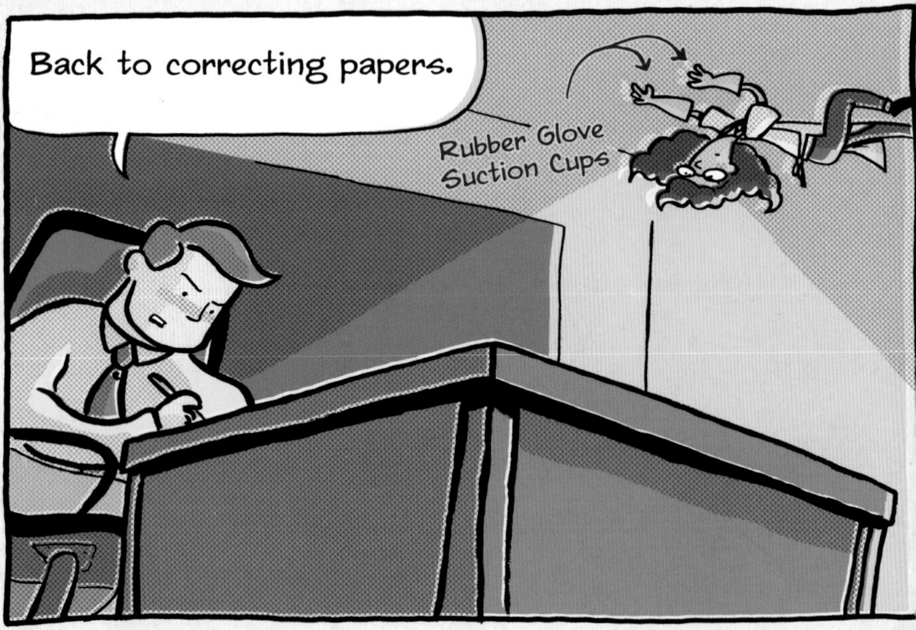
Back to correcting papers.
Rubber Glove Suction Cups

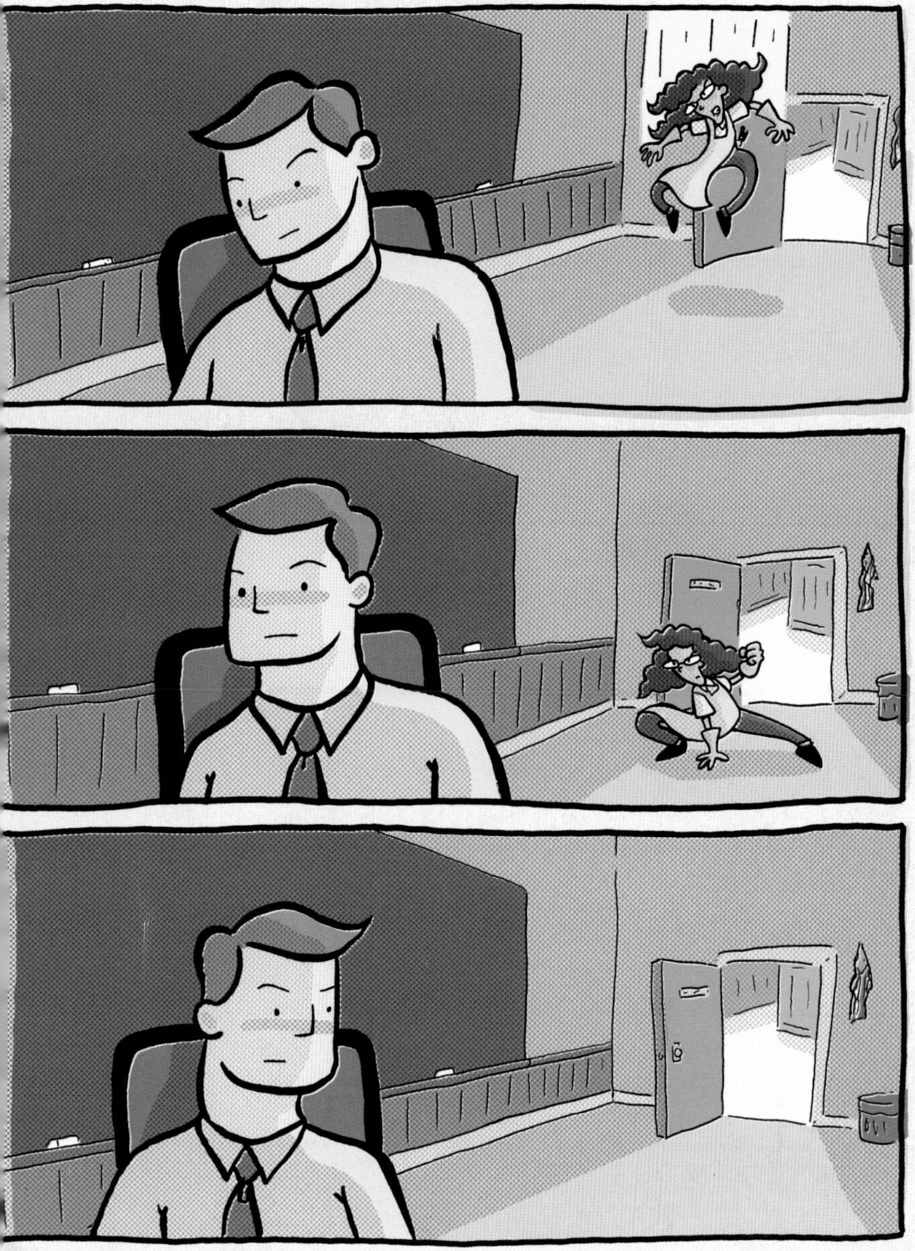

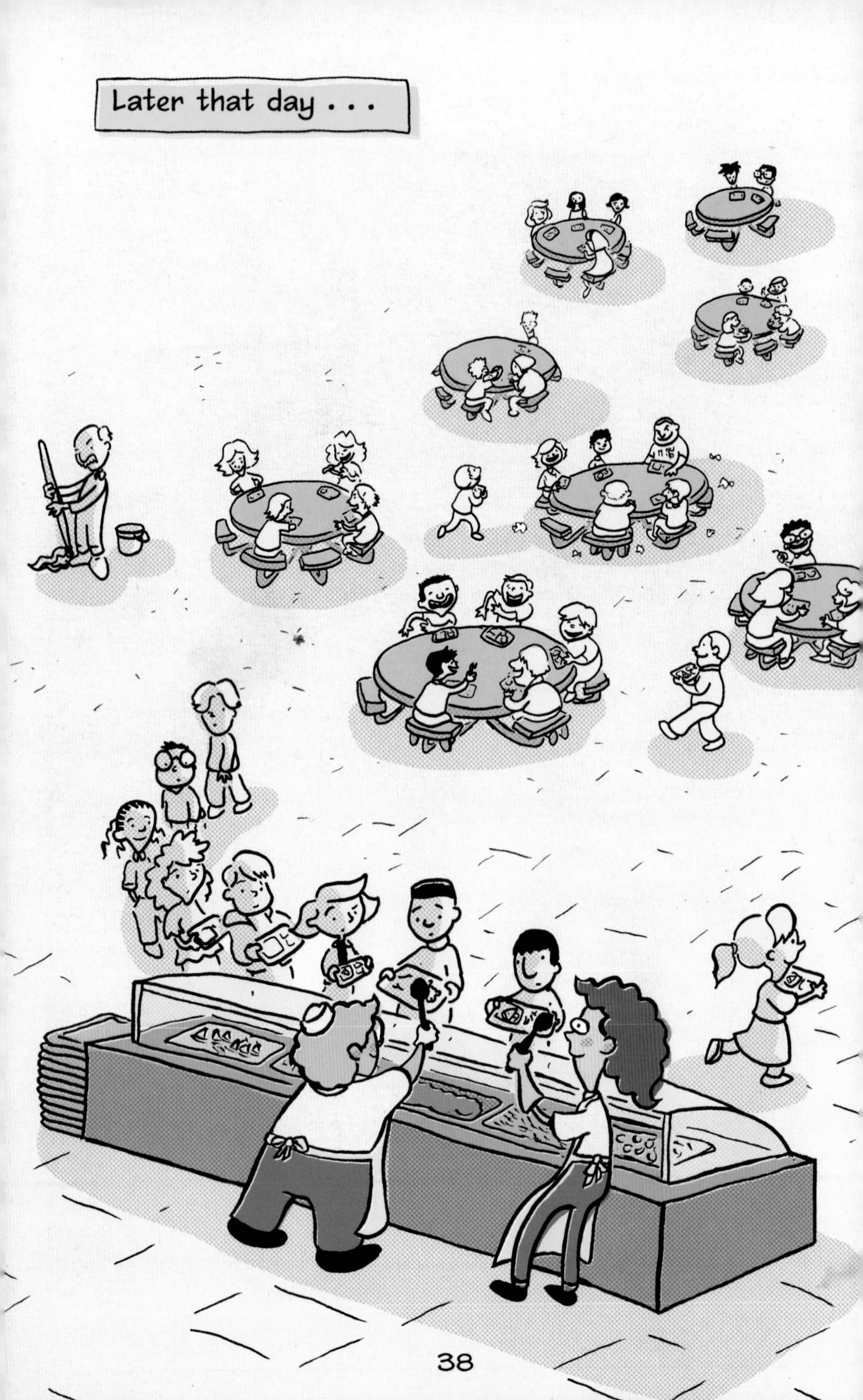
Later that day . . .

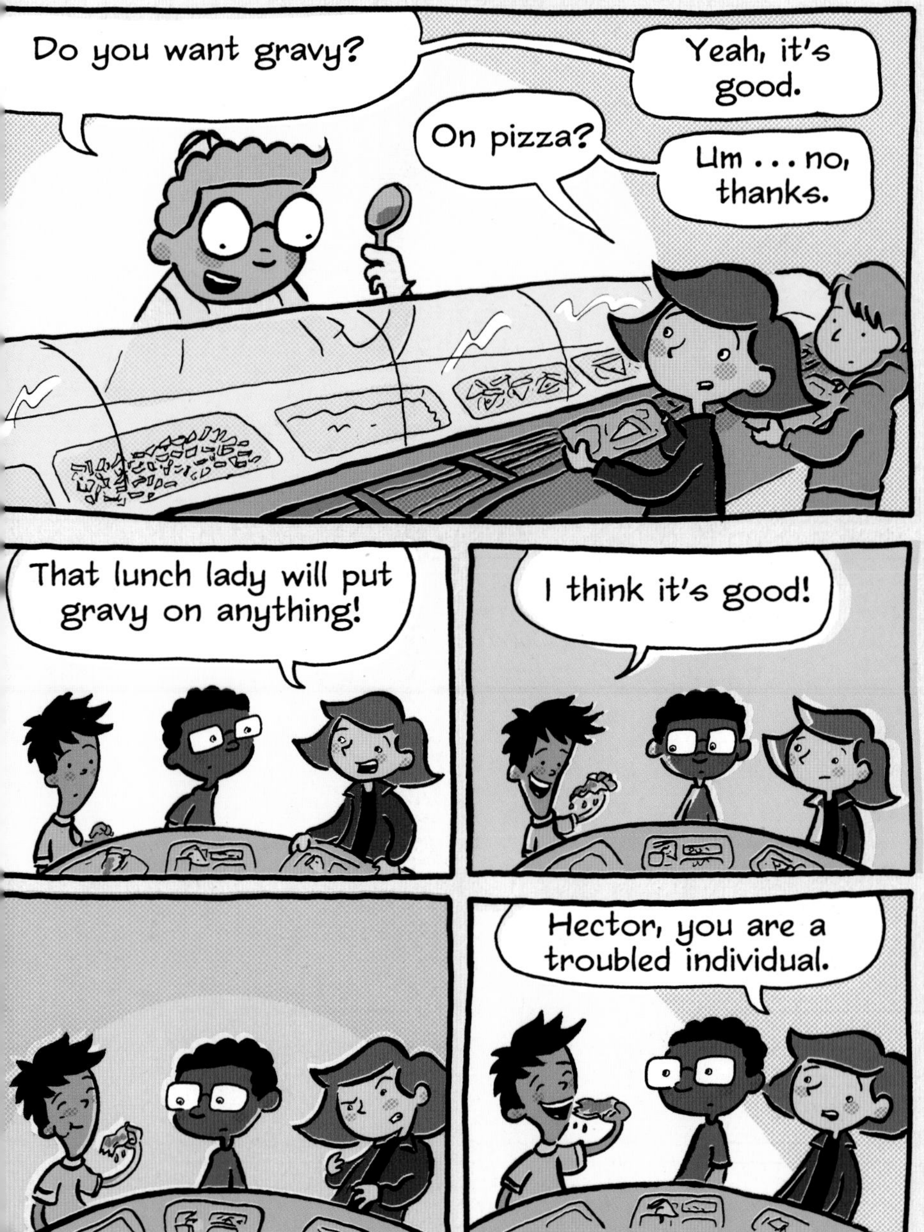
Do you want gravy?
Yeah, it's good.
On pizza?
Um . . . no, thanks.
That lunch lady will put gravy on anything!
I think it's good!
Hector, you are a troubled individual.

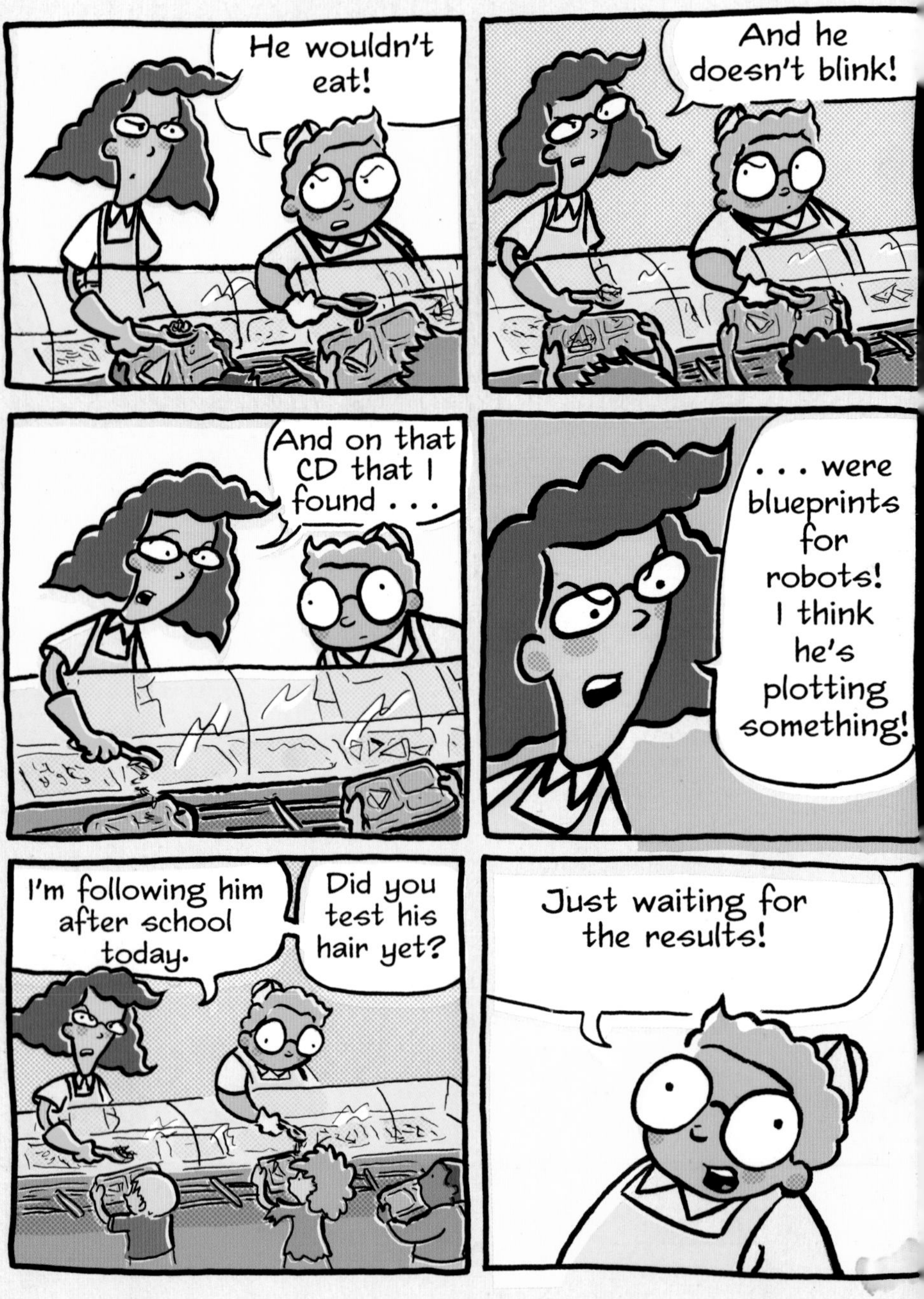
He wouldn't eat!
And he doesn't blink!
And on that CD that I found . . .
. . . were blueprints for robots! I think he's plotting something!
I'm following him after school today.
Did you test his hair yet?
Just waiting for the results!

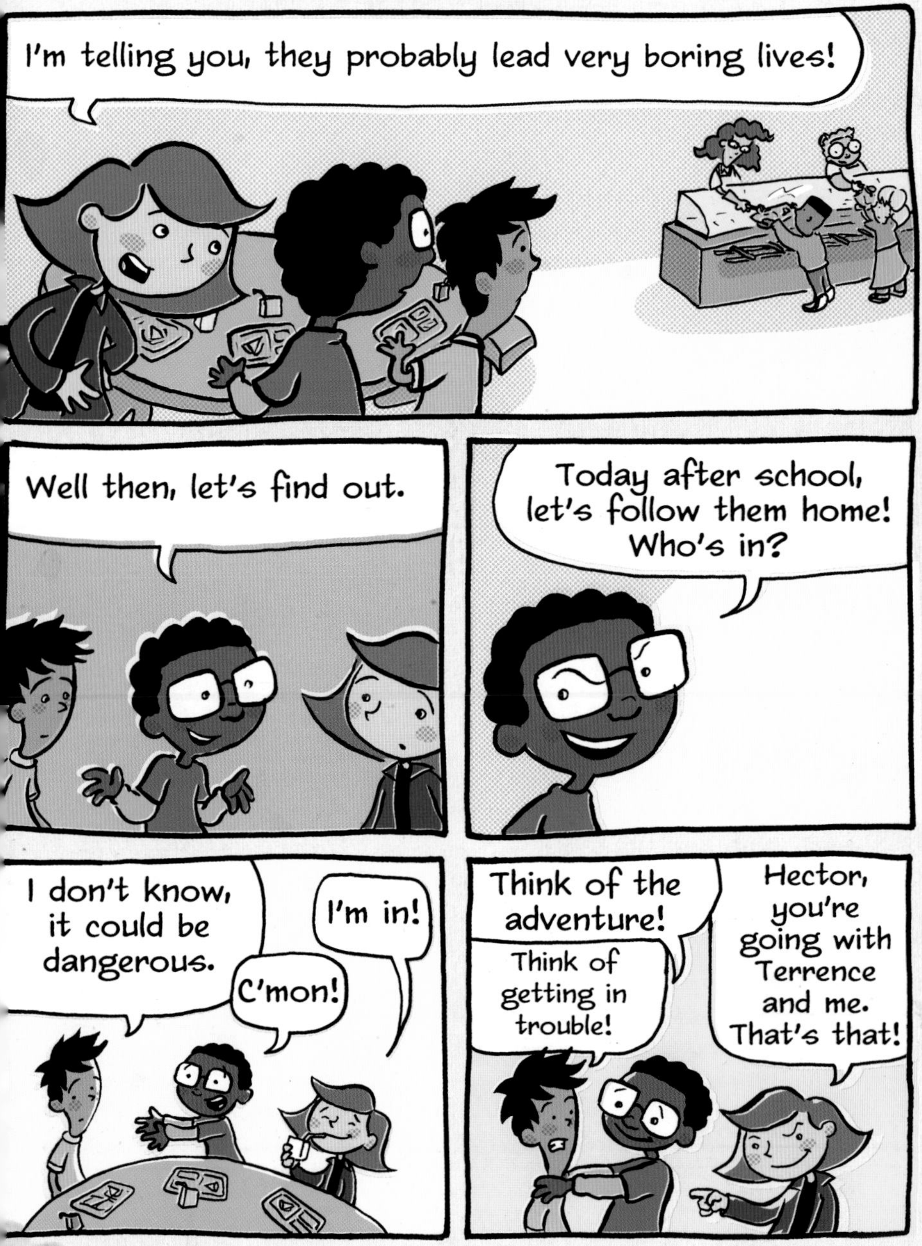
I'm telling you, they probably lead very boring lives!
Well then, let's find out.
Today after school, let's follow them home! Who's in?
I don't know, it could be dangerous.
C'mon!
I'm in!
Think of the adventure!
Think of getting in trouble!
Hector, you're going with Terrence and me. That's that!

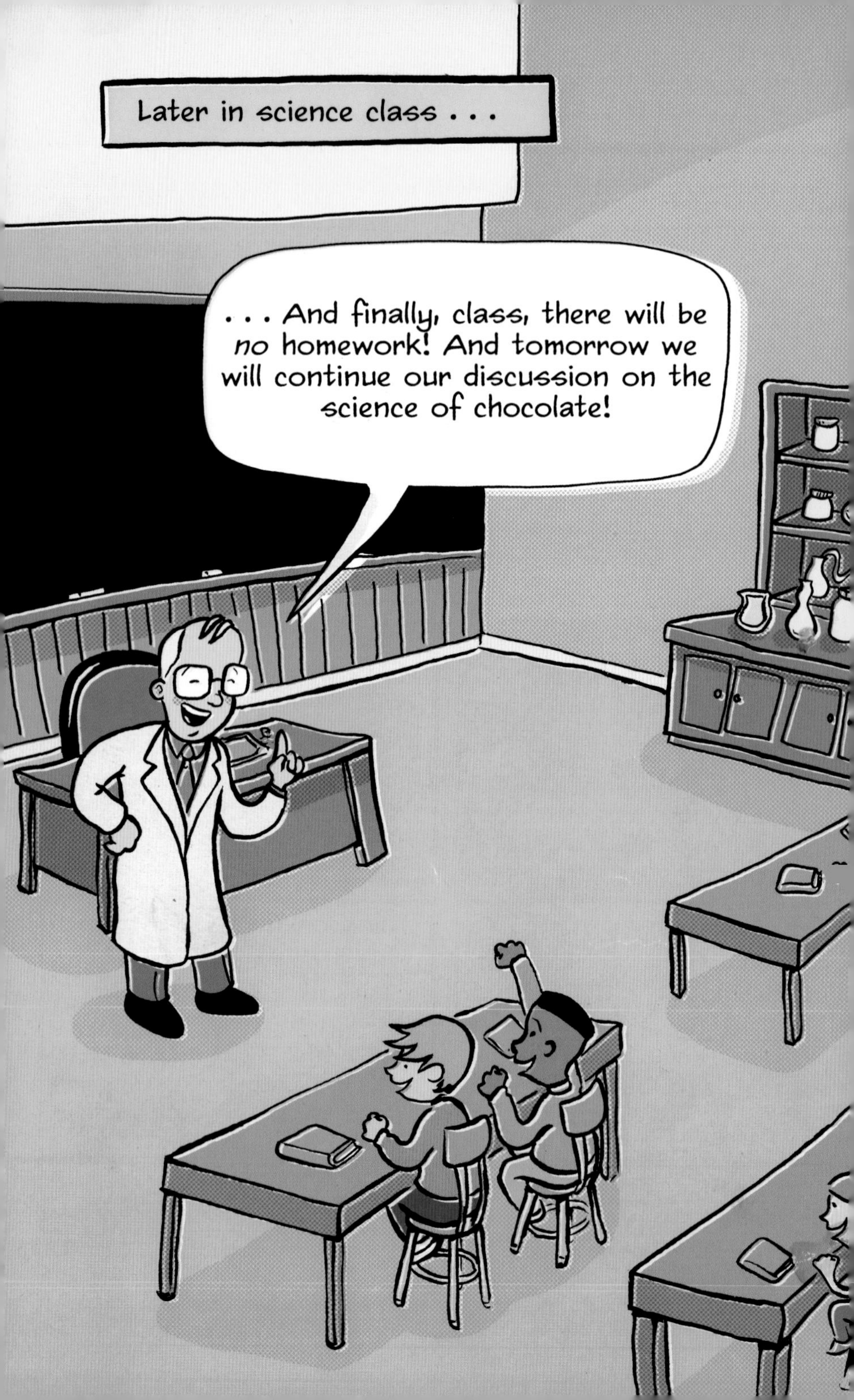
Later in science class . . .
. . . And finally, class, there will be *no* homework! And tomorrow we will continue our discussion on the science of chocolate!

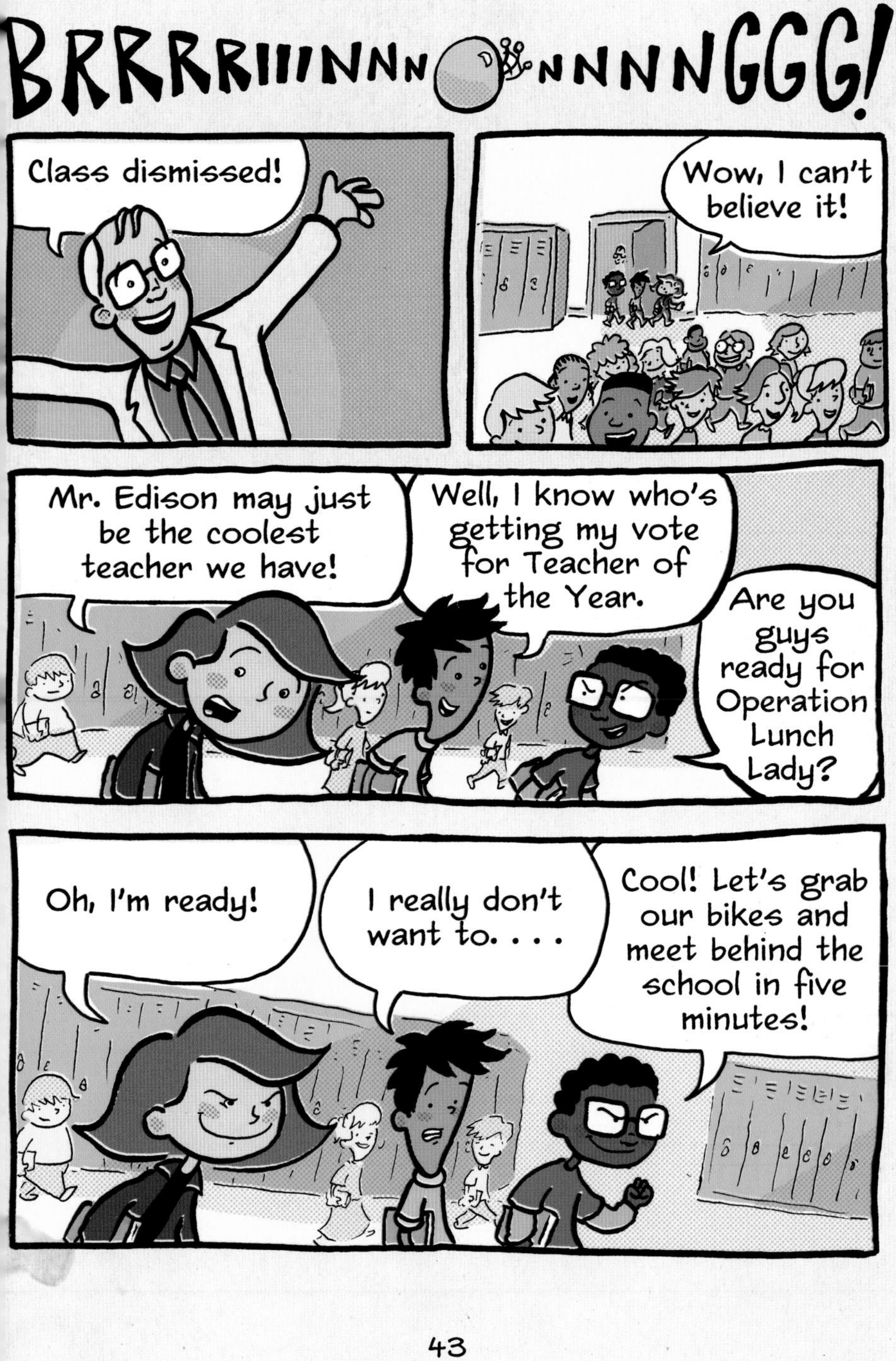
BRRRRIIIINNNN NNNNNGGG!
Class dismissed!
Wow, I can't believe it!
Mr. Edison may just be the coolest teacher we have!
Well, I know who's getting my vote for Teacher of the Year.
Are you guys ready for Operation Lunch Lady?
Oh, I'm ready!
I really don't want to. . . .
Cool! Let's grab our bikes and meet behind the school in five minutes!

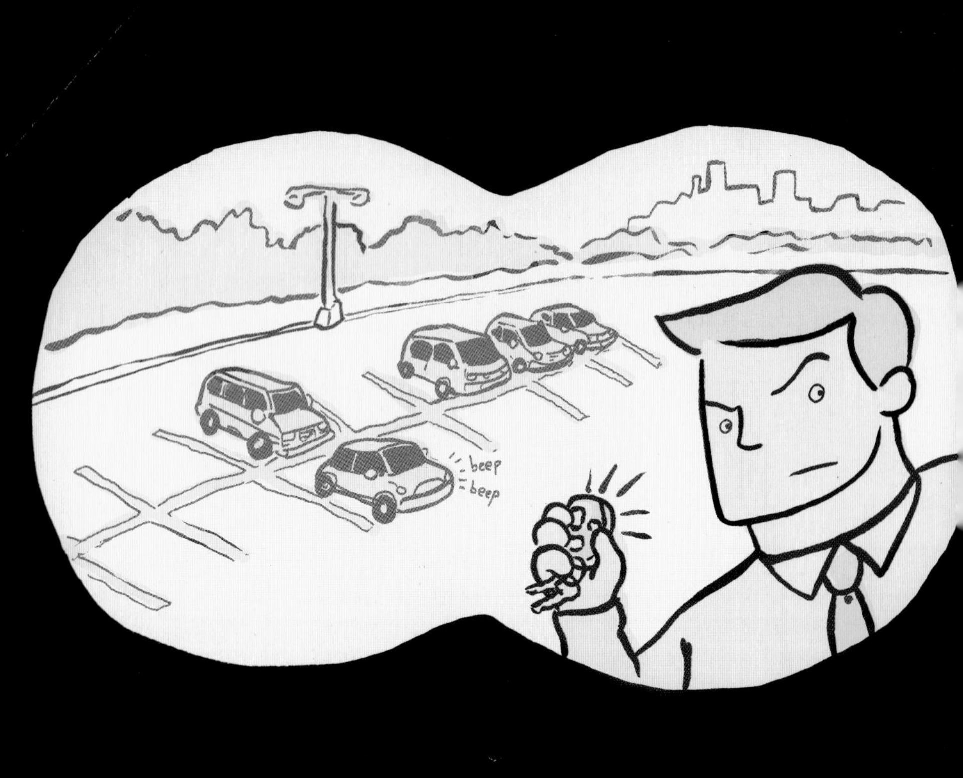
beep
beep

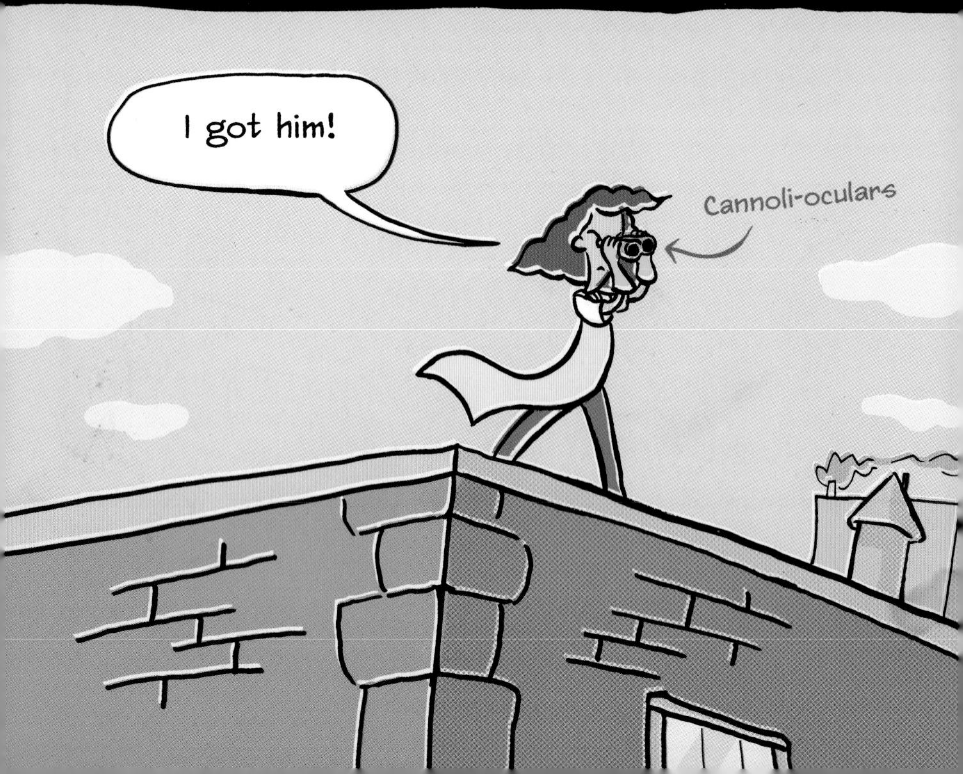
I got him!
Cannoli-oculars

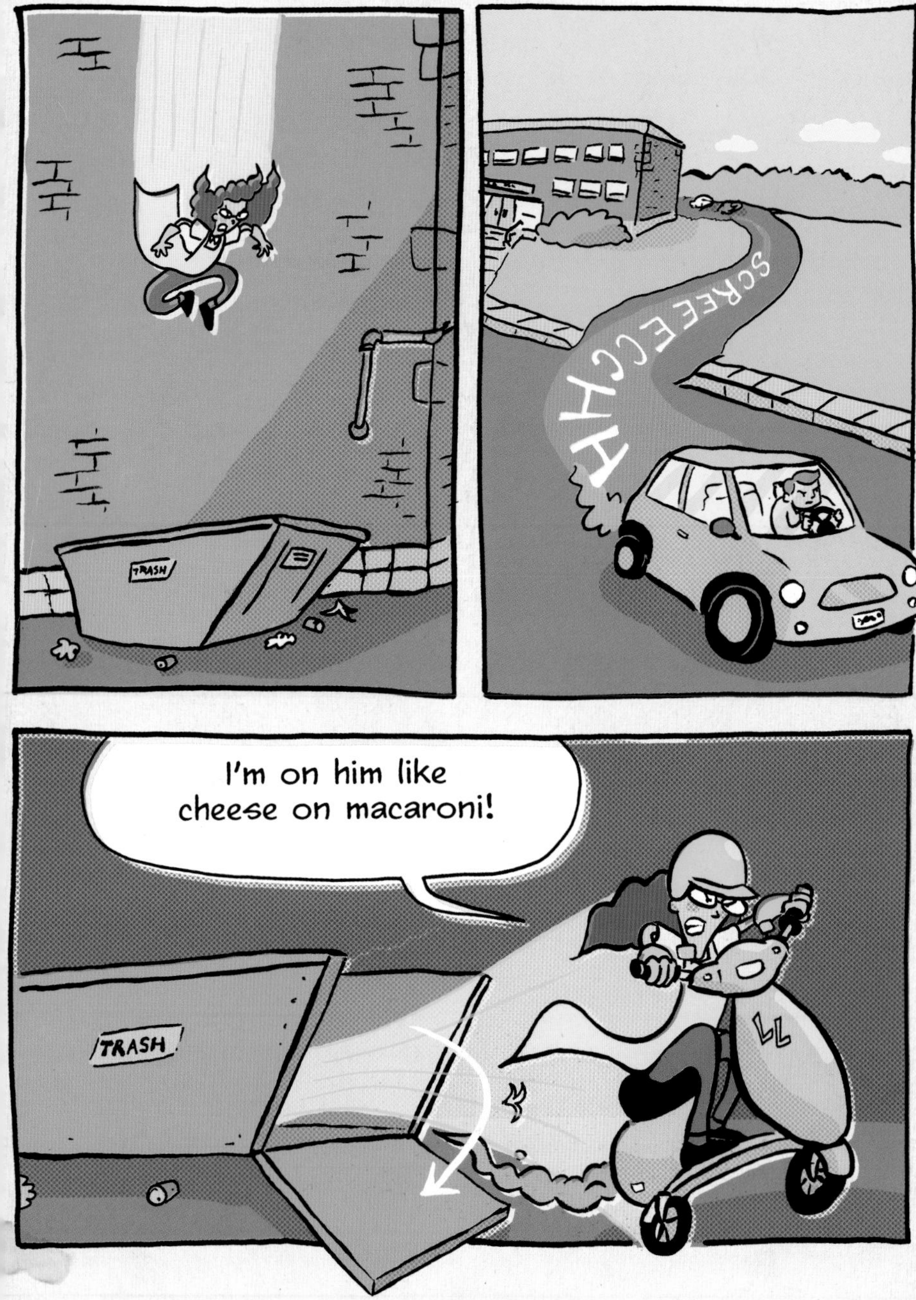
TRASH
SCREEECCHHH
I'm on him like cheese on macaroni!
TRASH

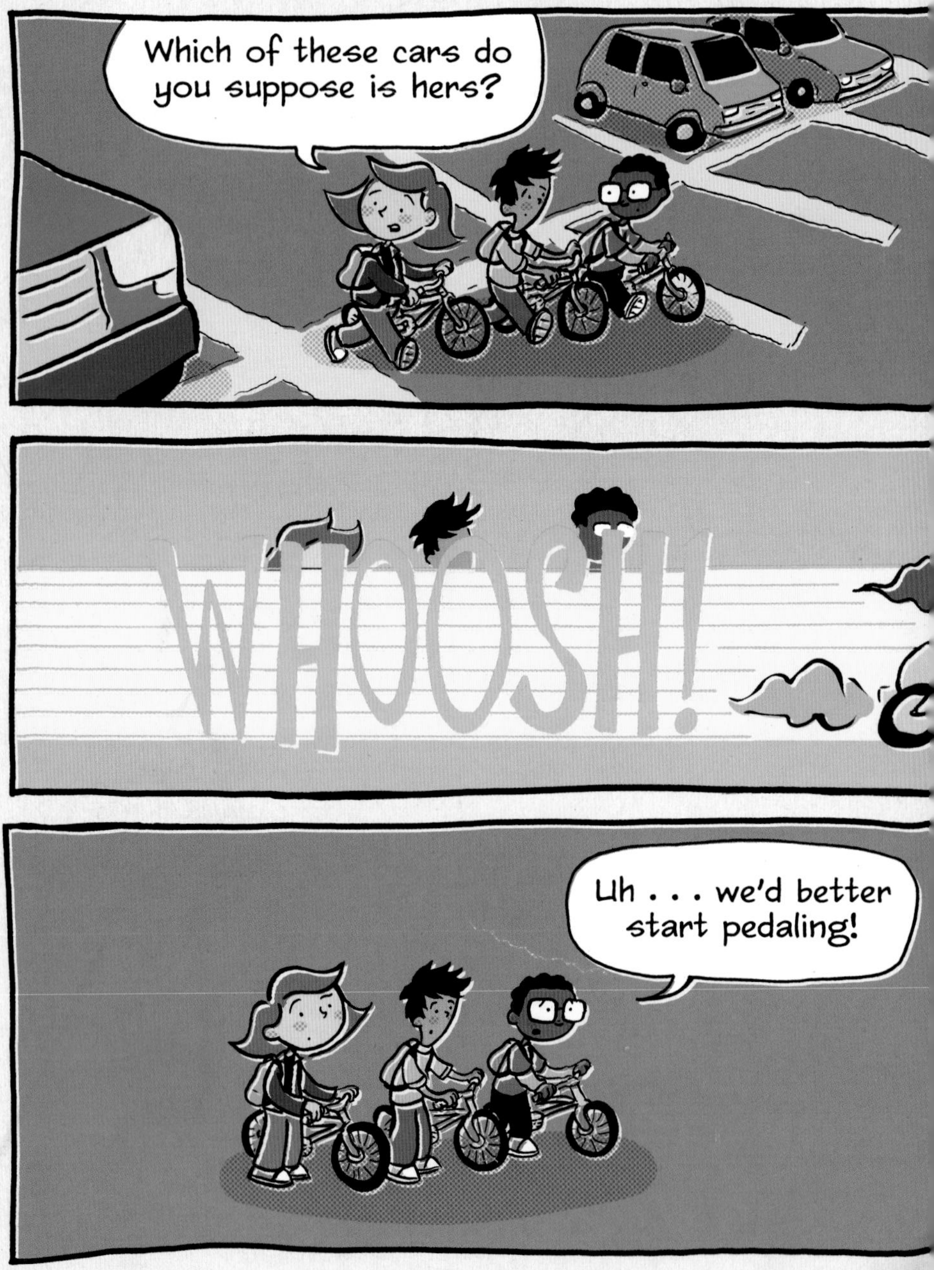
Which of these cars do you suppose is hers?
WHOOSH!
Uh . . . we'd better start pedaling!

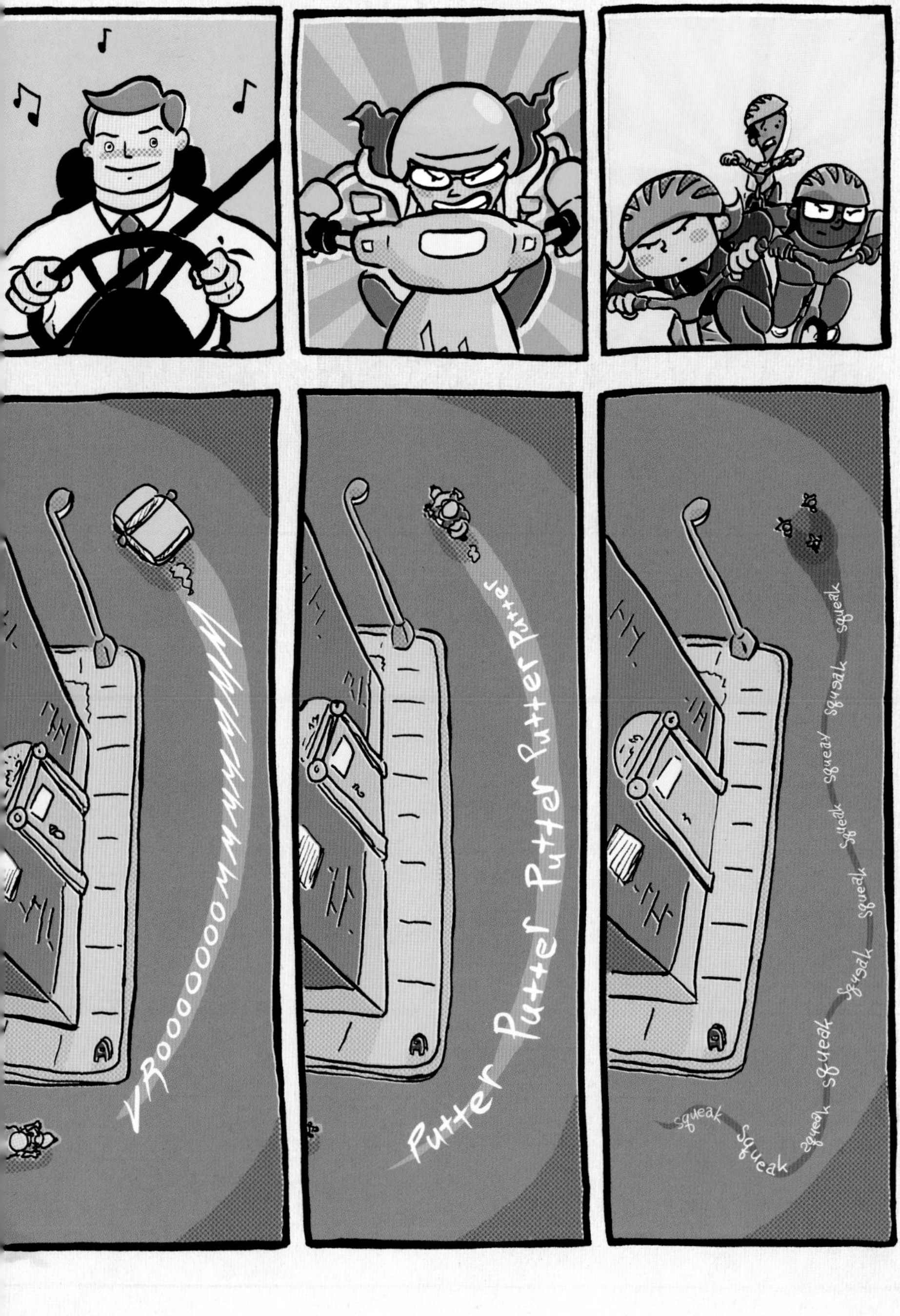

VROOOOOOOMMMMMMMMMM
Putter Putter Putter Putter Putter
squeak squeak squeak squeak squeak squeak squeaky squeak squeak squeak

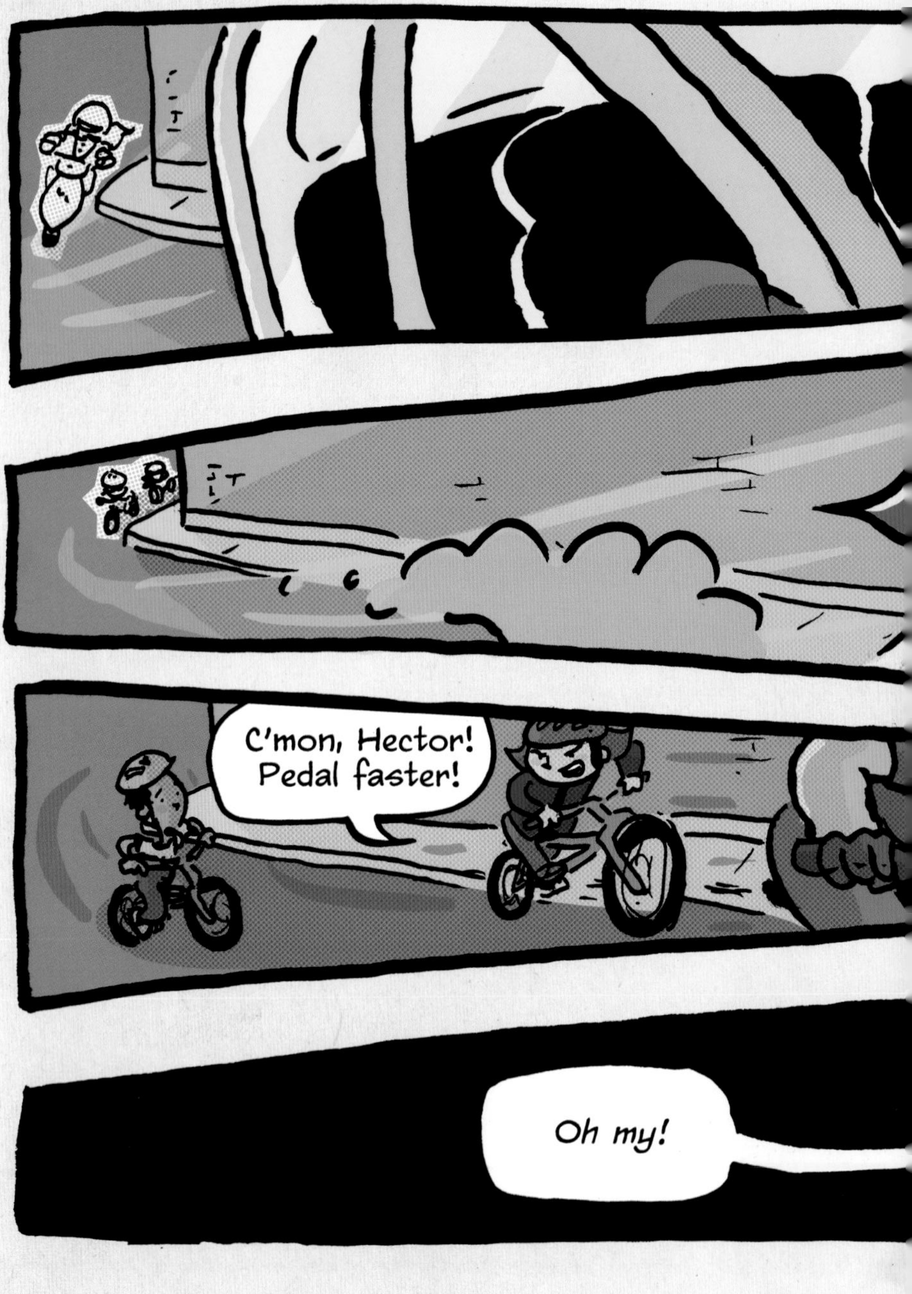
C'mon, Hector! Pedal faster!
Oh my!

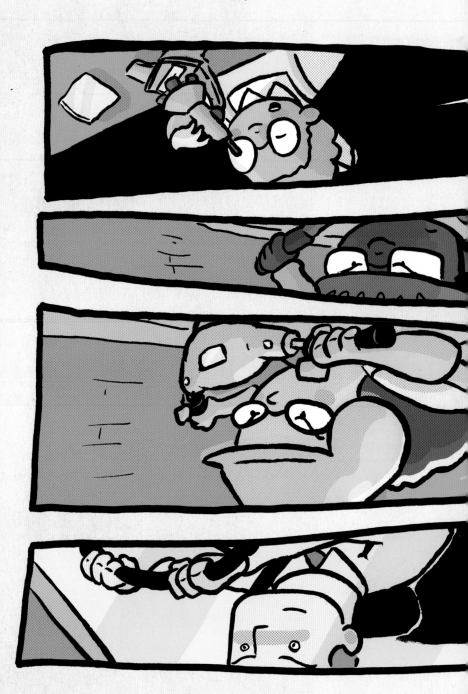

64

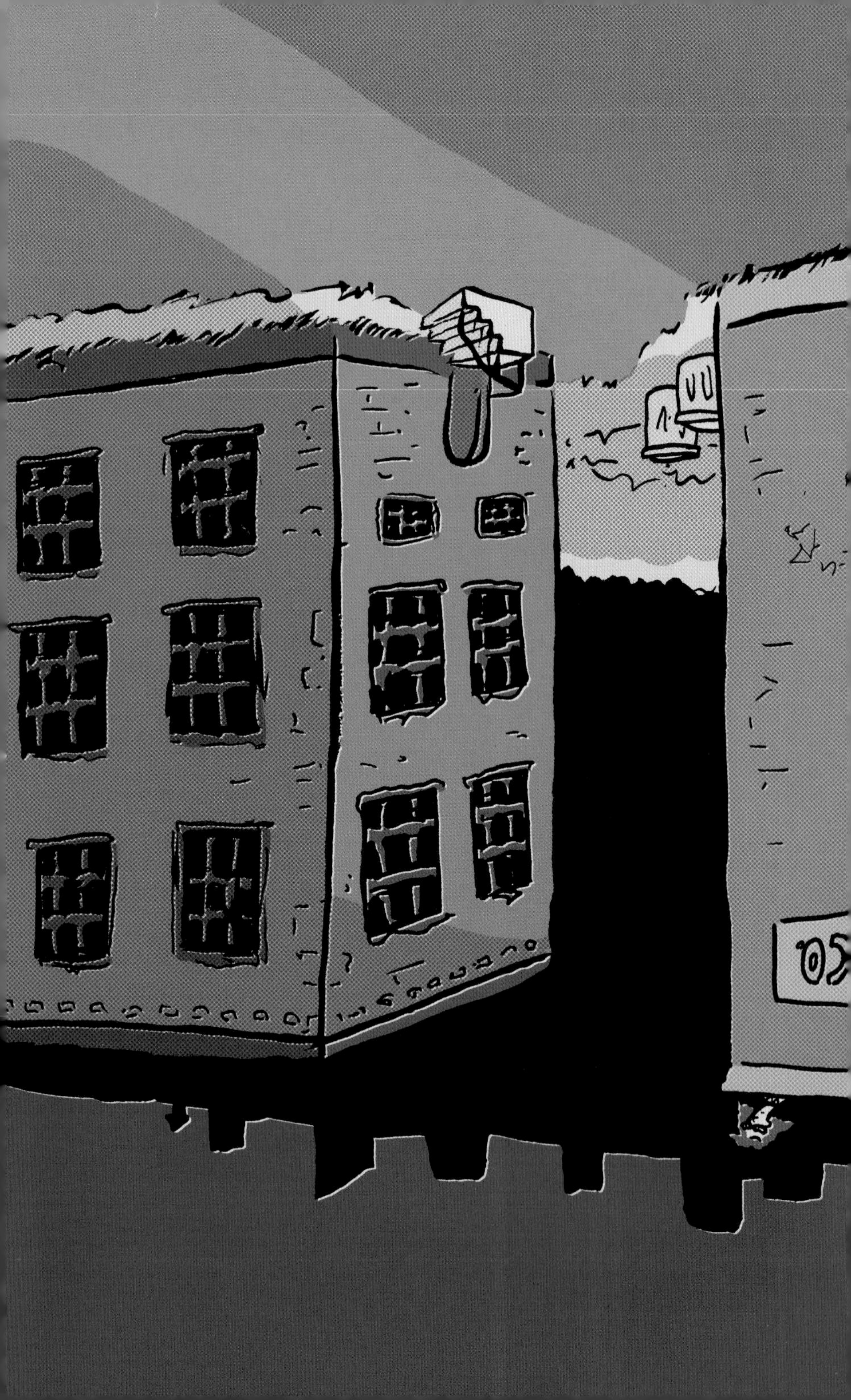

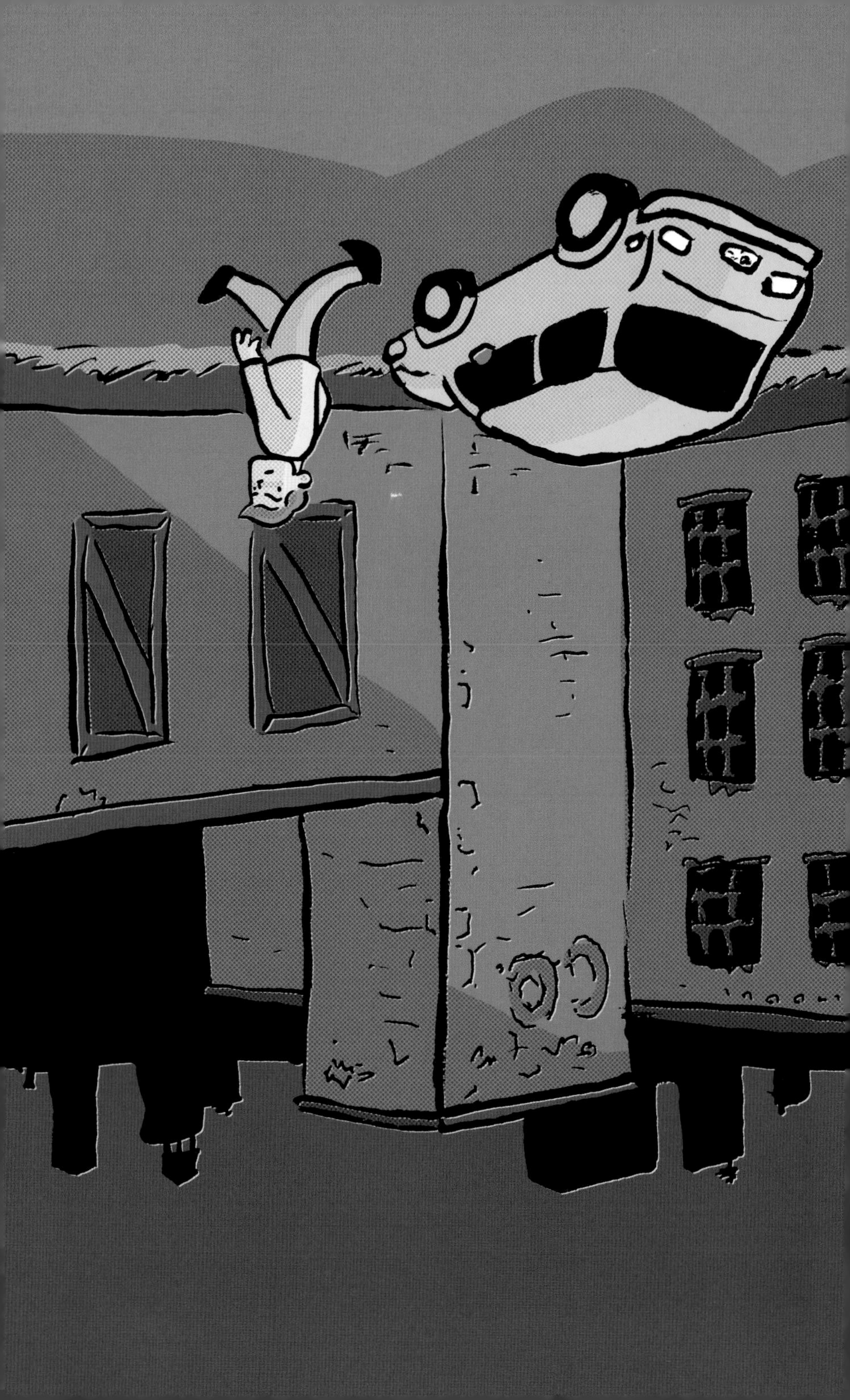

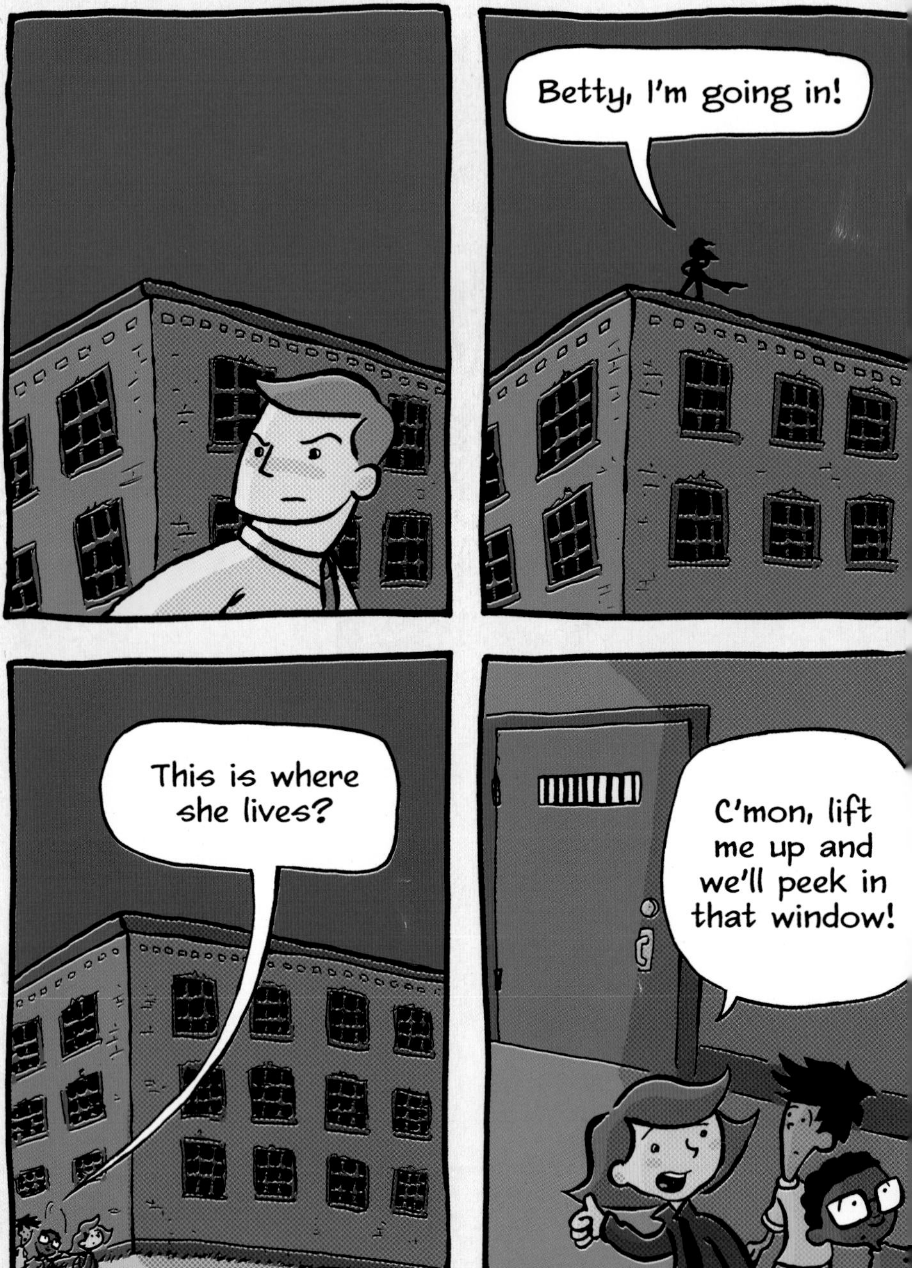
Betty, I'm going in!
This is where she lives?
C'mon, lift me up and we'll peek in that window!

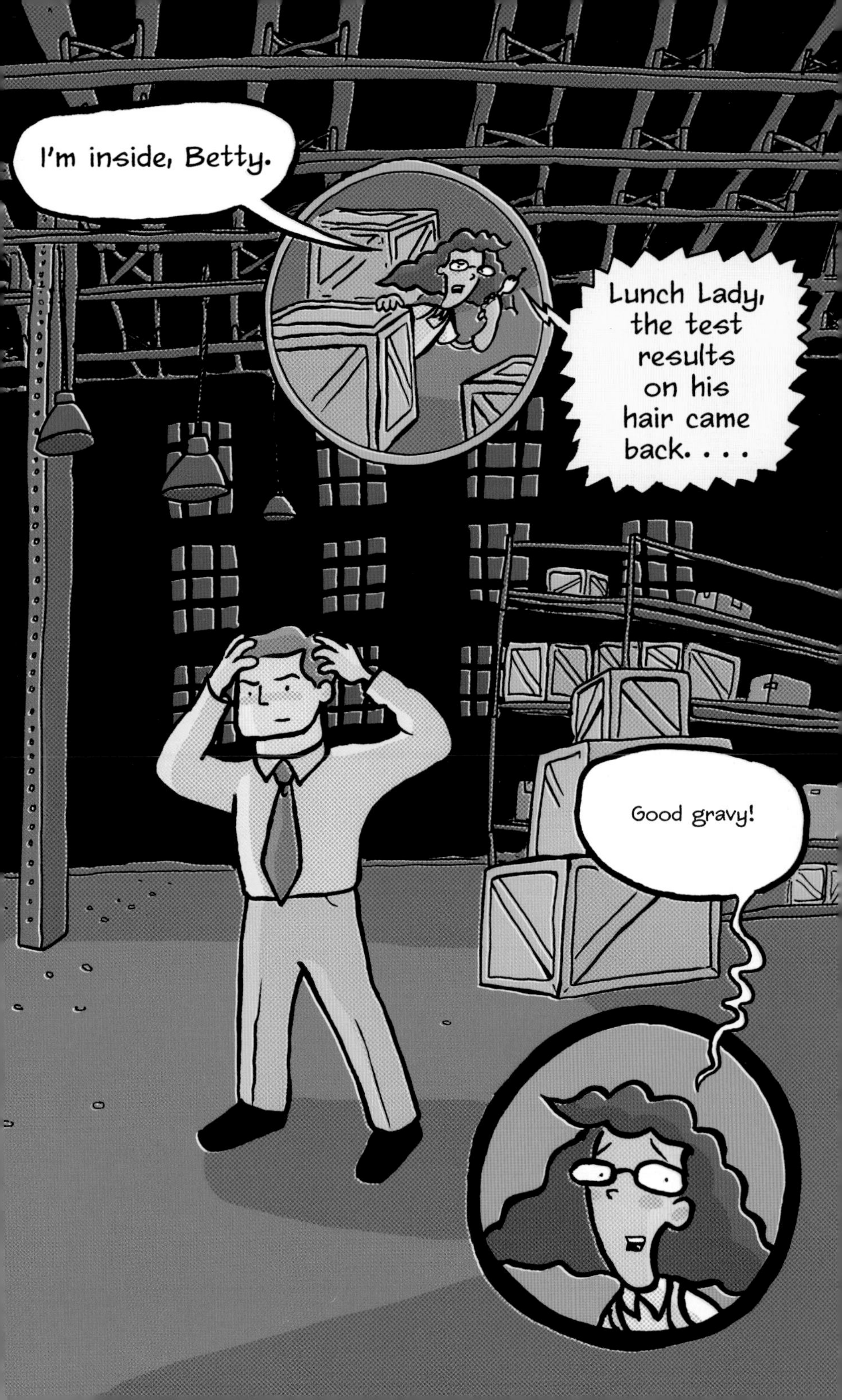
I'm inside, Betty.
Lunch Lady, the test results on his hair came back. . . .
Good gravy!

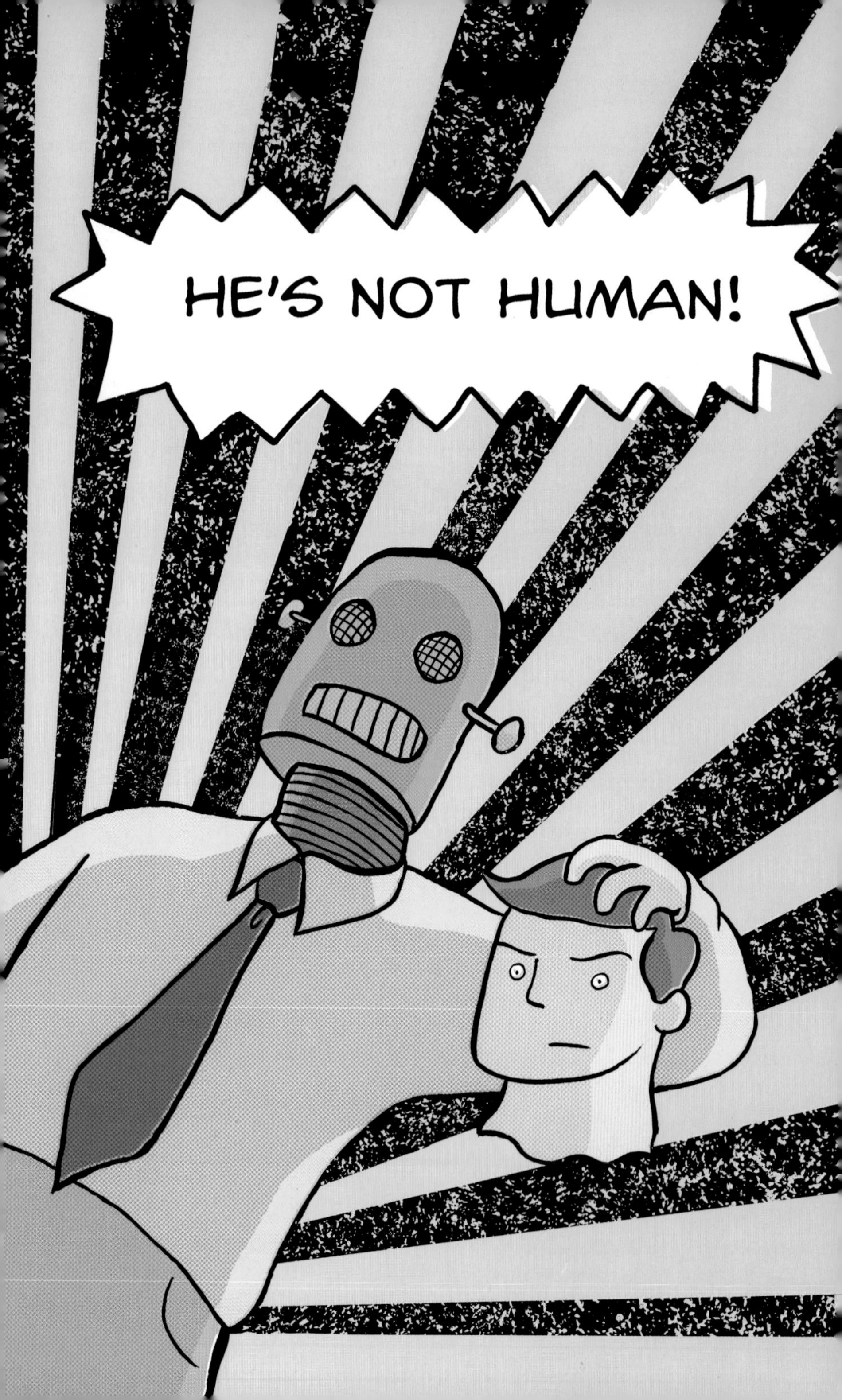
HE'S NOT HUMAN!

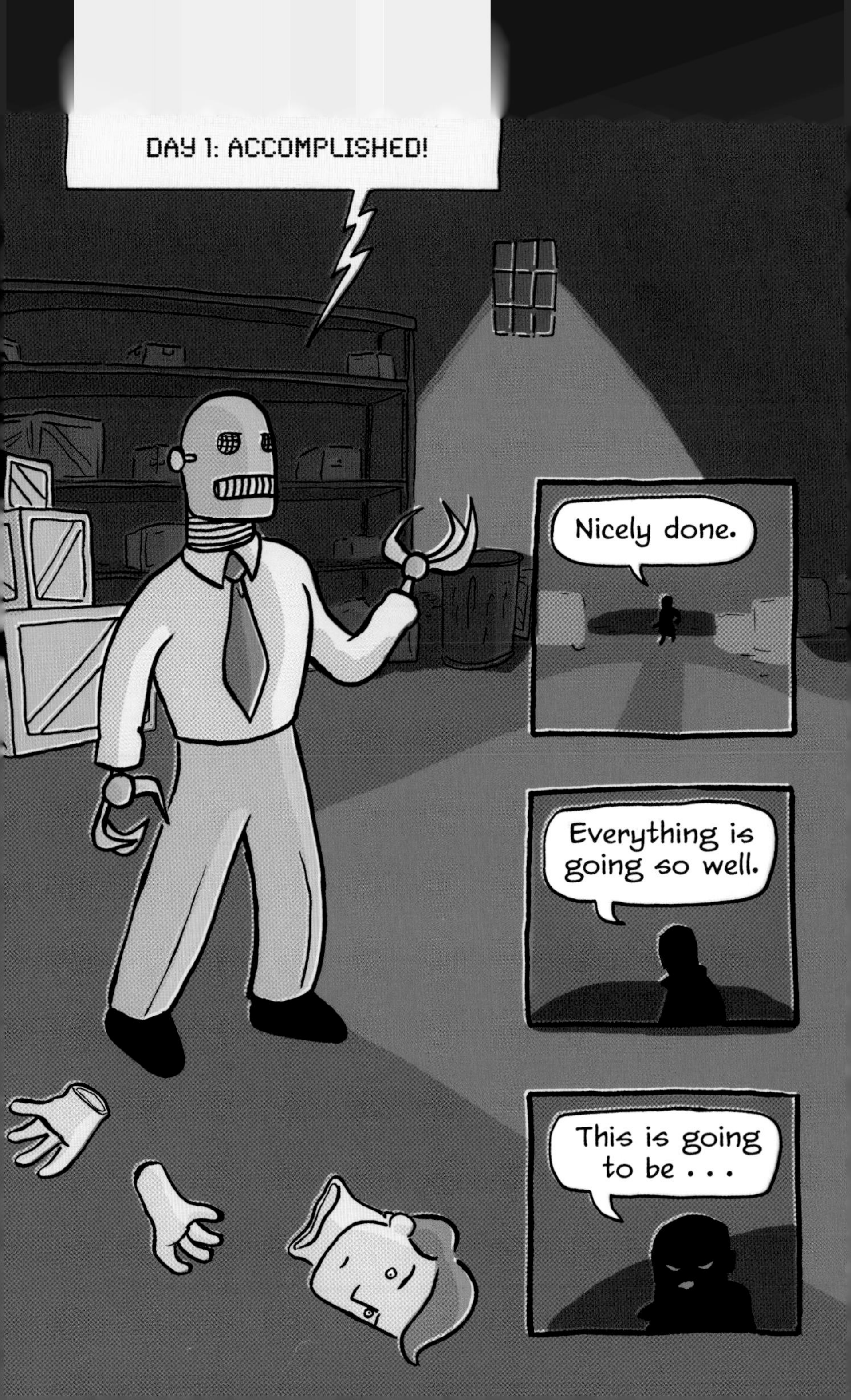
DAY 1: ACCOMPLISHED!
Nicely done.
Everything is going so well.
This is going to be . . .

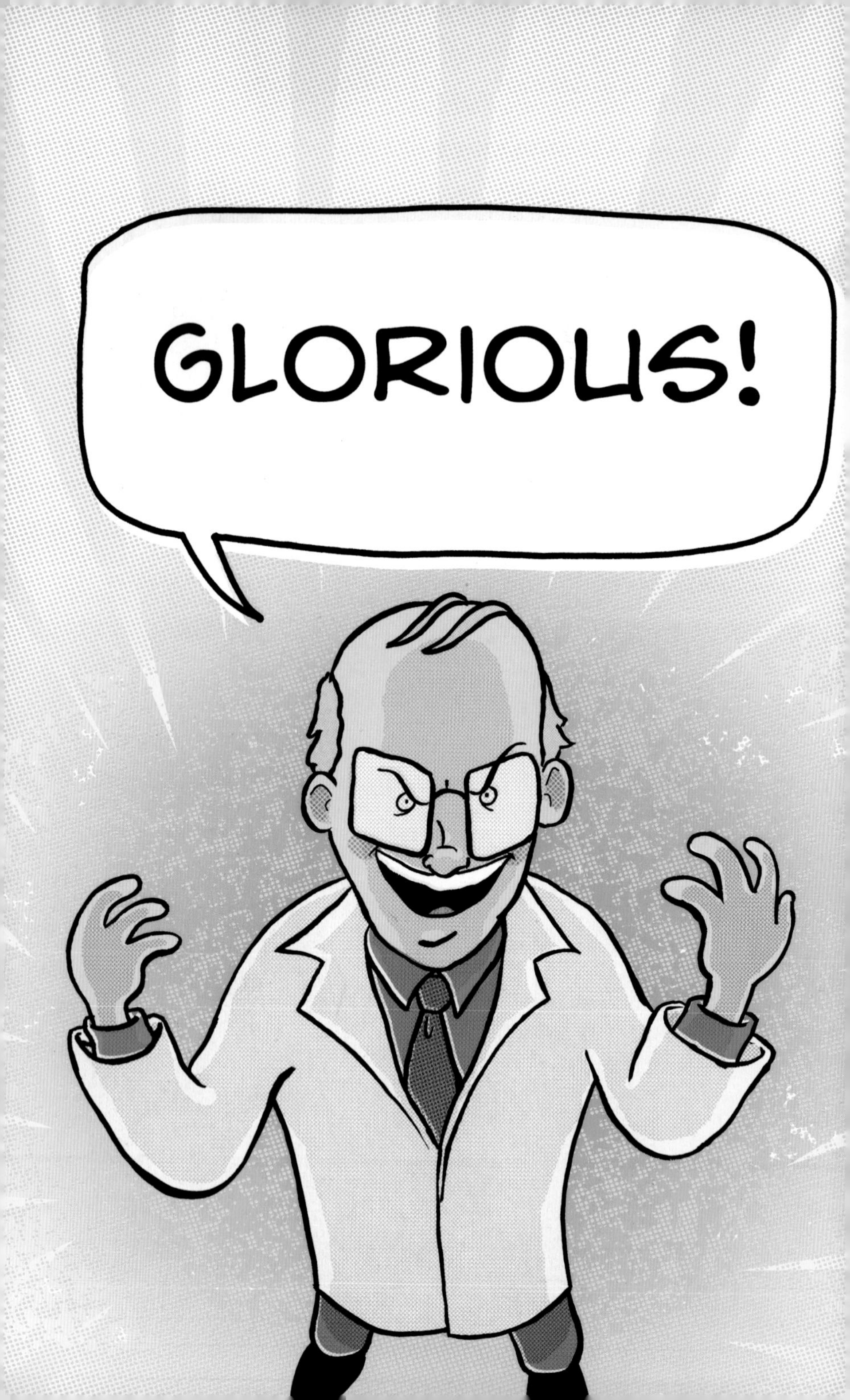
GLORIOUS!

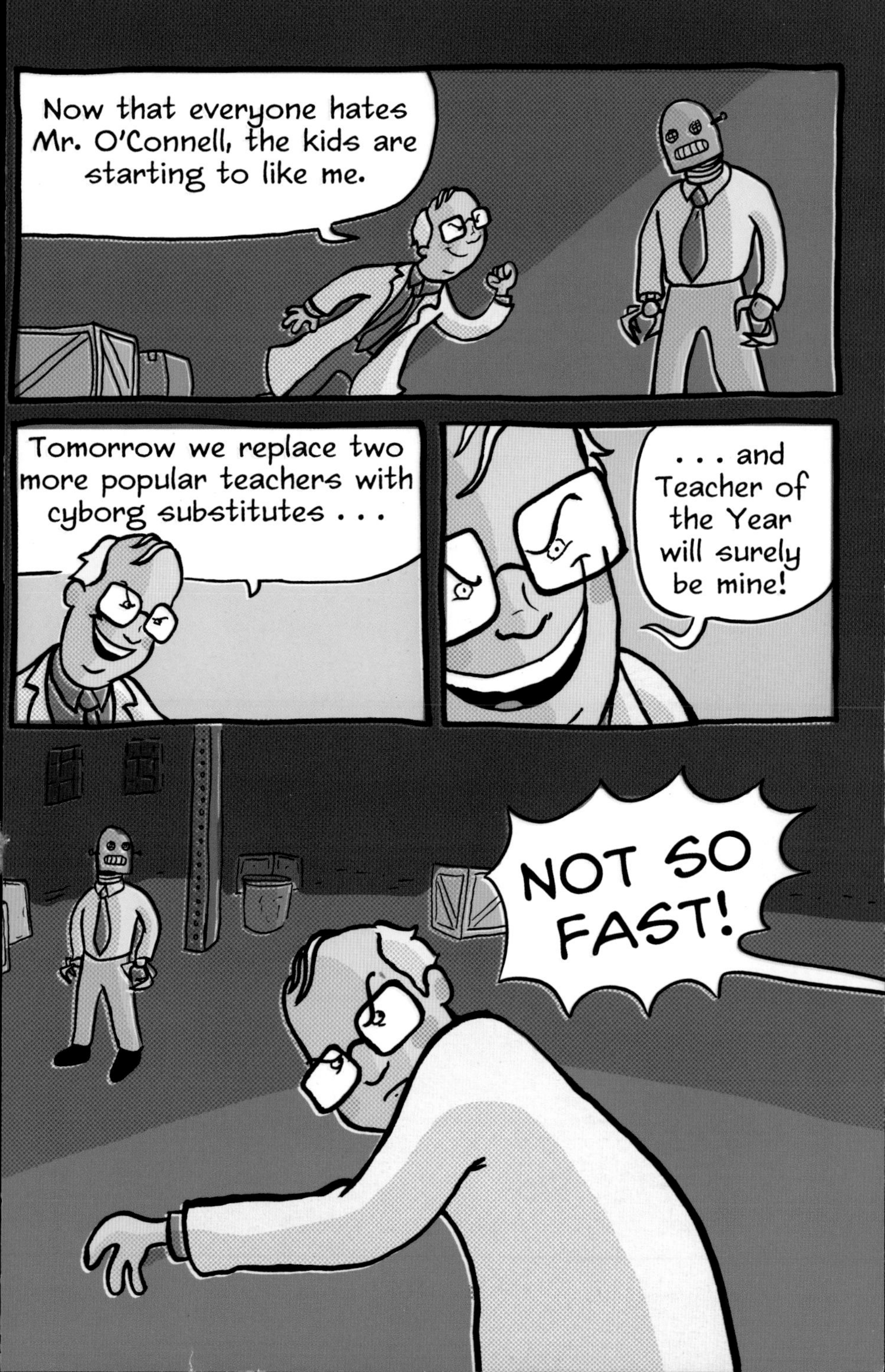
Now that everyone hates Mr. O'Connell, the kids are starting to like me.
Tomorrow we replace two more popular teachers with cyborg substitutes . . .
. . . and Teacher of the Year will surely be mine!
NOT SO FAST!

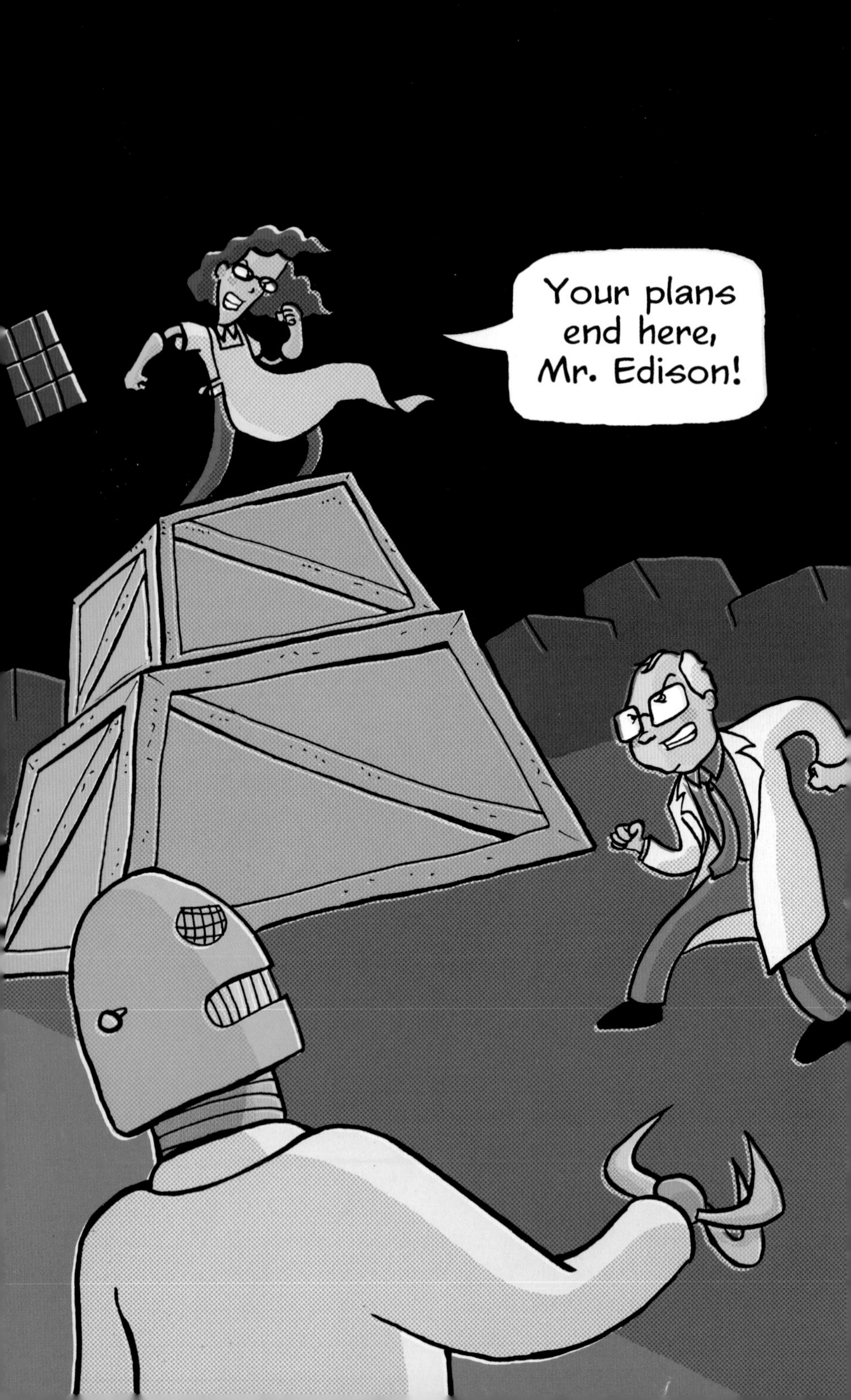
Your plans end here, Mr. Edison!

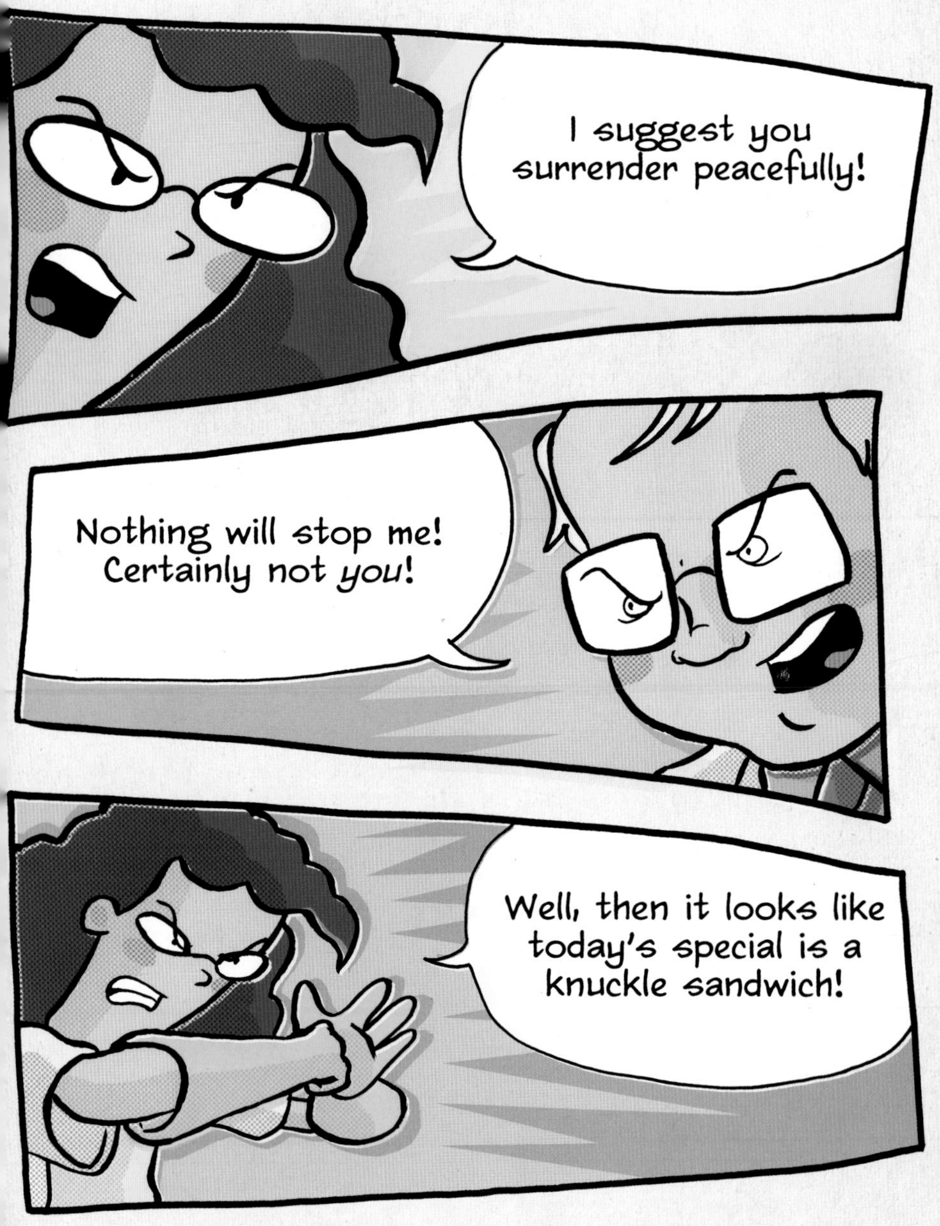
I suggest you surrender peacefully!
Nothing will stop me! Certainly not *you*!
Well, then it looks like today's special is a knuckle sandwich!

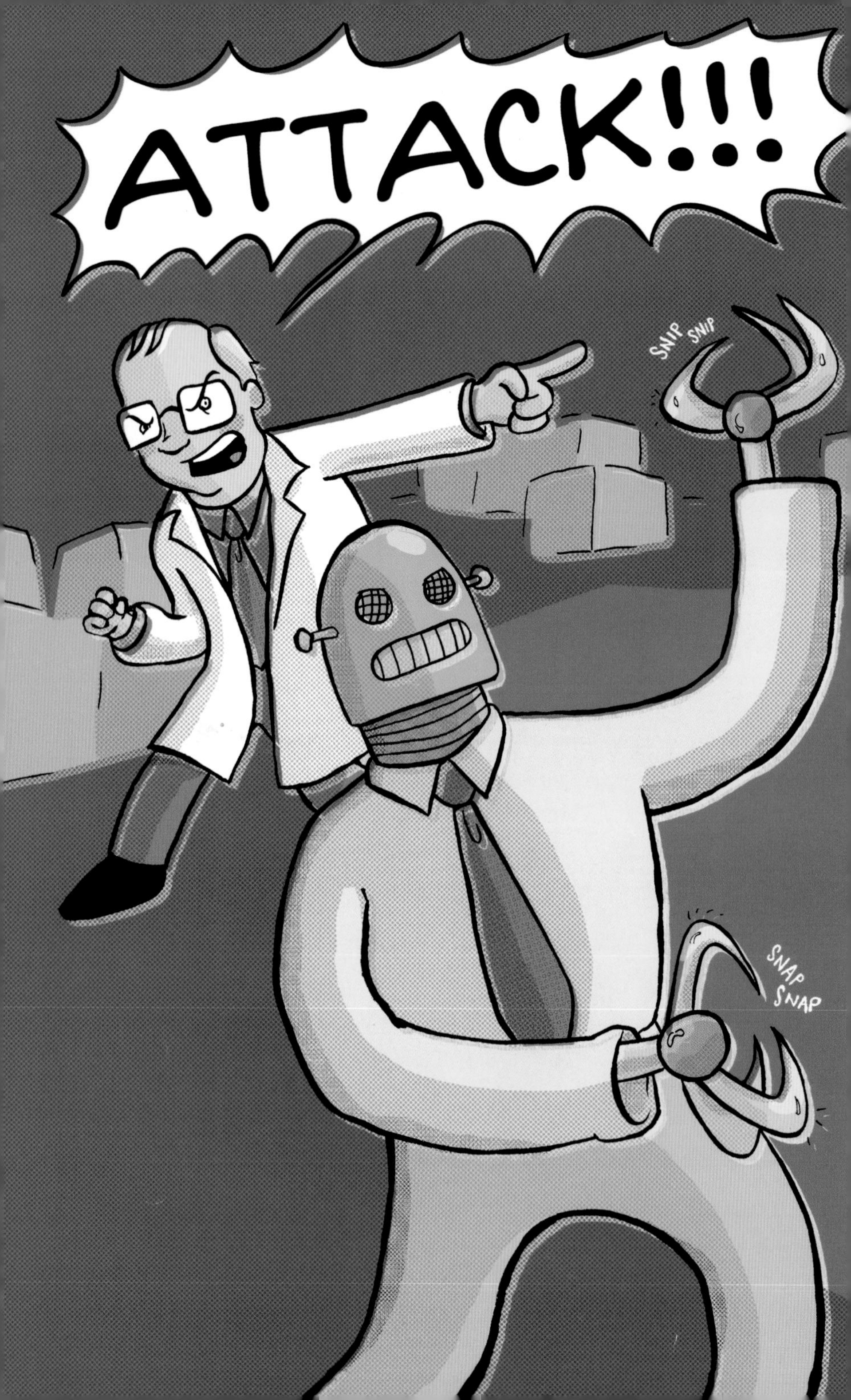
ATTACK!!!
SNIP SNIP
SNAP SNAP

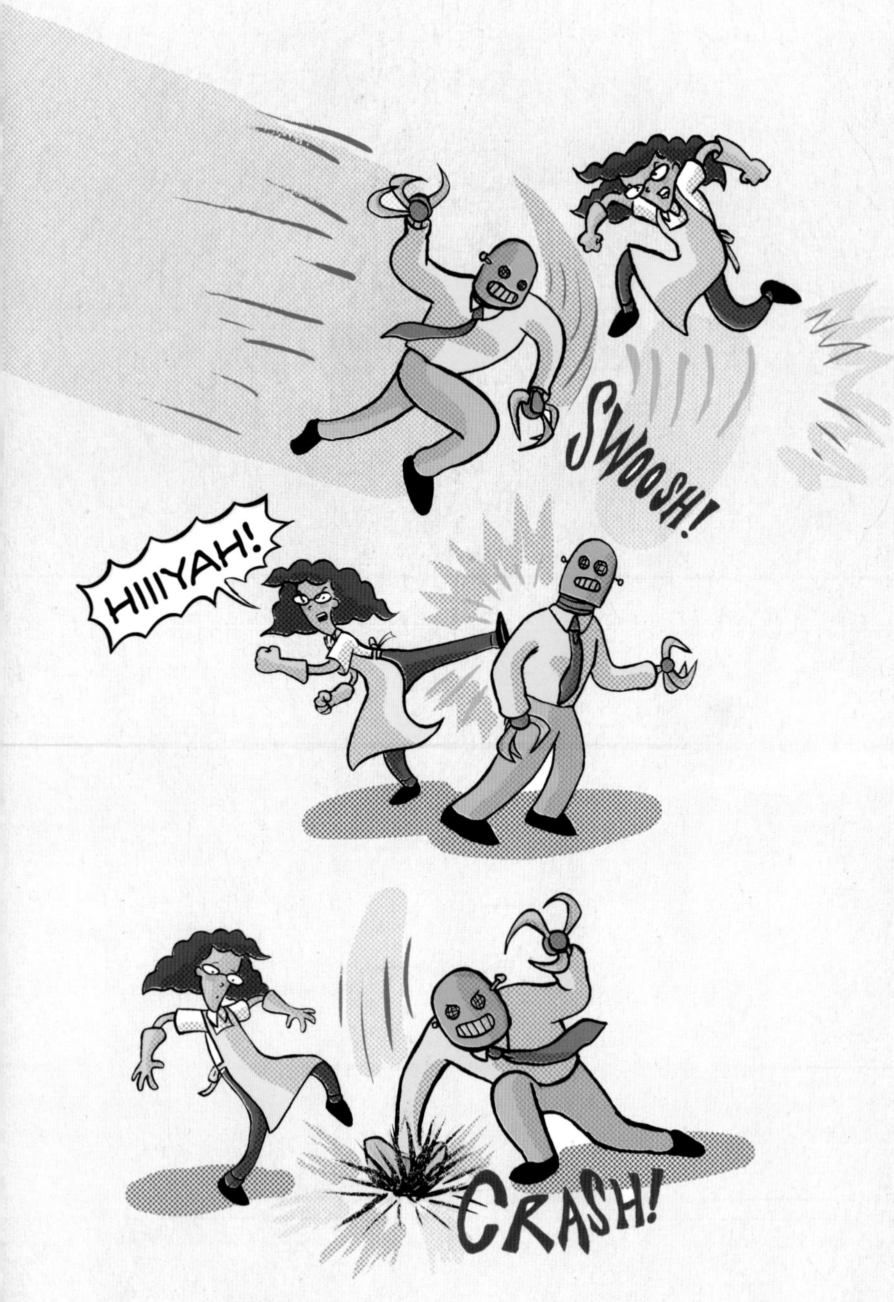
SWOOSH!
HIIIYAH!
CRASH!

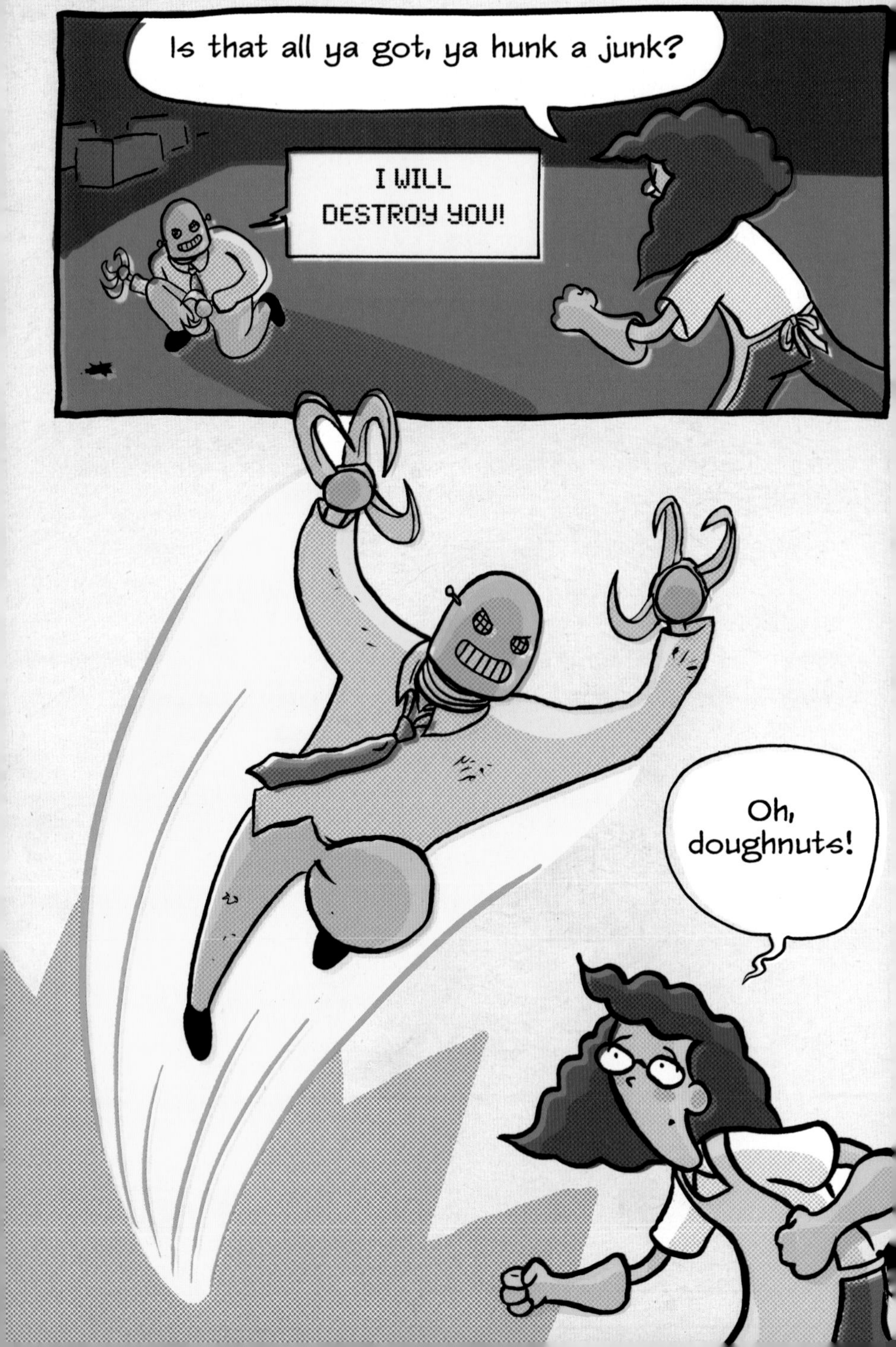
Is that all ya got, ya hunk a junk?
I WILL DESTROY YOU!
Oh, doughnuts!

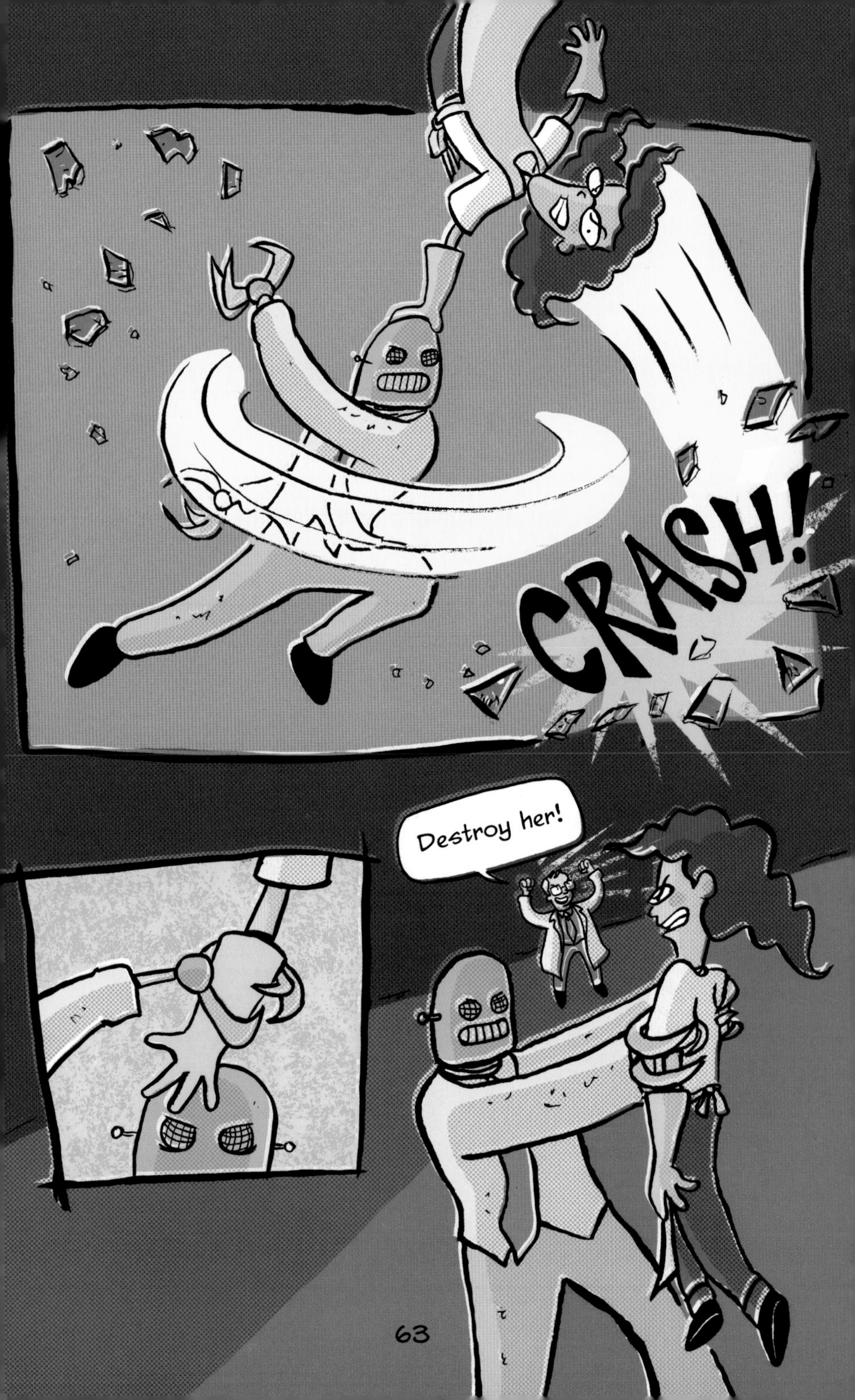
CRASH!
Destroy her!

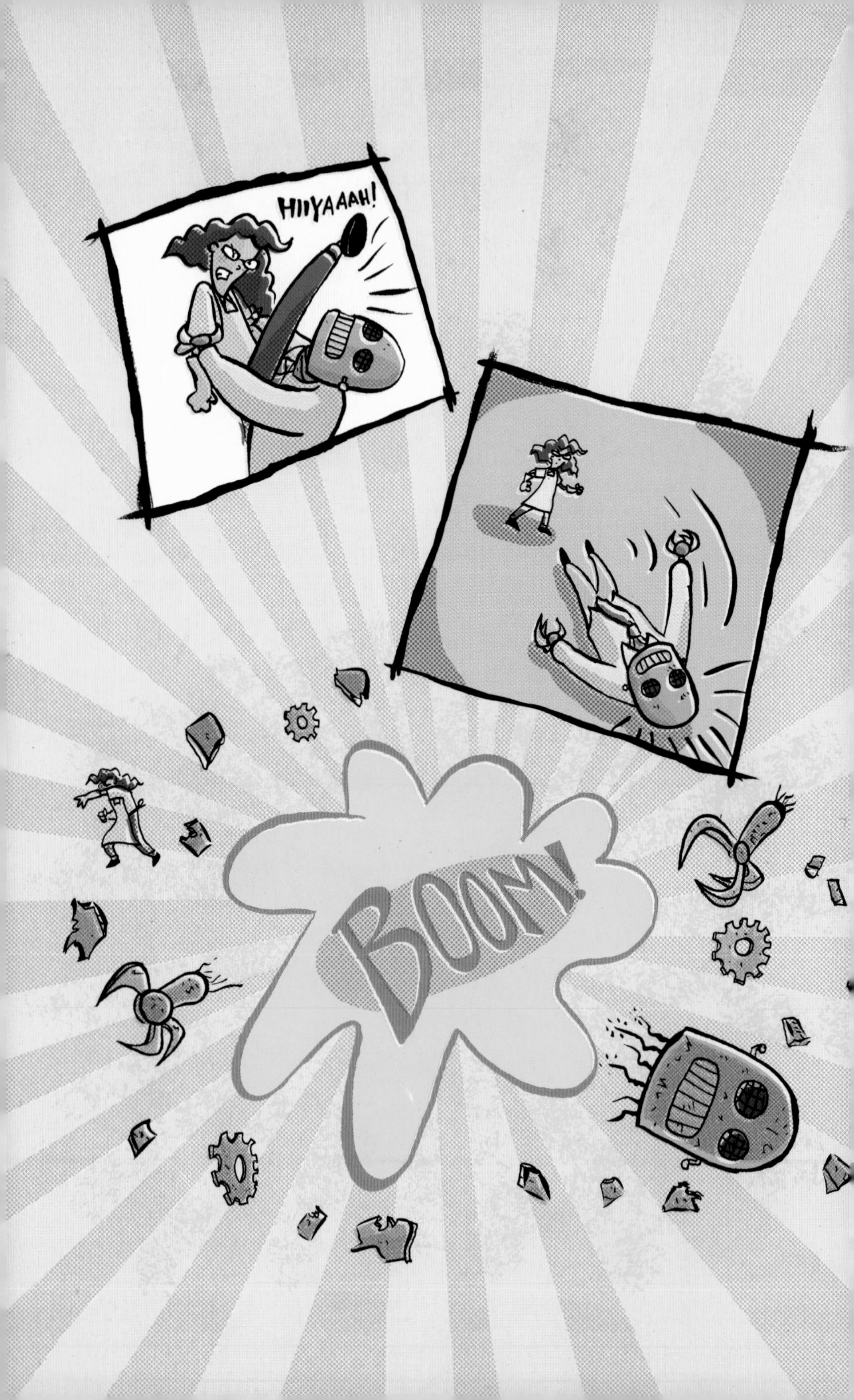
HIIYAAAH!
BOOM!

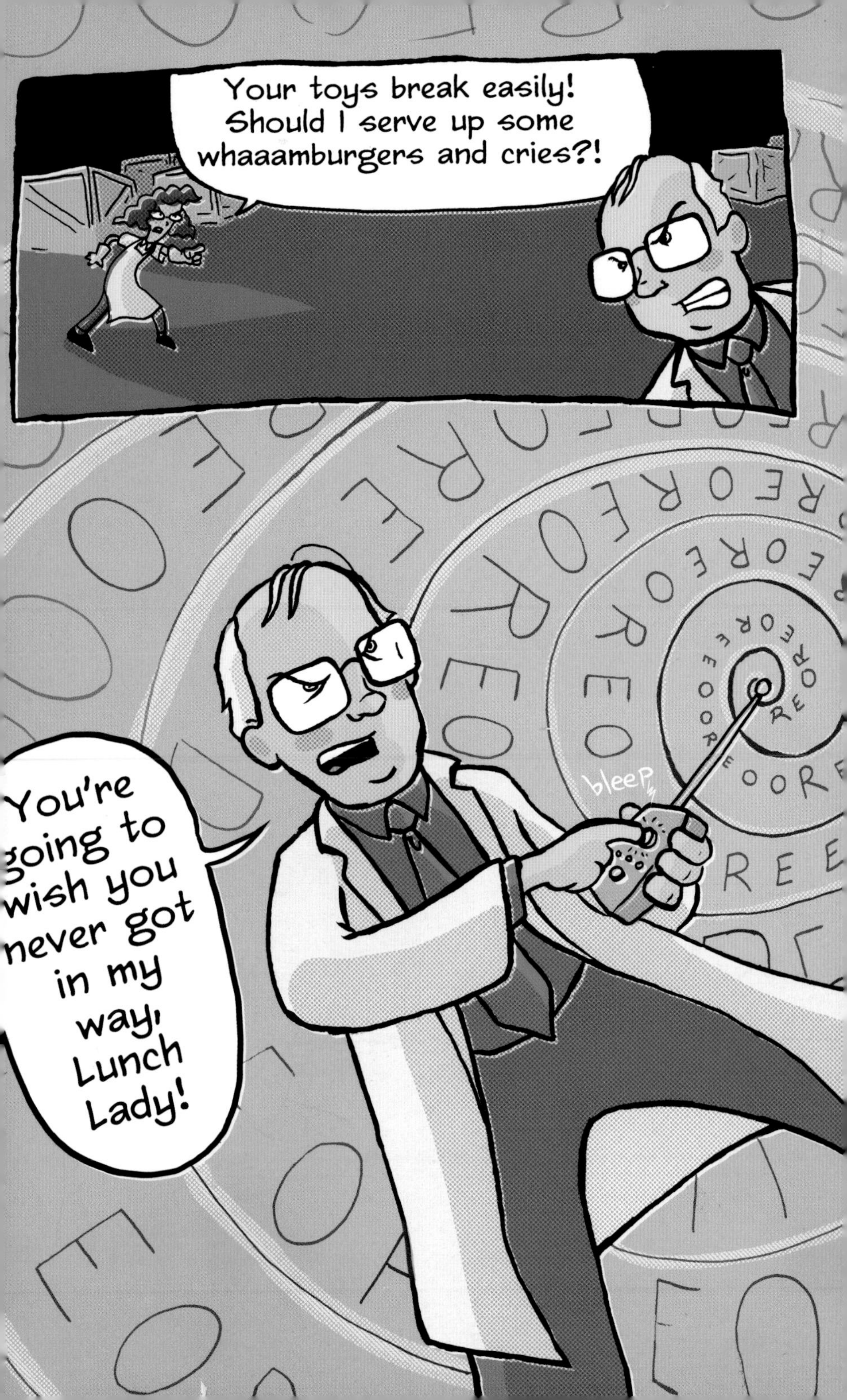
Your toys break easily! Should I serve up some whaaamburgers and cries?!
You're going to wish you never got in my way, Lunch Lady!
bleep

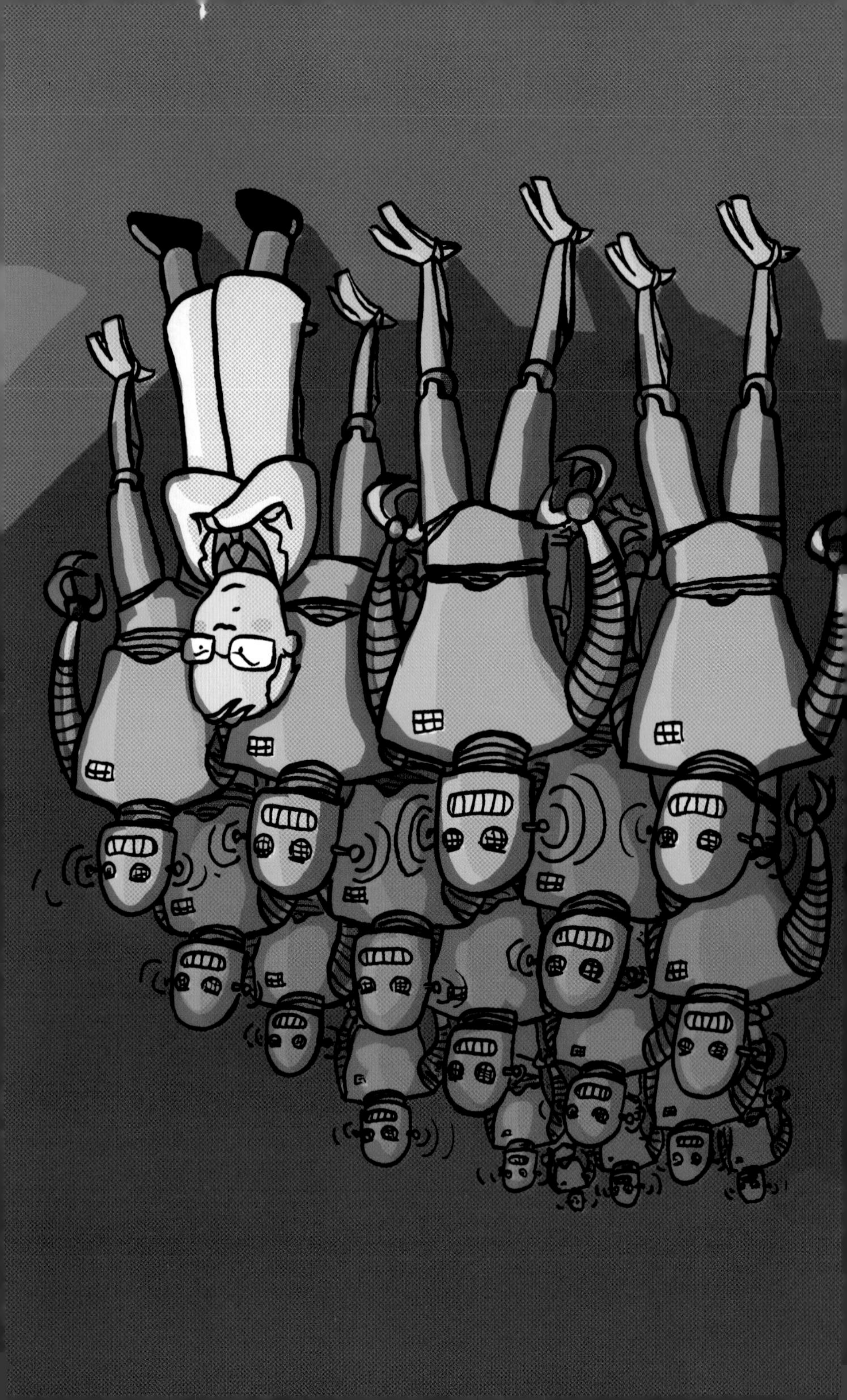

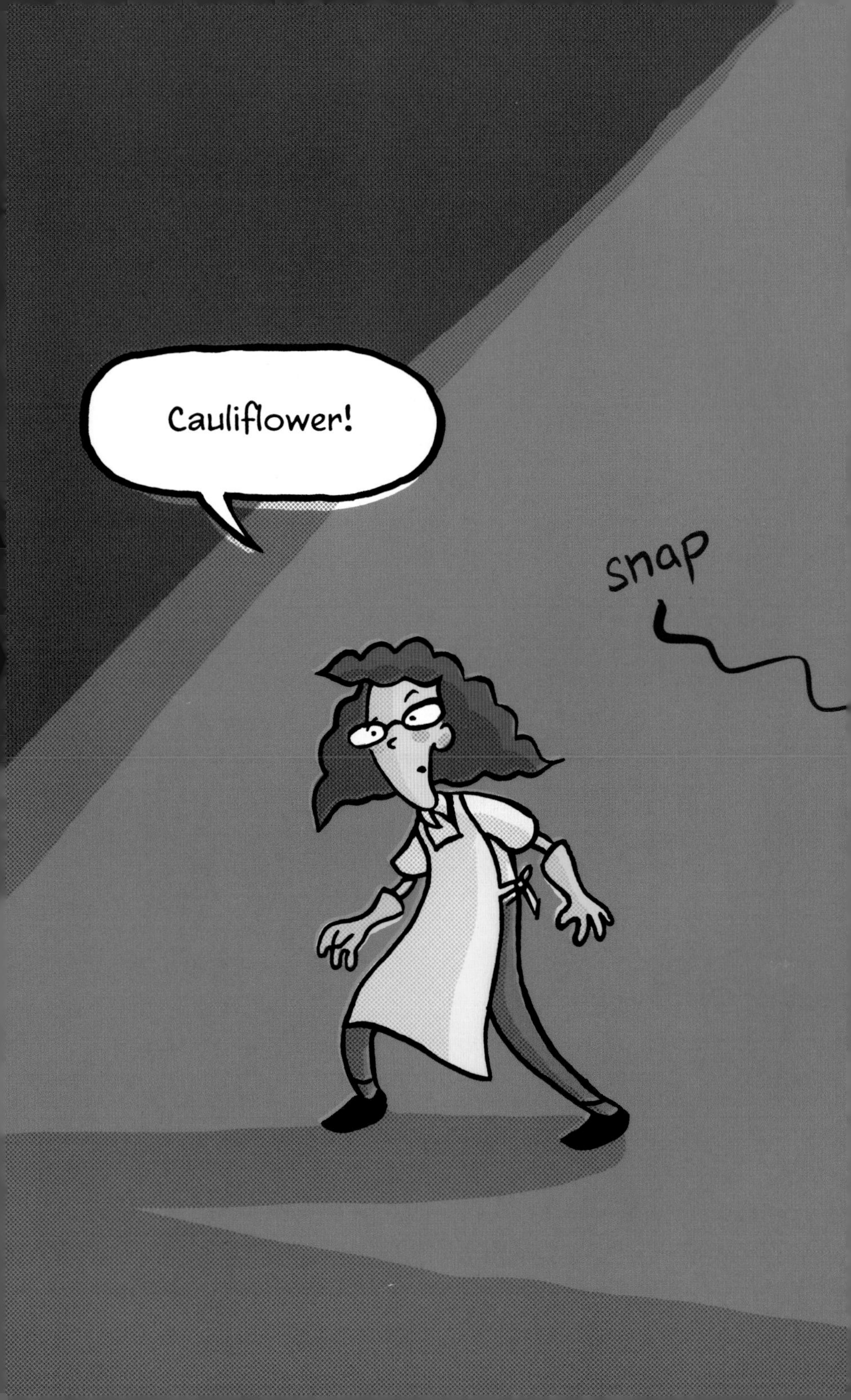
Cauliflower!
snap

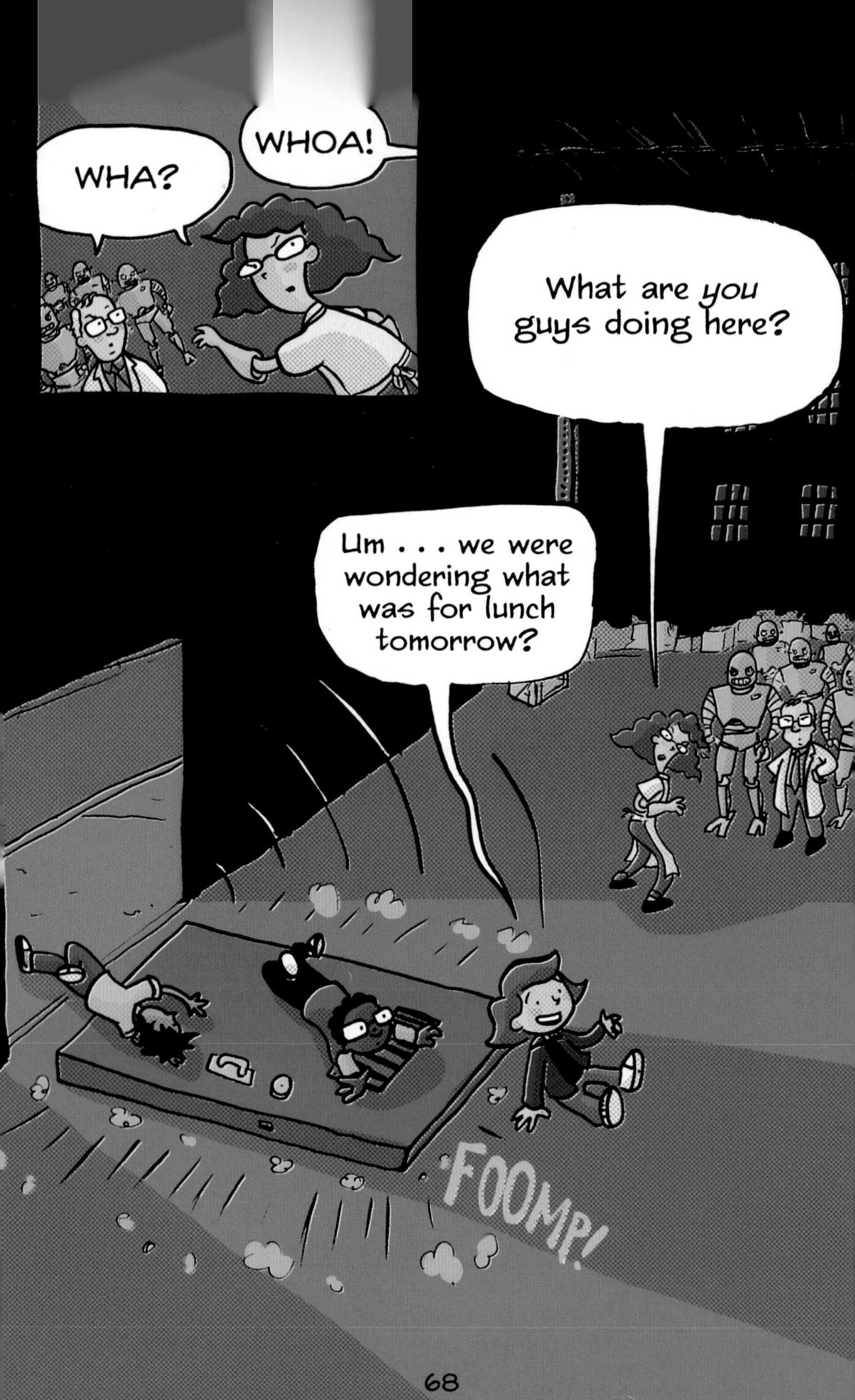
WHA?
WHOA!
What are *you* guys doing here?
Um . . . we were wondering what was for lunch tomorrow?
FOOMP!

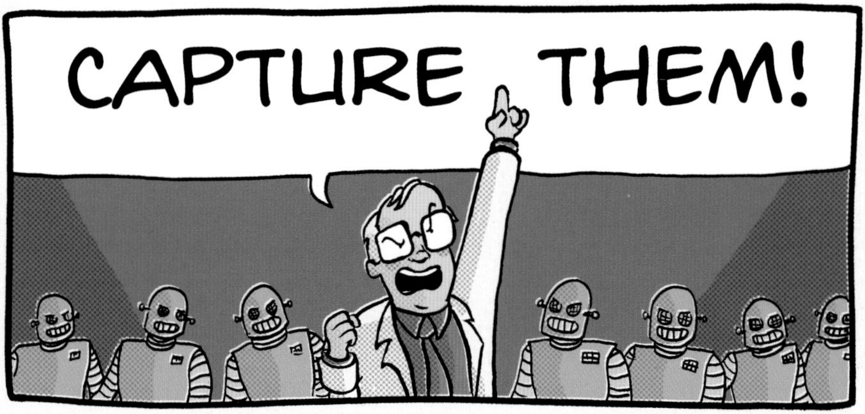
CAPTURE THEM!

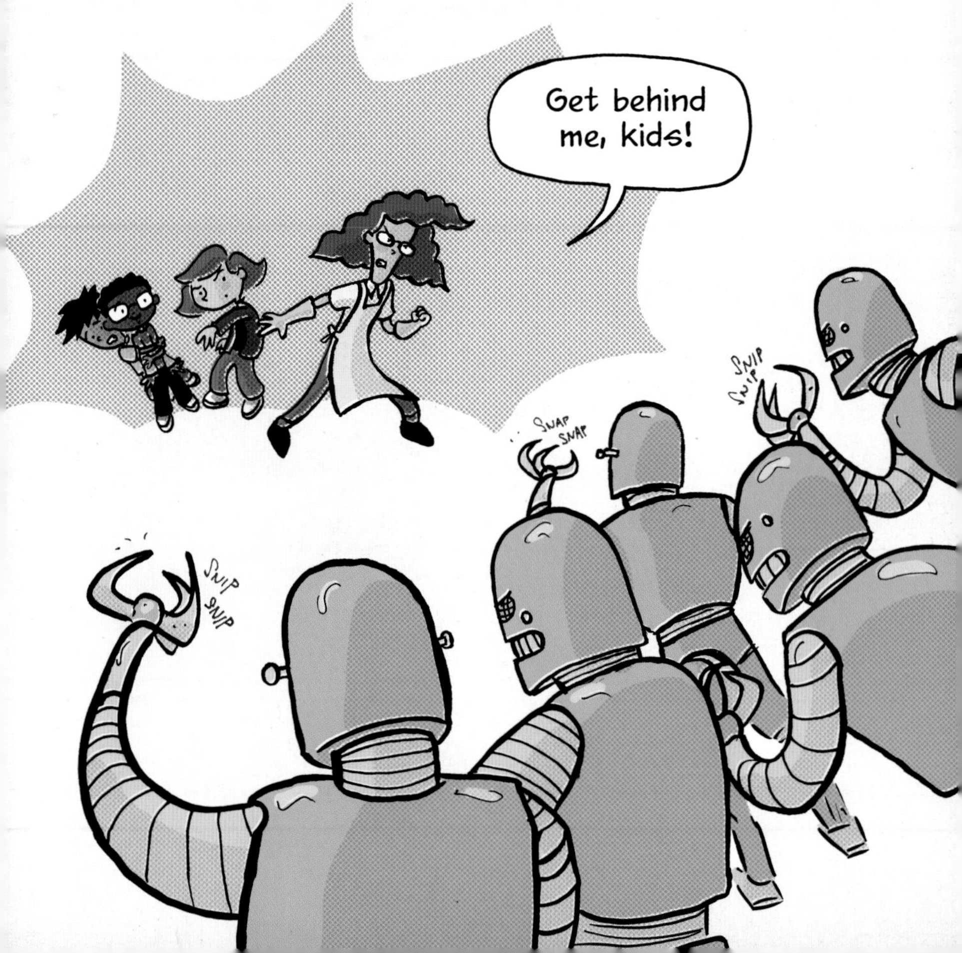
Get behind me, kids!
SNIP SNIP
SNAP SNAP
SNIP SNIP

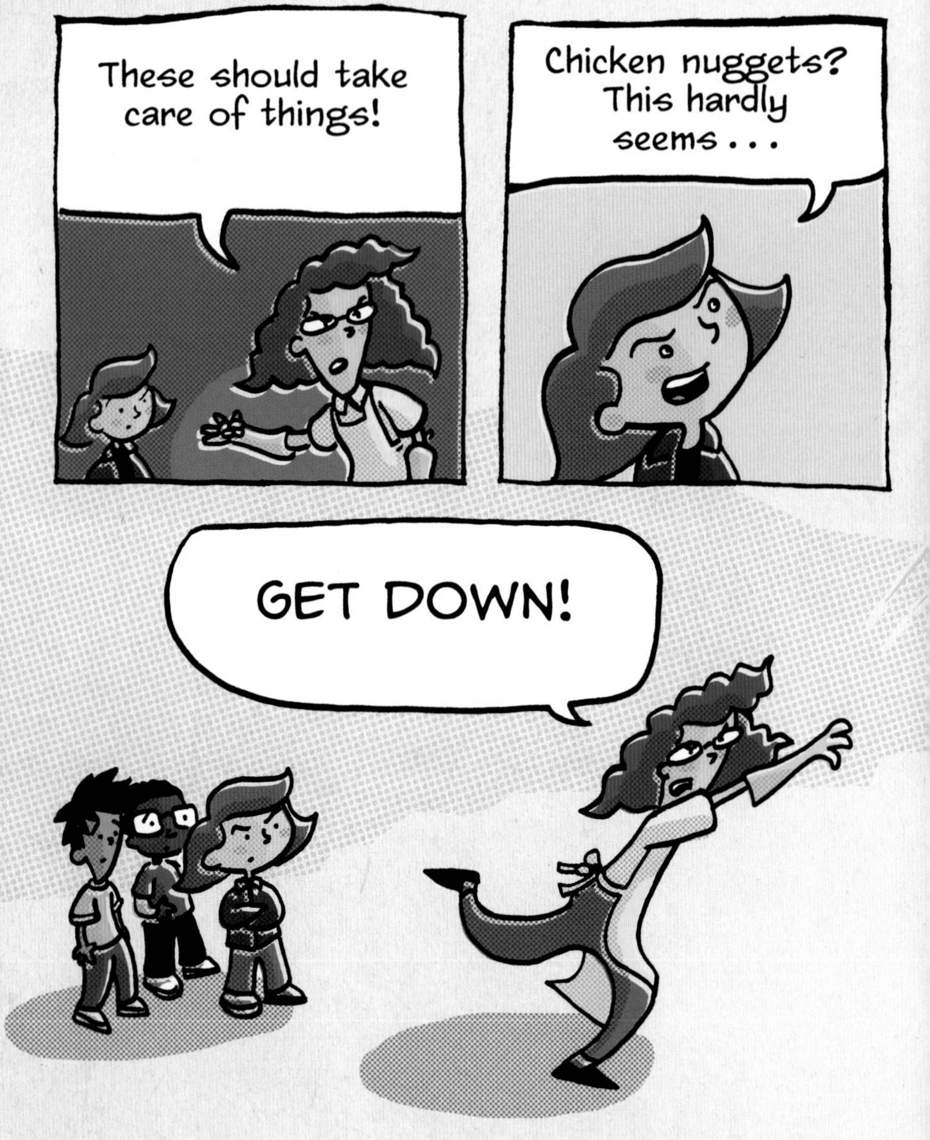
These should take care of things!
Chicken nuggets? This hardly seems . . .
GET DOWN!

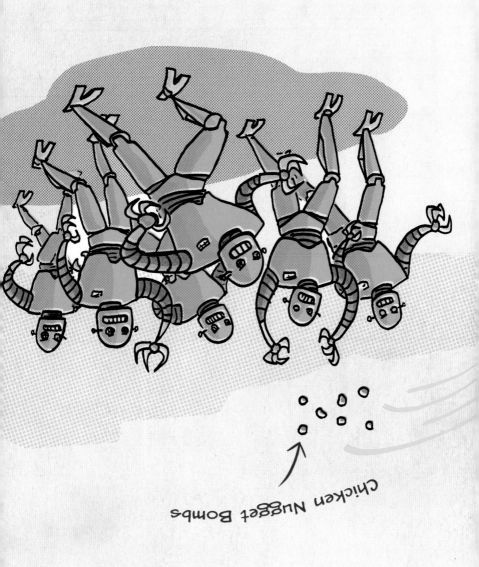

Chicken Nugget Bombs

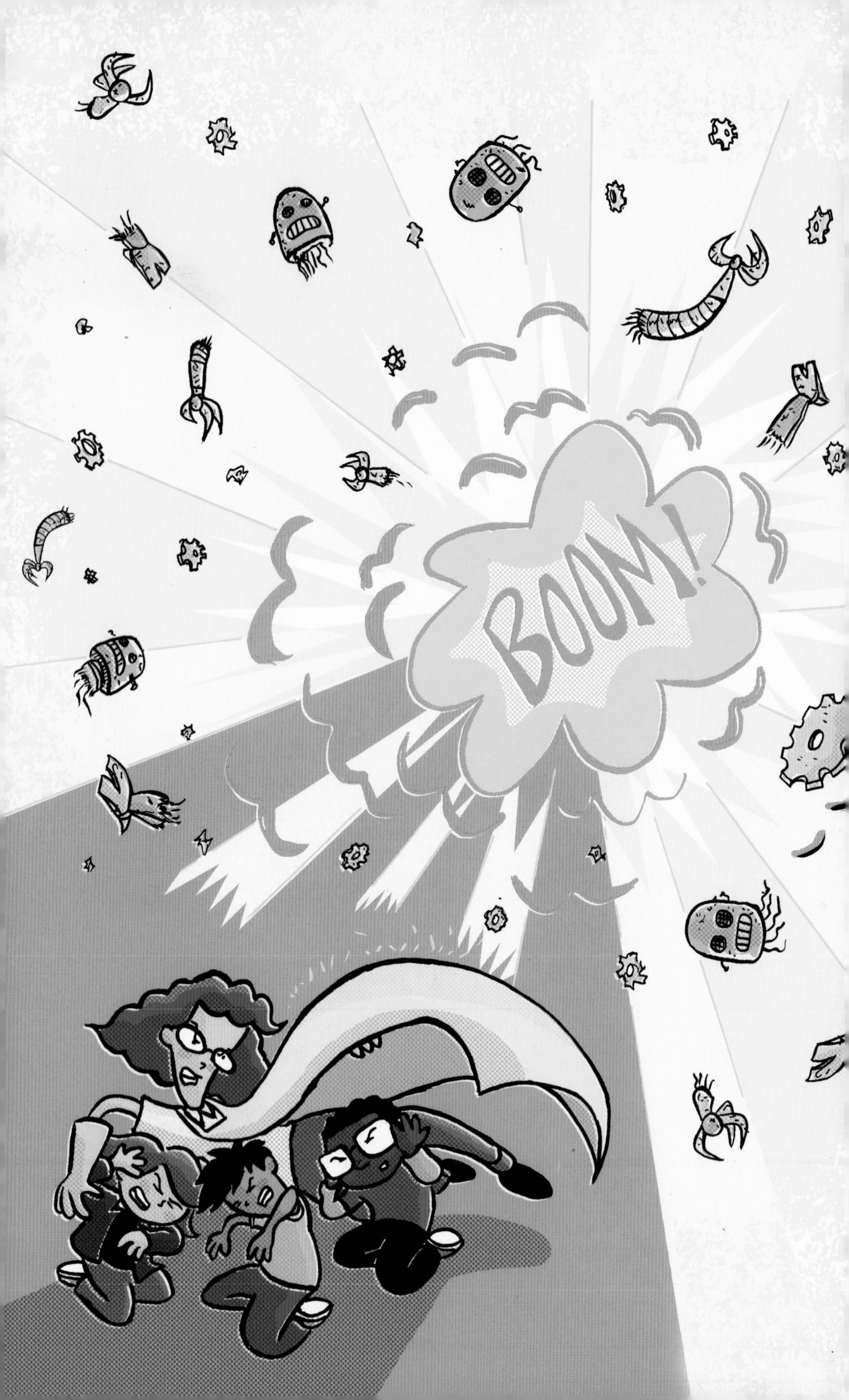
BOOM!

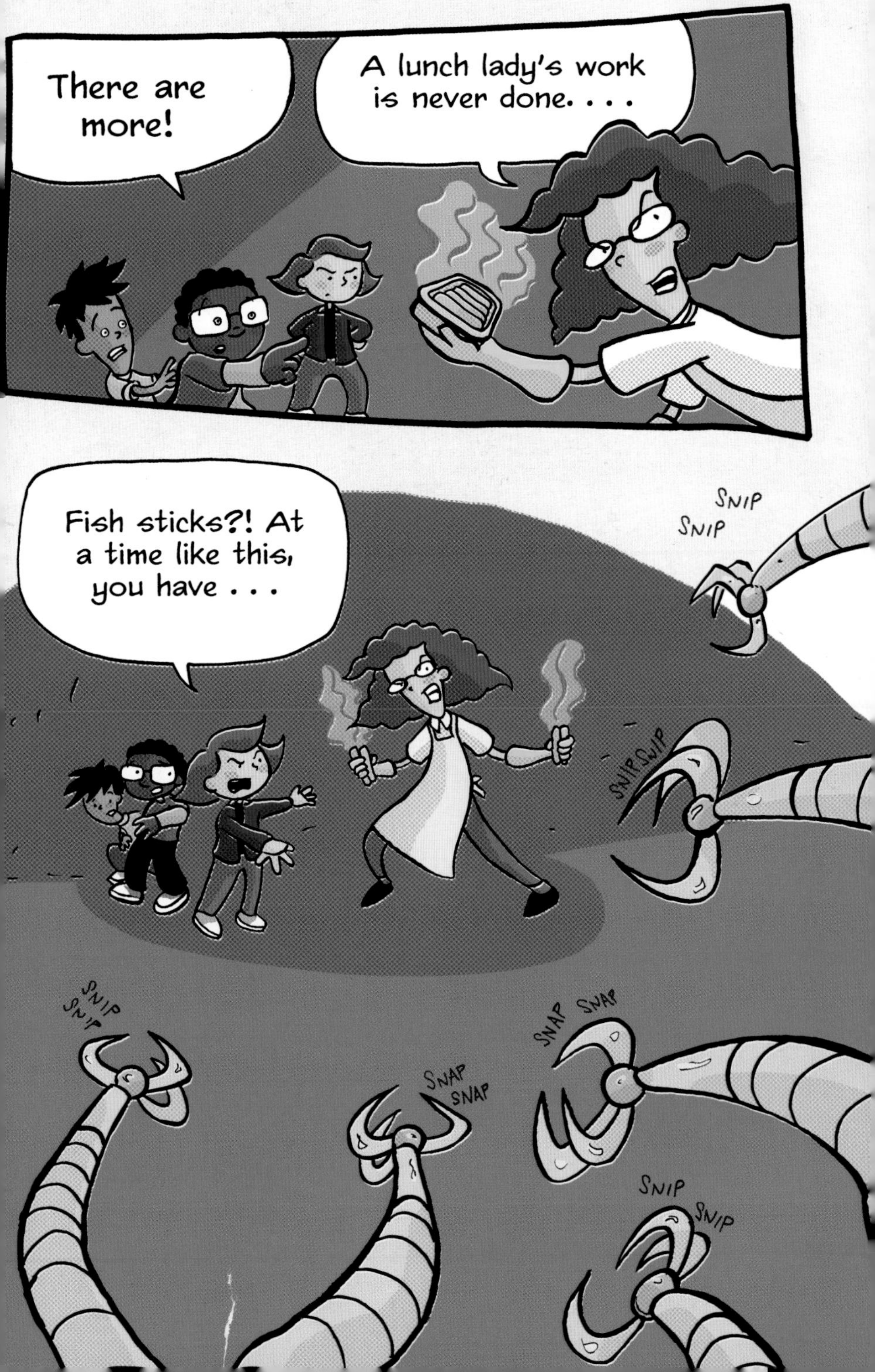
There are more!
A lunch lady's work is never done. . . .
Fish sticks?! At a time like this, you have . . .
SNIP
SNIP
SNIP SNIP
SNIP
SNIP
SNAP
SNAP
SNAP SNAP
SNIP
SNIP

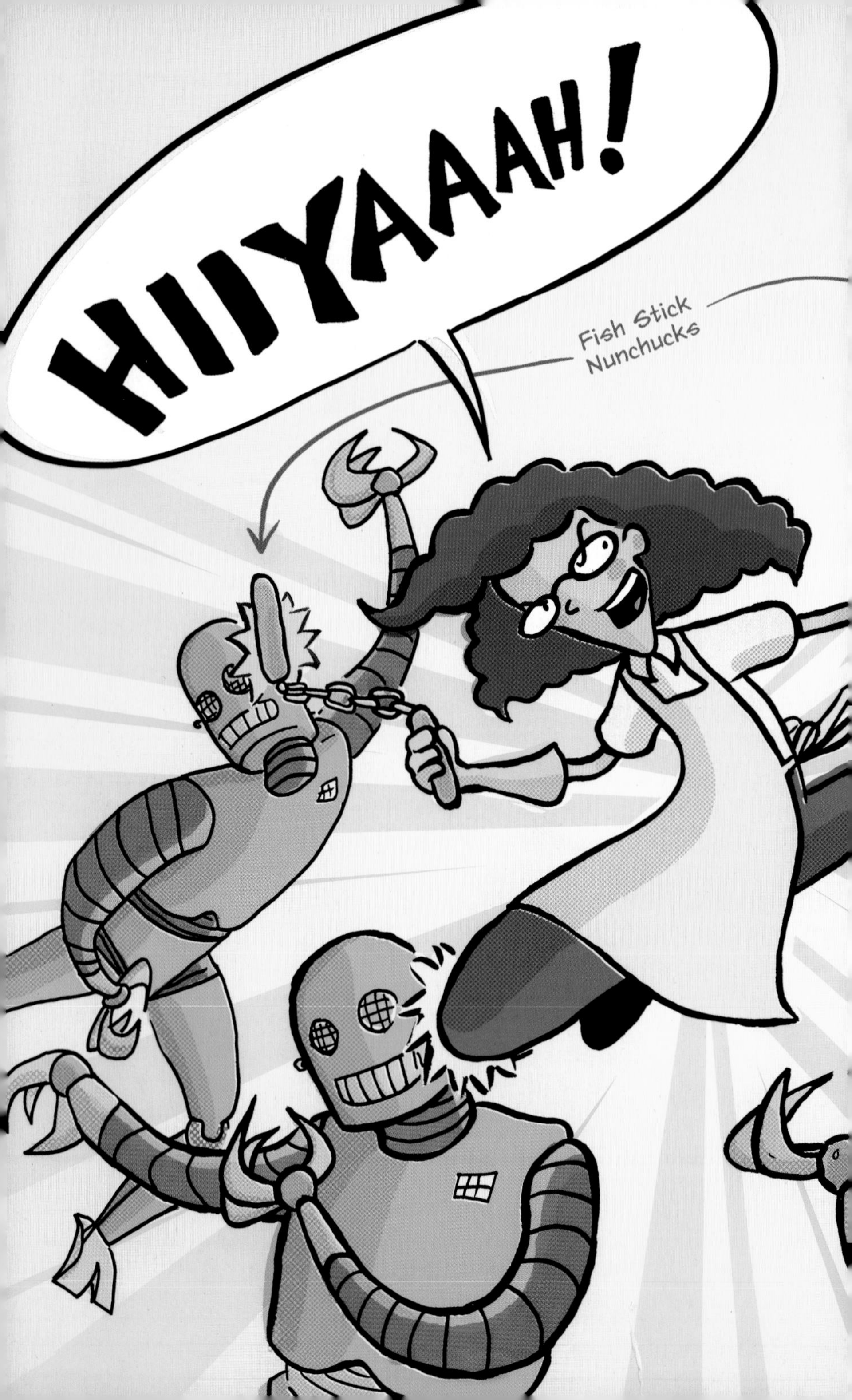
HIIYAAAH!
Fish Stick Nunchucks

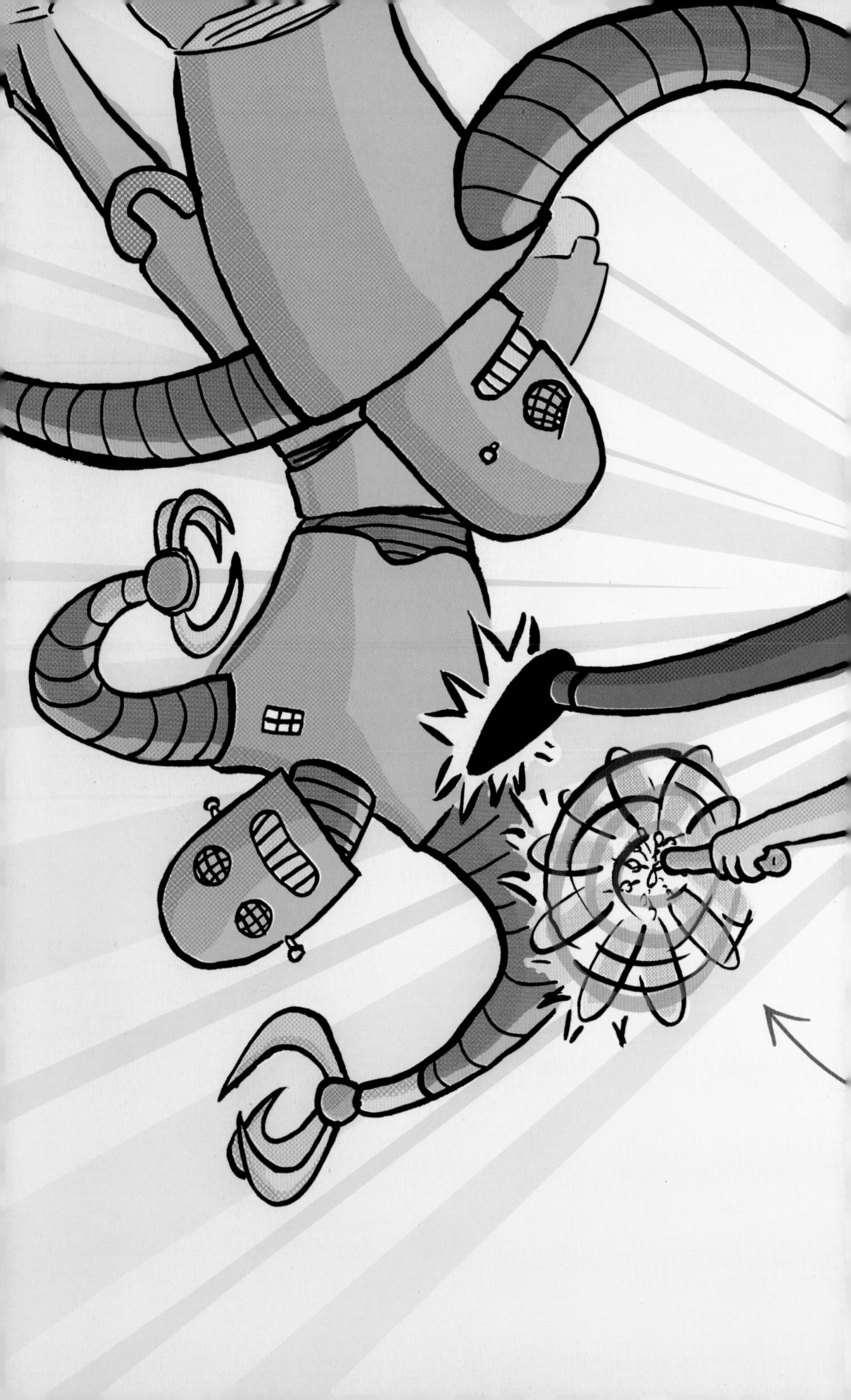

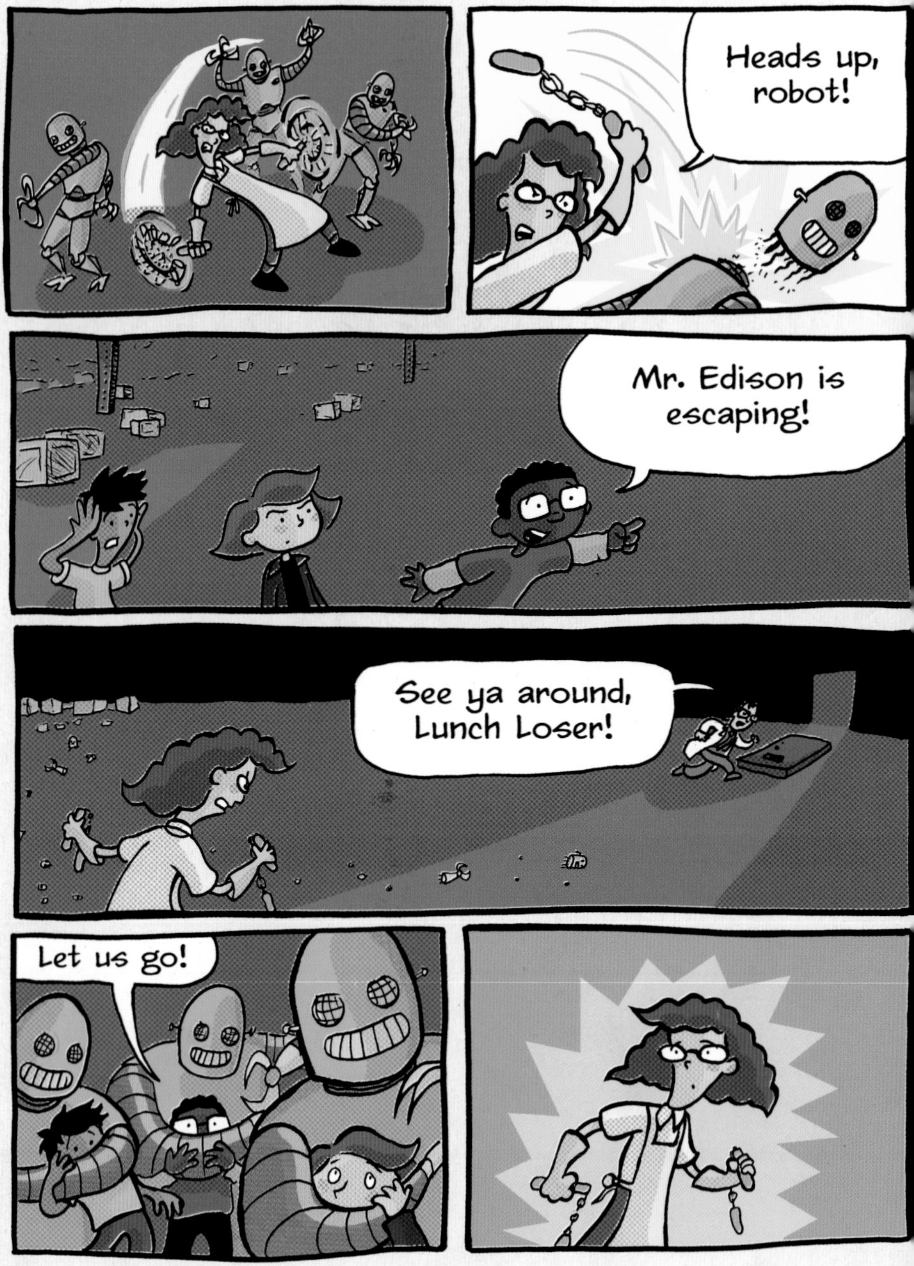
Heads up, robot!
Mr. Edison is escaping!
See ya around, Lunch Loser!
Let us go!

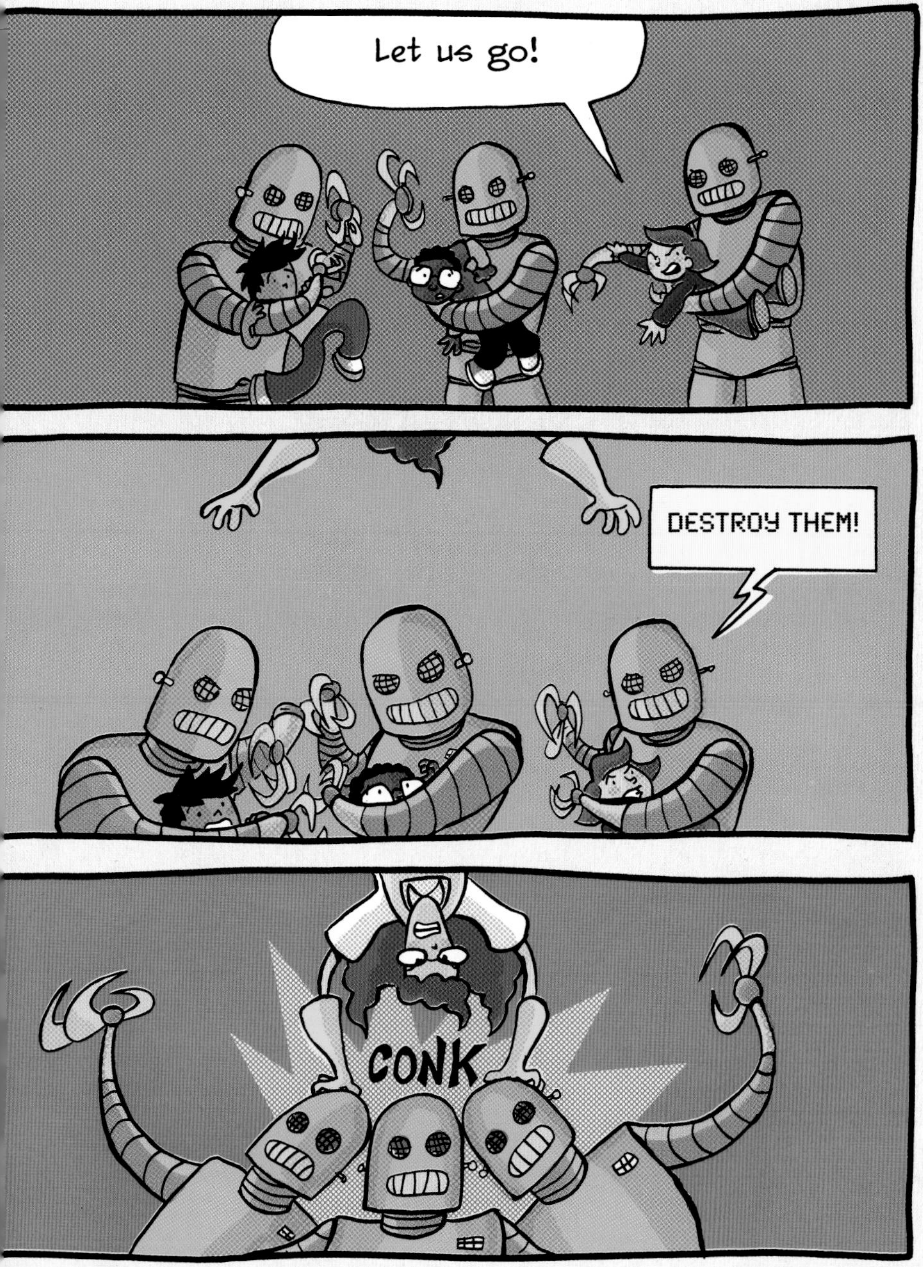
Let us go!
DESTROY THEM!
CONK

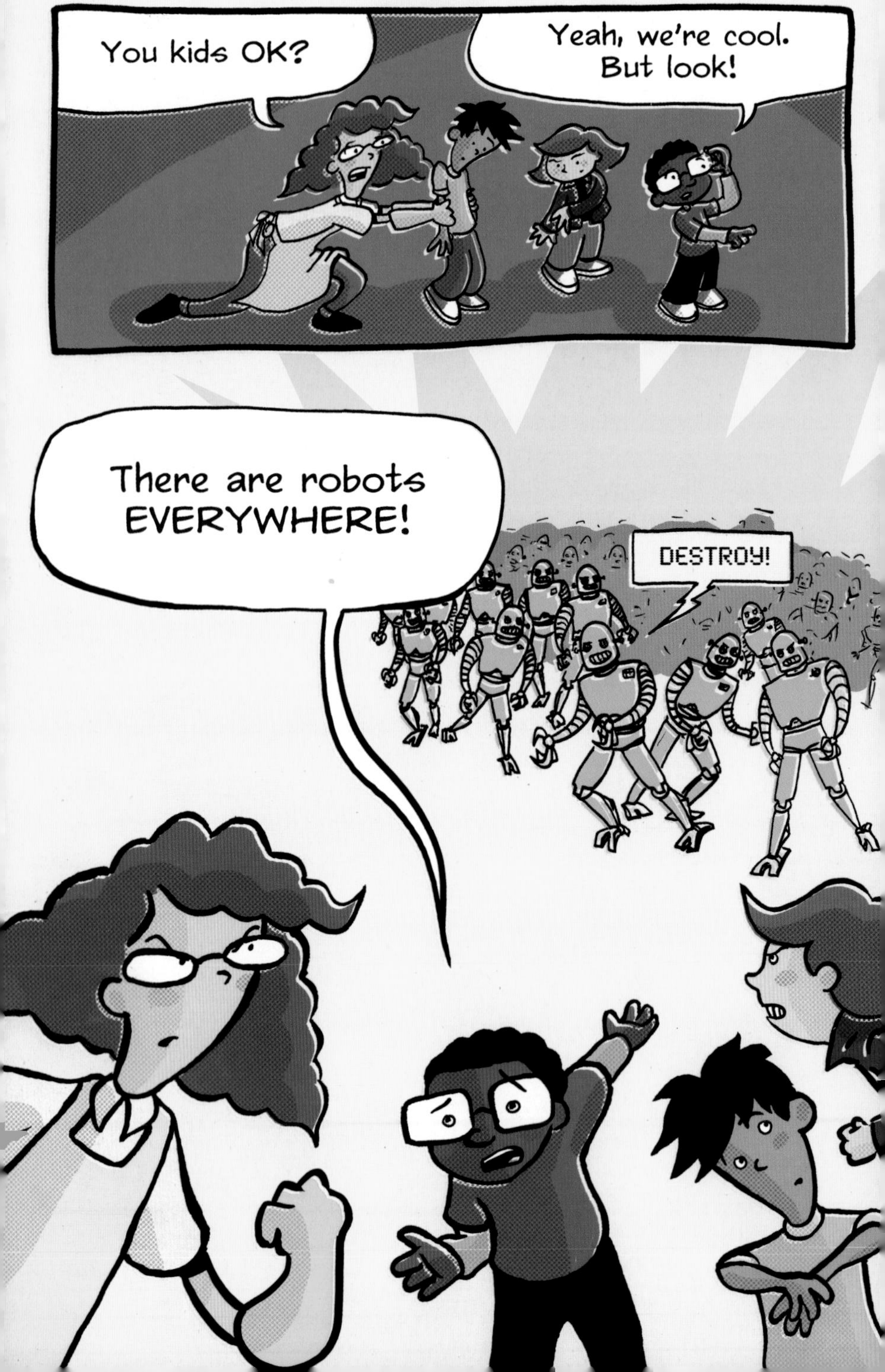
You kids OK?
Yeah, we're cool. But look!
There are robots EVERYWHERE!
DESTROY!

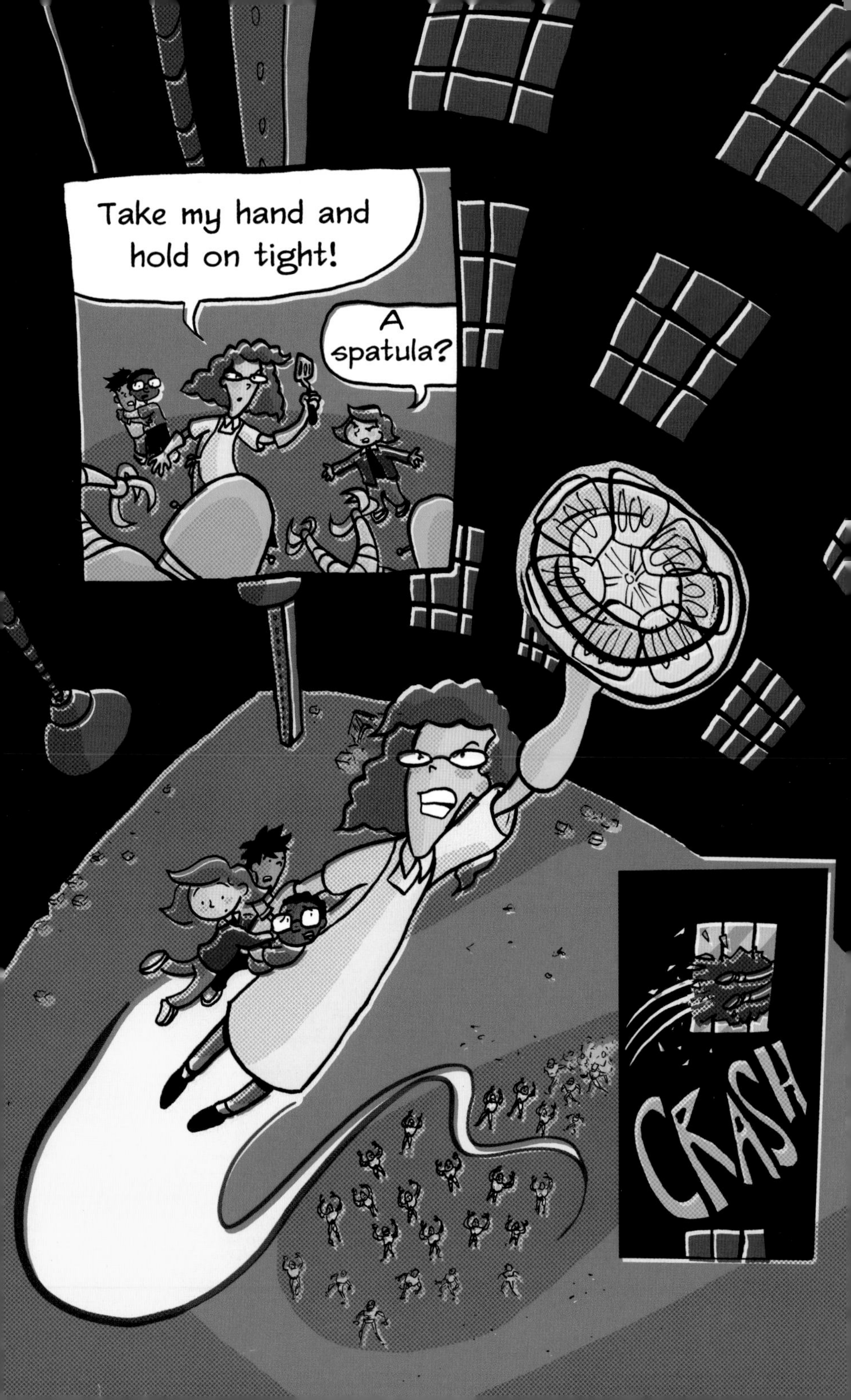
Take my hand and hold on tight!
A spatula?
CRASH

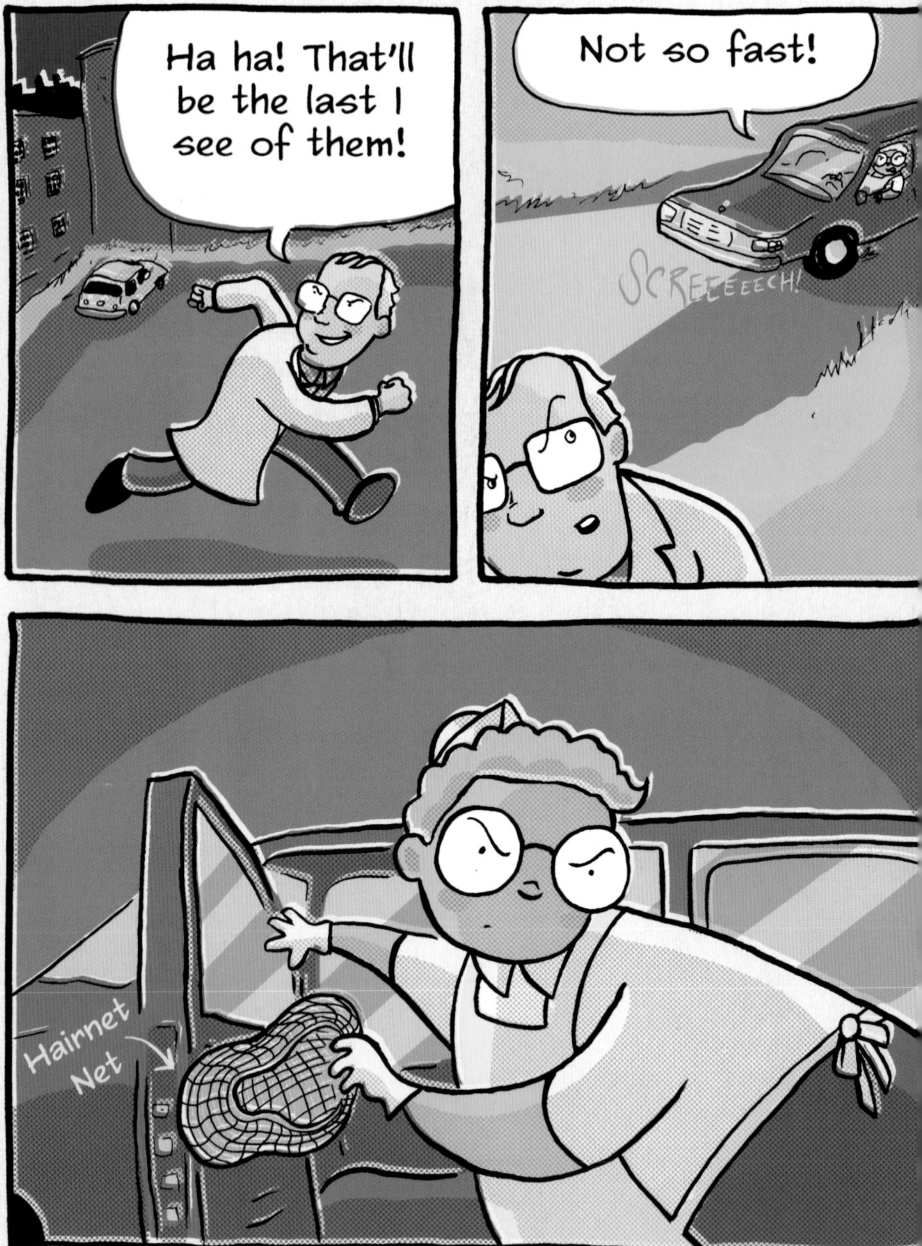
Ha ha! That'll be the last I see of them!
Not so fast!
SCREEEEECH!
Hairnet Net

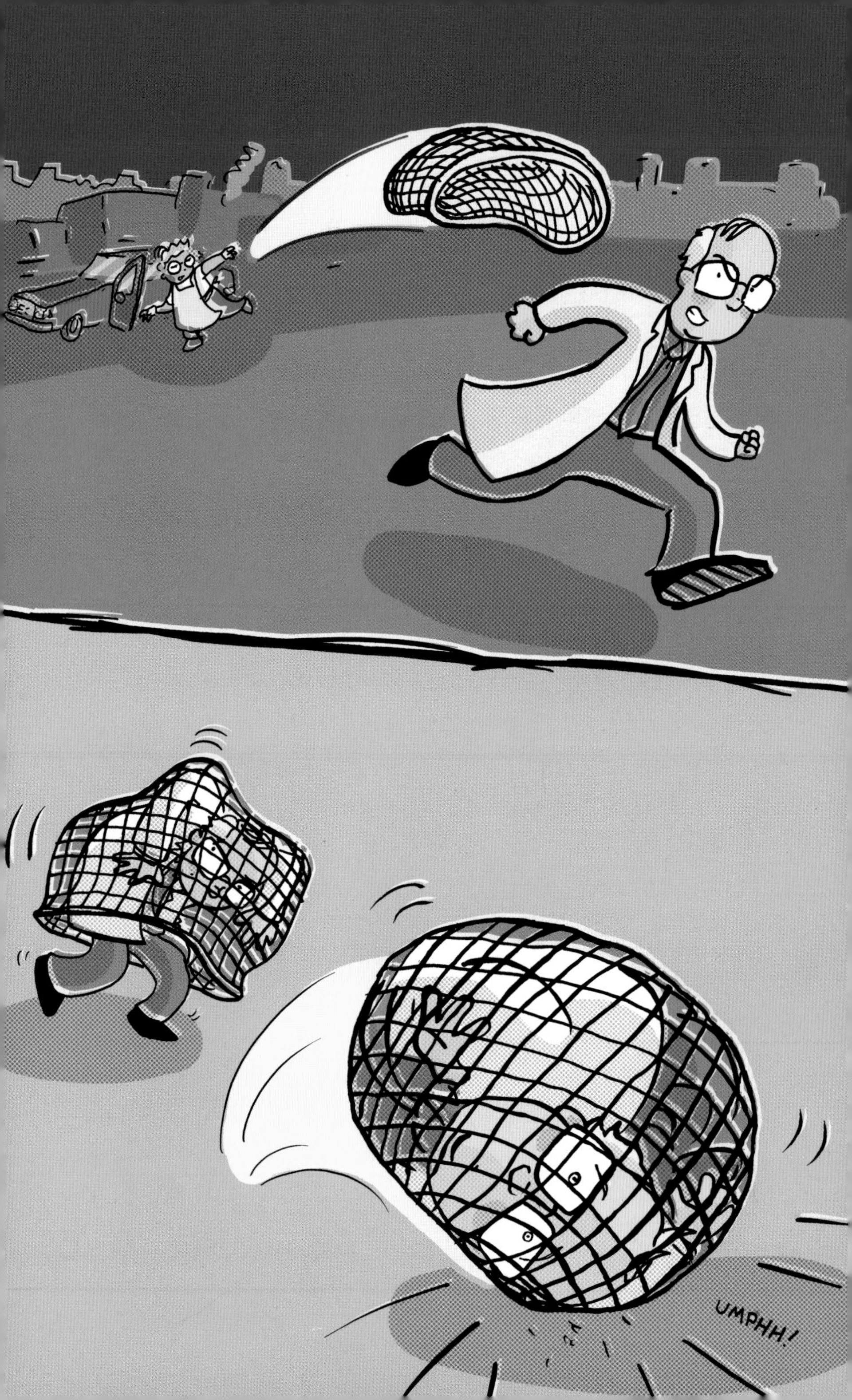
UMPHH!

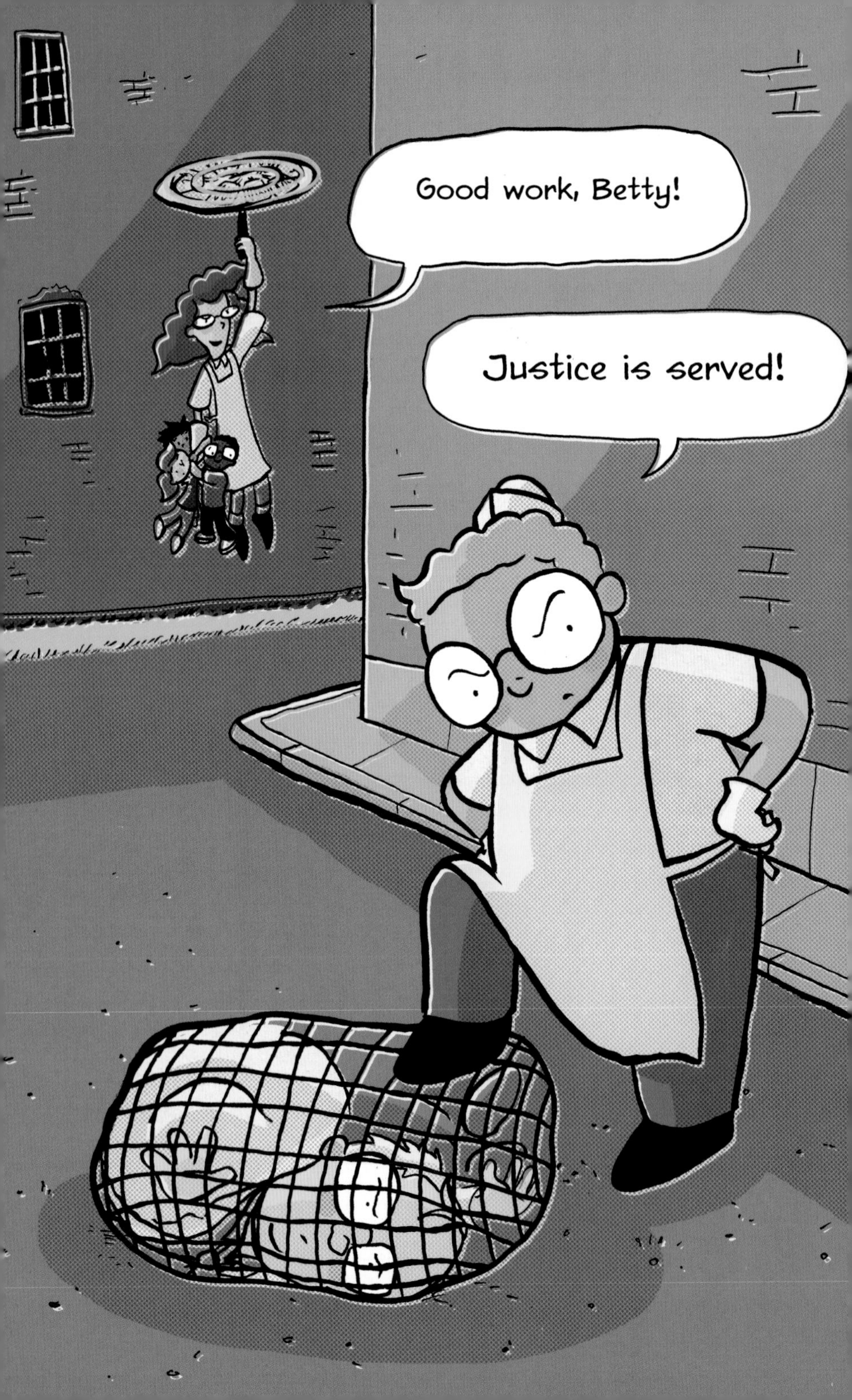
Good work, Betty!
Justice is served!

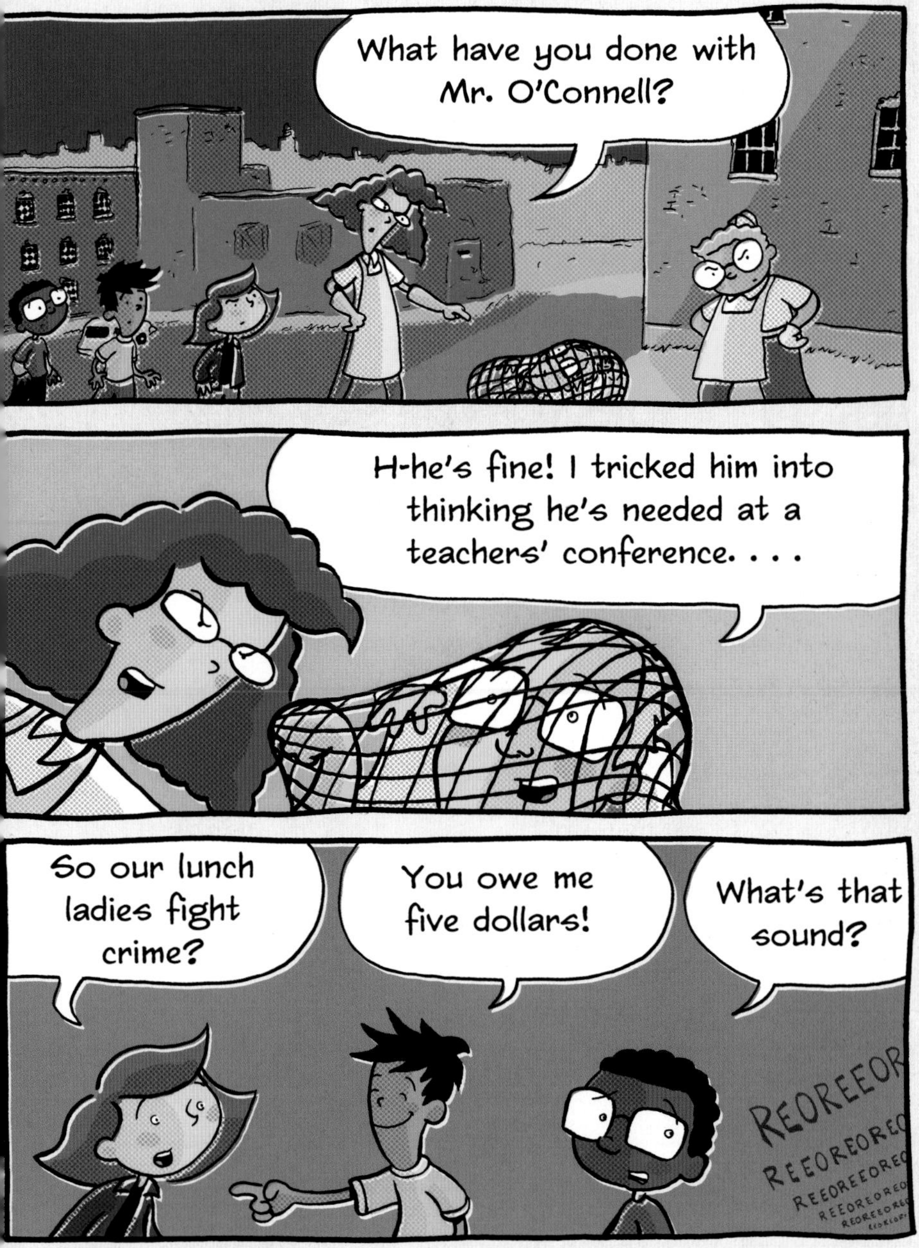
What have you done with Mr. O'Connell?
H-he's fine! I tricked him into thinking he's needed at a teachers' conference. . . .
So our lunch ladies fight crime?
You owe me five dollars!
What's that sound?
REOREEOR
REEOREEOREO

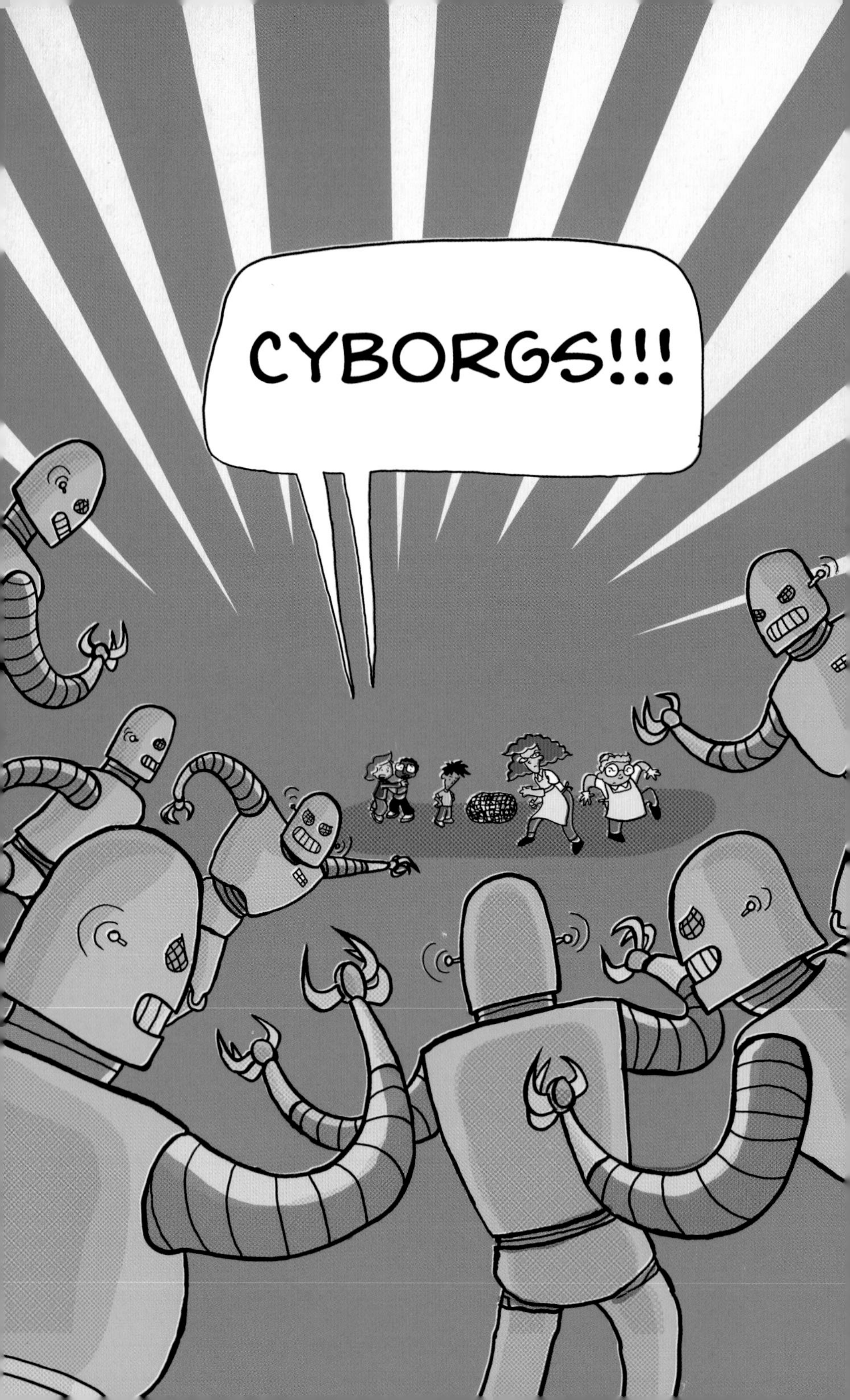
CYBORGS!!!

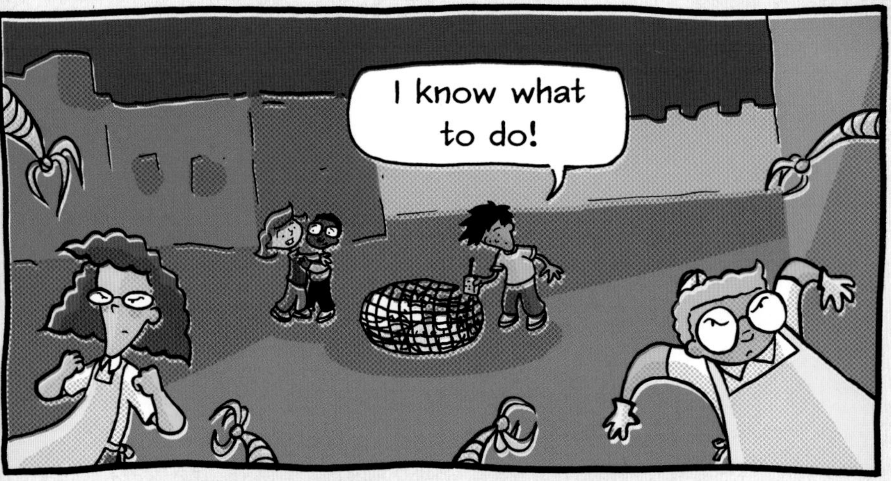
I know what to do!

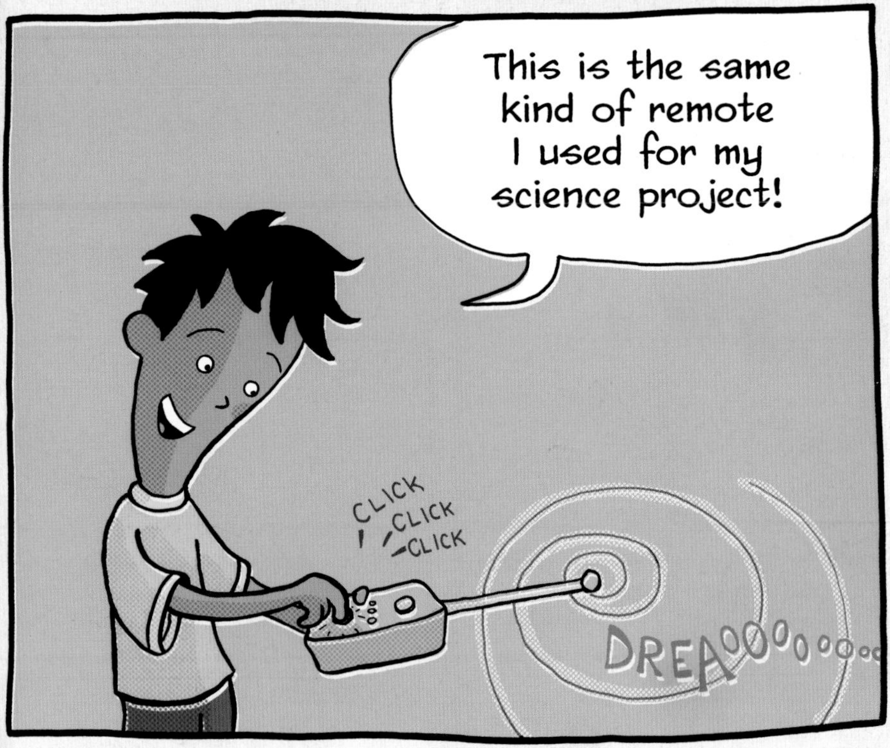
This is the same kind of remote I used for my science project!
CLICK CLICK CLICK
DREAOOOooo...

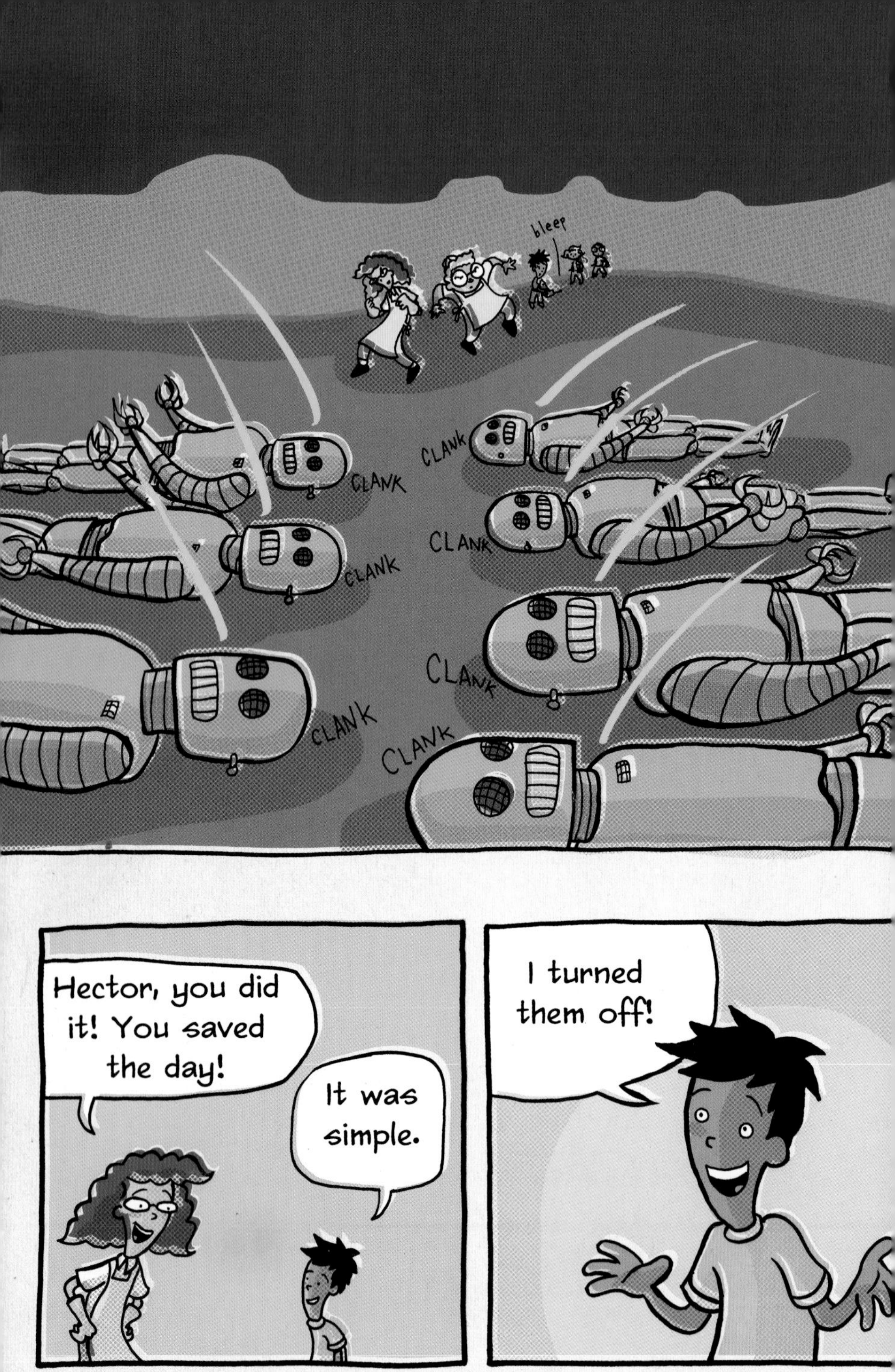
bleep
CLANK
CLANK
CLANK
CLANK
CLANK
CLANK
CLANK
CLANK
Hector, you did it! You saved the day!
It was simple.
I turned them off!

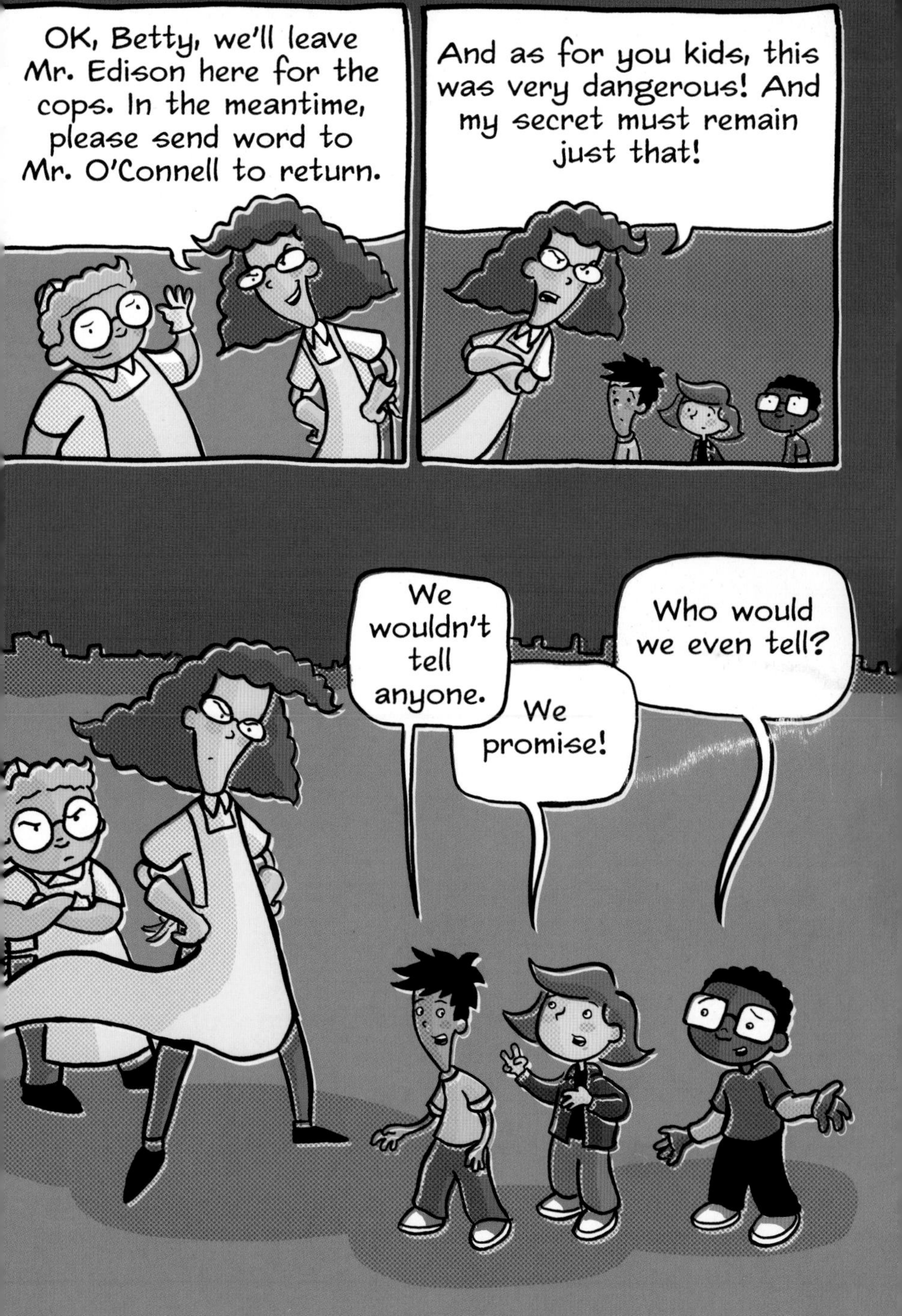
OK, Betty, we'll leave Mr. Edison here for the cops. In the meantime, please send word to Mr. O'Connell to return.
And as for you kids, this was very dangerous! And my secret must remain just that!
We wouldn't tell anyone.
We promise!
Who would we even tell?

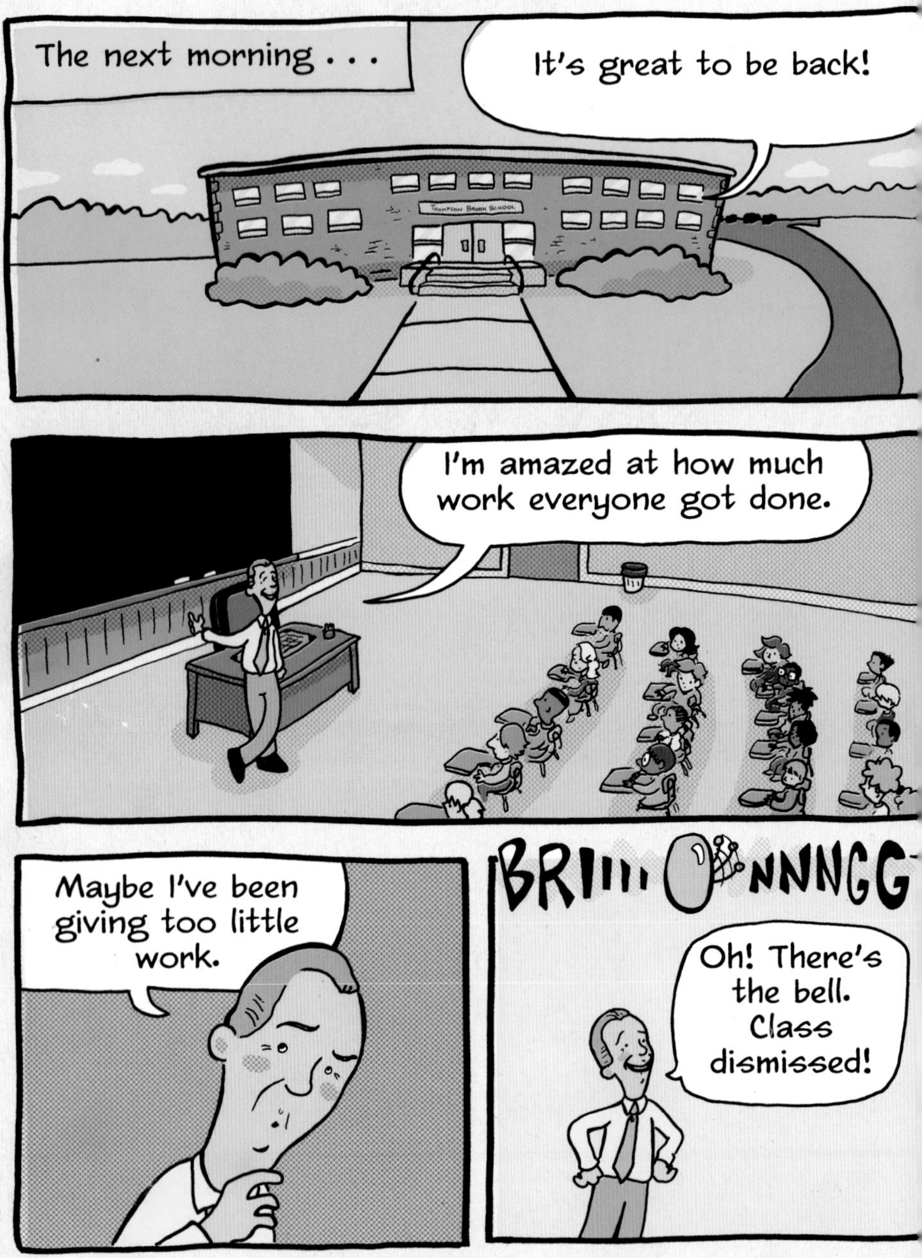
The next morning . . .
It's great to be back!
THOMPSON BROOK SCHOOL
I'm amazed at how much work everyone got done.
Maybe I've been giving too little work.
BRIIIIONNNGG
Oh! There's the bell. Class dismissed!

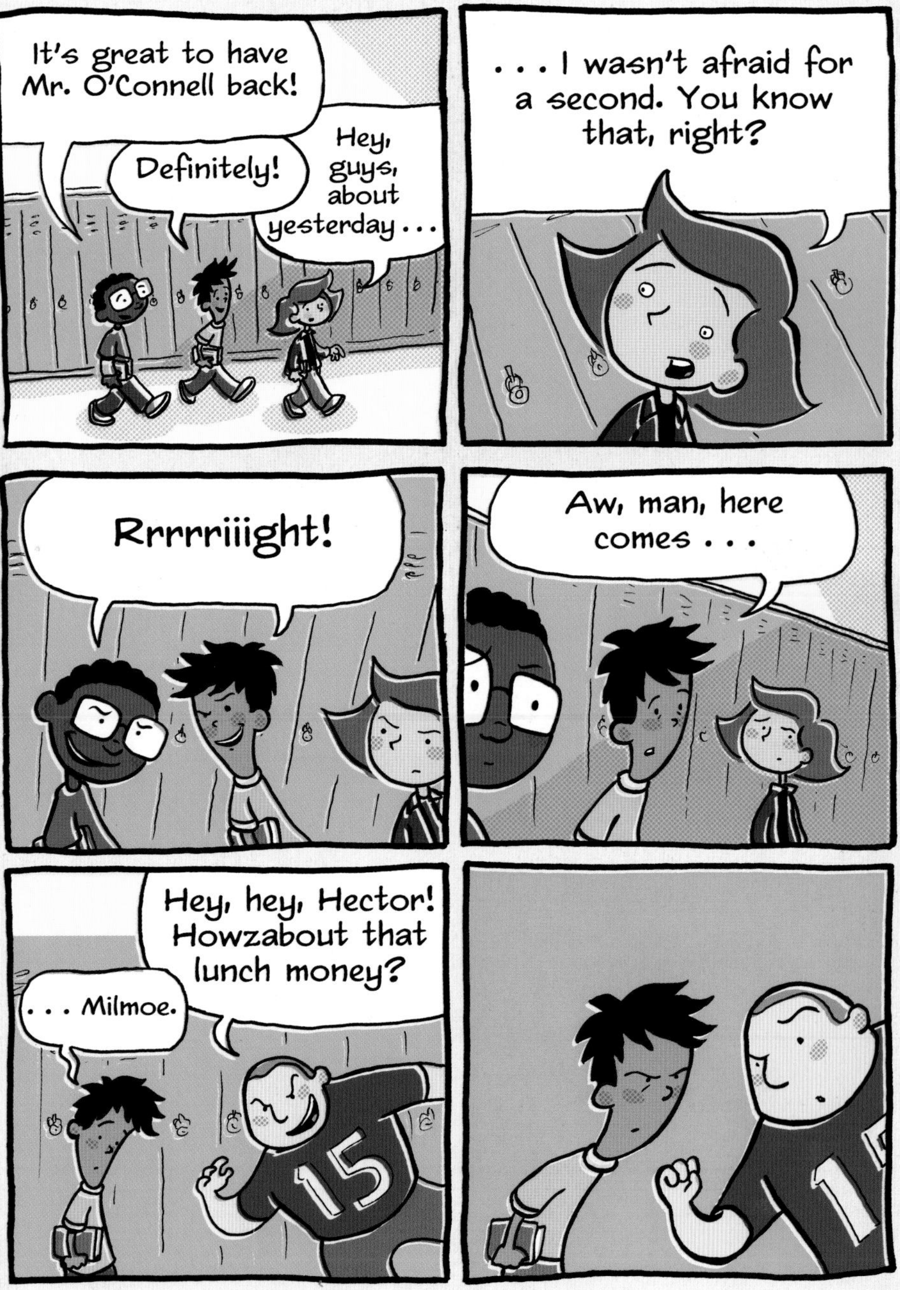
It's great to have Mr. O'Connell back!
Definitely!
Hey, guys, about yesterday . . .
. . . I wasn't afraid for a second. You know that, right?
Rrrrriiight!
Aw, man, here comes . . .
Hey, hey, Hector! Howzabout that lunch money?
. . . Milmoe.
15
15

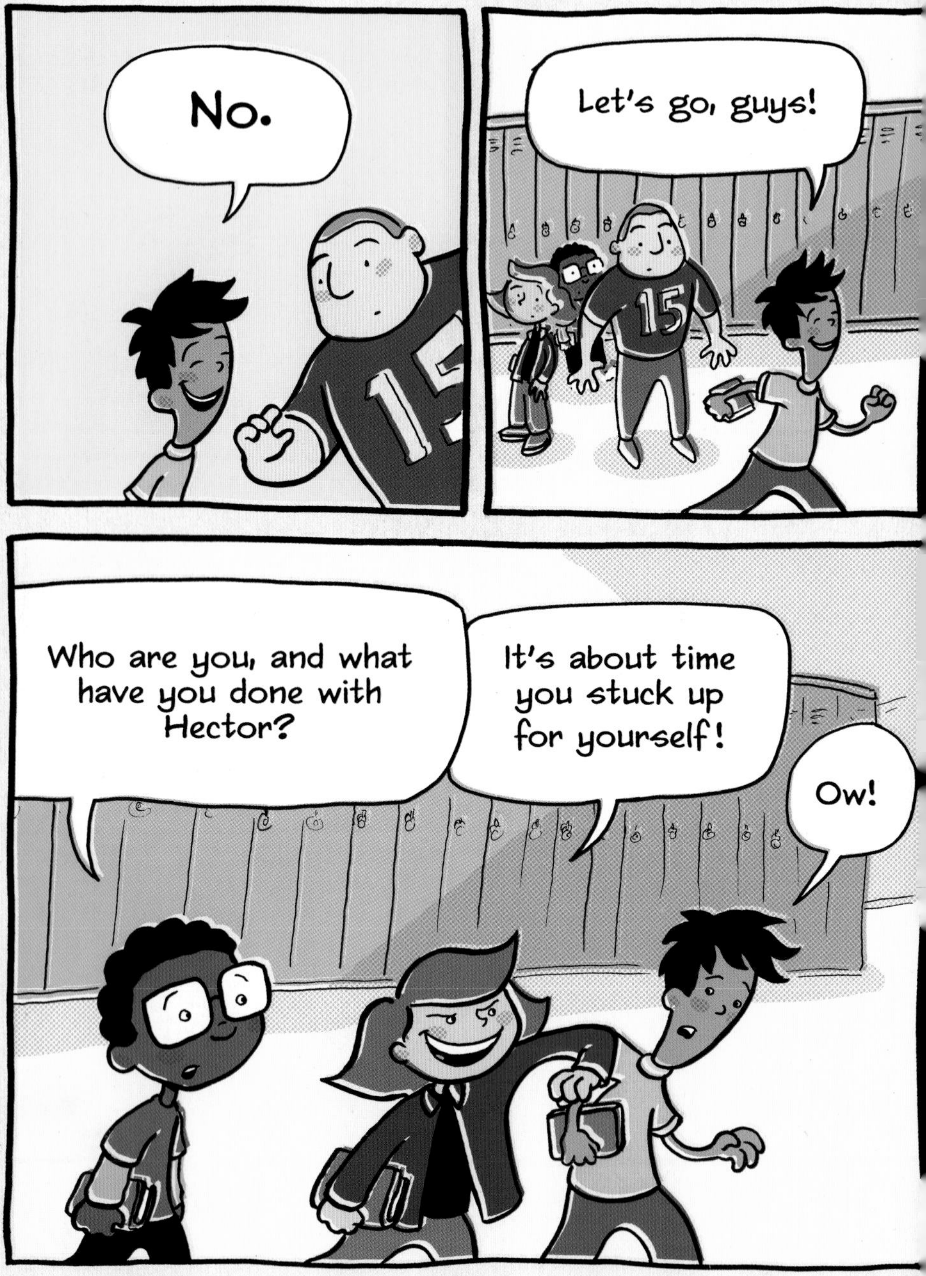
No.
Let's go, guys!
Who are you, and what have you done with Hector?
It's about time you stuck up for yourself!
Ow!

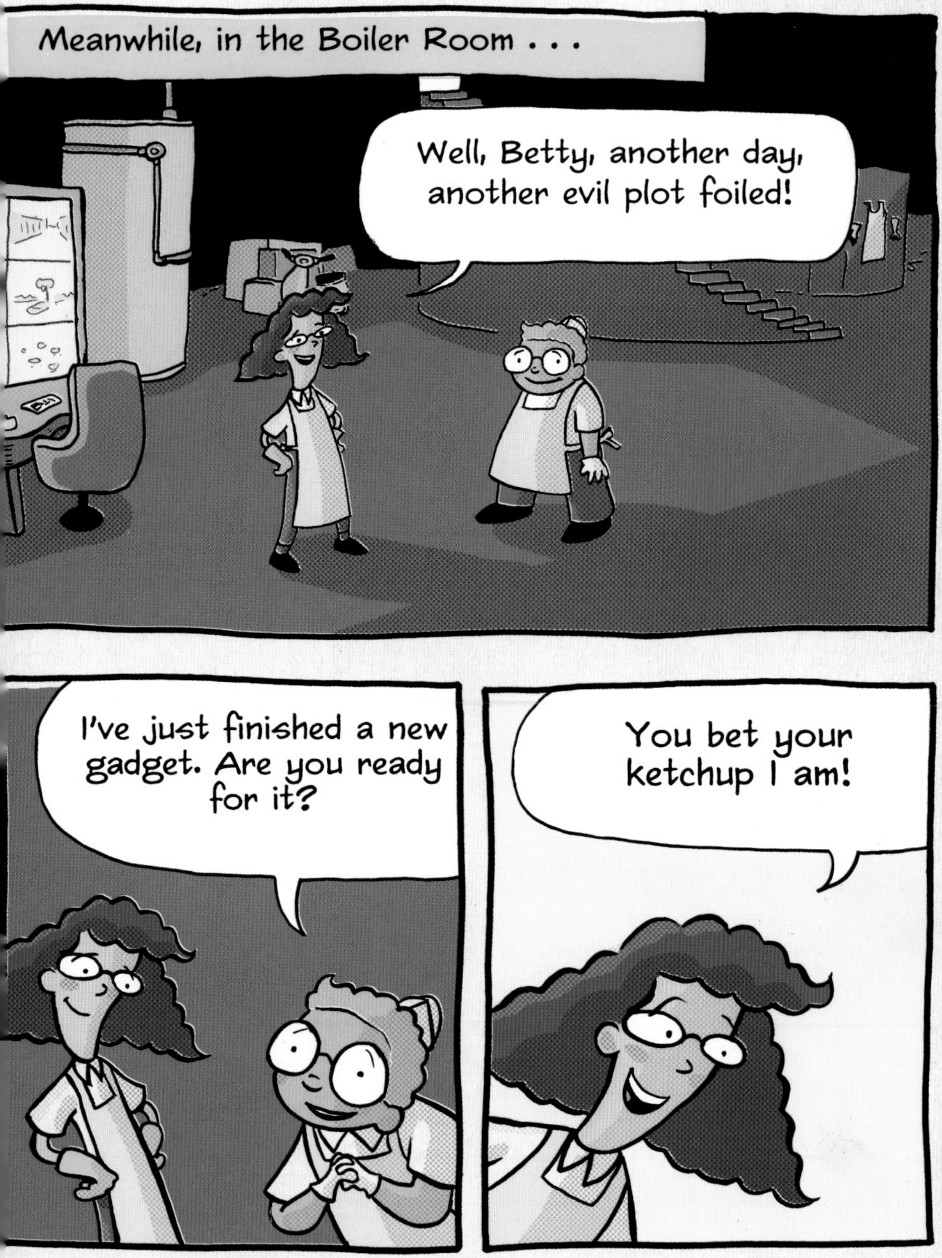
Meanwhile, in the Boiler Room . . .
Well, Betty, another day, another evil plot foiled!
I've just finished a new gadget. Are you ready for it?
You bet your ketchup I am!

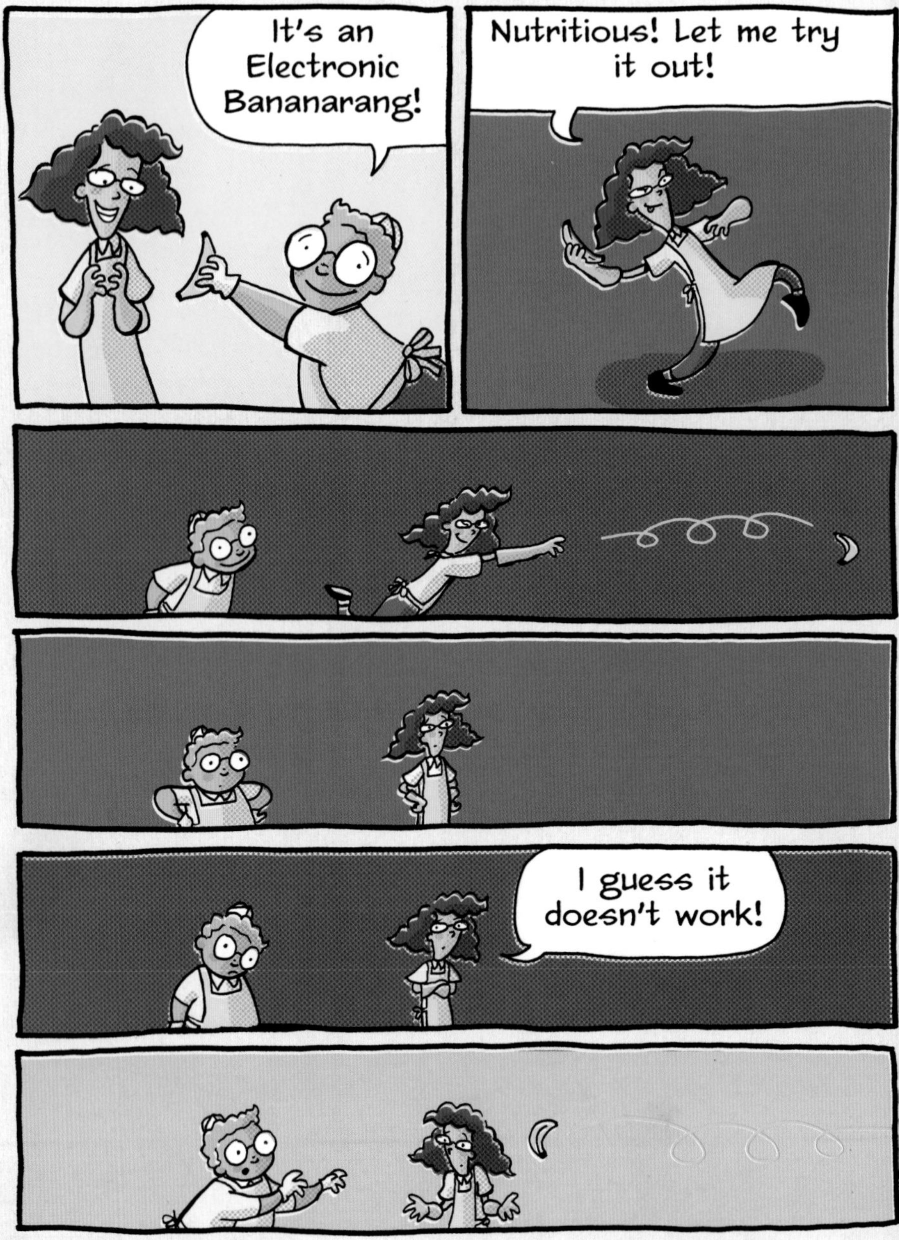

It's an Electronic Bananarang!
Nutritious! Let me try it out!
I guess it doesn't work!

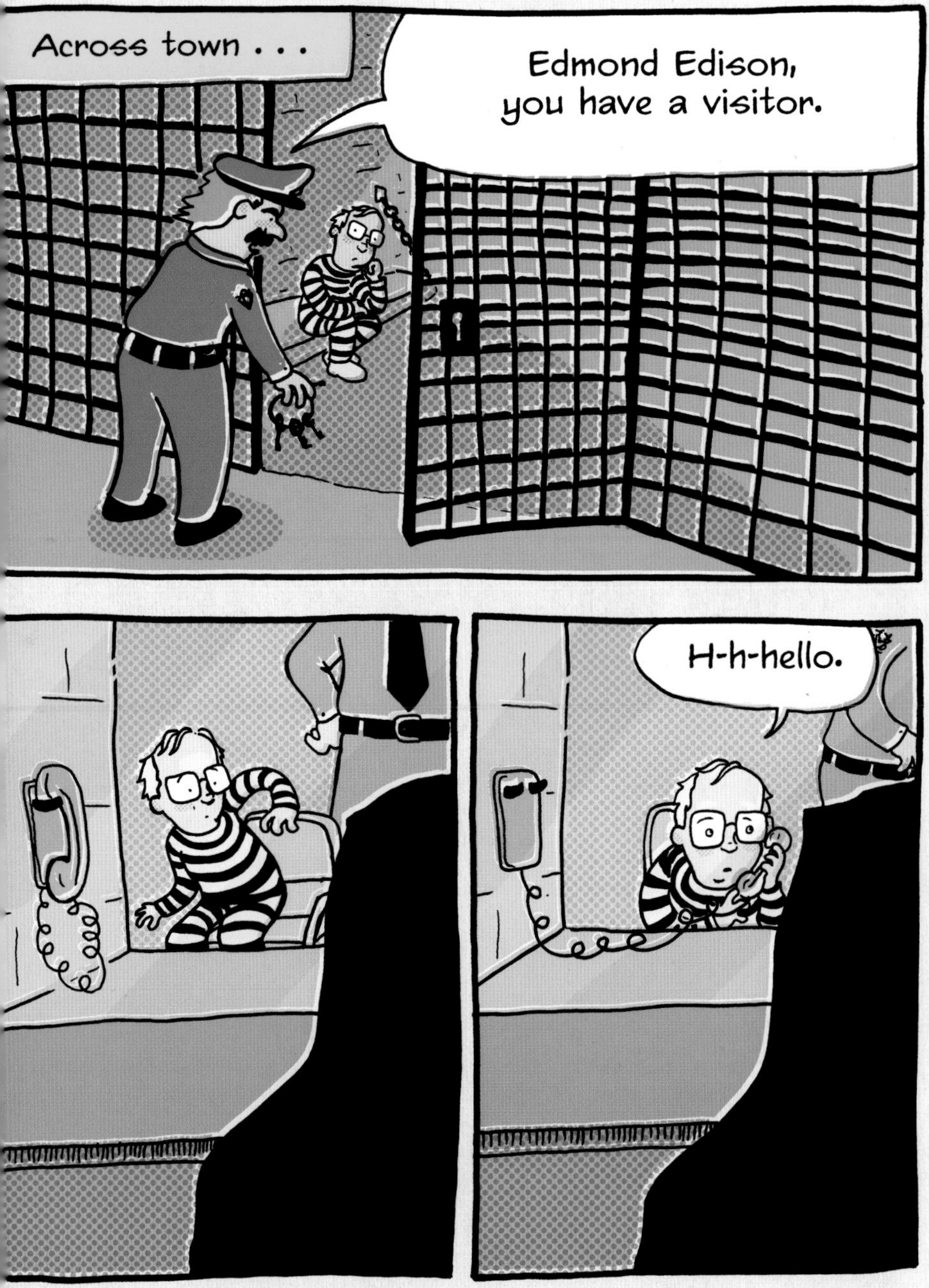
Across town . . .
Edmond Edison, you have a visitor.
H-h-hello.

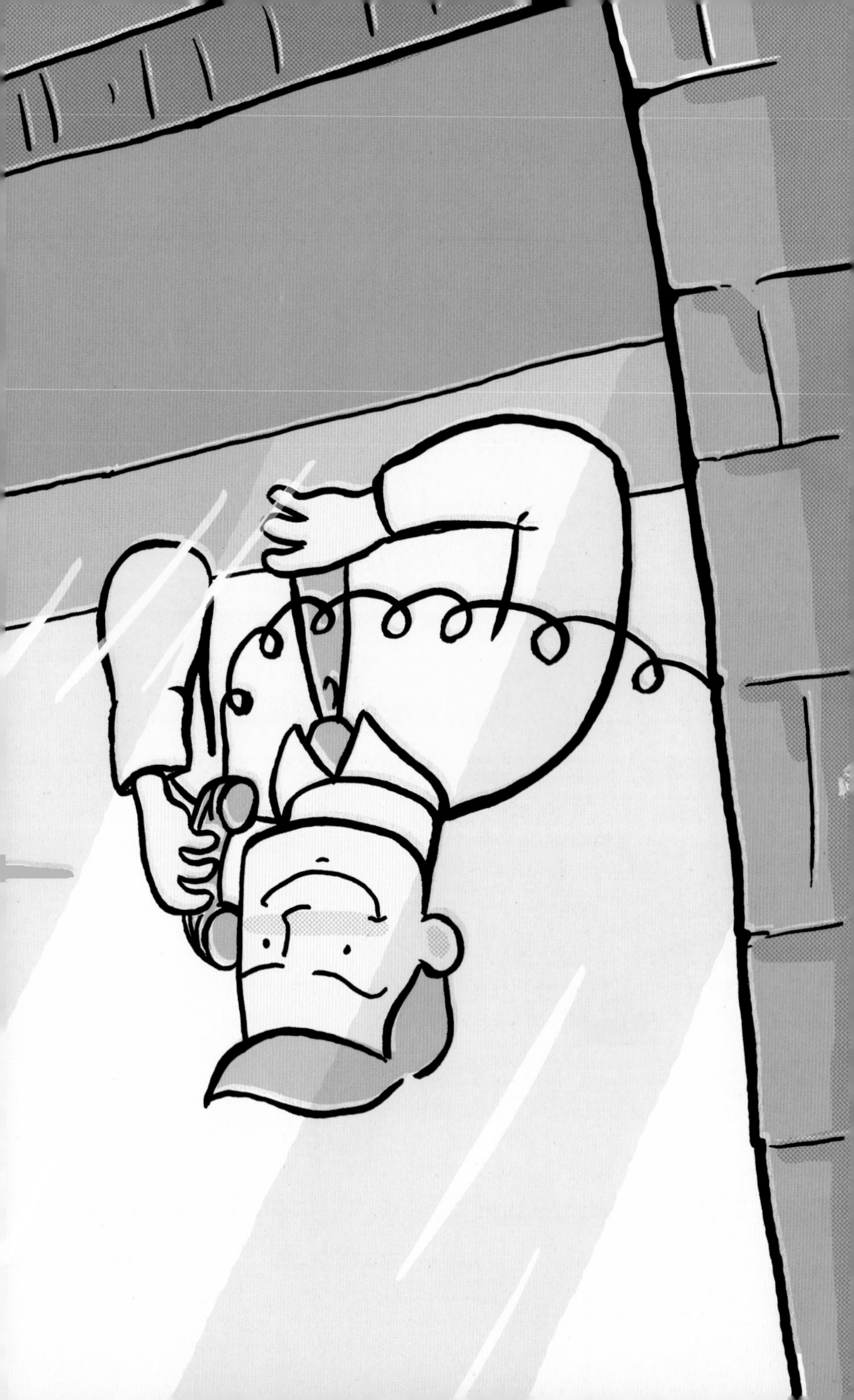

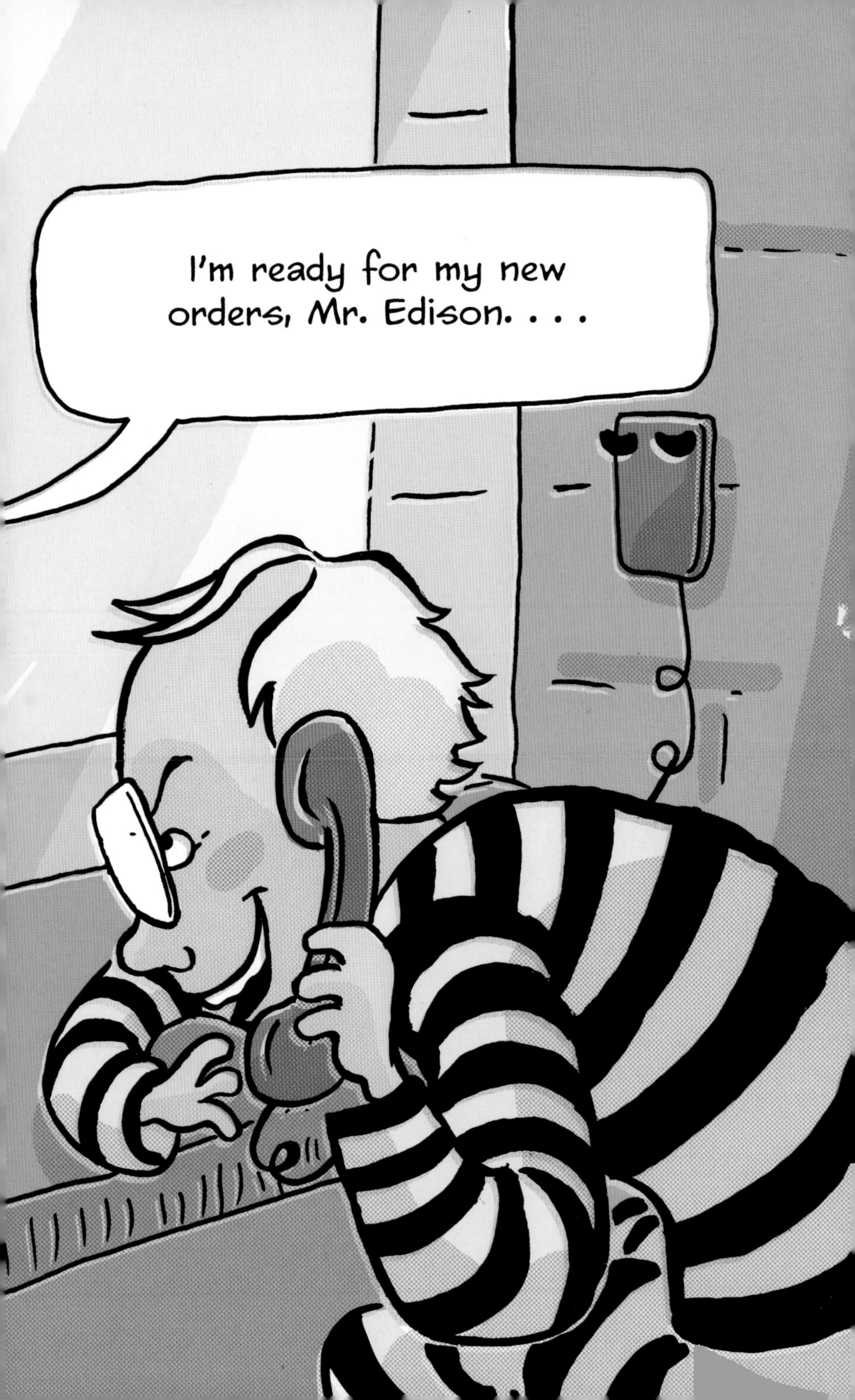
I'm ready for my new orders, Mr. Edison. . . .

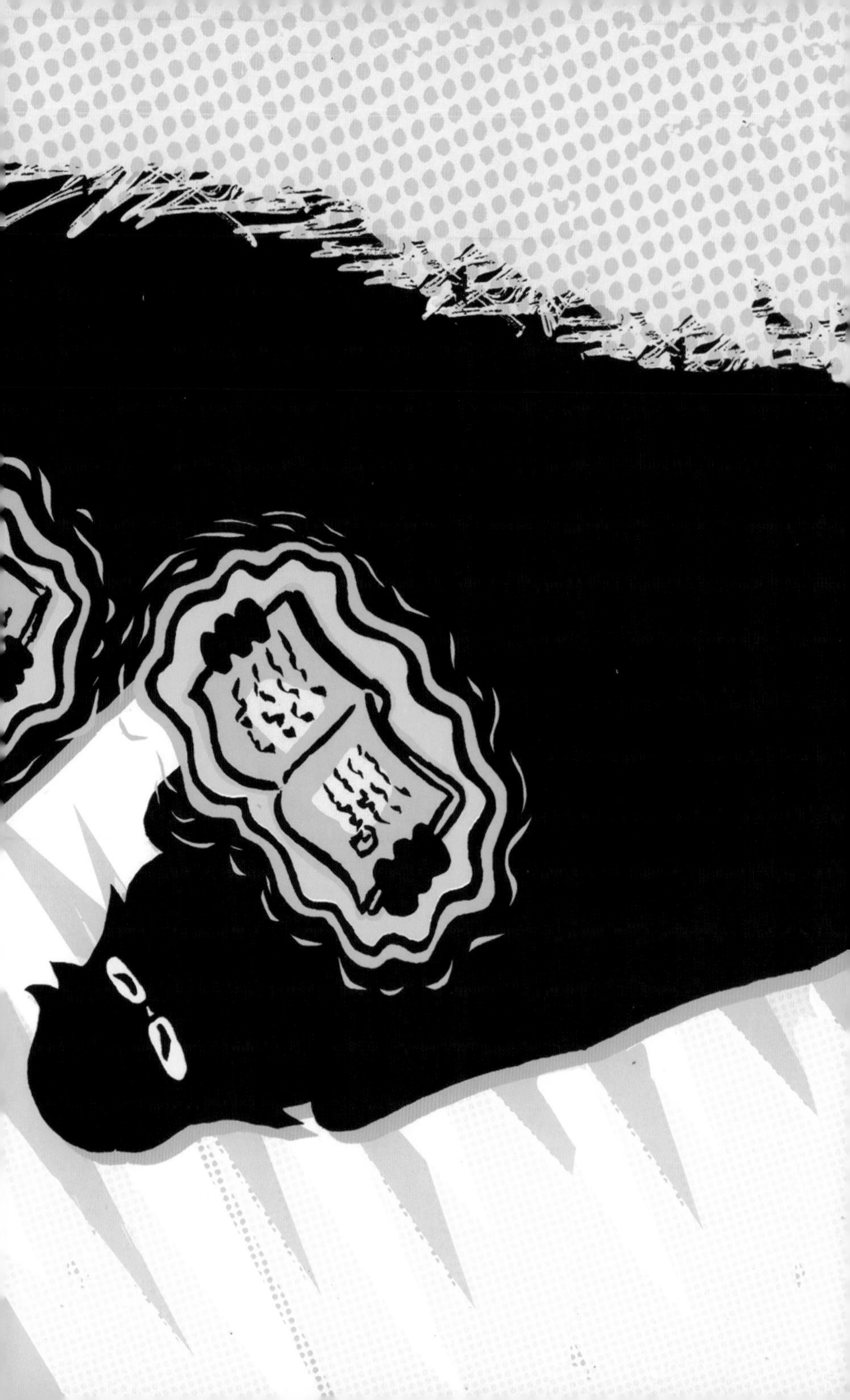

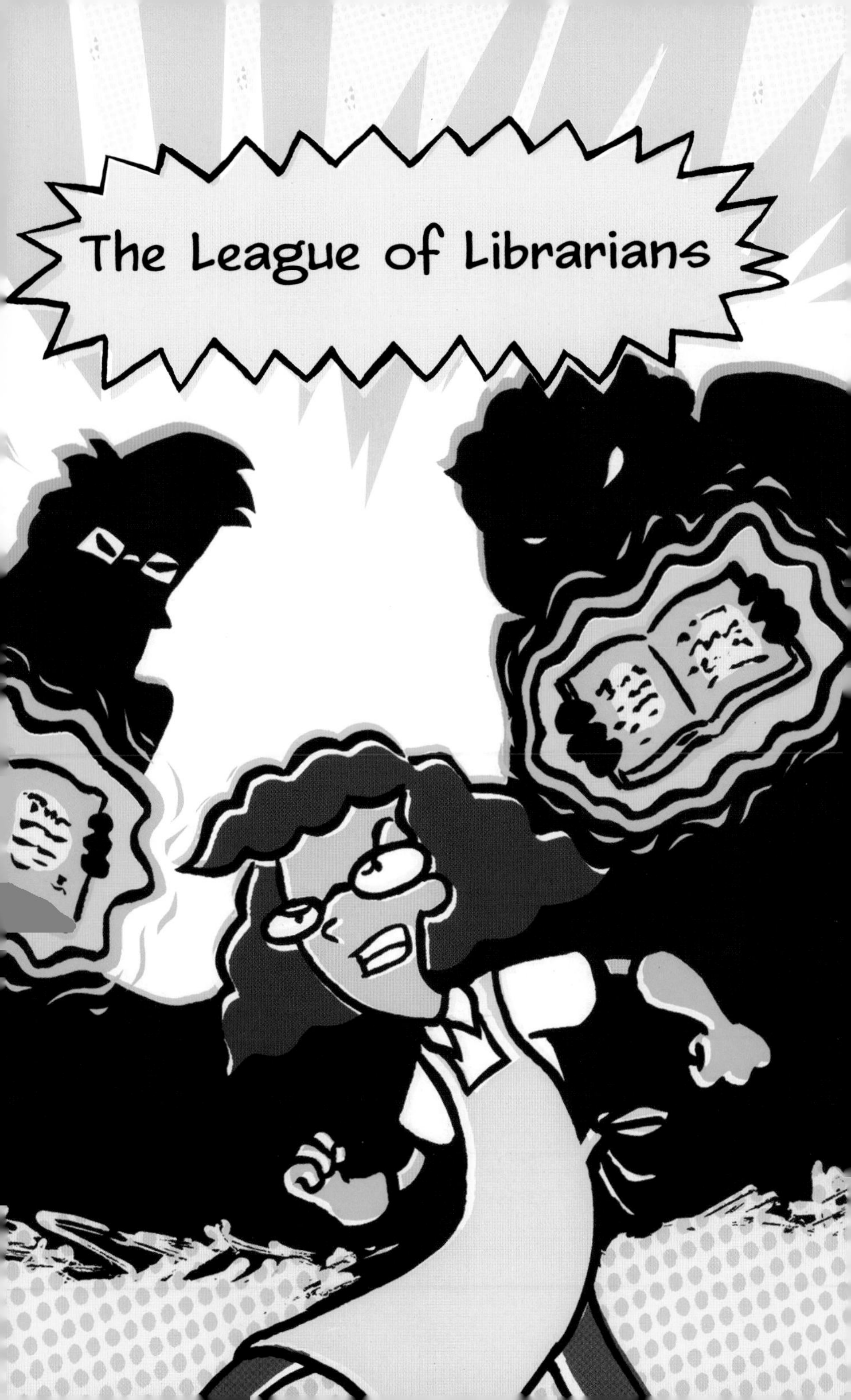
The League of Librarians

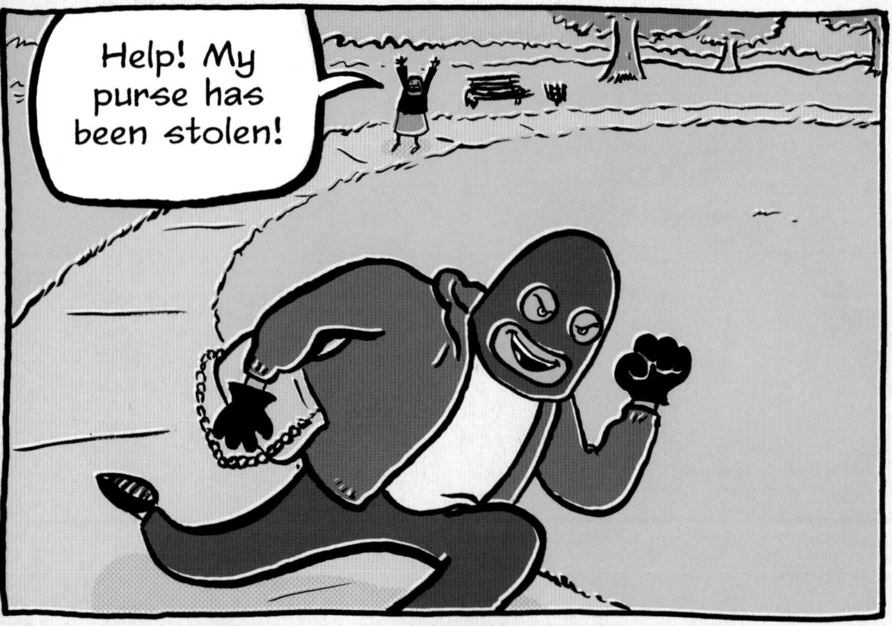
Help! My purse has been stolen!

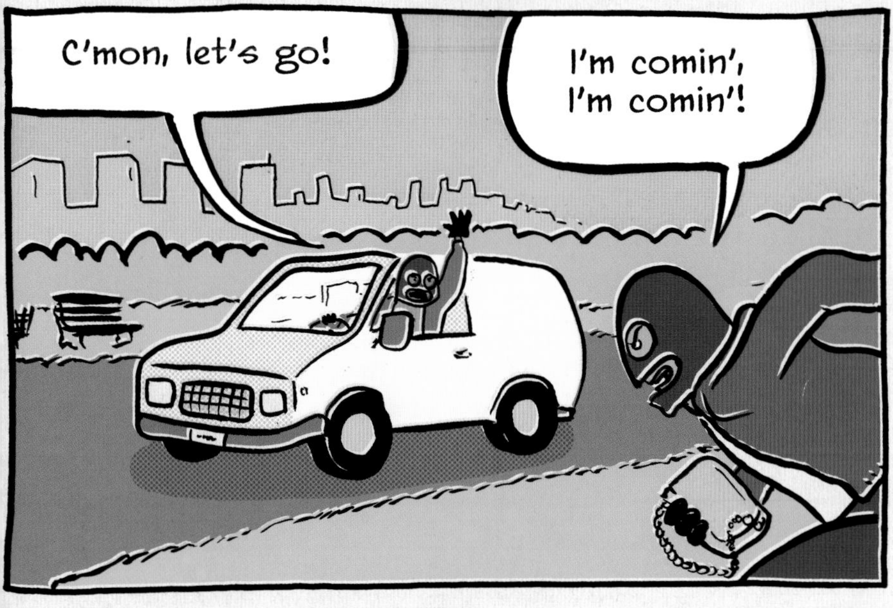
C'mon, let's go!
I'm comin', I'm comin'!

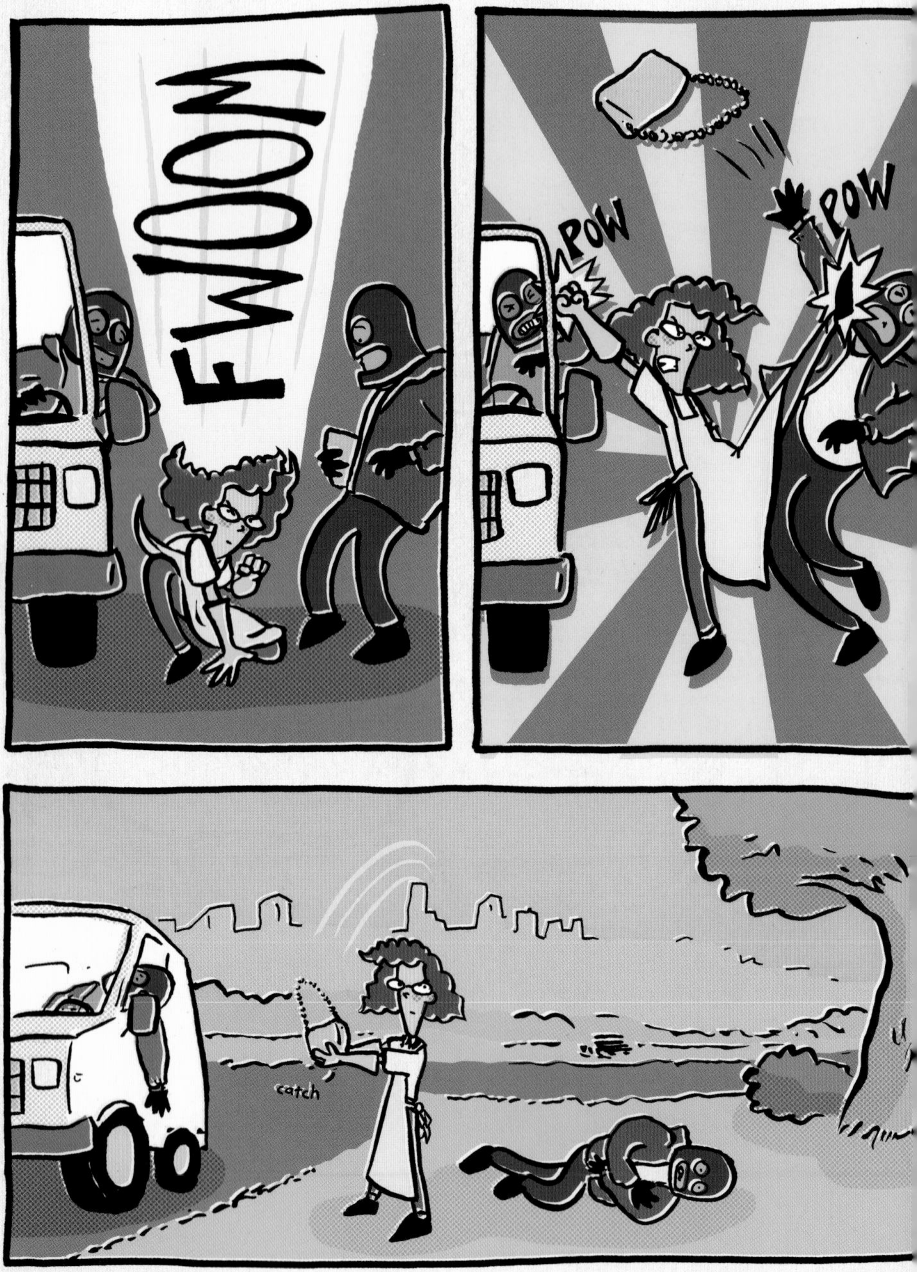
FWOOM
POW
POW
catch

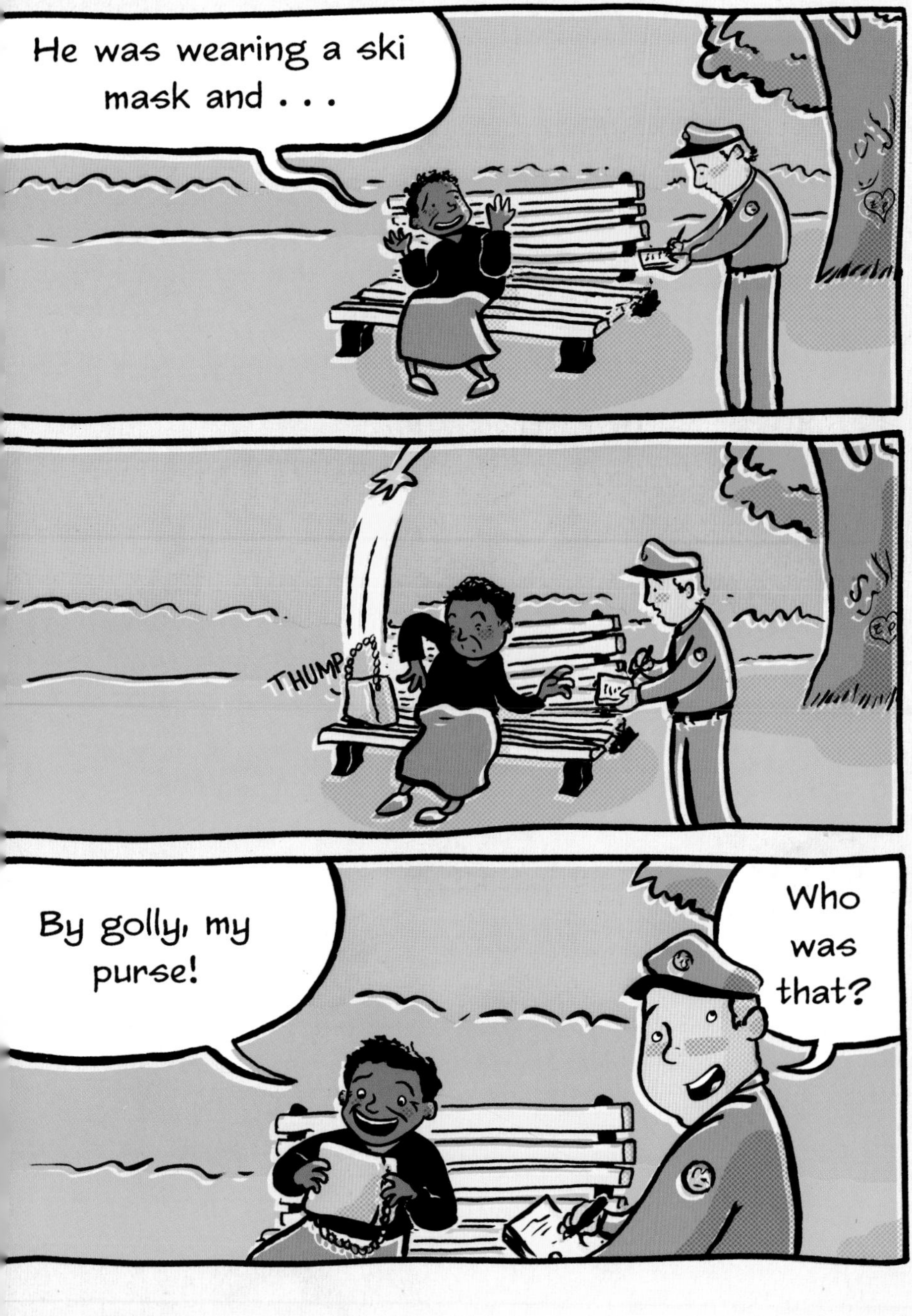
He was wearing a ski mask and . . .
THUMP
By golly, my purse!
Who was that?

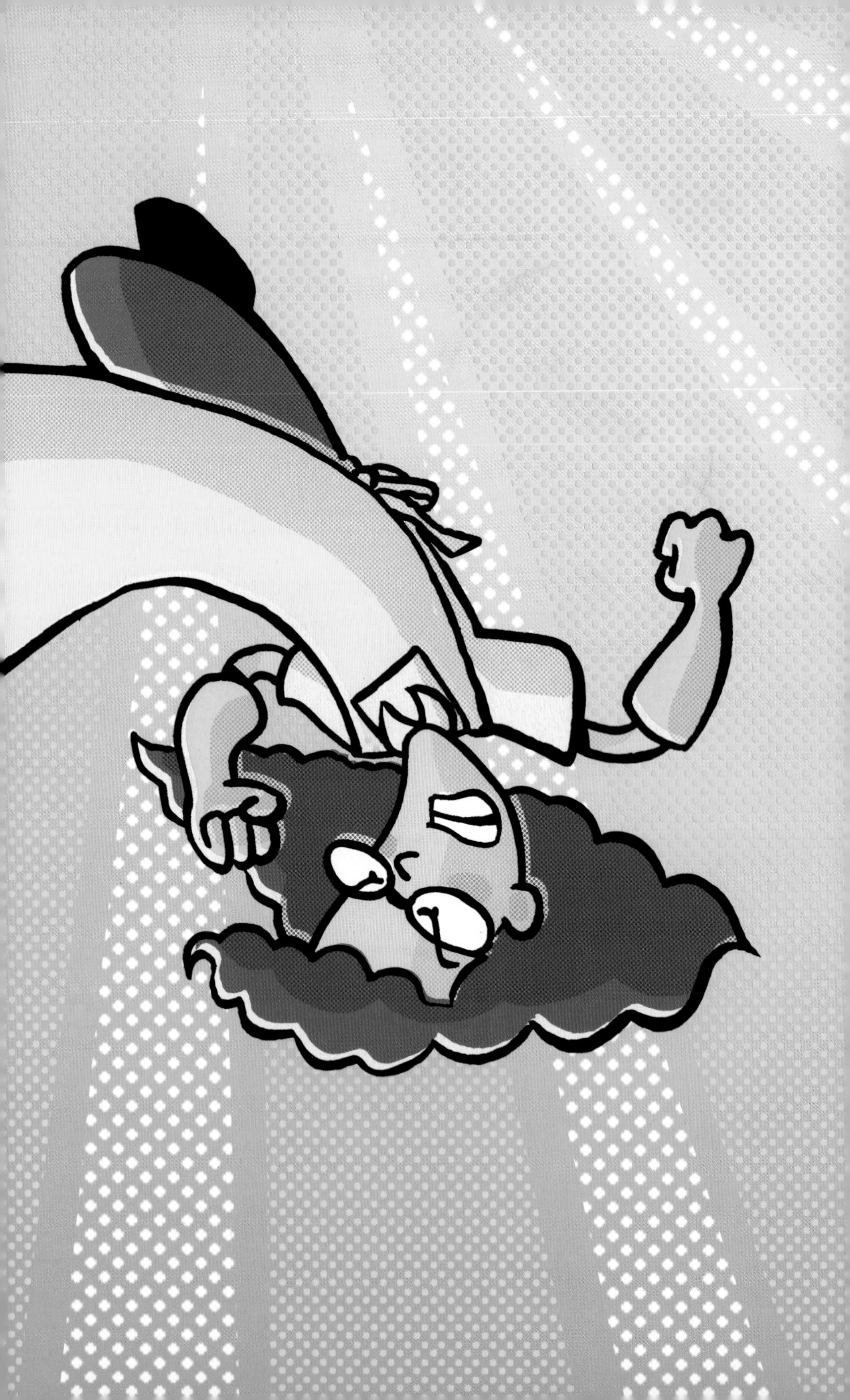

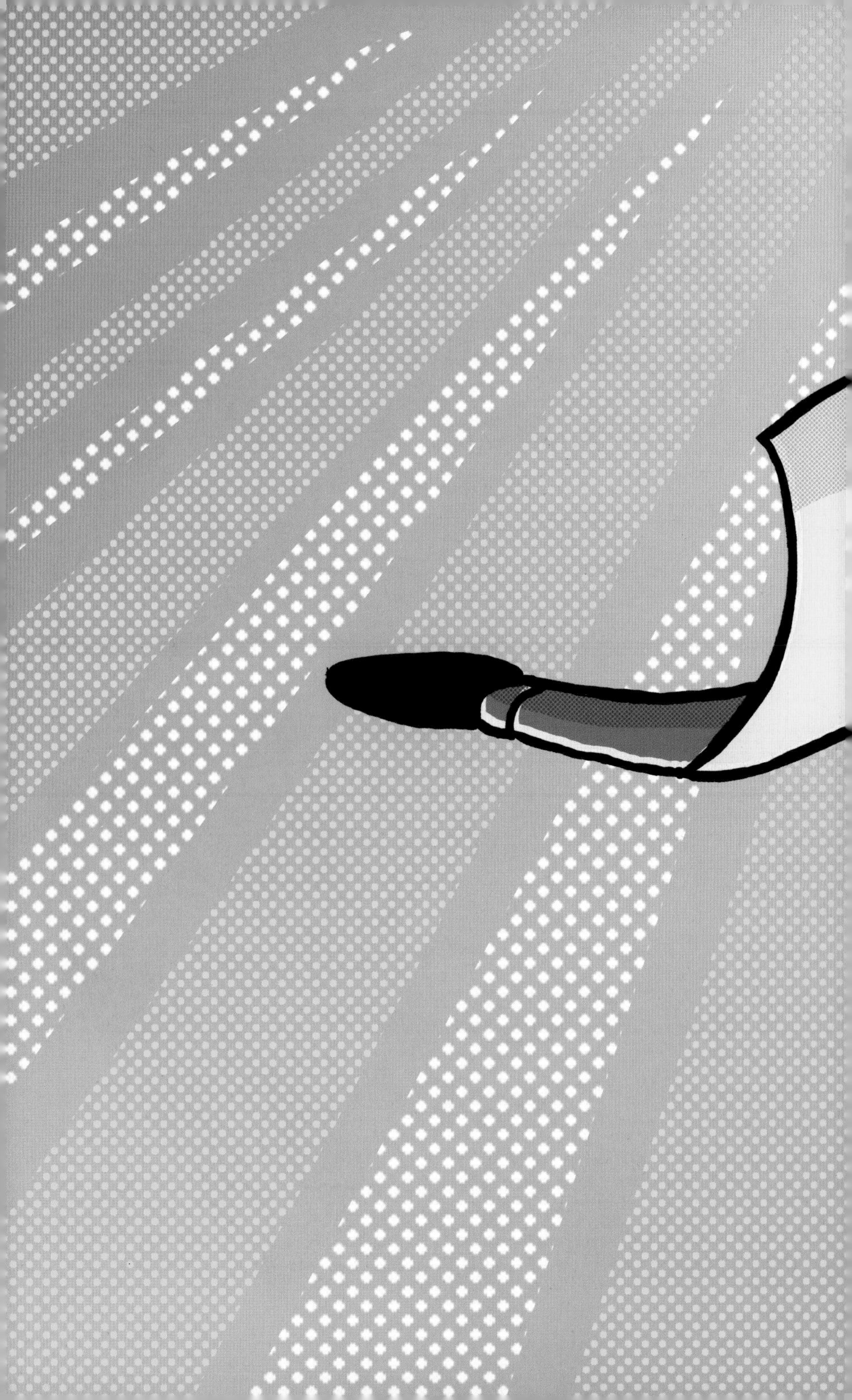

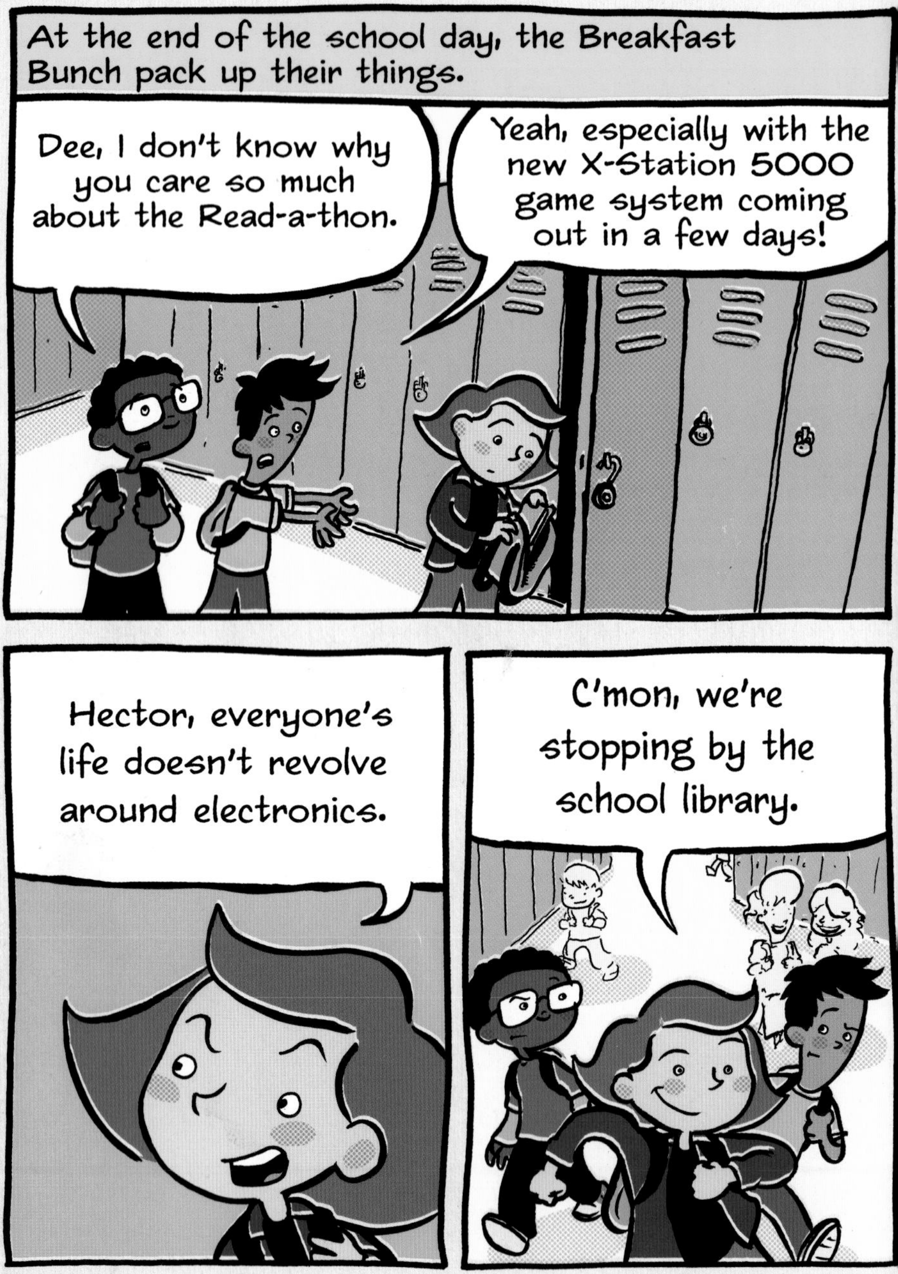
At the end of the school day, the Breakfast Bunch pack up their things.
Dee, I don't know why you care so much about the Read-a-thon.
Yeah, especially with the new X-Station 5000 game system coming out in a few days!
Hector, everyone's life doesn't revolve around electronics.
C'mon, we're stopping by the school library.

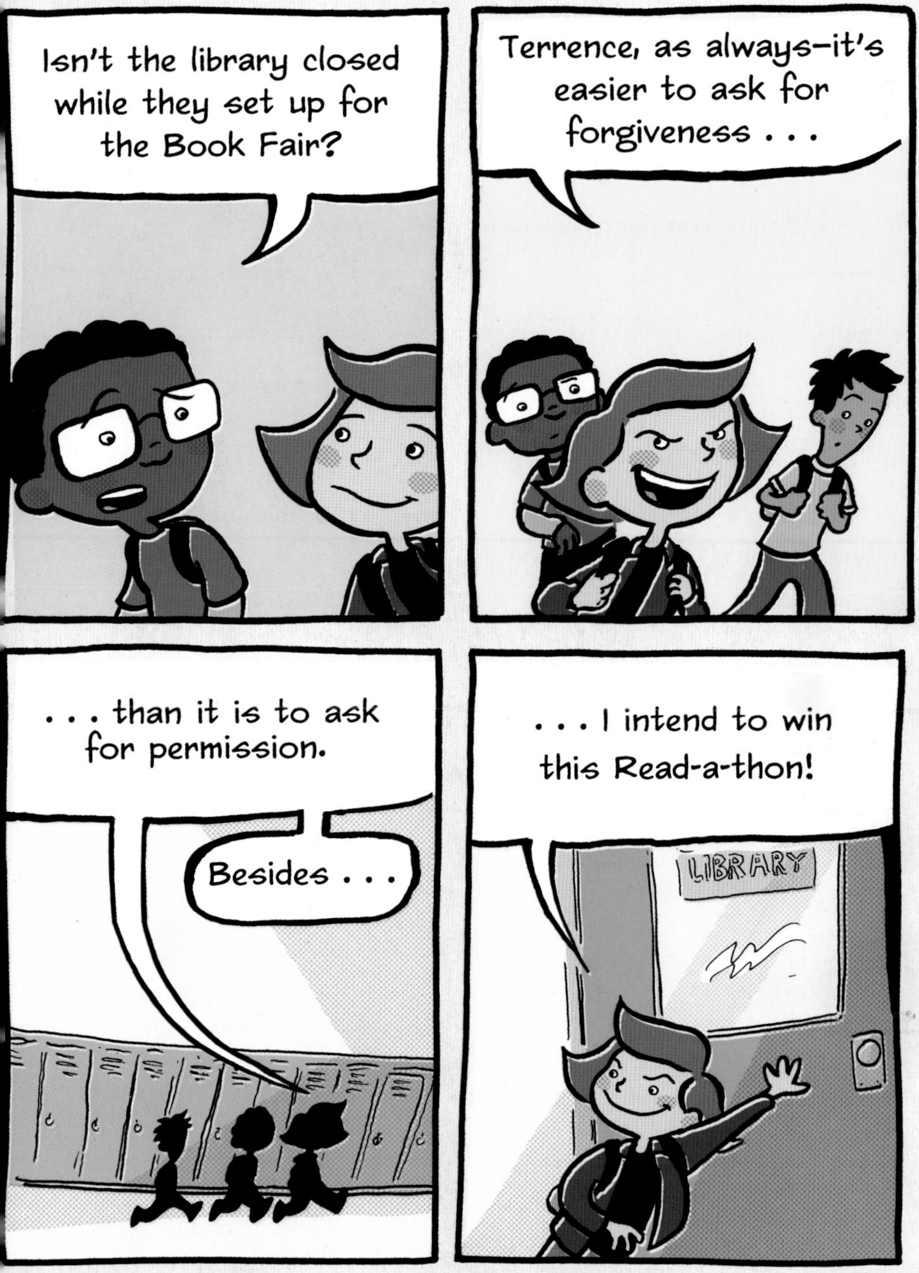
Isn't the library closed while they set up for the Book Fair?
Terrence, as always—it's easier to ask for forgiveness . . .
. . . than it is to ask for permission.
Besides . . .
. . . I intend to win this Read-a-thon!
LIBRARY

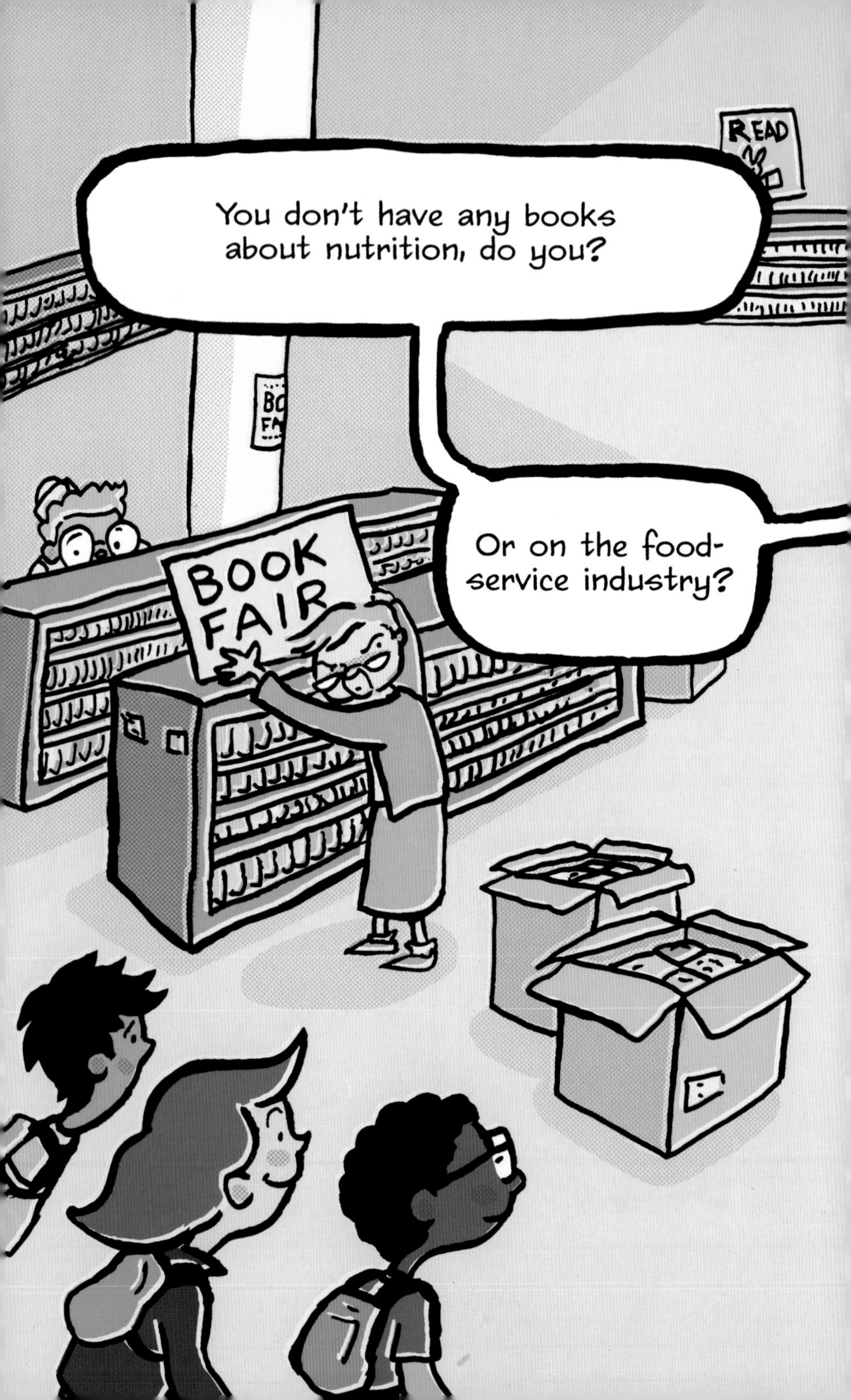
READ
You don't have any books about nutrition, do you?
Or on the food-service industry?
BOOK FAIR

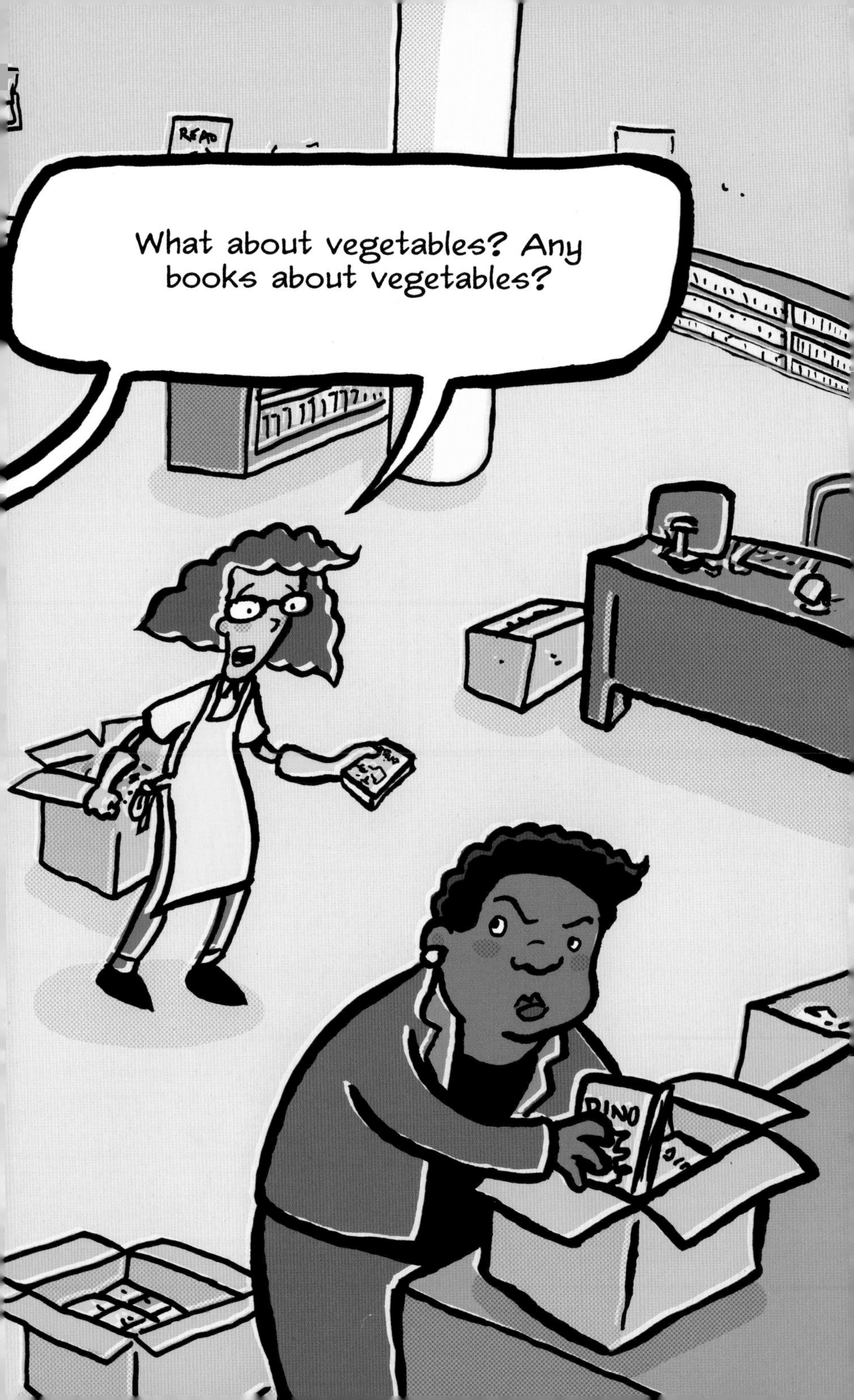
What about vegetables? Any books about vegetables?
READ
DINO

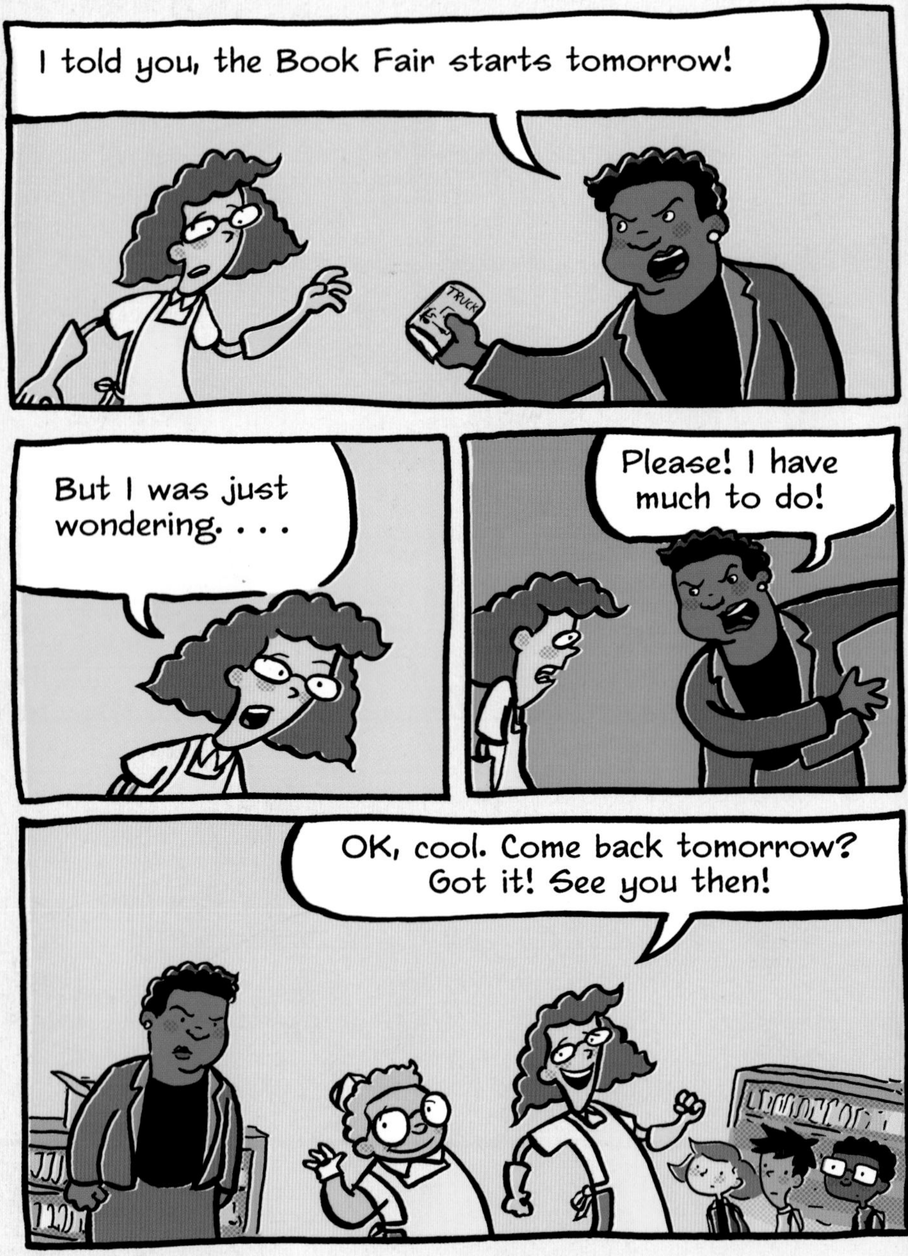
I told you, the Book Fair starts tomorrow!
TRUCK
But I was just wondering. . . .
Please! I have much to do!
OK, cool. Come back tomorrow? Got it! See you then!

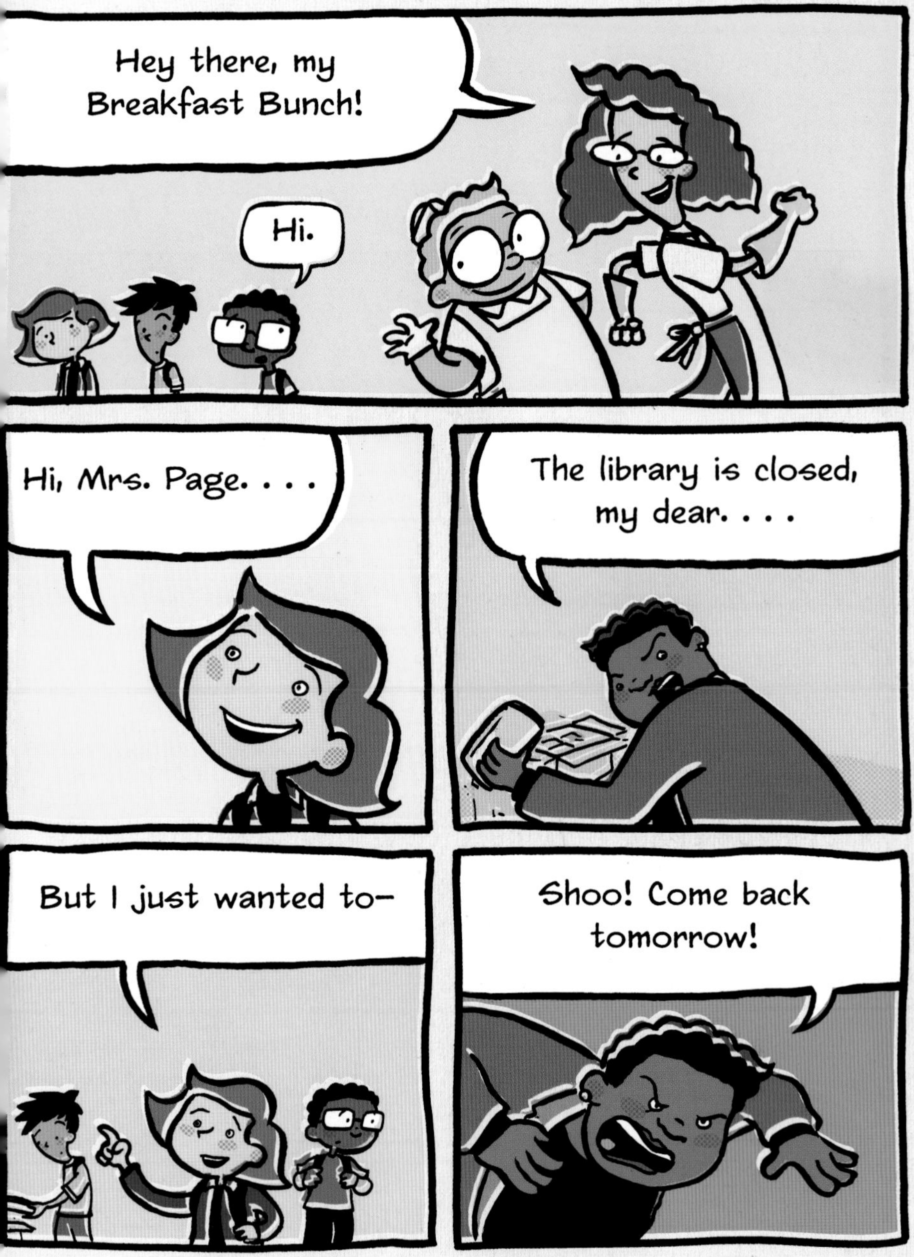
Hey there, my Breakfast Bunch!
Hi.
Hi, Mrs. Page. . . .
The library is closed, my dear. . . .
But I just wanted to—
Shoo! Come back tomorrow!

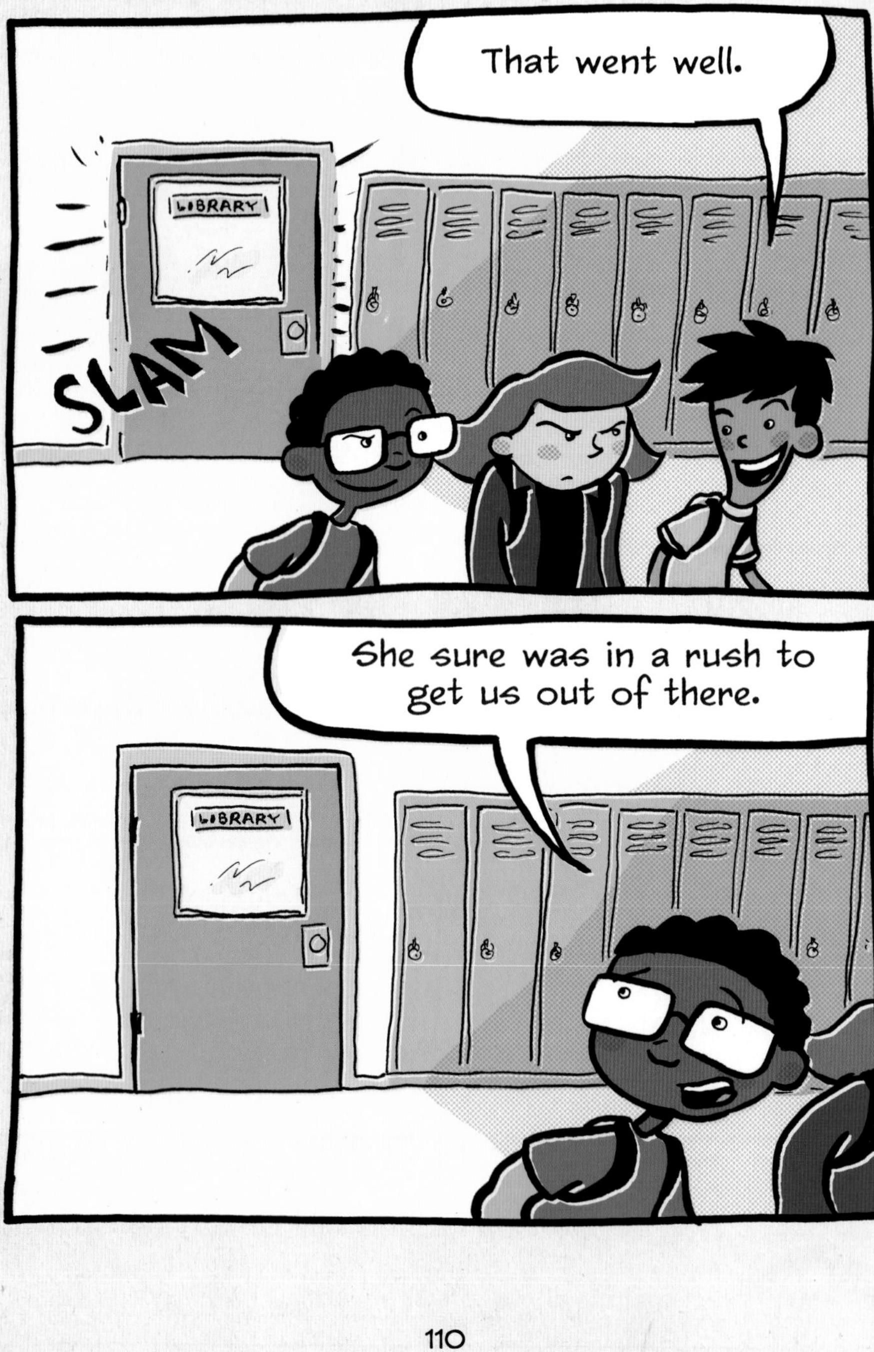
That went well.
LIBRARY
SLAM
She sure was in a rush to get us out of there.
LIBRARY

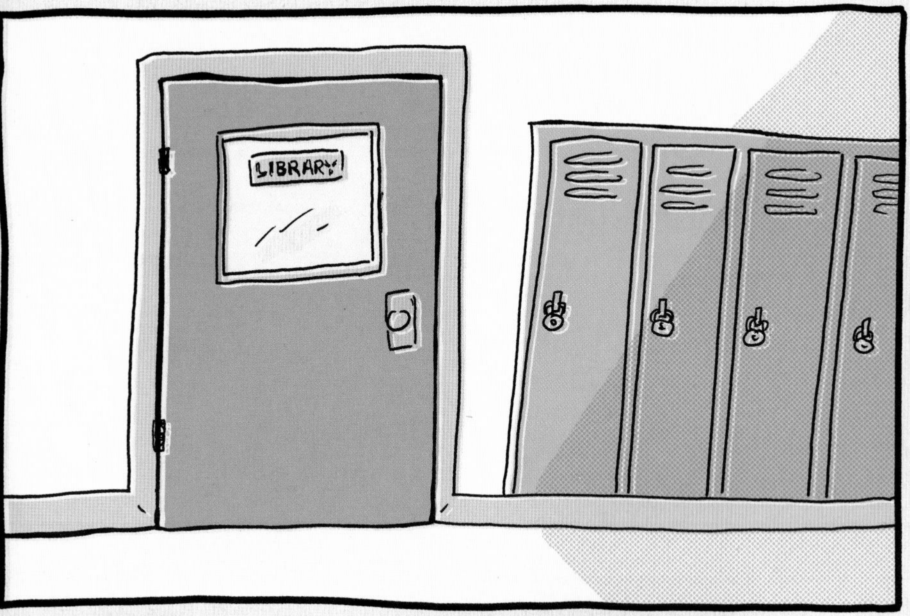
LIBRARY

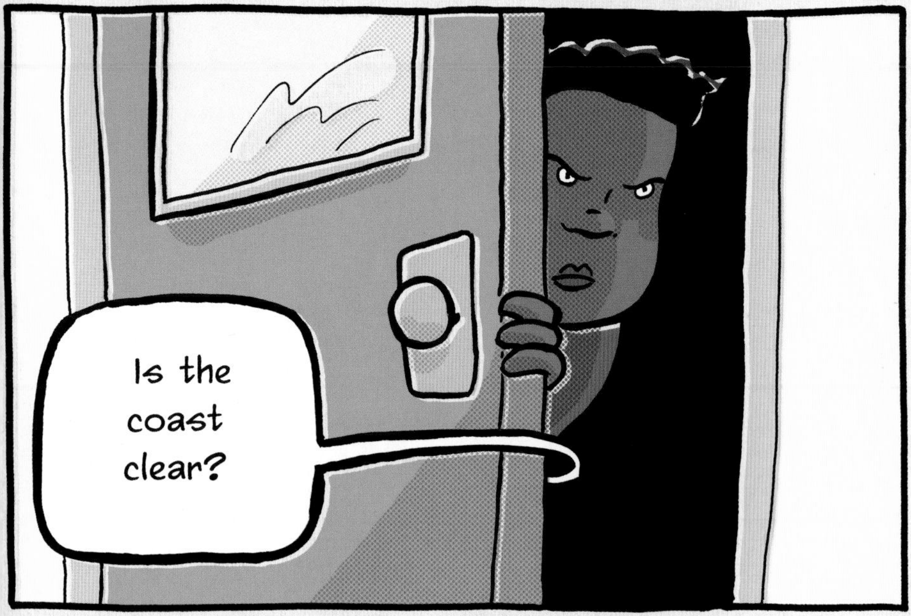
Is the coast clear?

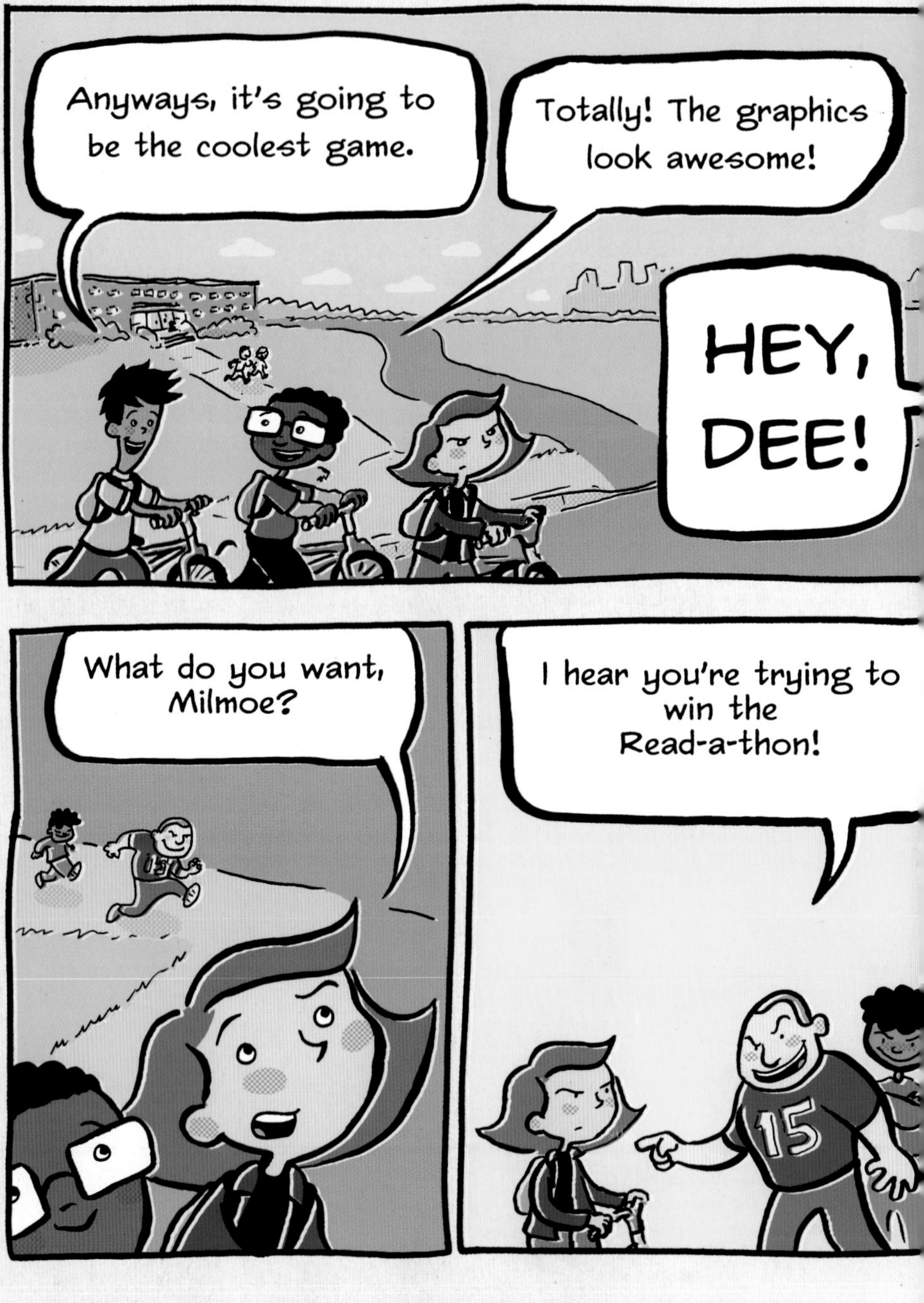
Anyways, it's going to be the coolest game.
Totally! The graphics look awesome!
HEY, DEE!
What do you want, Milmoe?
I hear you're trying to win the Read-a-thon!
15

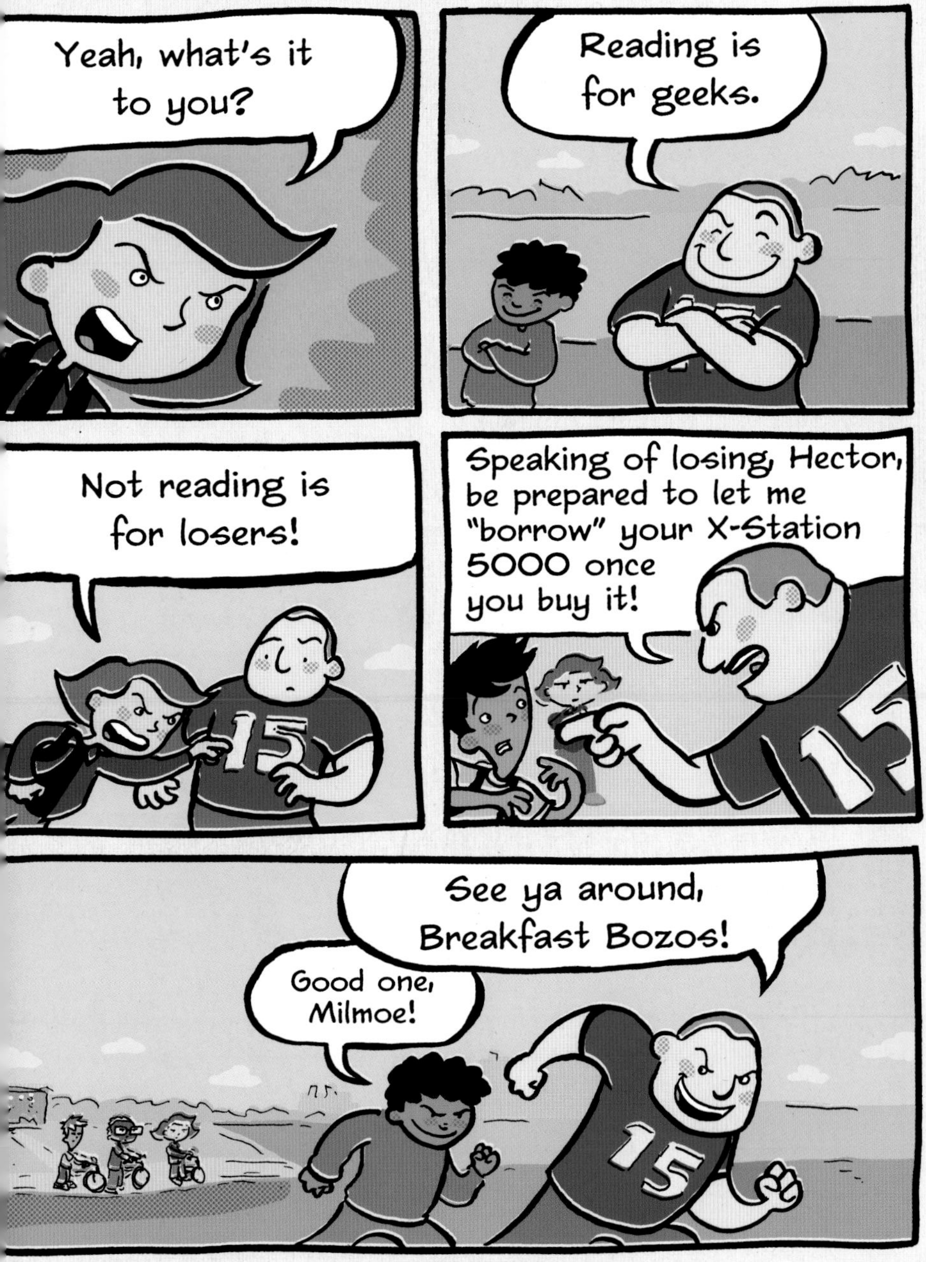
Yeah, what's it to you?
Reading is for geeks.
Not reading is for losers!
Speaking of losing, Hector, be prepared to let me "borrow" your X-Station 5000 once you buy it!
See ya around, Breakfast Bozos!
Good one, Milmoe!

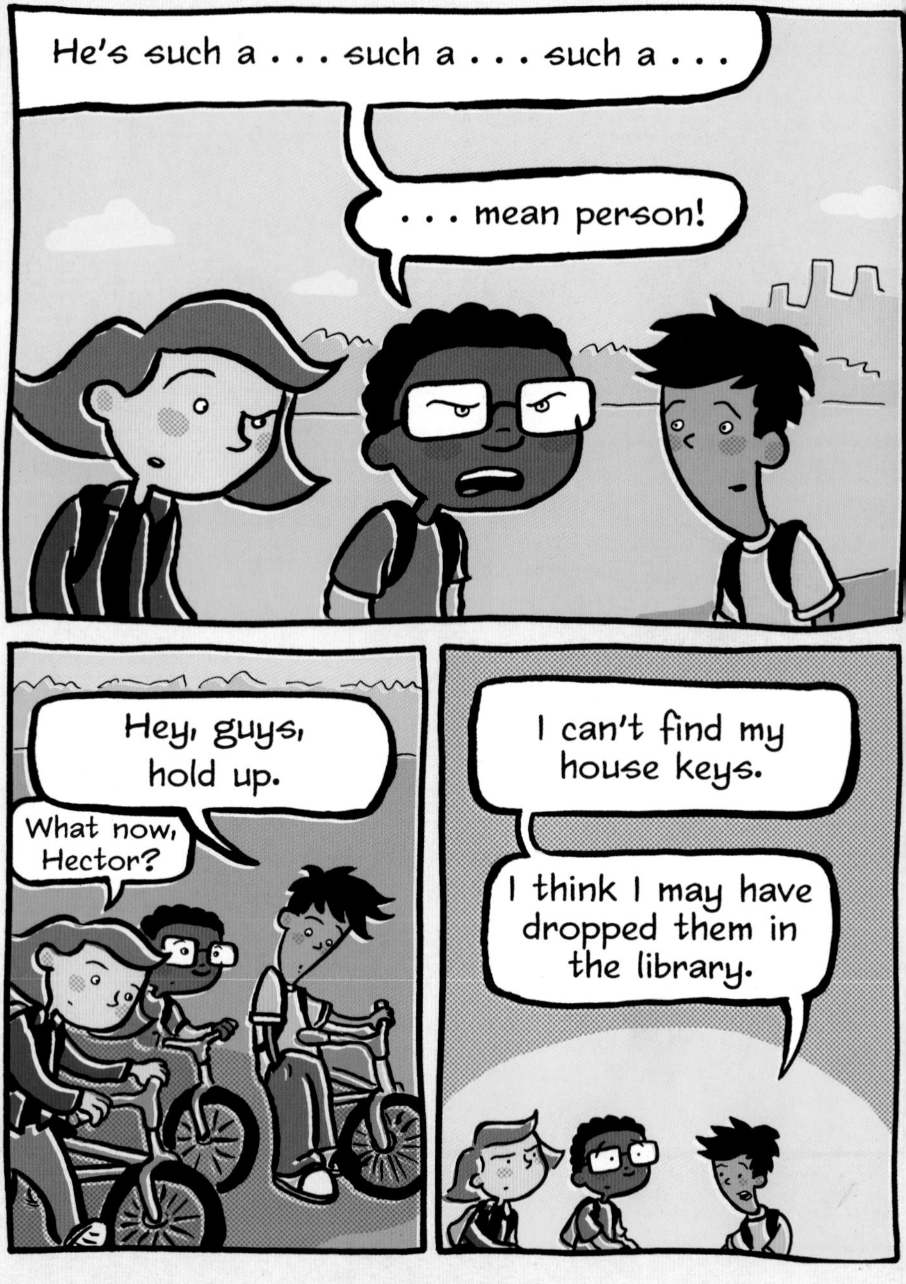
He's such a . . . such a . . . such a . . .
. . . mean person!
Hey, guys, hold up.
What now, Hector?
I can't find my house keys.
I think I may have dropped them in the library.

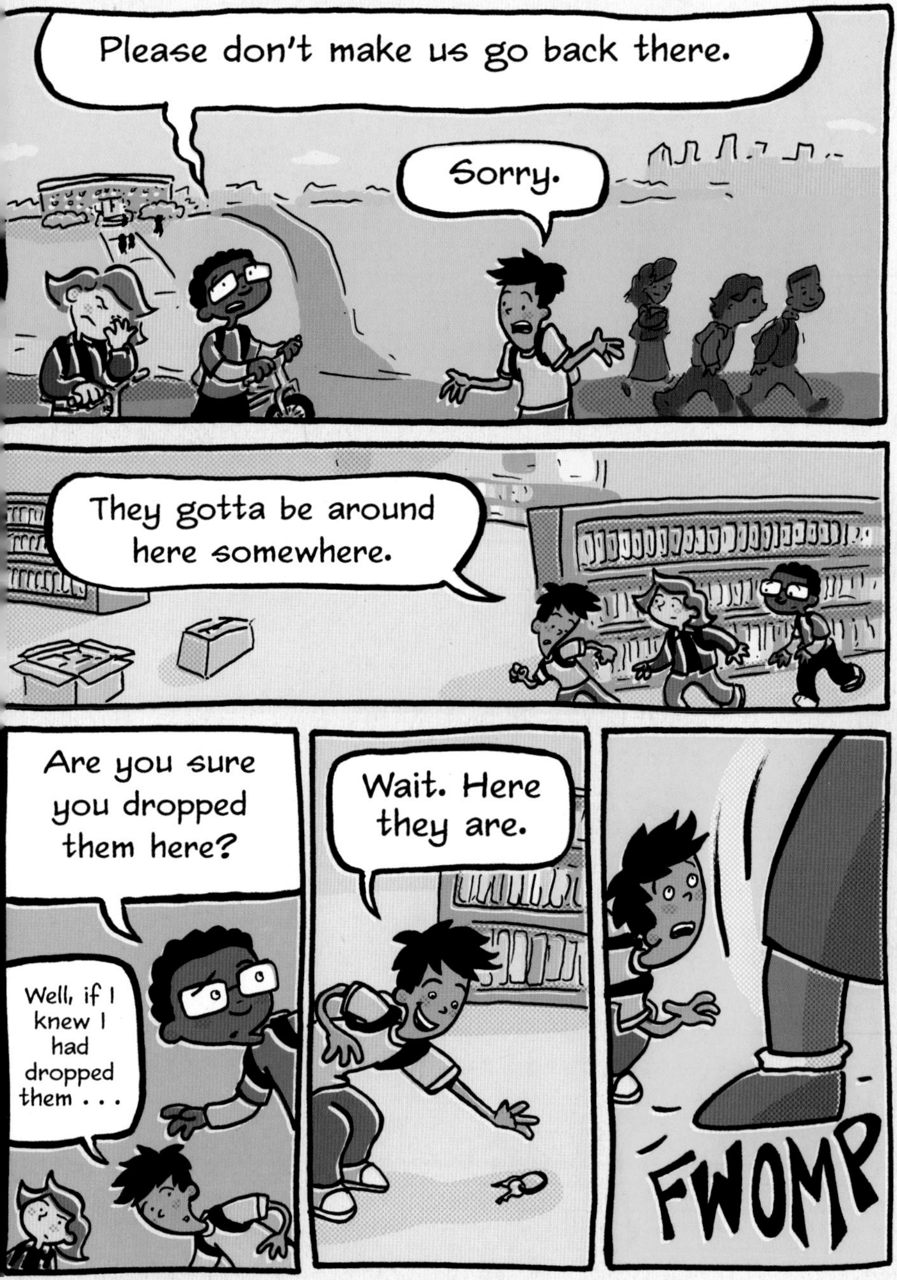
Please don't make us go back there.
Sorry.
They gotta be around here somewhere.
Are you sure you dropped them here?
Well, if I knew I had dropped them . . .
Wait. Here they are.
FWOMP

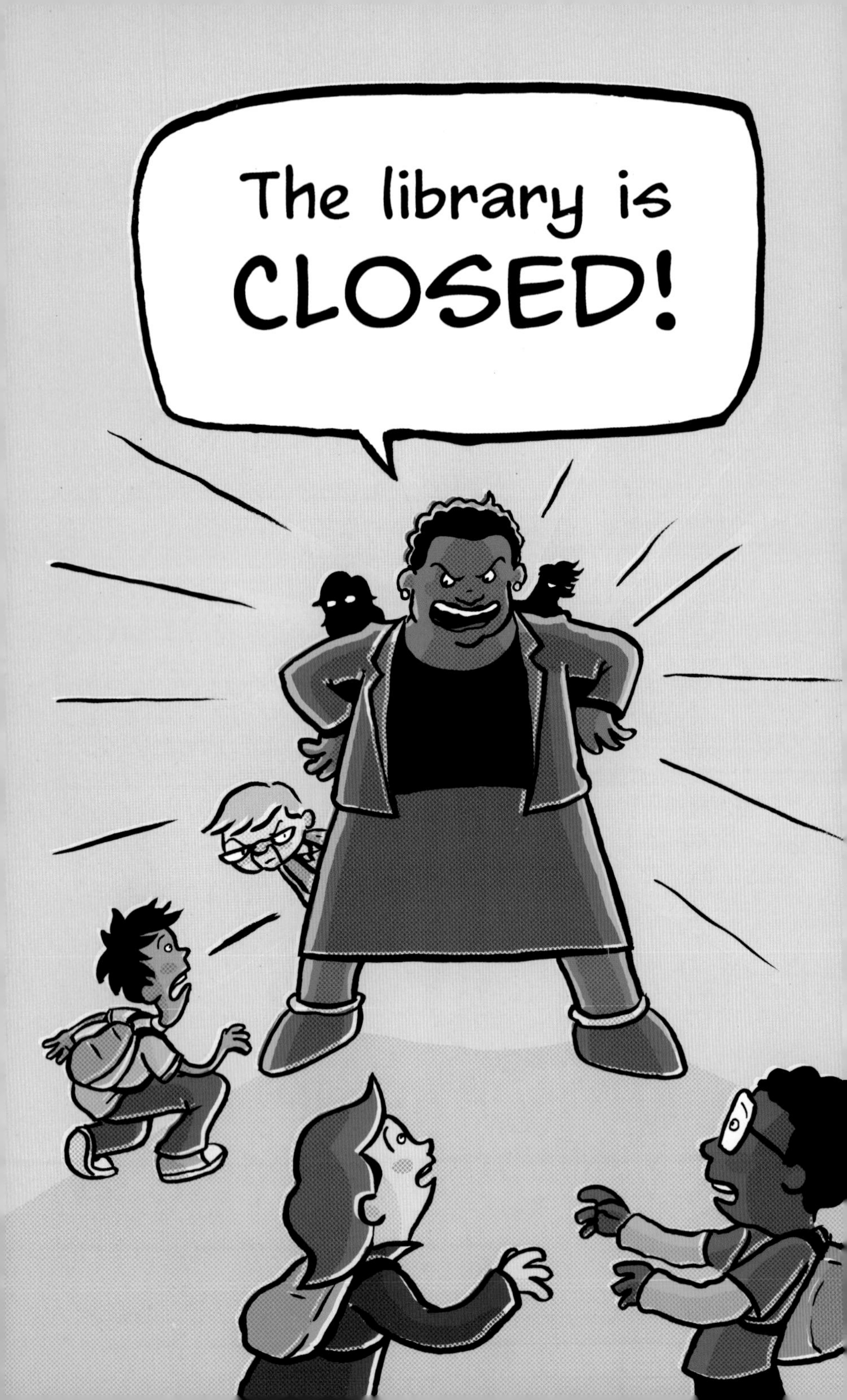
The library is CLOSED!

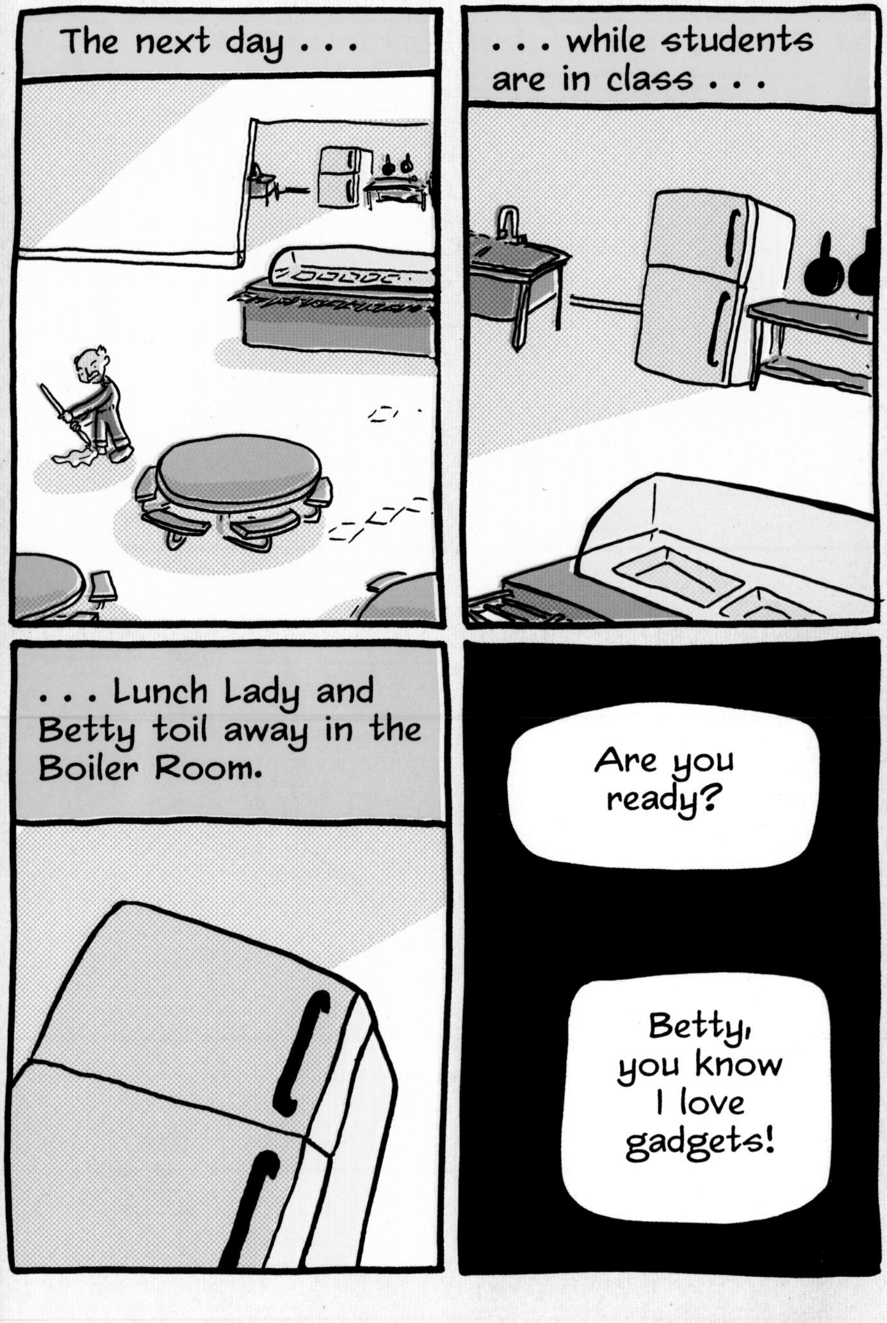
The next day . . .
. . . while students are in class . . .
. . . Lunch Lady and Betty toil away in the Boiler Room.
Are you ready?
Betty, you know I love gadgets!

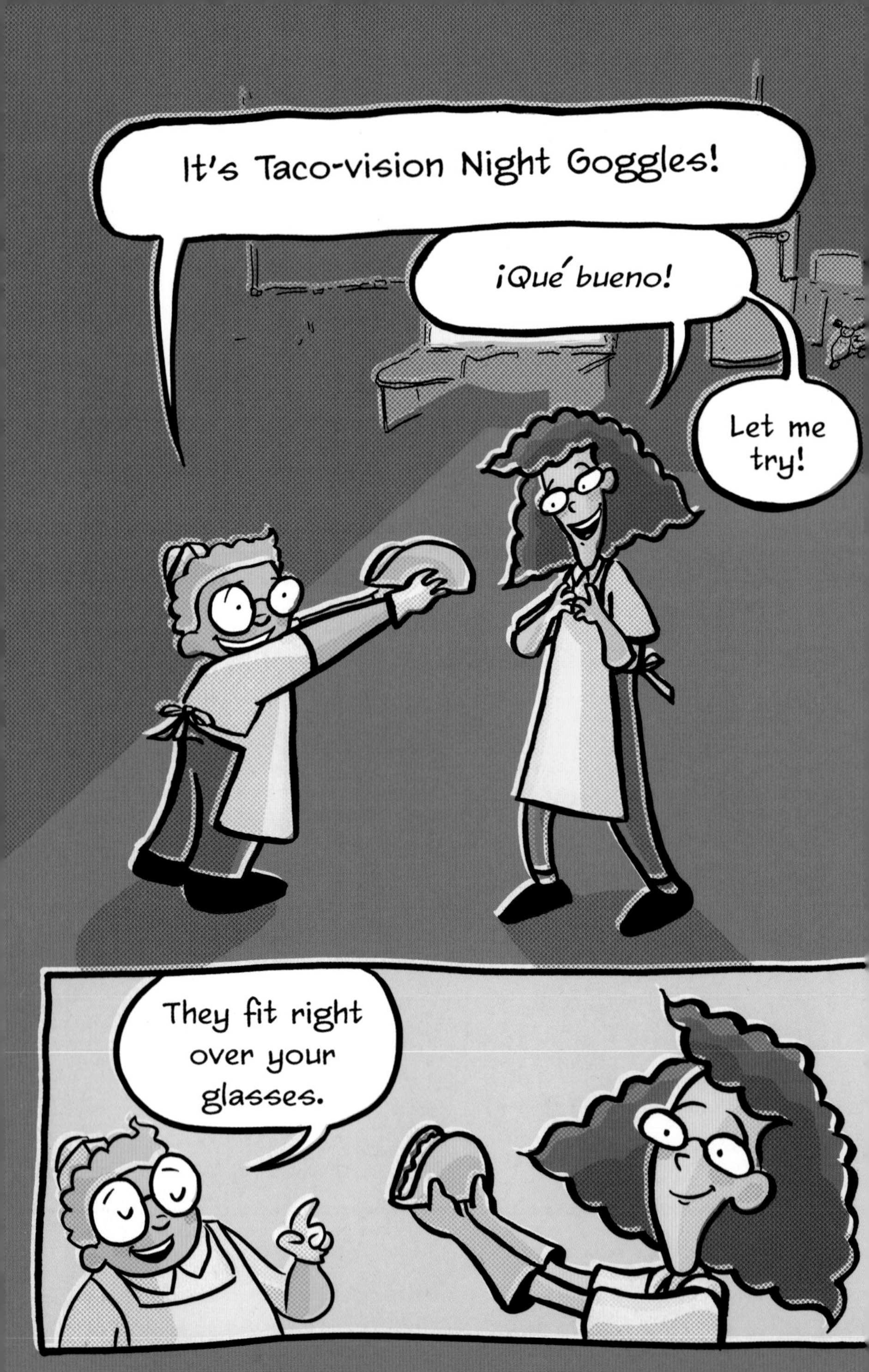
It's Taco-vision Night Goggles!
¡Qué bueno!
Let me try!
They fit right over your glasses.

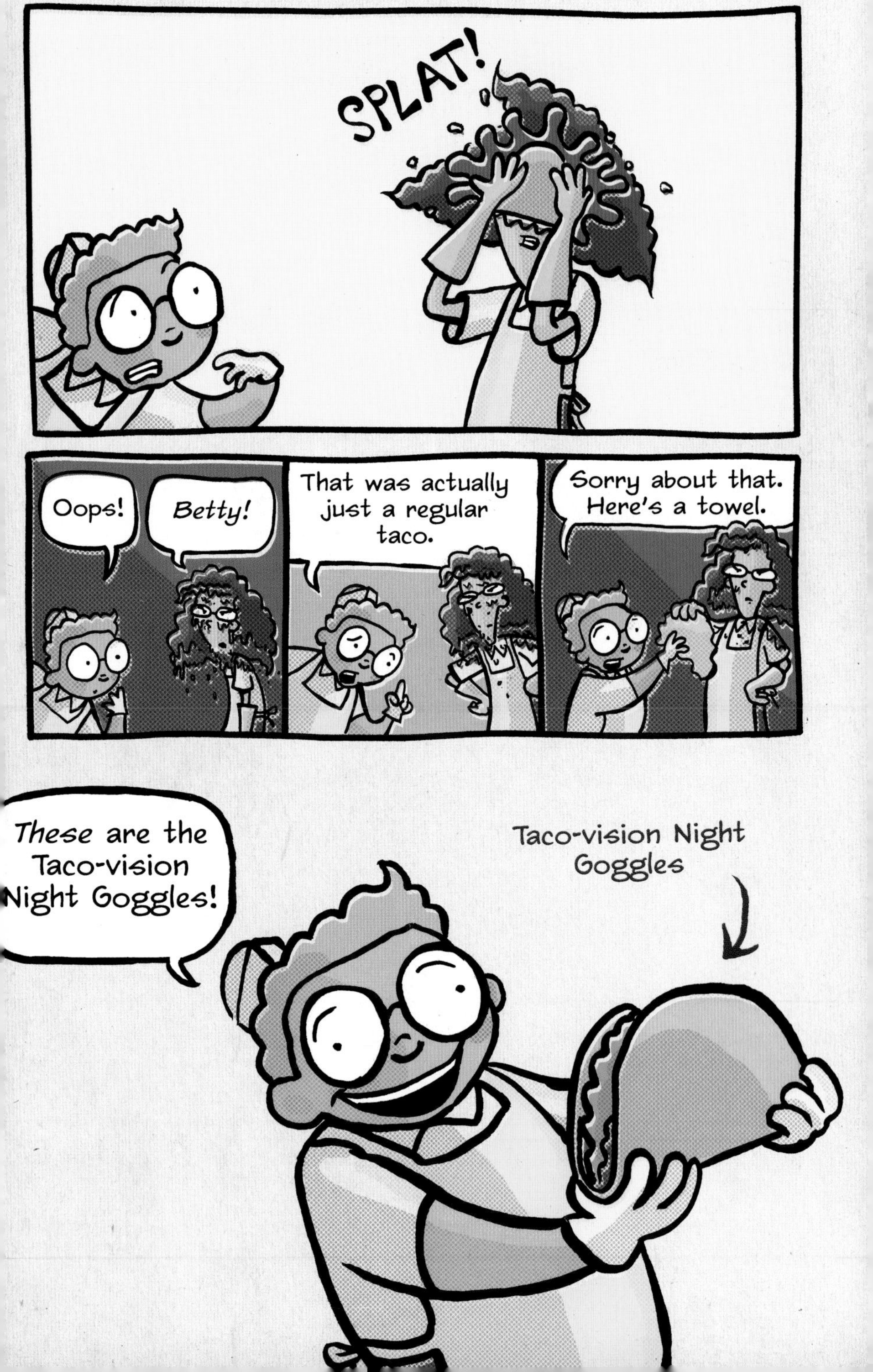
SPLAT!
Oops!
Betty!
That was actually just a regular taco.
Sorry about that. Here's a towel.
These are the Taco-vision Night Goggles!
Taco-vision Night Goggles

Hit the lights, Betty!
Sure thing.
clap clap

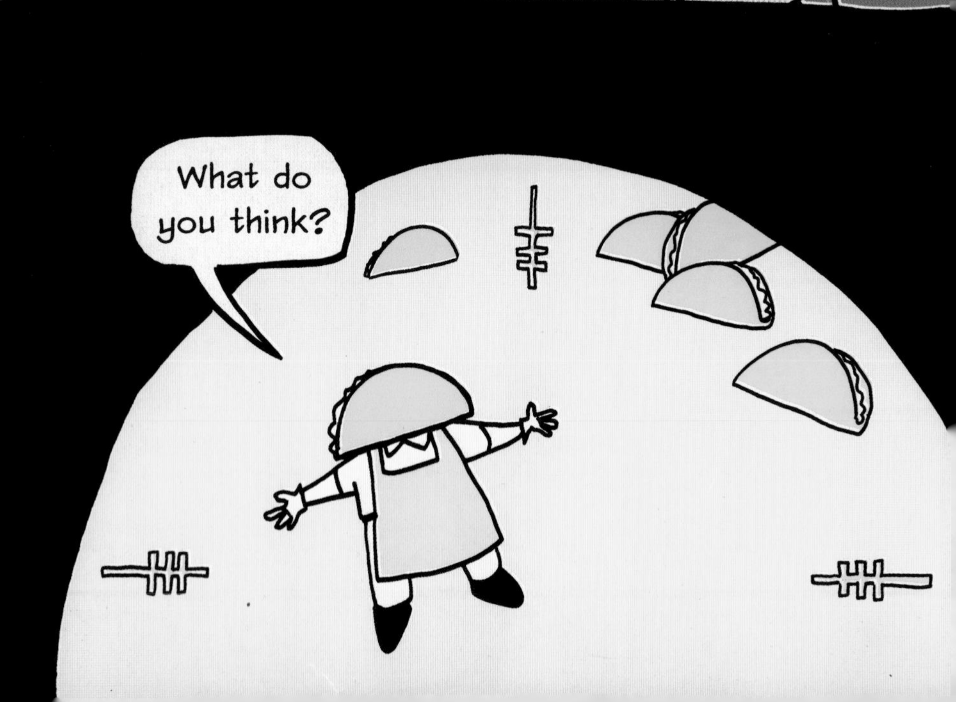
What do you think?

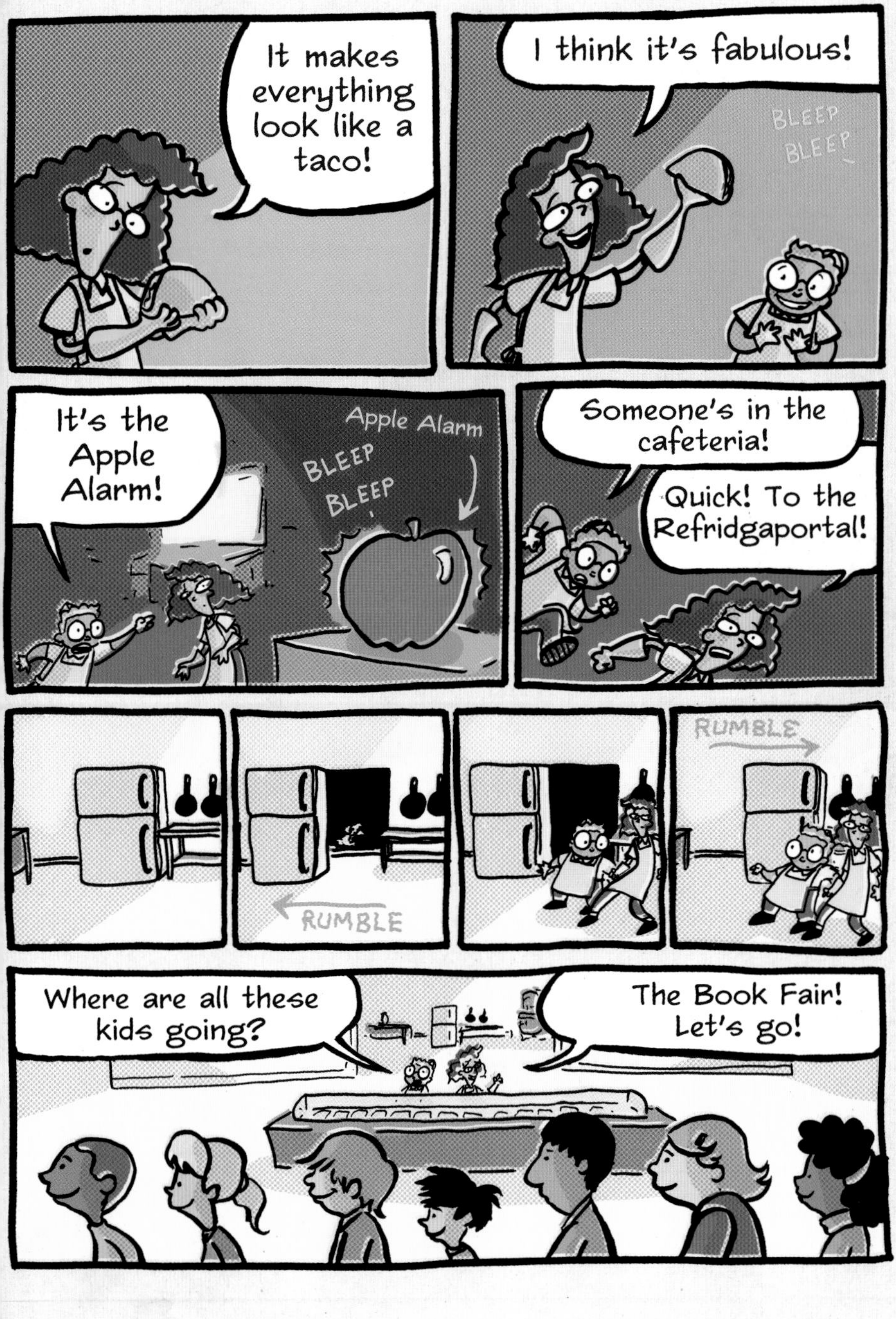
It makes everything look like a taco!
I think it's fabulous!
BLEEP
BLEEP
It's the Apple Alarm!
Apple Alarm
BLEEP
BLEEP
Someone's in the cafeteria!
Quick! To the Refridgaportal!
RUMBLE
RUMBLE
Where are all these kids going?
The Book Fair! Let's go!

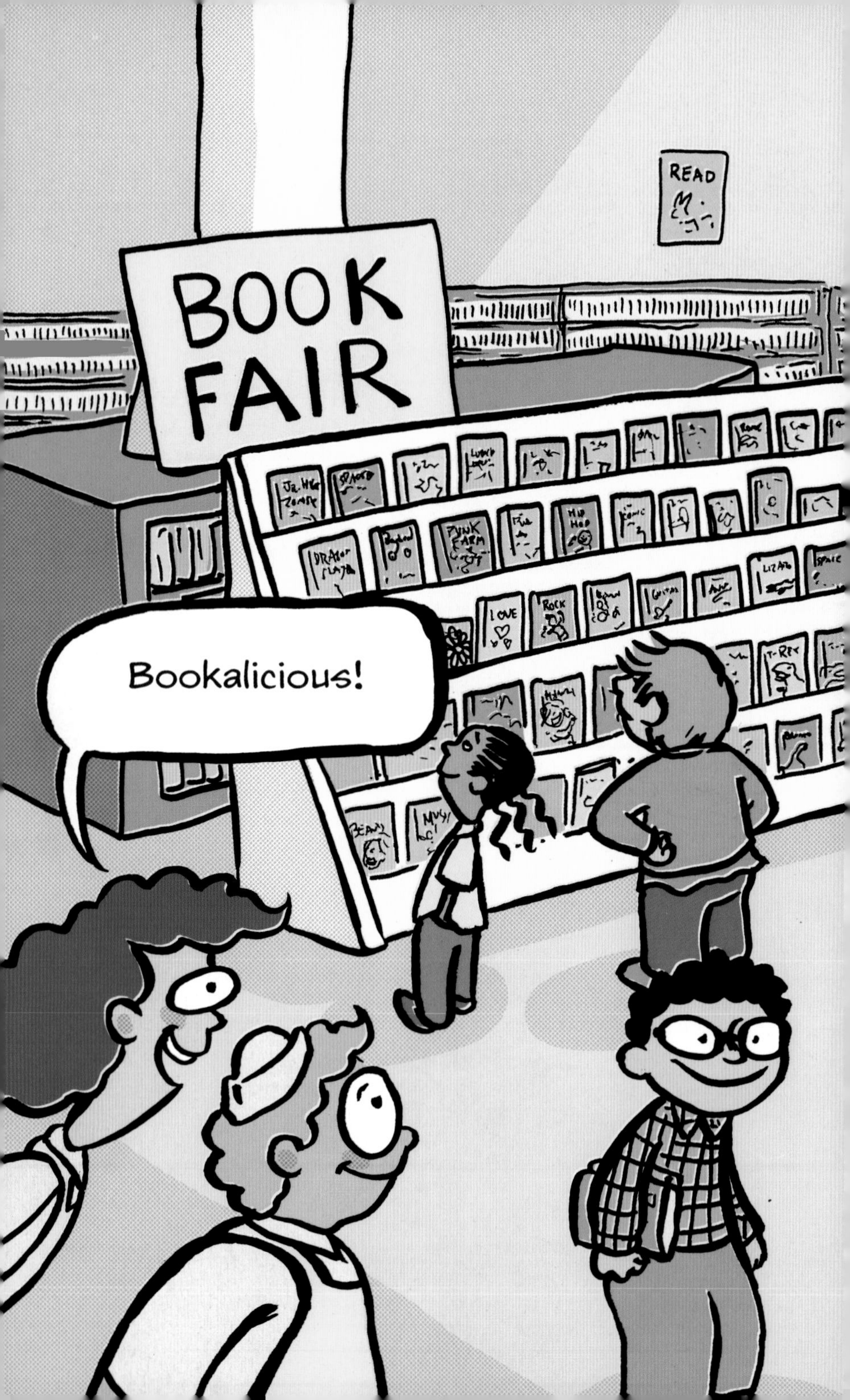
BOOK FAIR
READ
Bookalicious!

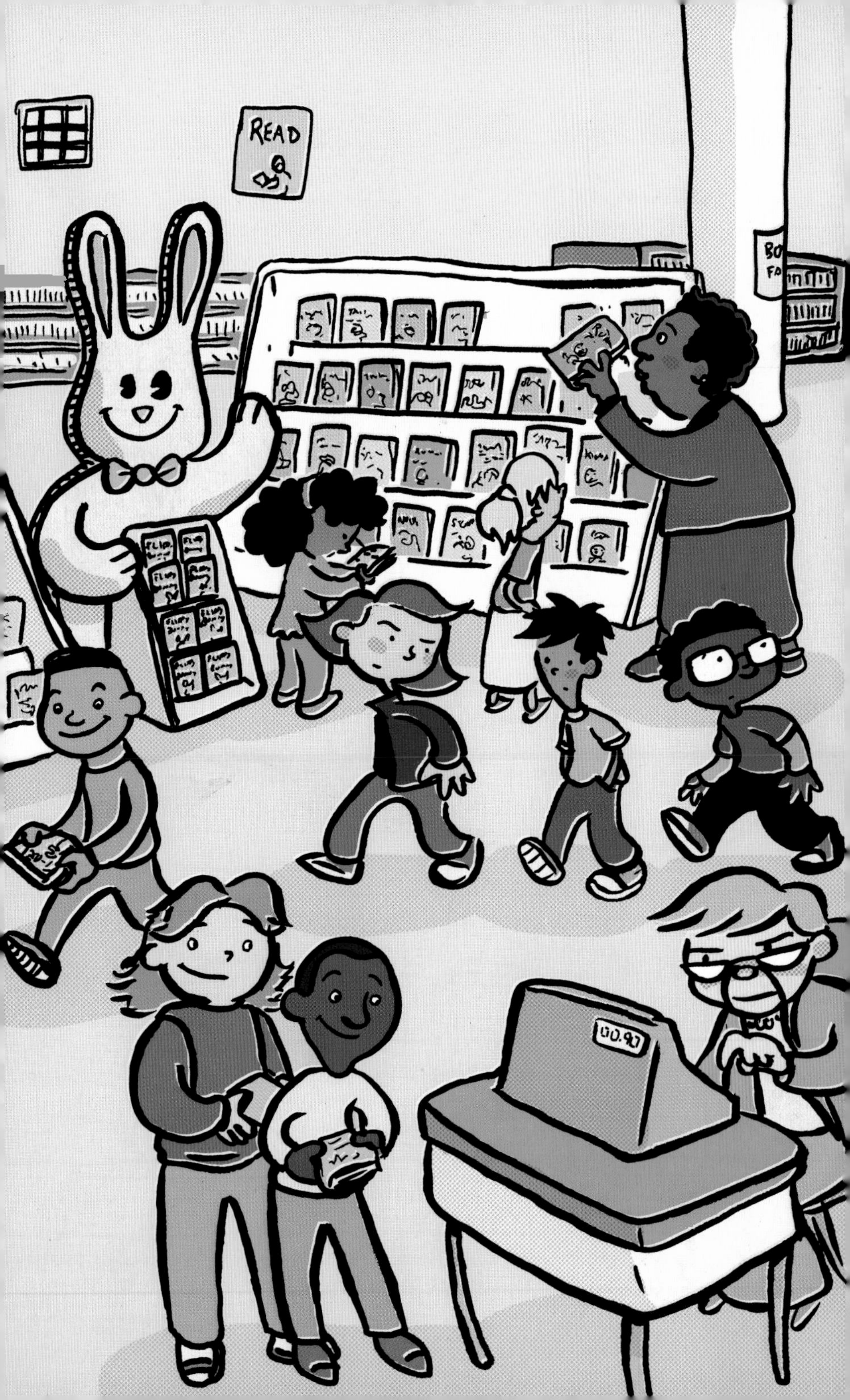
READ

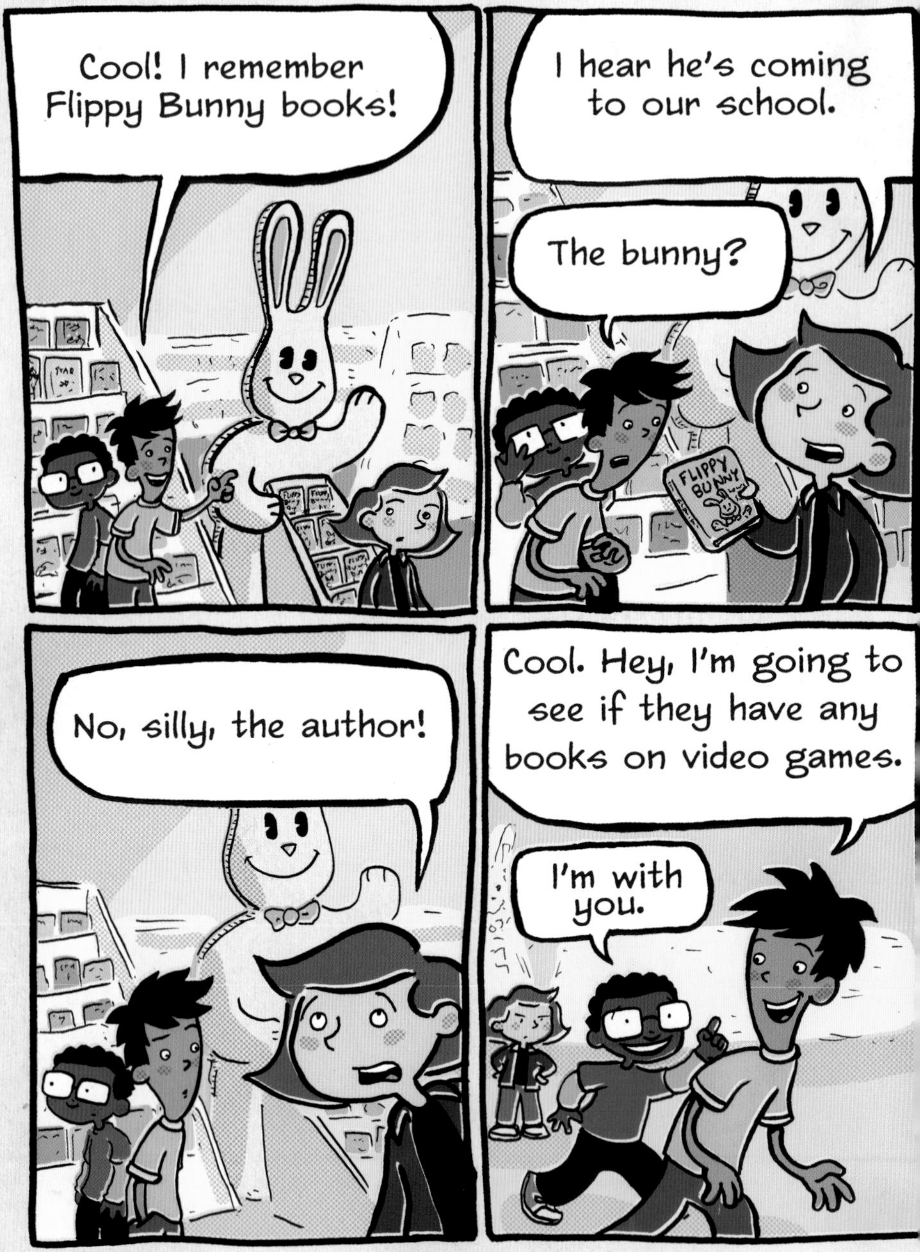
Cool! I remember Flippy Bunny books!
I hear he's coming to our school.
The bunny?
FLIPPY BUNNY
No, silly, the author!
Cool. Hey, I'm going to see if they have any books on video games.
I'm with you.

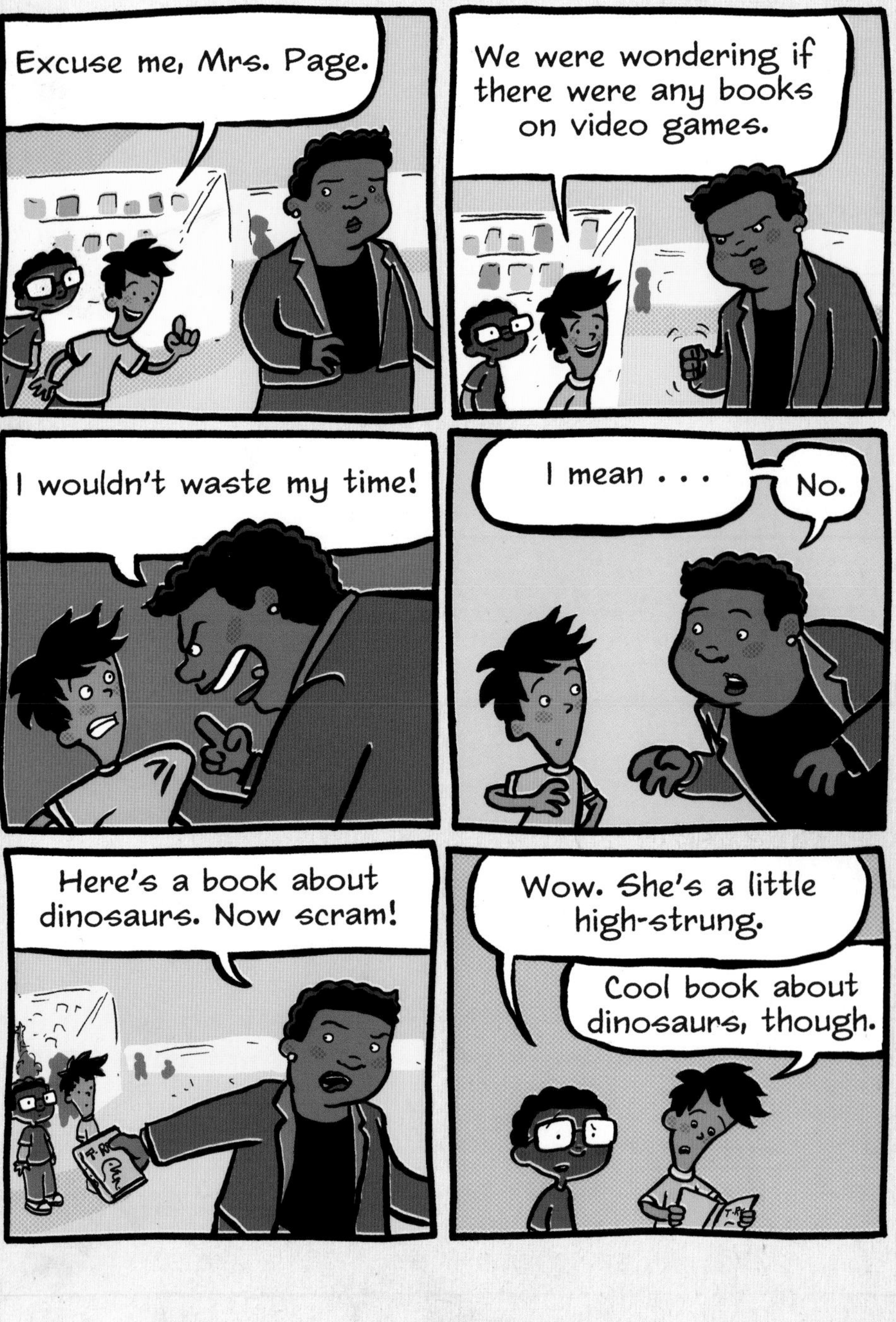
Excuse me, Mrs. Page.
We were wondering if there were any books on video games.
I wouldn't waste my time!
I mean . . .
No.
Here's a book about dinosaurs. Now scram!
Wow. She's a little high-strung.
Cool book about dinosaurs, though.

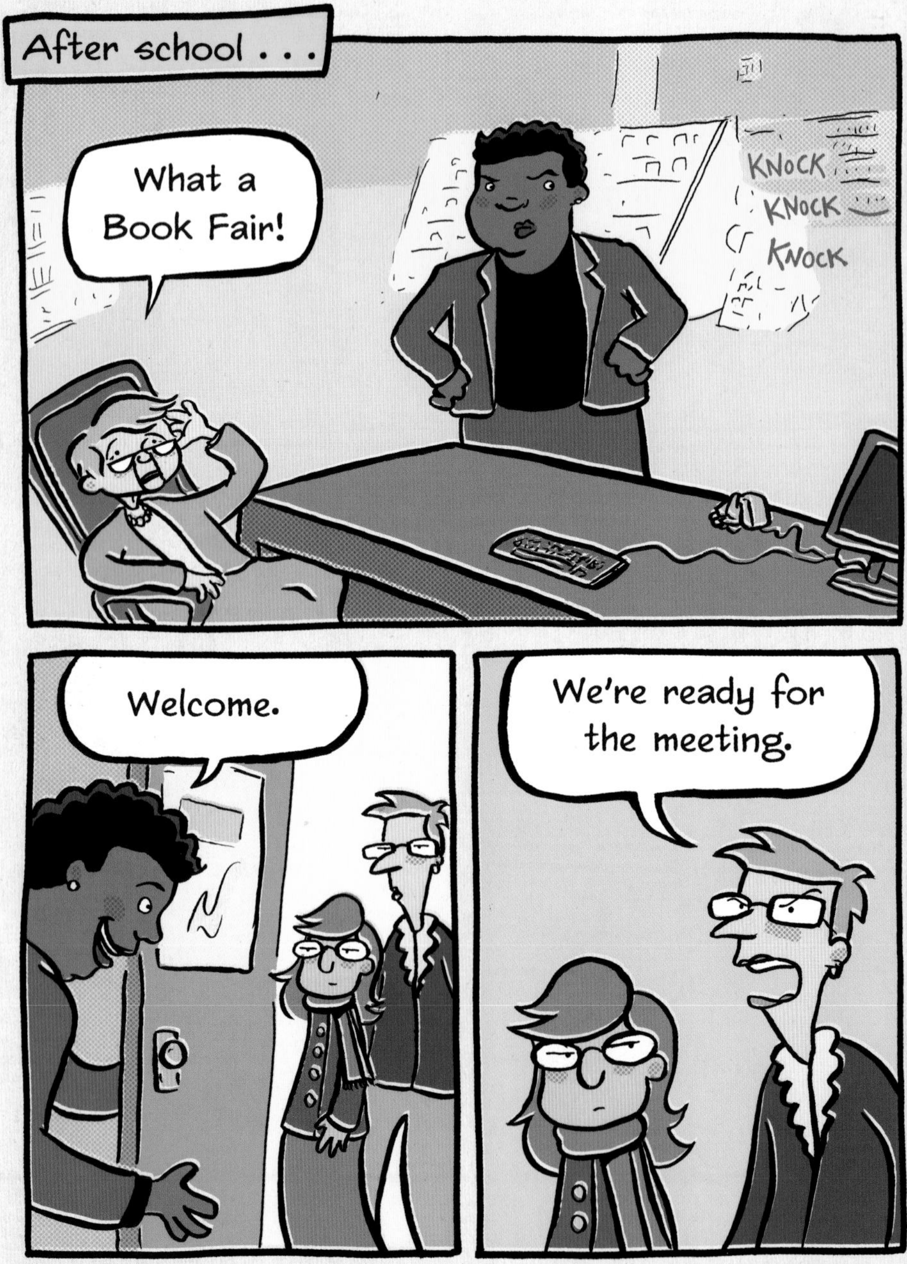
After school . . .
What a Book Fair!
KNOCK
KNOCK
KNOCK
Welcome.
We're ready for the meeting.

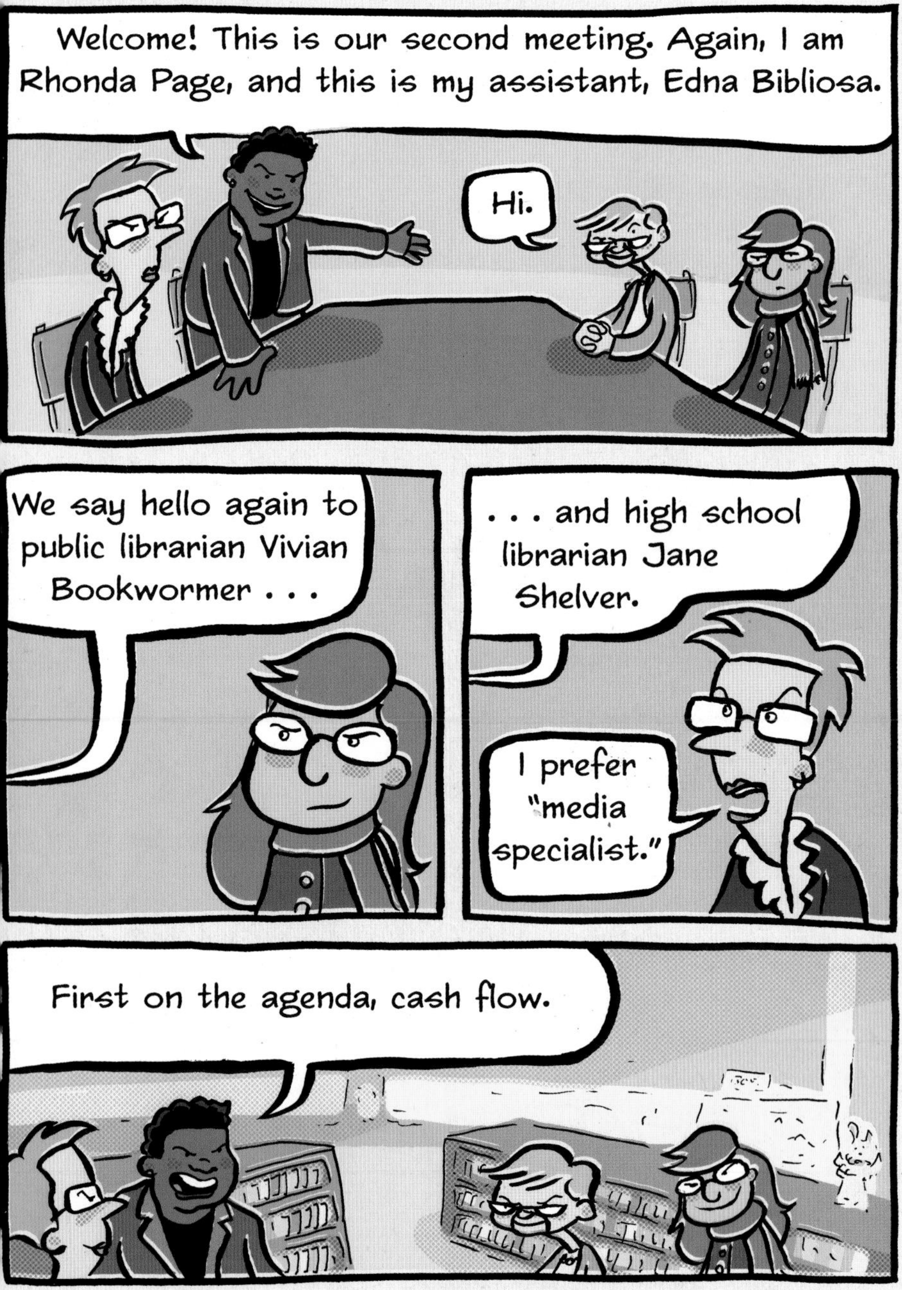
Welcome! This is our second meeting. Again, I am Rhonda Page, and this is my assistant, Edna Bibliosa.
Hi.
We say hello again to public librarian Vivian Bookwormer . . .
. . . and high school librarian Jane Shelver.
I prefer "media specialist."
First on the agenda, cash flow.

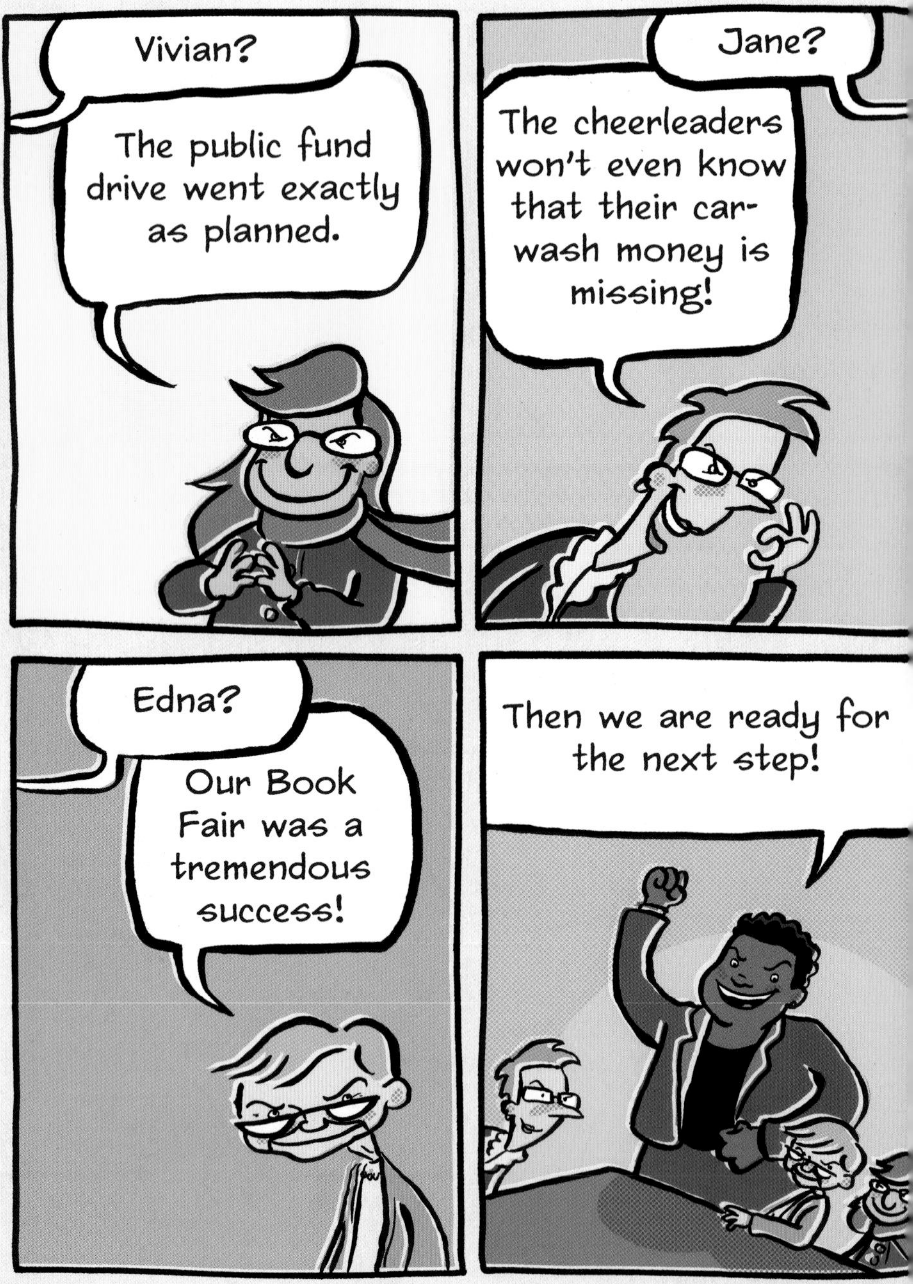
Vivian?
The public fund drive went exactly as planned.
Jane?
The cheerleaders won't even know that their car-wash money is missing!
Edna?
Our Book Fair was a tremendous success!
Then we are ready for the next step!

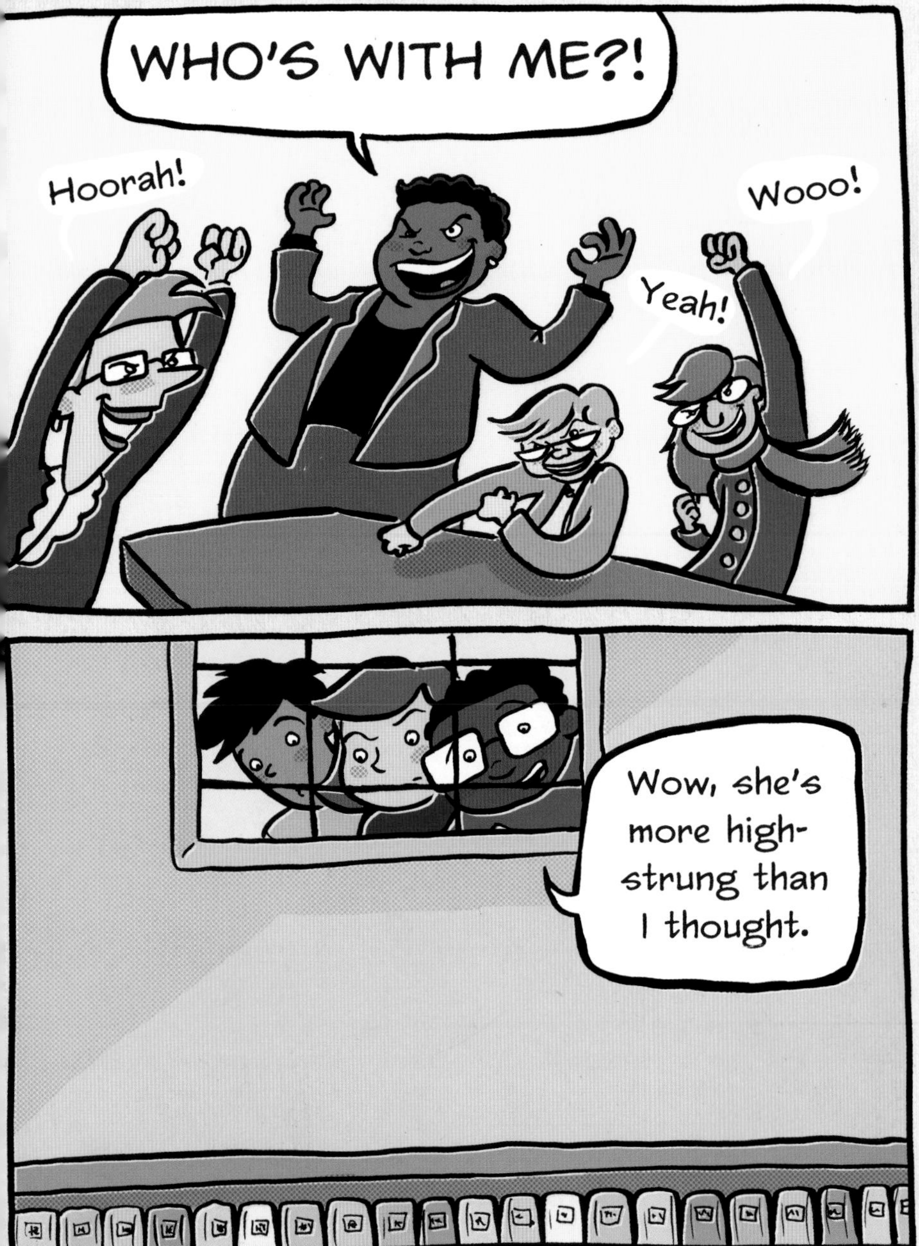
WHO'S WITH ME?!
Hoorah!
Yeah!
Wooo!
Wow, she's more high-strung than I thought.

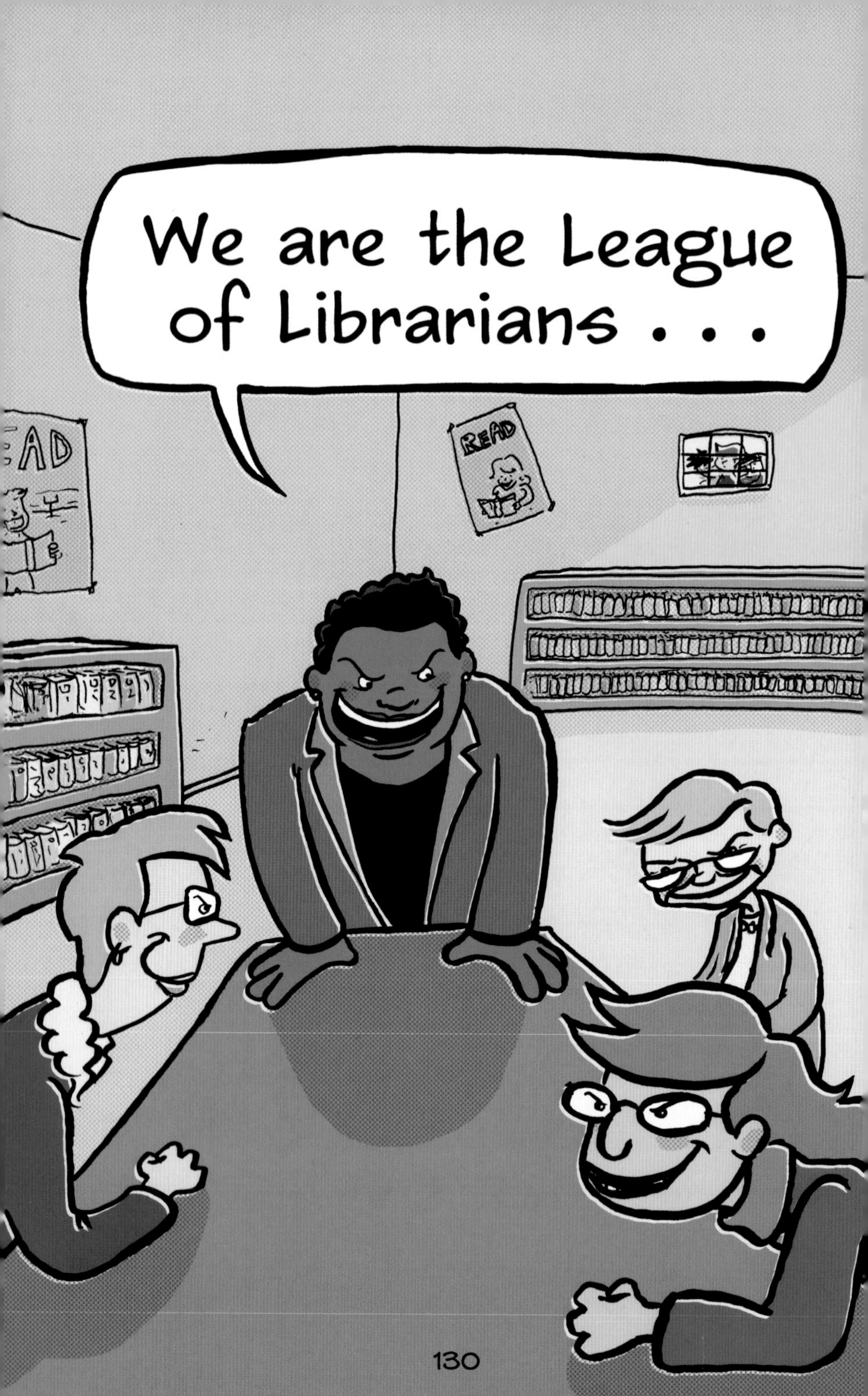
We are the League of Librarians . . .
READ
READ

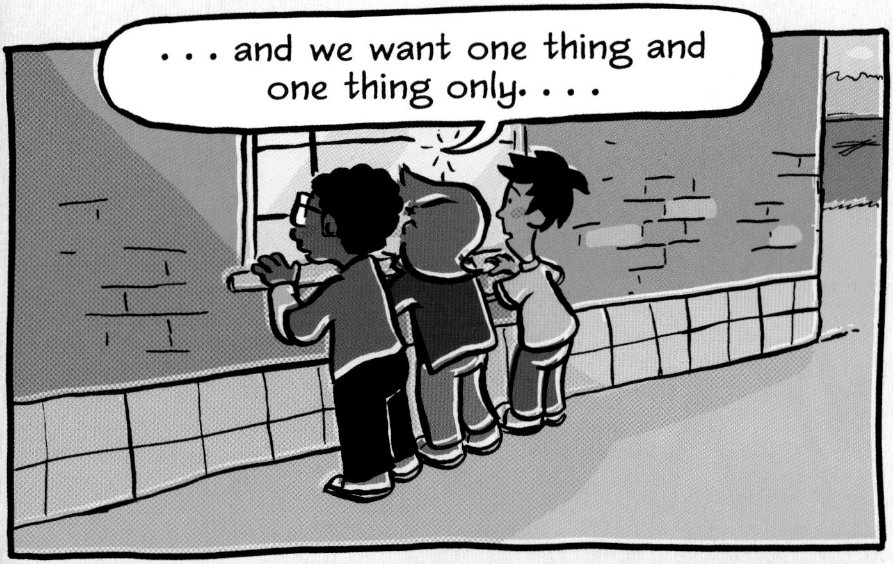
. . . and we want one thing and one thing only. . . .

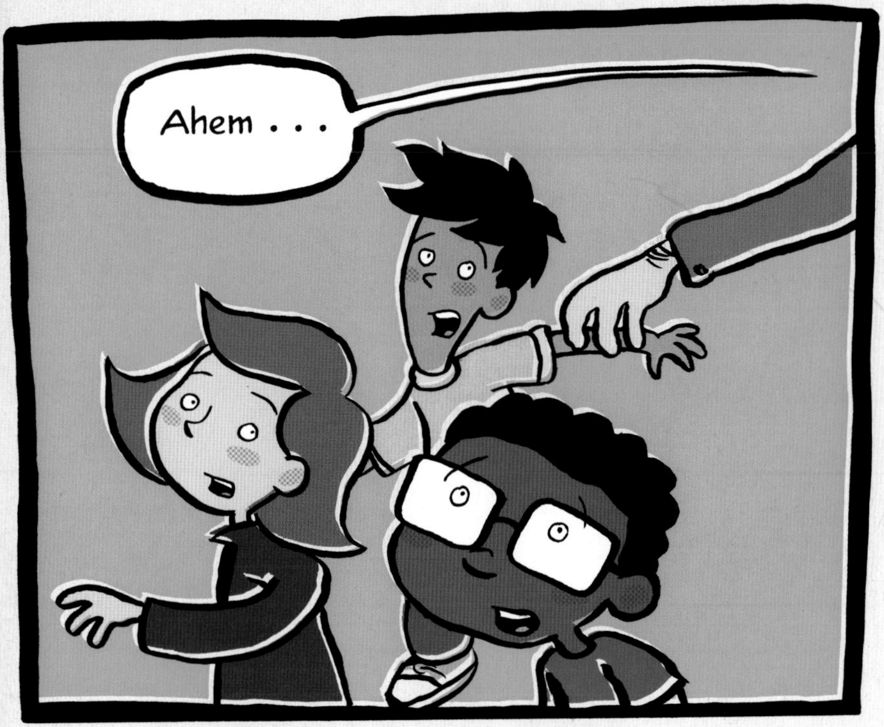
Ahem . . .

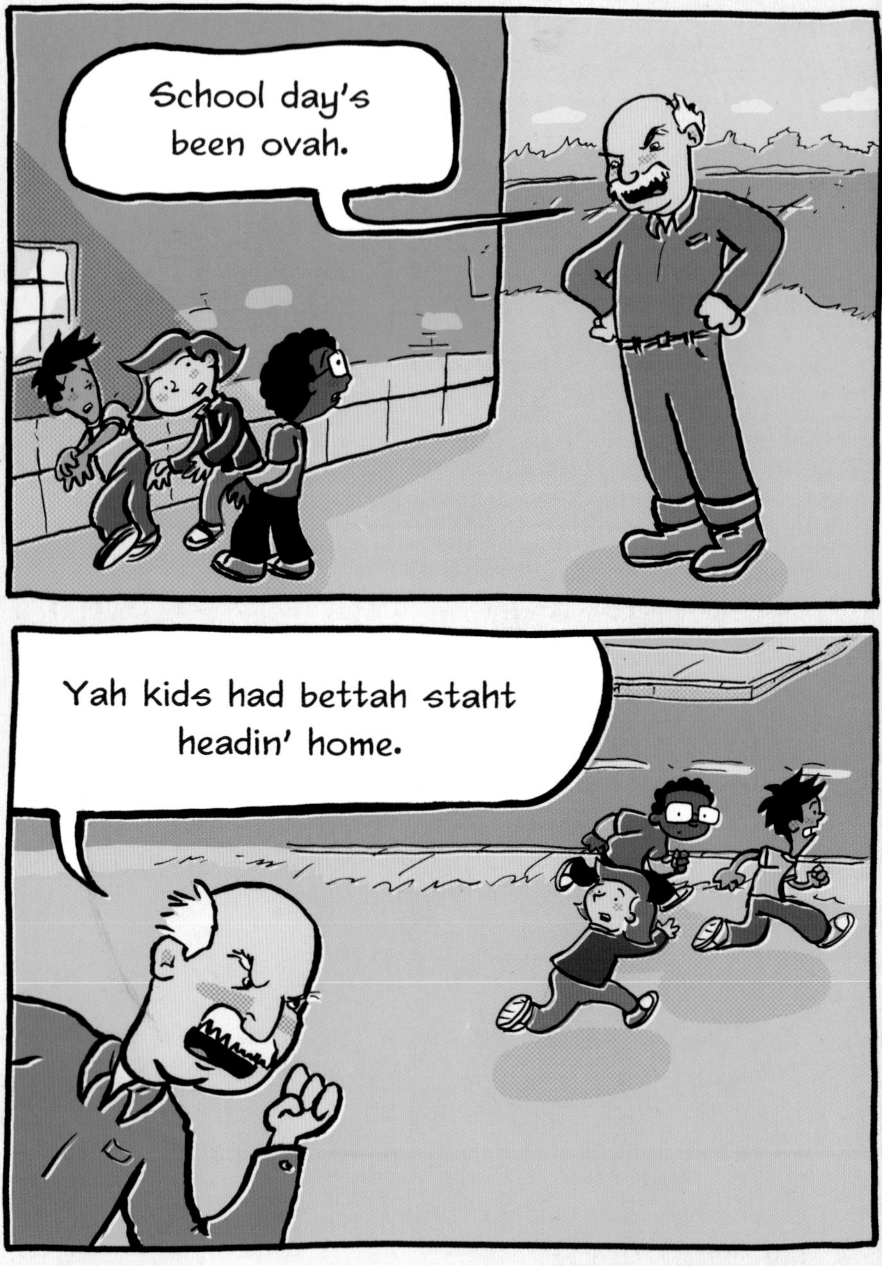
School day's been ovah.
Yah kids had bettah staht headin' home.

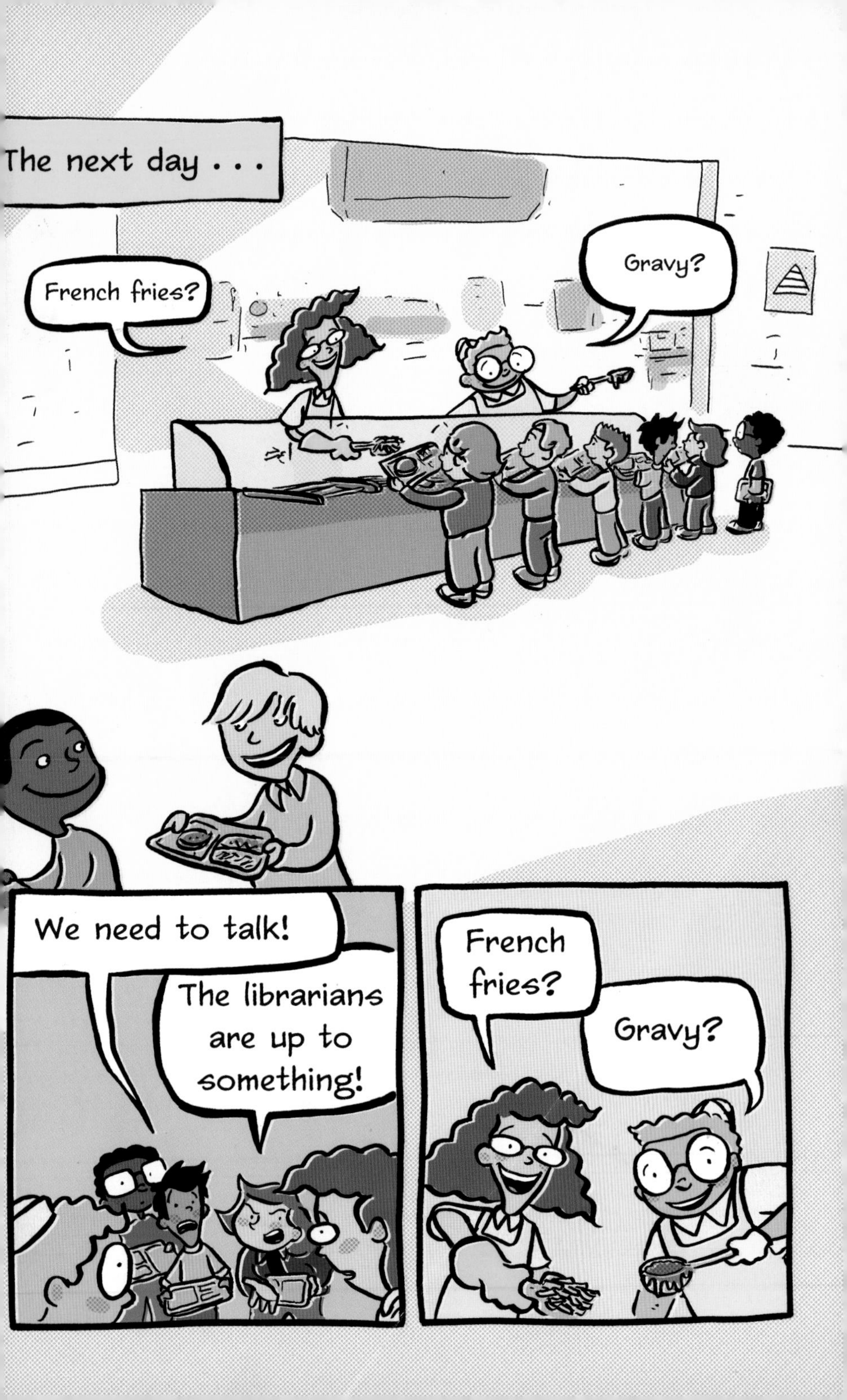
The next day . . .
French fries?
Gravy?
We need to talk!
The librarians are up to something!
French fries?
Gravy?

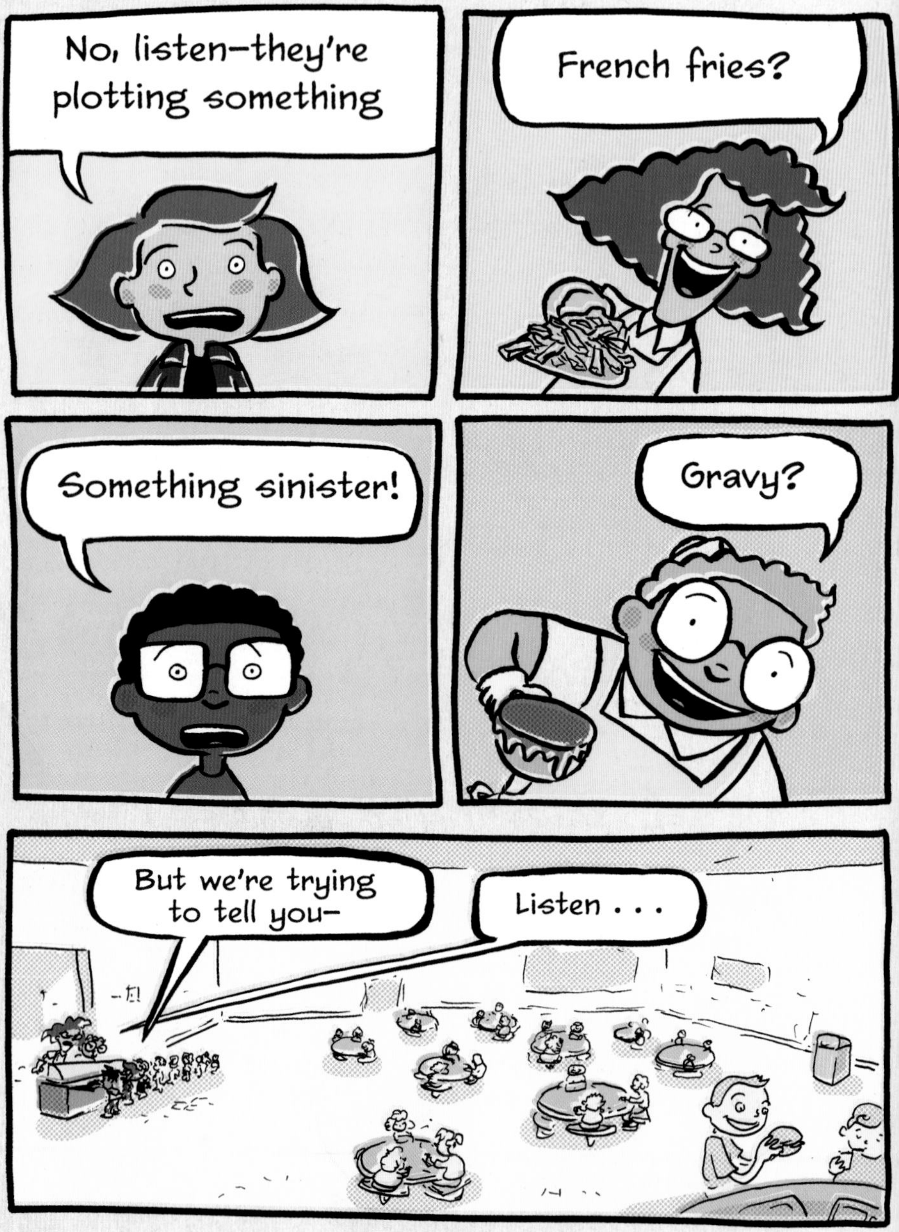
No, listen—they're plotting something
French fries?
Something sinister!
Gravy?
But we're trying to tell you—
Listen . . .

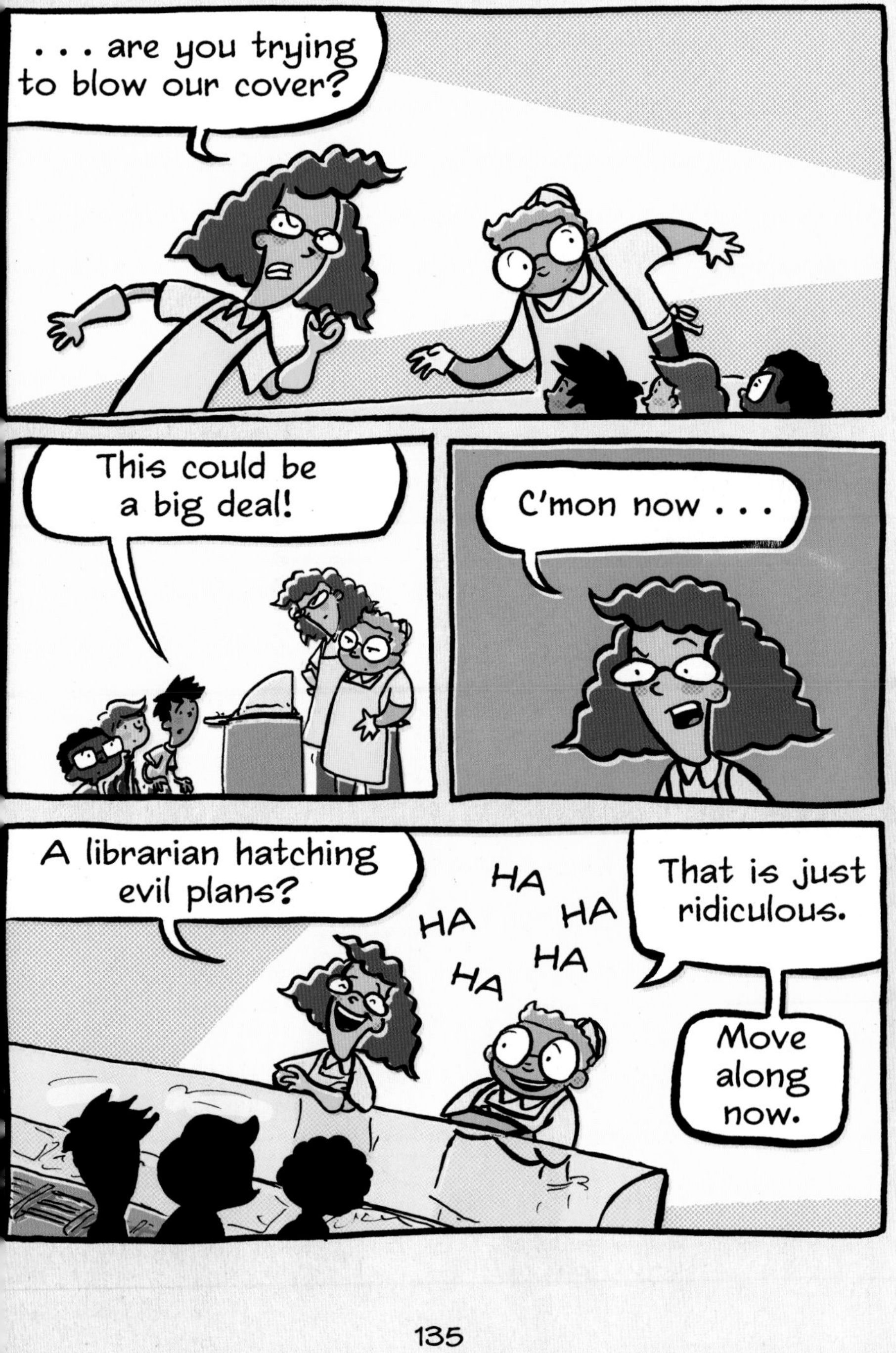
. . . are you trying to blow our cover?
This could be a big deal!
C'mon now . . .
A librarian hatching evil plans?
HA HA HA HA HA
That is just ridiculous.
Move along now.

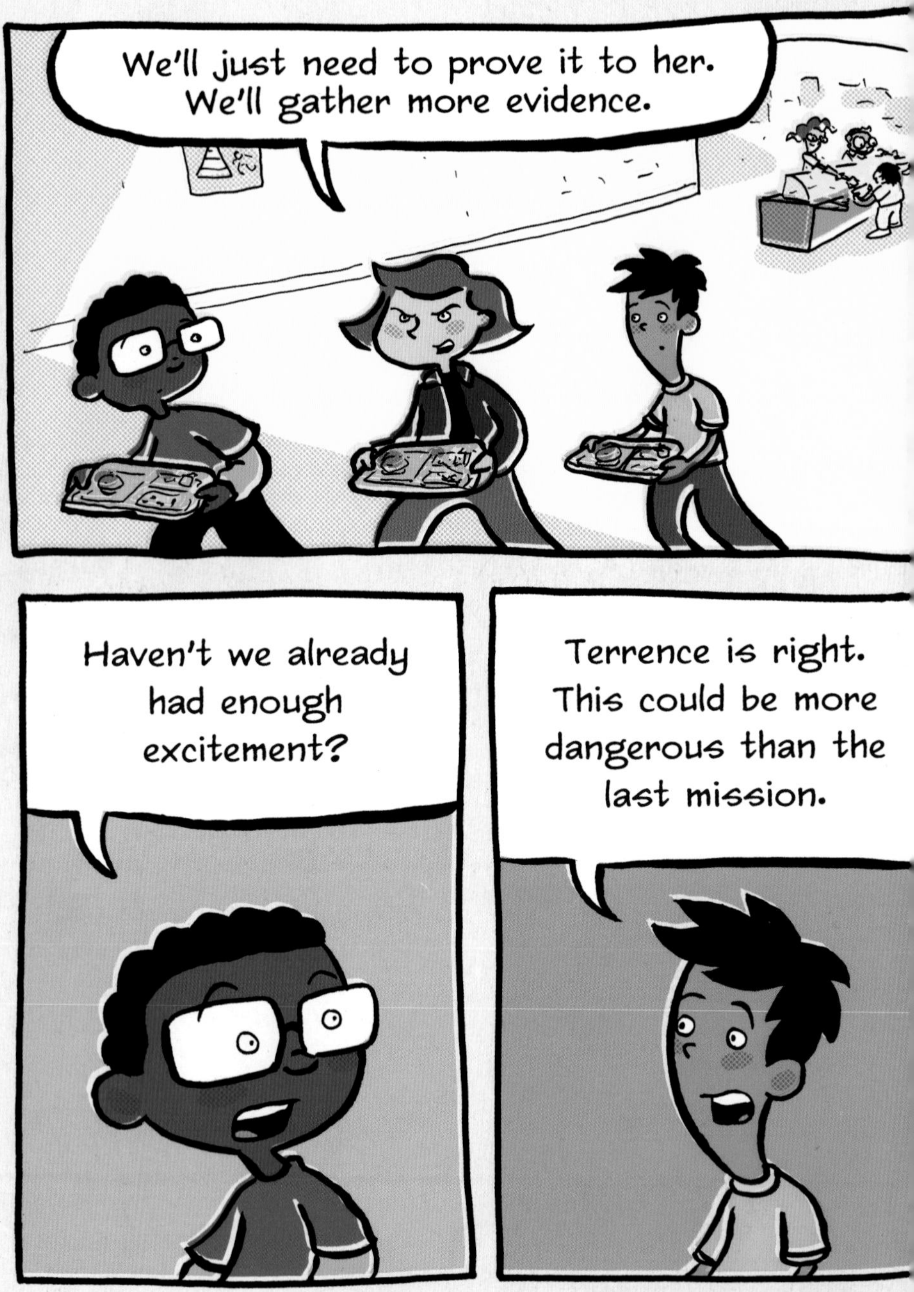
We'll just need to prove it to her. We'll gather more evidence.
Haven't we already had enough excitement?
Terrence is right. This could be more dangerous than the last mission.

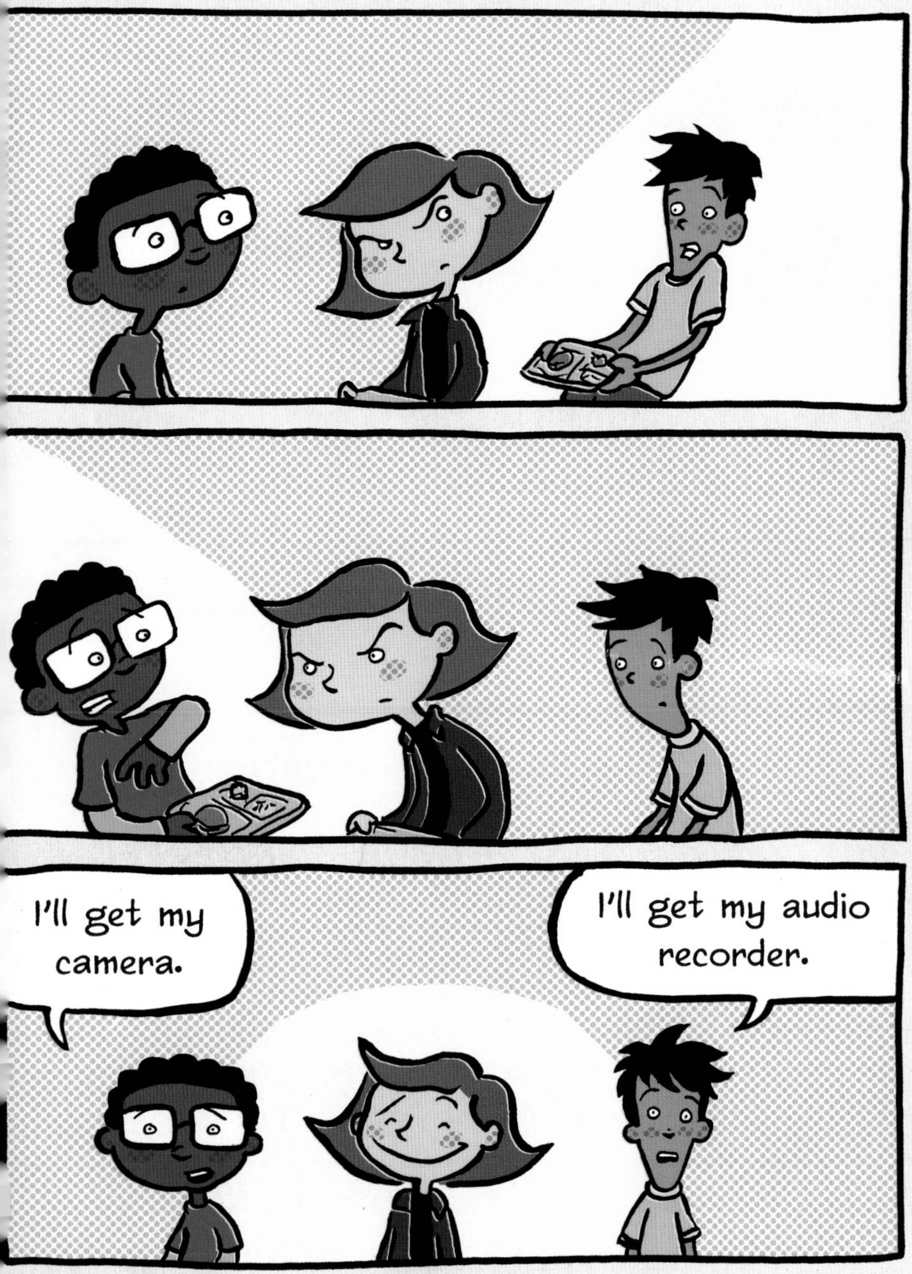
I'll get my camera.
I'll get my audio recorder.

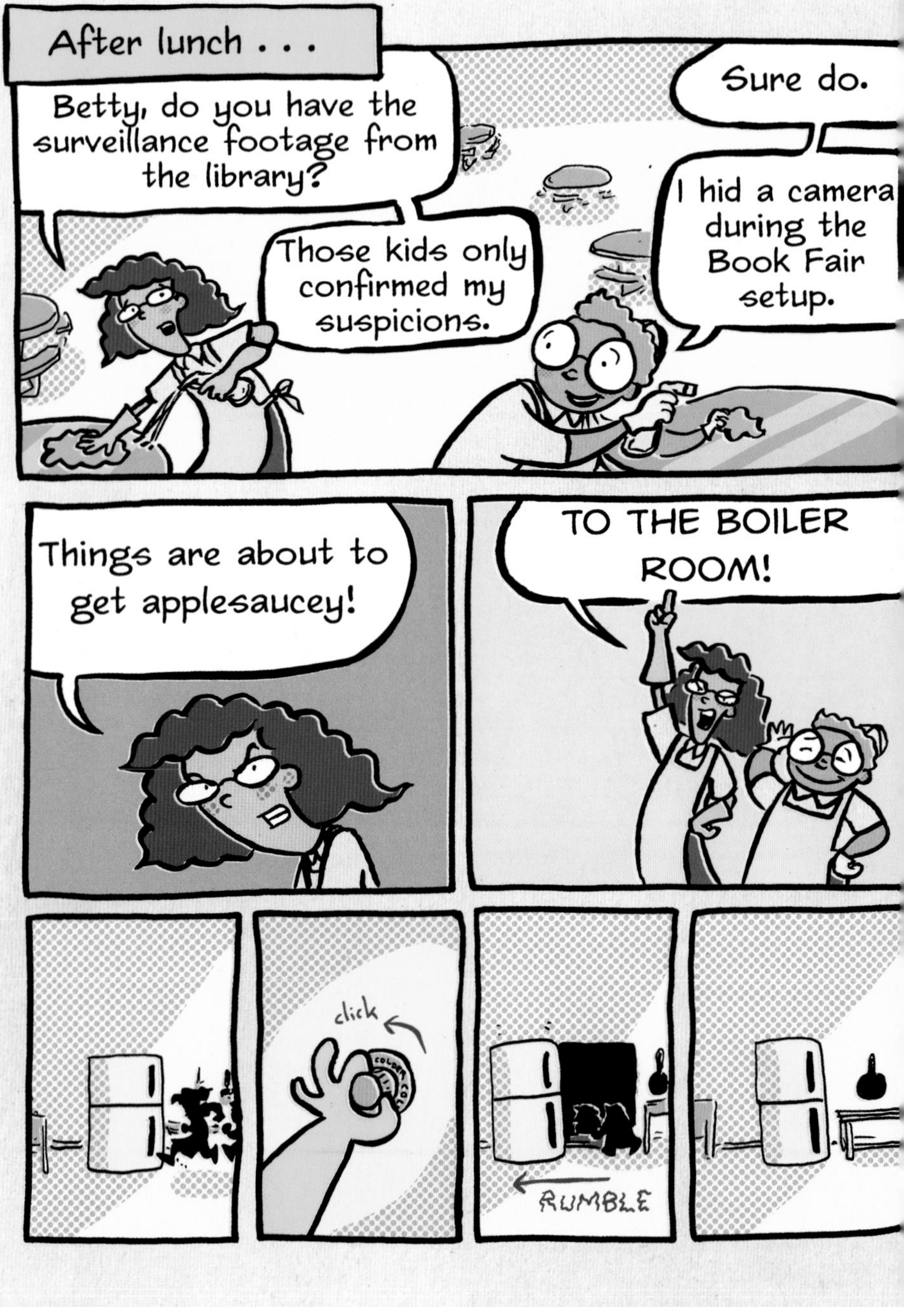
After lunch . . .
Betty, do you have the surveillance footage from the library?
Those kids only confirmed my suspicions.
Sure do.
I hid a camera during the Book Fair setup.
Things are about to get applesaucey!
TO THE BOILER ROOM!
click
RUMBLE

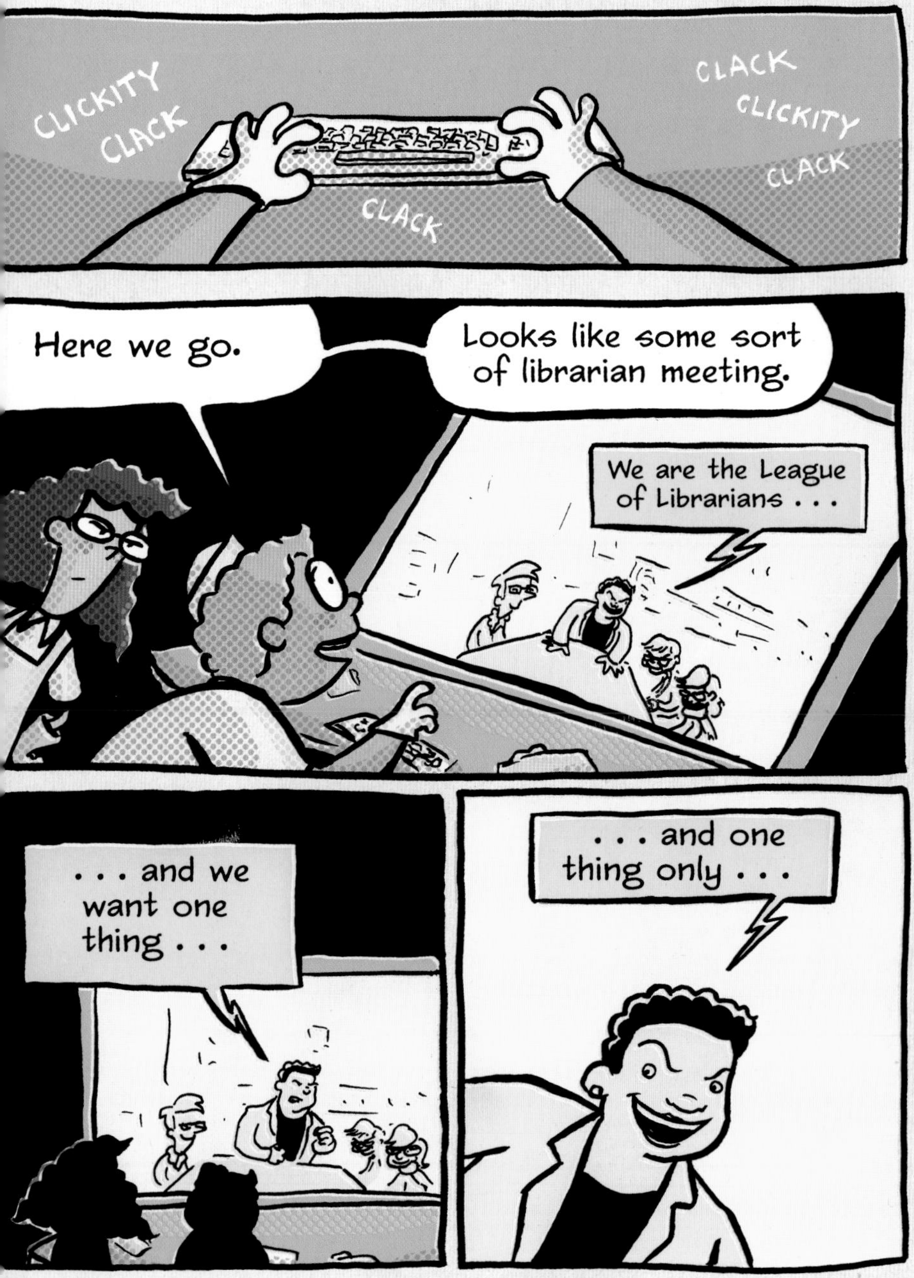
CLICKITY
CLACK
CLACK
CLACK
CLICKITY
CLACK
Here we go.
Looks like some sort of librarian meeting.
We are the League of Librarians . . .
. . . and we want one thing . . .
. . . and one thing only . . .

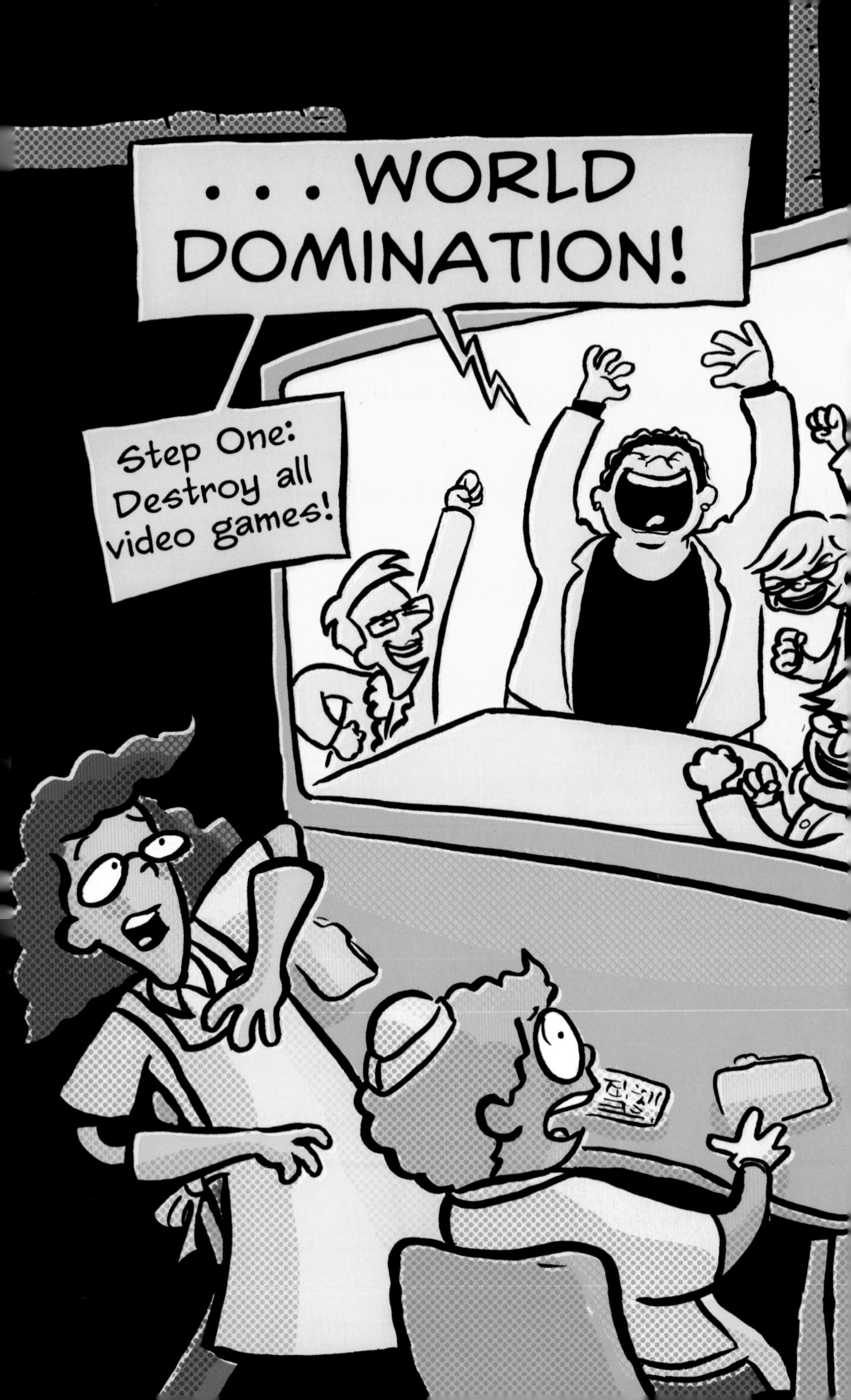
. . . WORLD DOMINATION!
Step One: Destroy all video games!

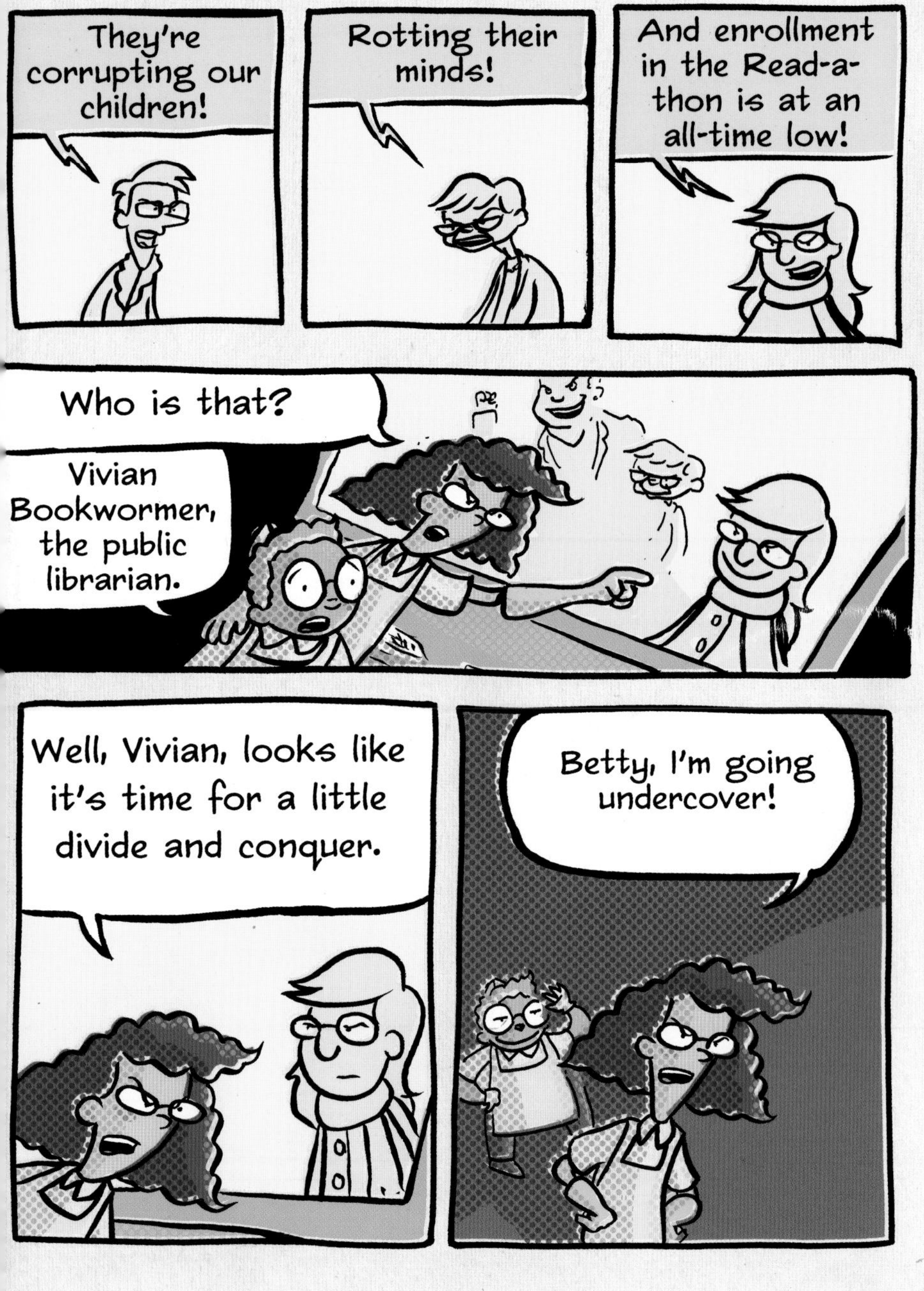
They're corrupting our children!
Rotting their minds!
And enrollment in the Read-a-thon is at an all-time low!
Who is that?
Vivian Bookwormer, the public librarian.
Well, Vivian, looks like it's time for a little divide and conquer.
Betty, I'm going undercover!

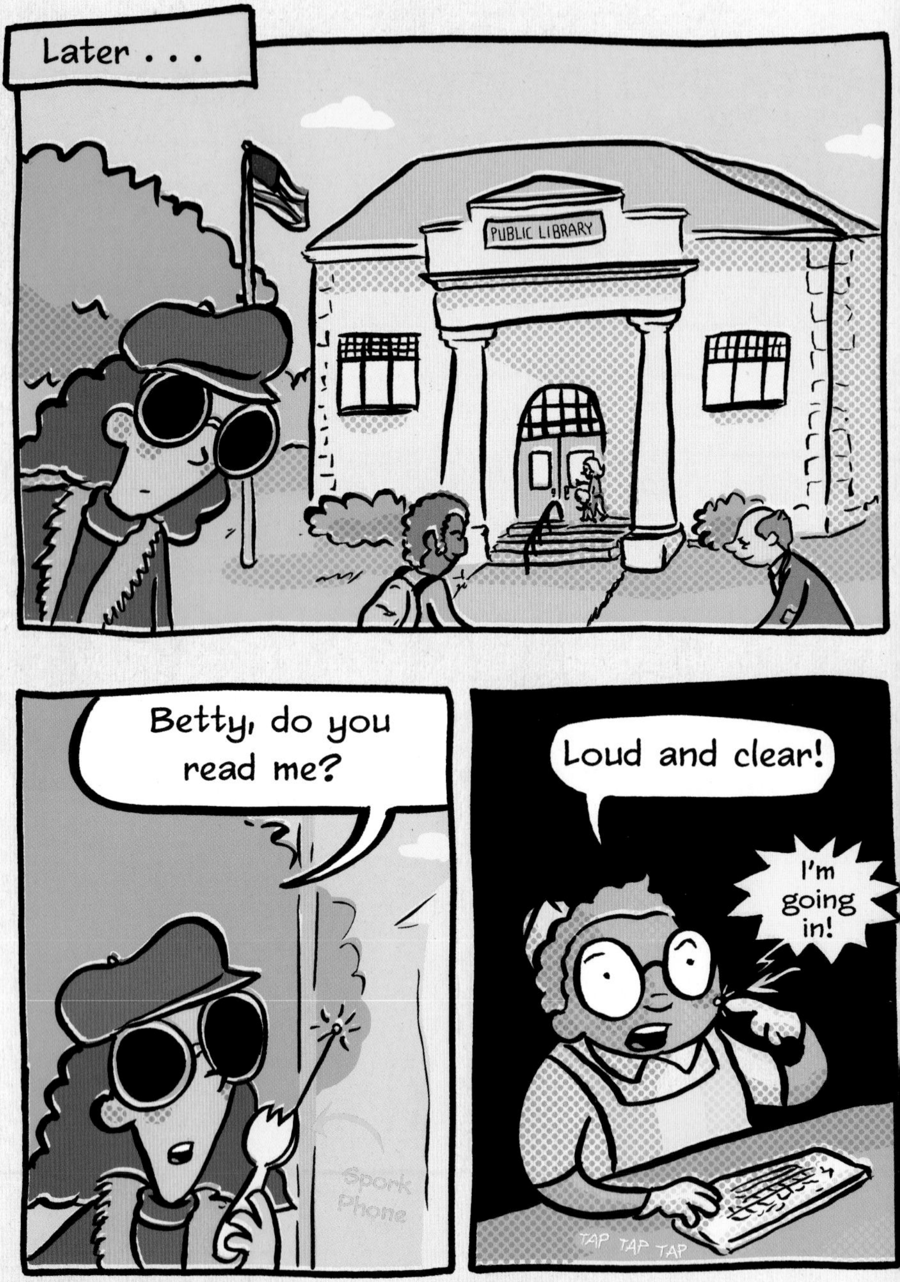
Later . . .
PUBLIC LIBRARY
Betty, do you read me?
Spork Phone
Loud and clear!
I'm going in!
TAP TAP TAP

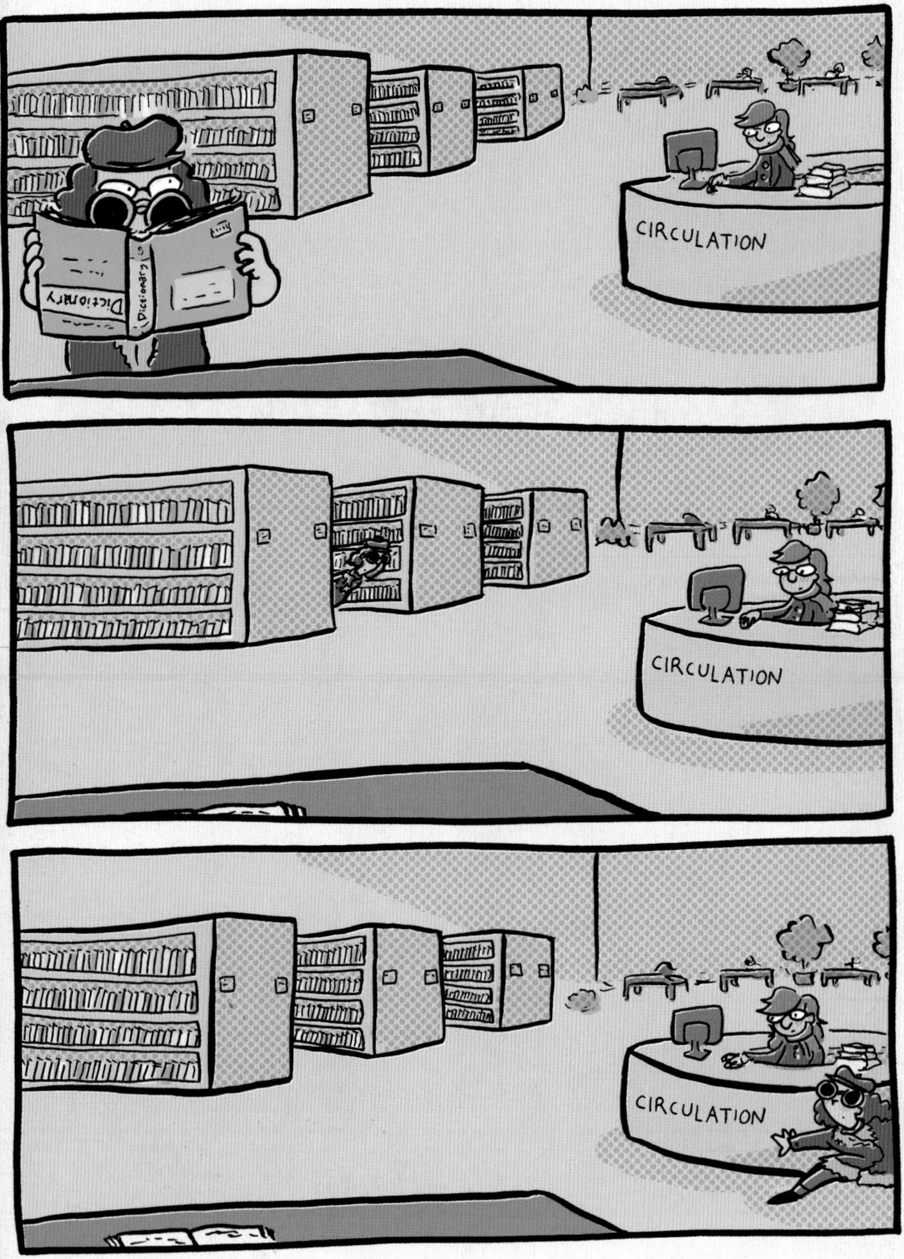
Dictionary
Dictionary
CIRCULATION
CIRCULATION
CIRCULATION

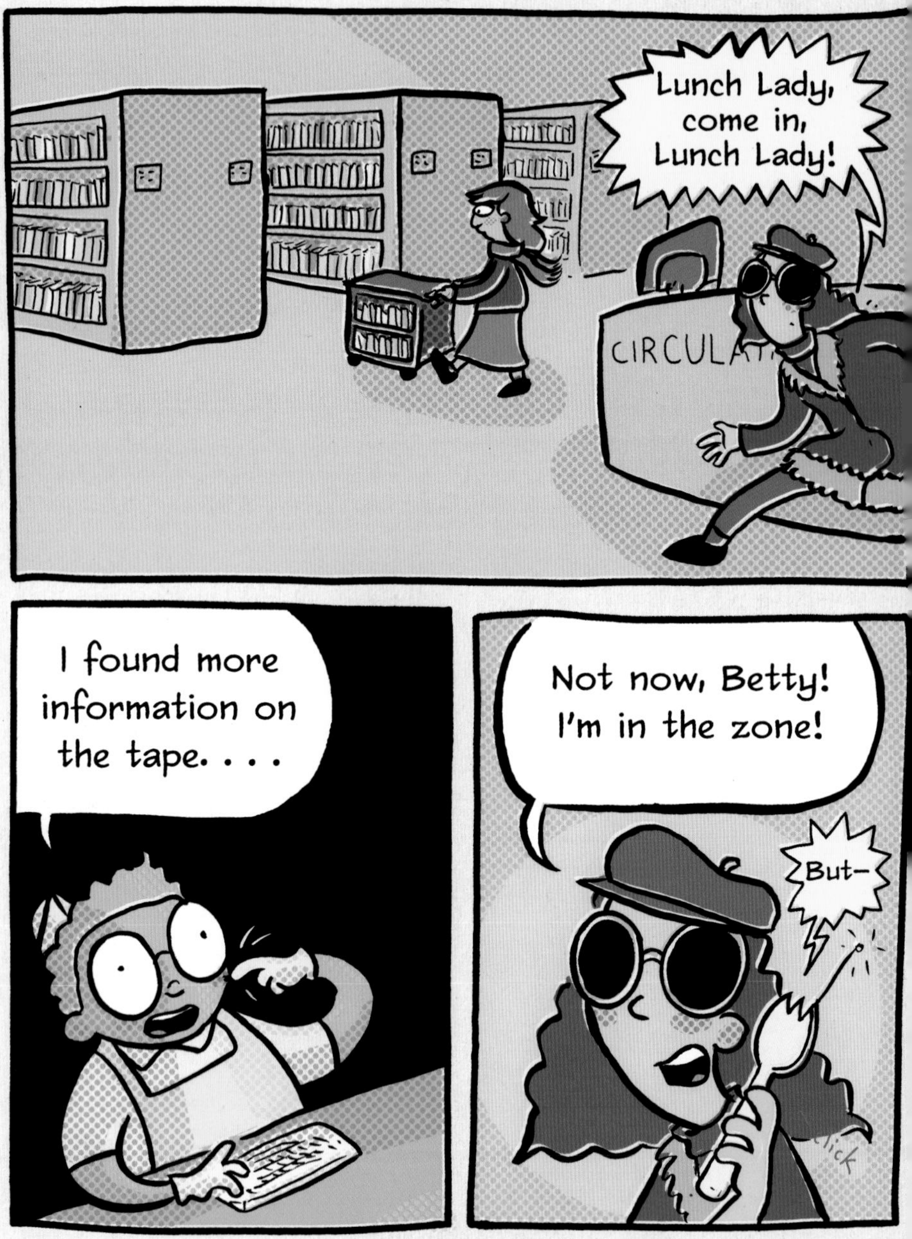

Lunch Lady, come in, Lunch Lady!
CIRCULA
I found more information on the tape. . . .
Not now, Betty! I'm in the zone!
But–

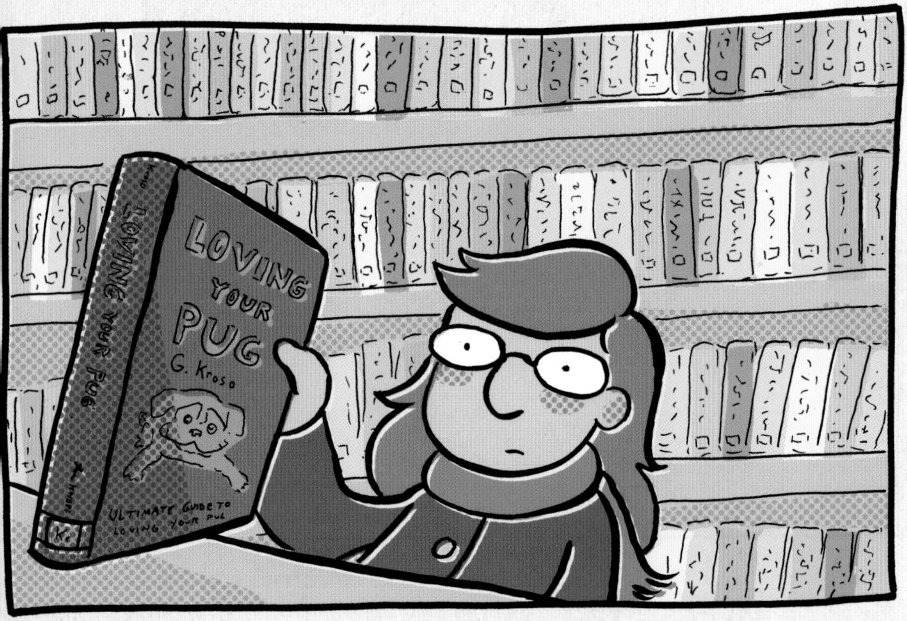
LOVING YOUR PUG
G. Kroso
LOVING YOUR PUG
ULTIMATE GUIDE TO LOVING YOUR PUG

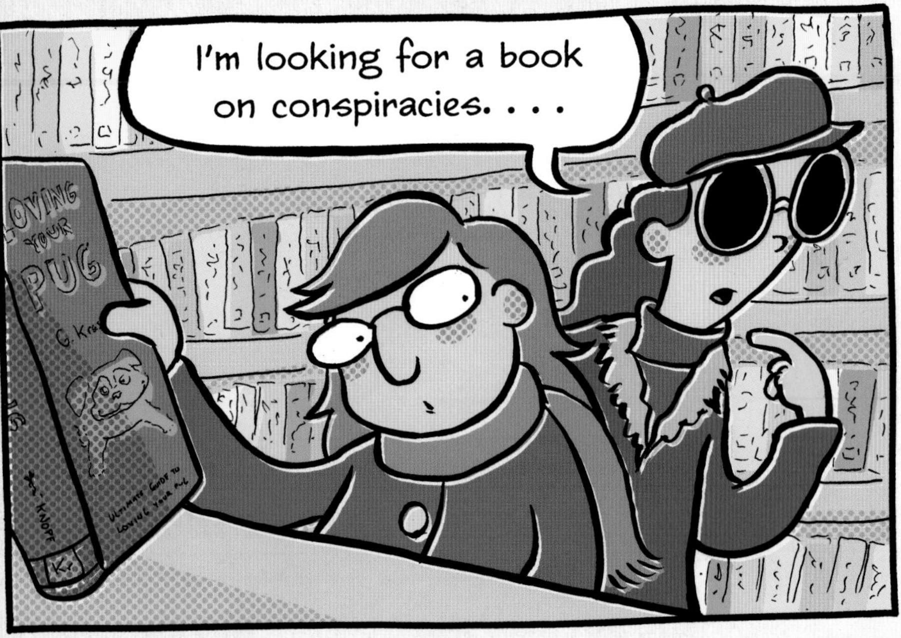
I'm looking for a book on conspiracies. . . .

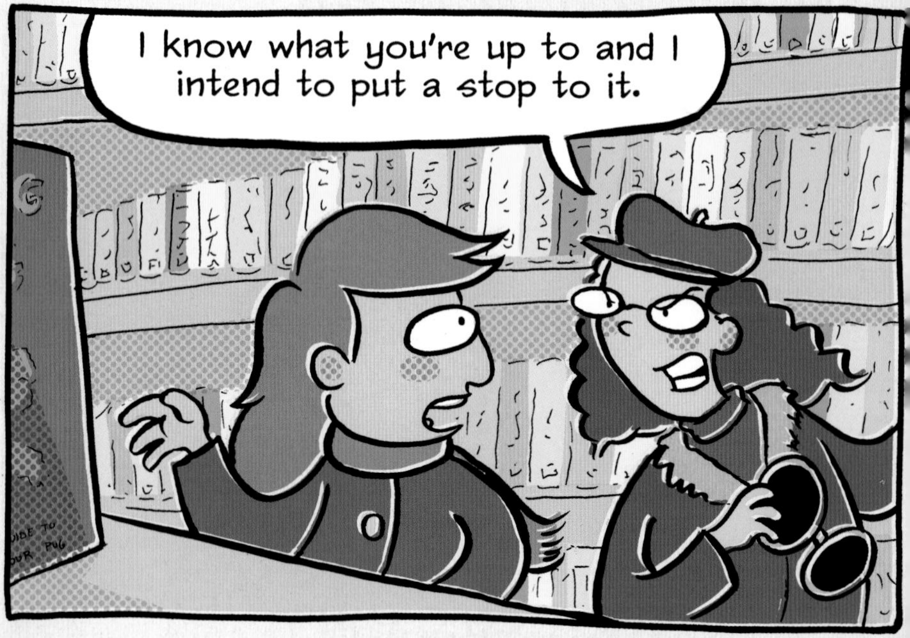
I know what you're up to and I intend to put a stop to it.

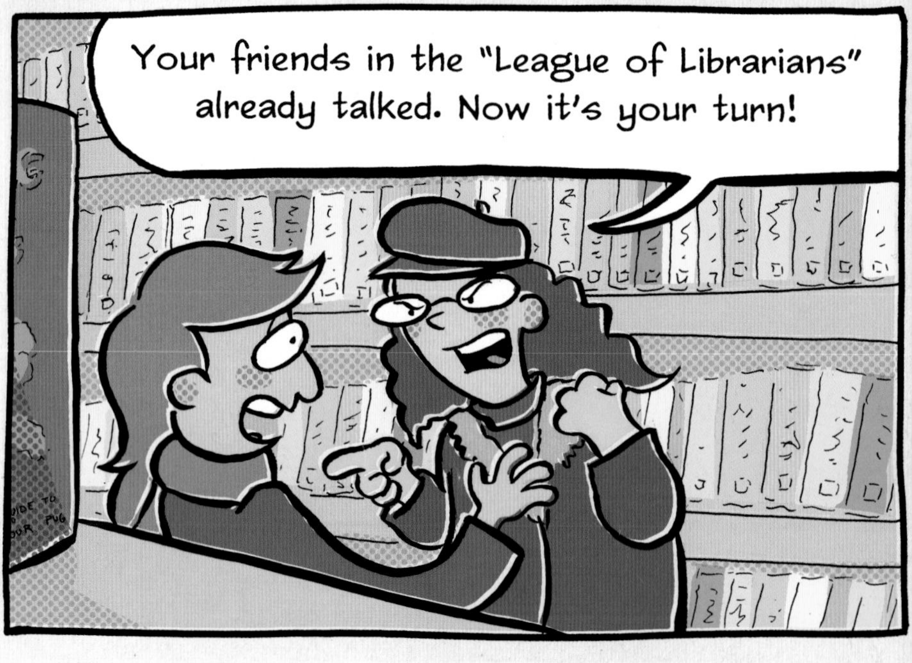
Your friends in the "League of Librarians" already talked. Now it's your turn!

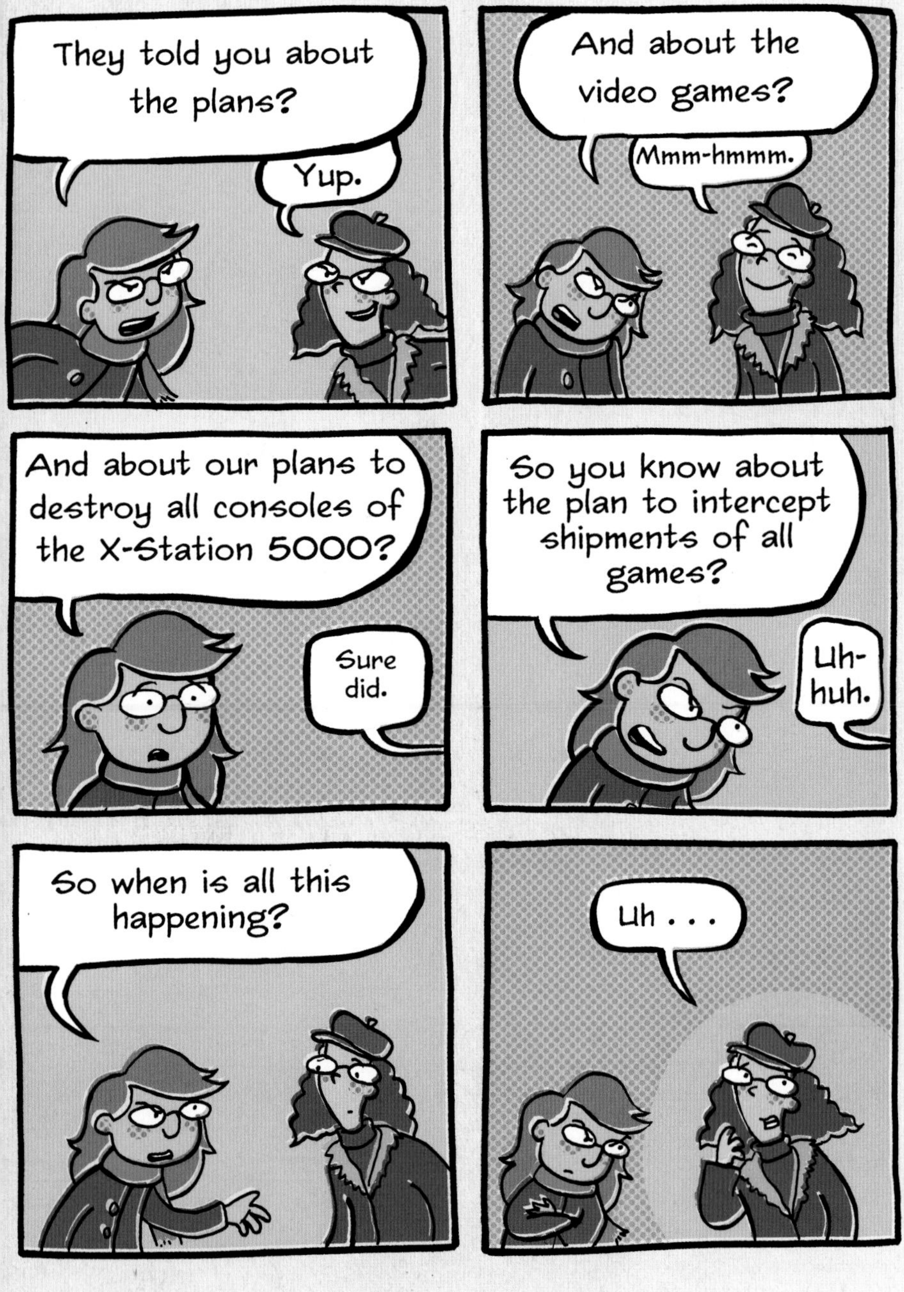
They told you about the plans?
Yup.
And about the video games?
Mmm-hmmm.
And about our plans to destroy all consoles of the X-Station 5000?
Sure did.
So you know about the plan to intercept shipments of all games?
Uh-huh.
So when is all this happening?
Uh . . .

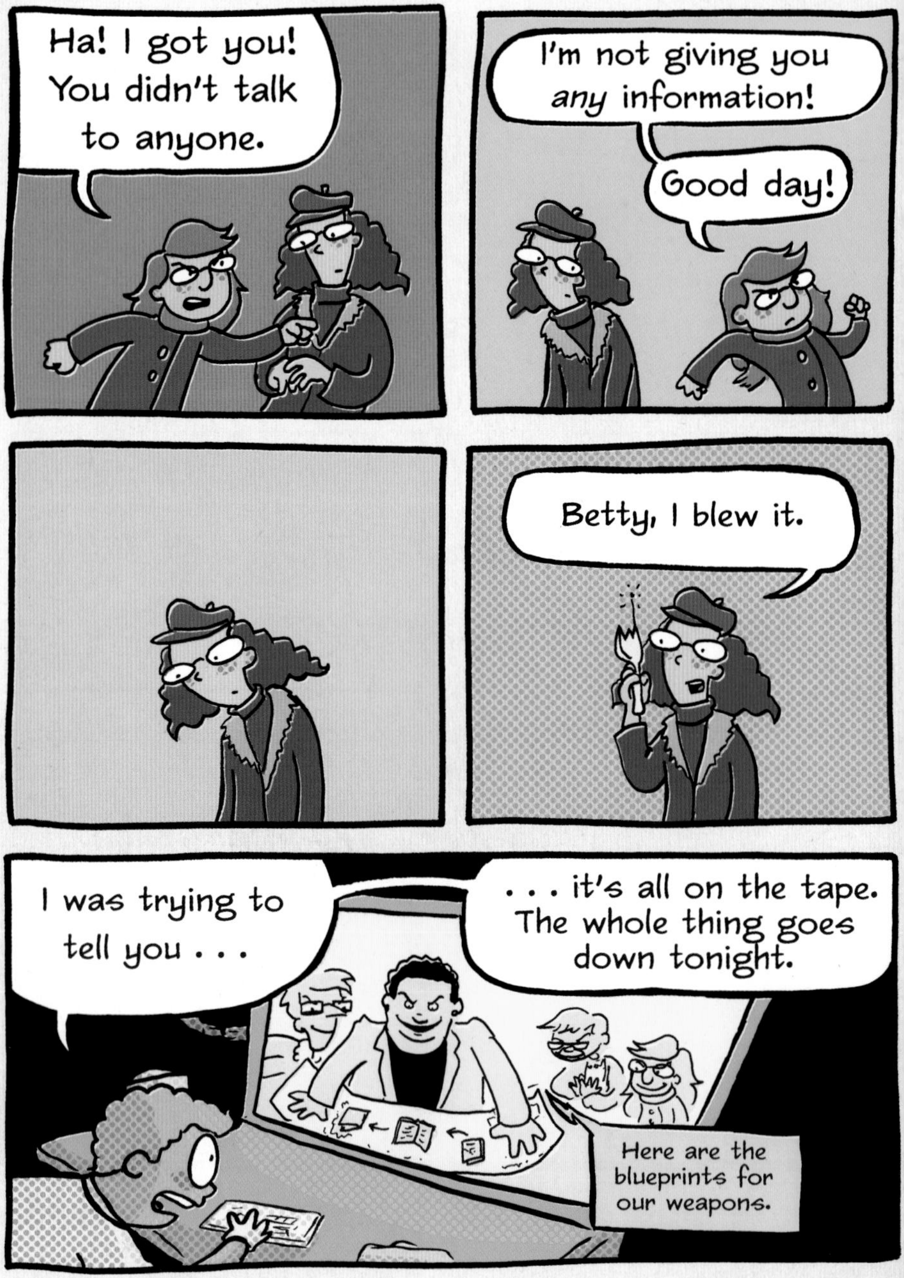
Ha! I got you! You didn't talk to anyone.
I'm not giving you *any* information!
Good day!
Betty, I blew it.
I was trying to tell you . . .
. . . it's all on the tape. The whole thing goes down tonight.
Here are the blueprints for our weapons.

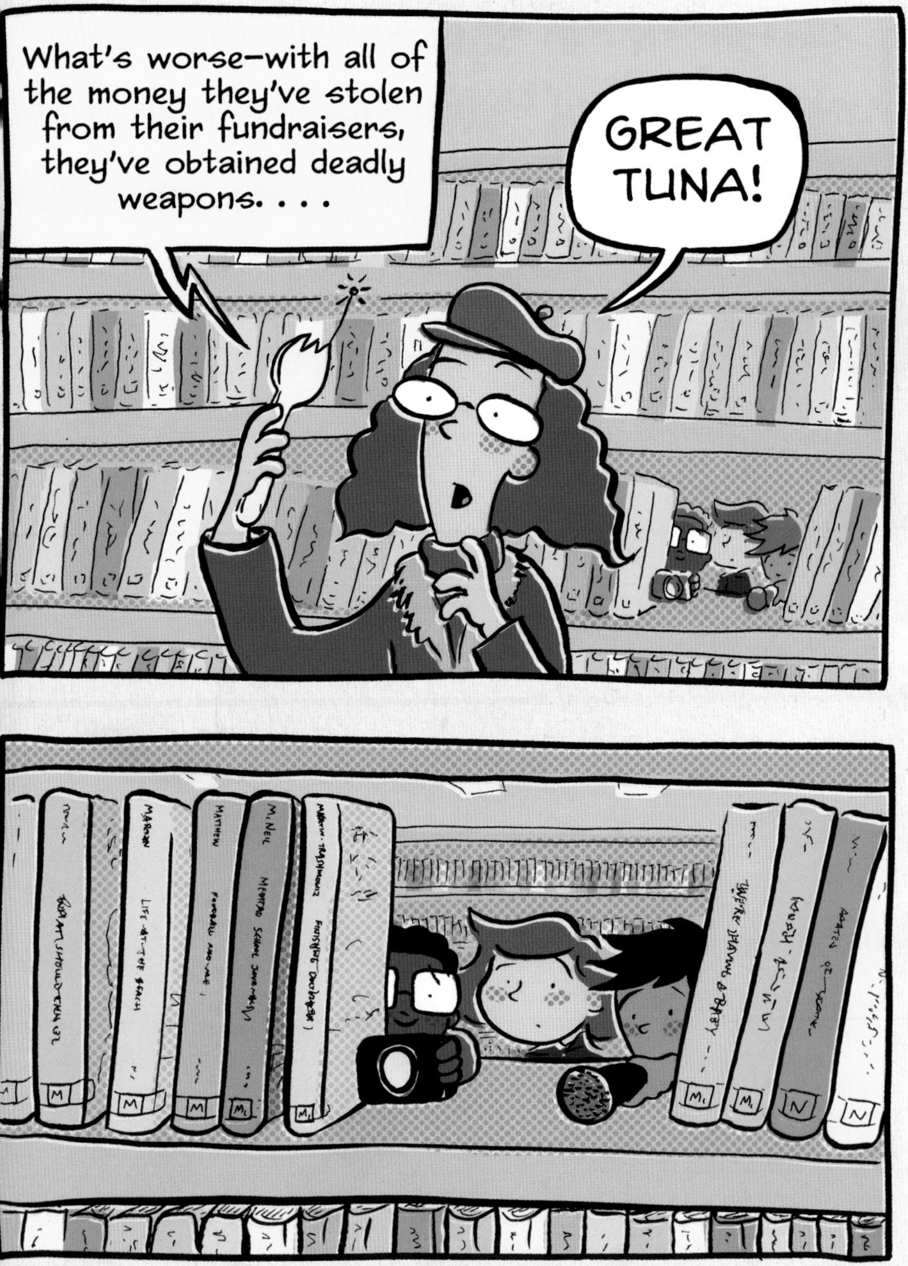
What's worse—with all of the money they've stolen from their fundraisers, they've obtained deadly weapons. . . .
GREAT TUNA!

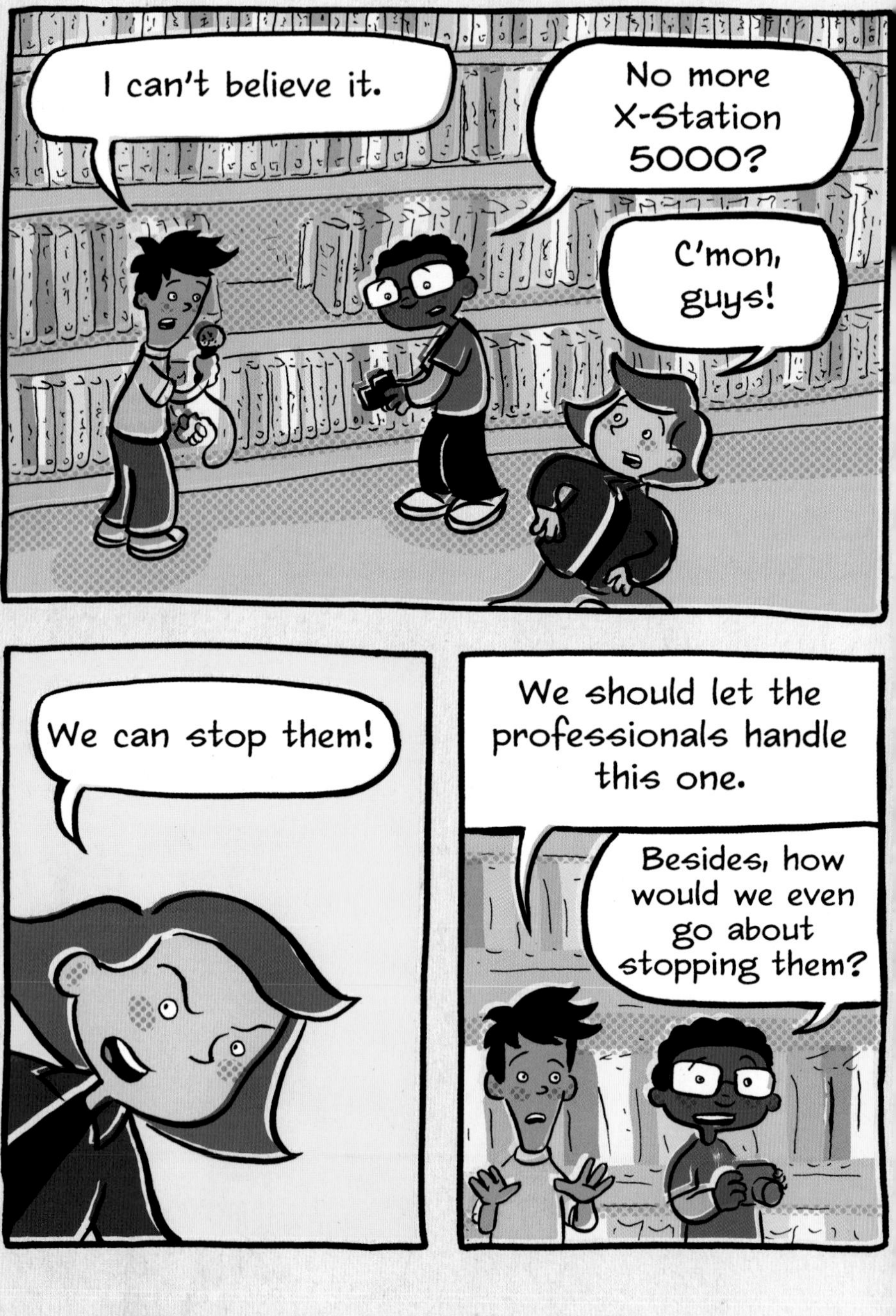
I can't believe it.
No more X-Station 5000?
C'mon, guys!
We can stop them!
We should let the professionals handle this one.
Besides, how would we even go about stopping them?

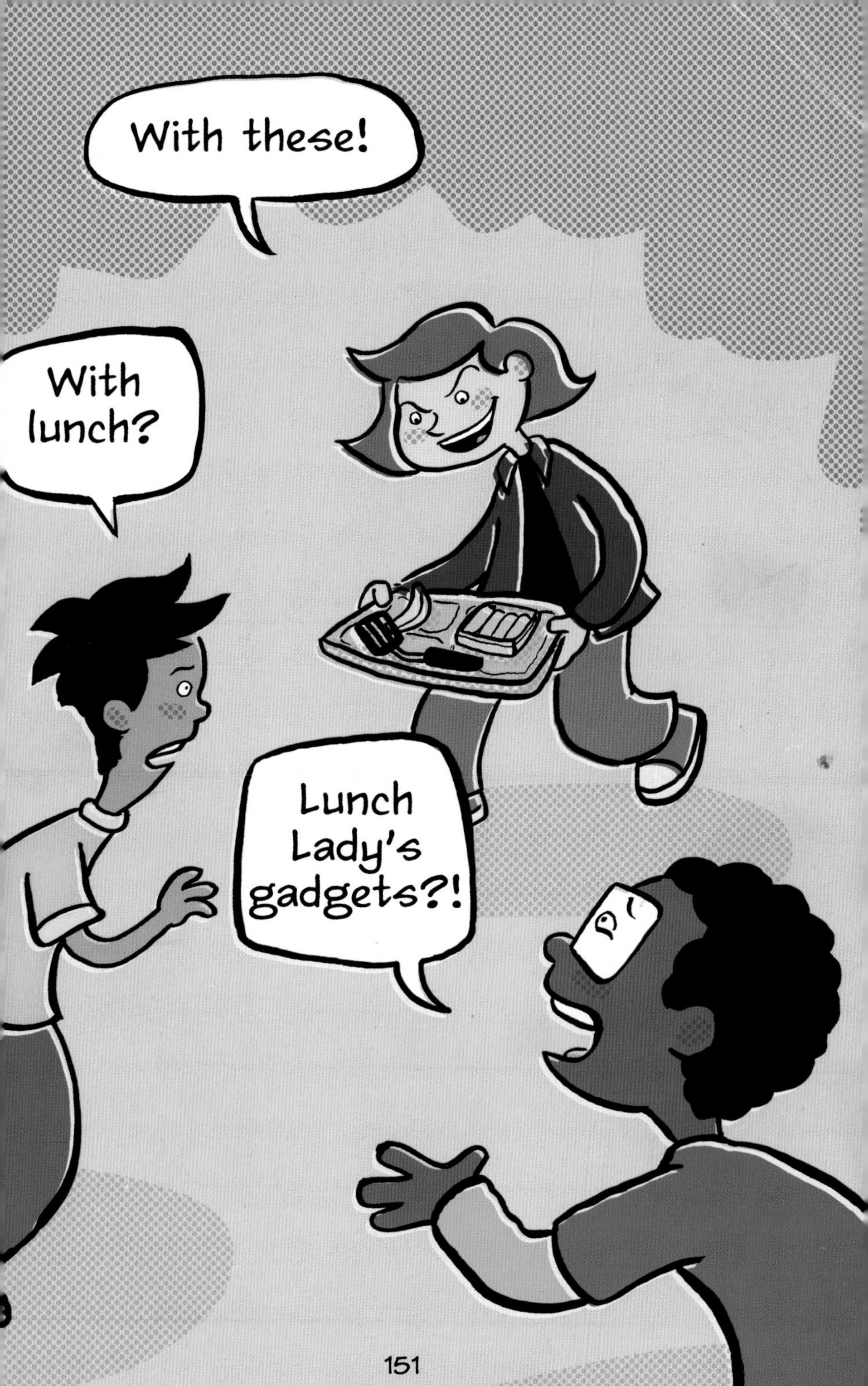
With these!
With lunch?
Lunch Lady's gadgets?!

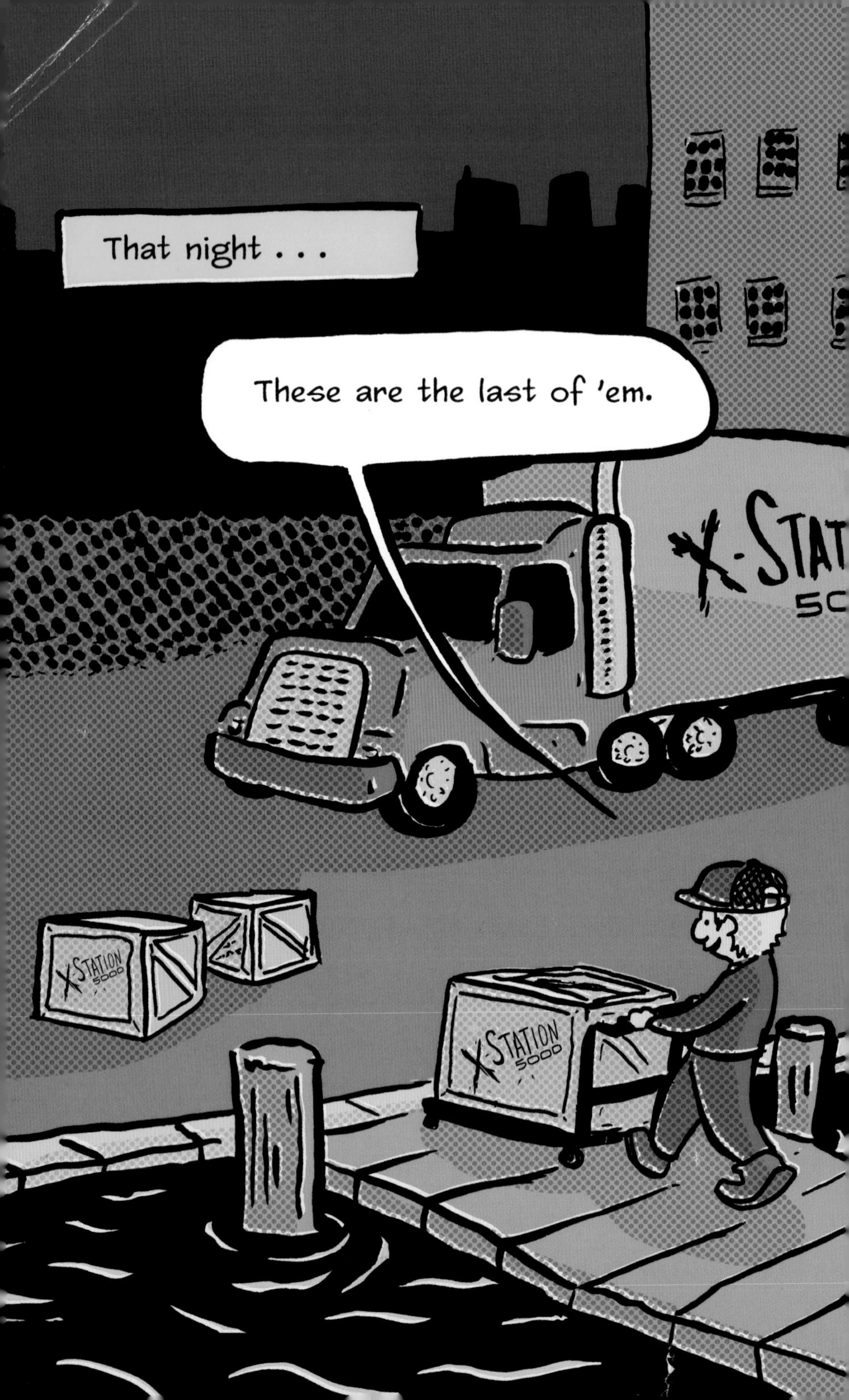
That night . . .
These are the last of 'em.
X-STATION 5000
X-STATION 5000
X-STATION 5000

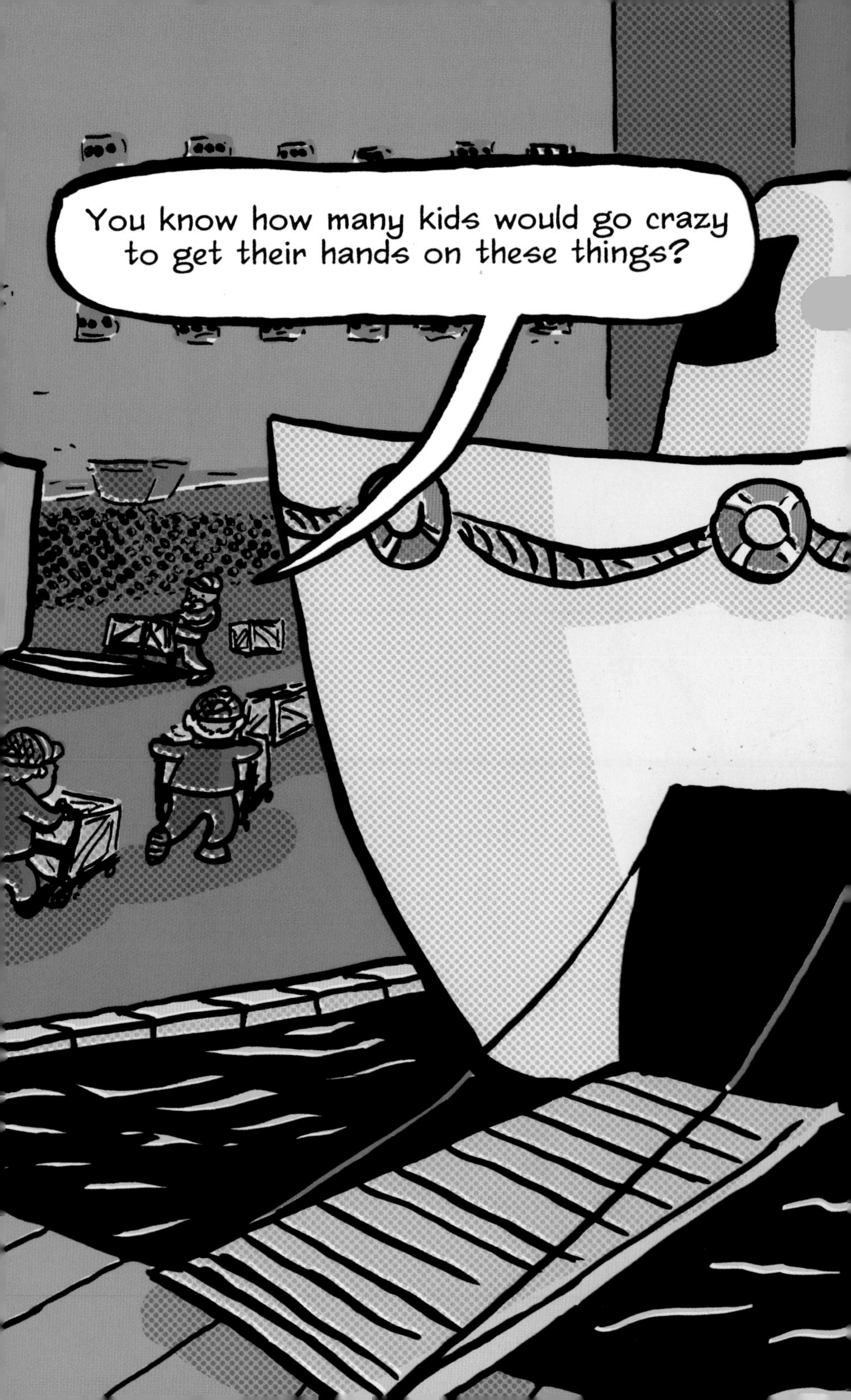
You know how many kids would go crazy to get their hands on these things?

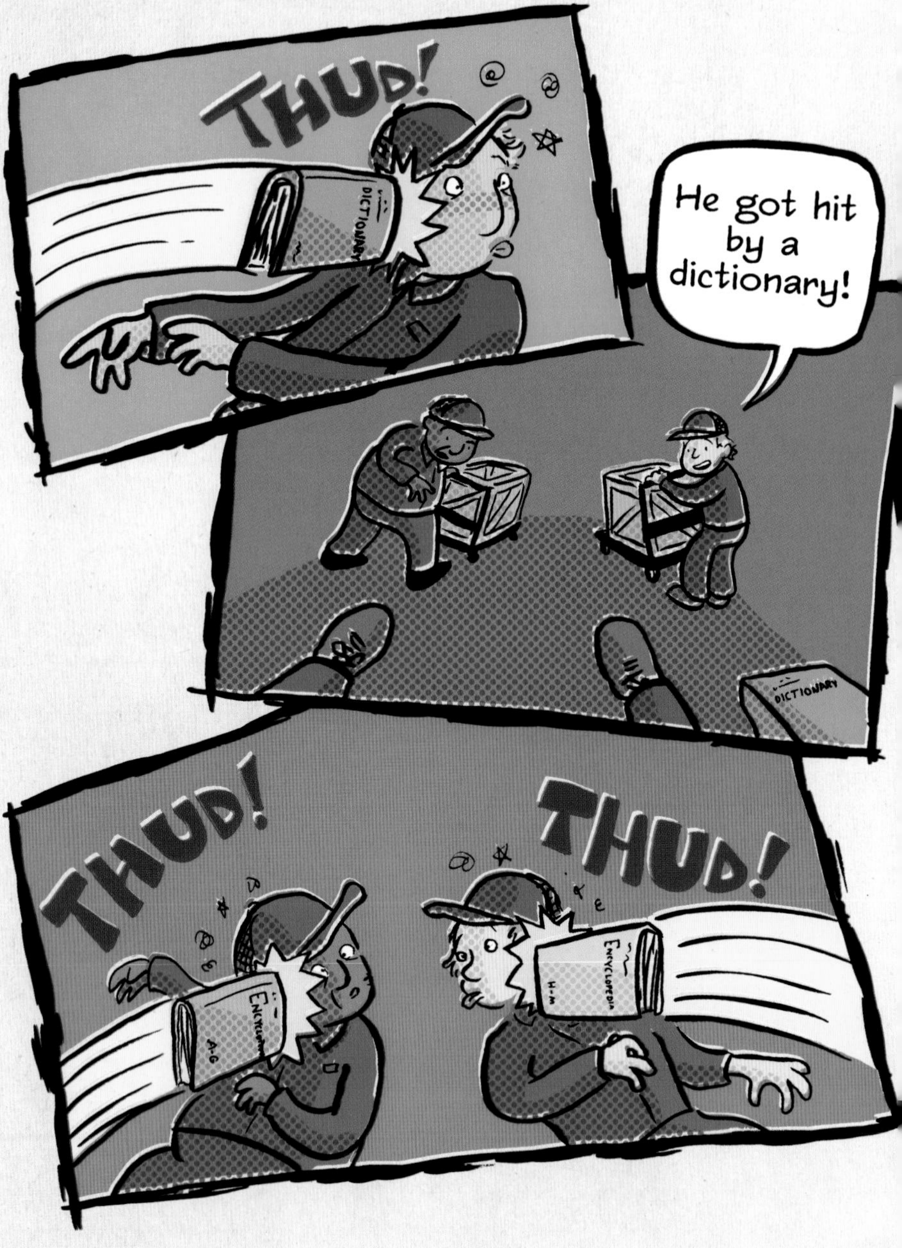
THUD!
DICTIONARY
He got hit by a dictionary!
DICTIONARY
THUD!
THUD!
ENCYCLOPEDIA
A-G
ENCYCLOPEDIA
H-M

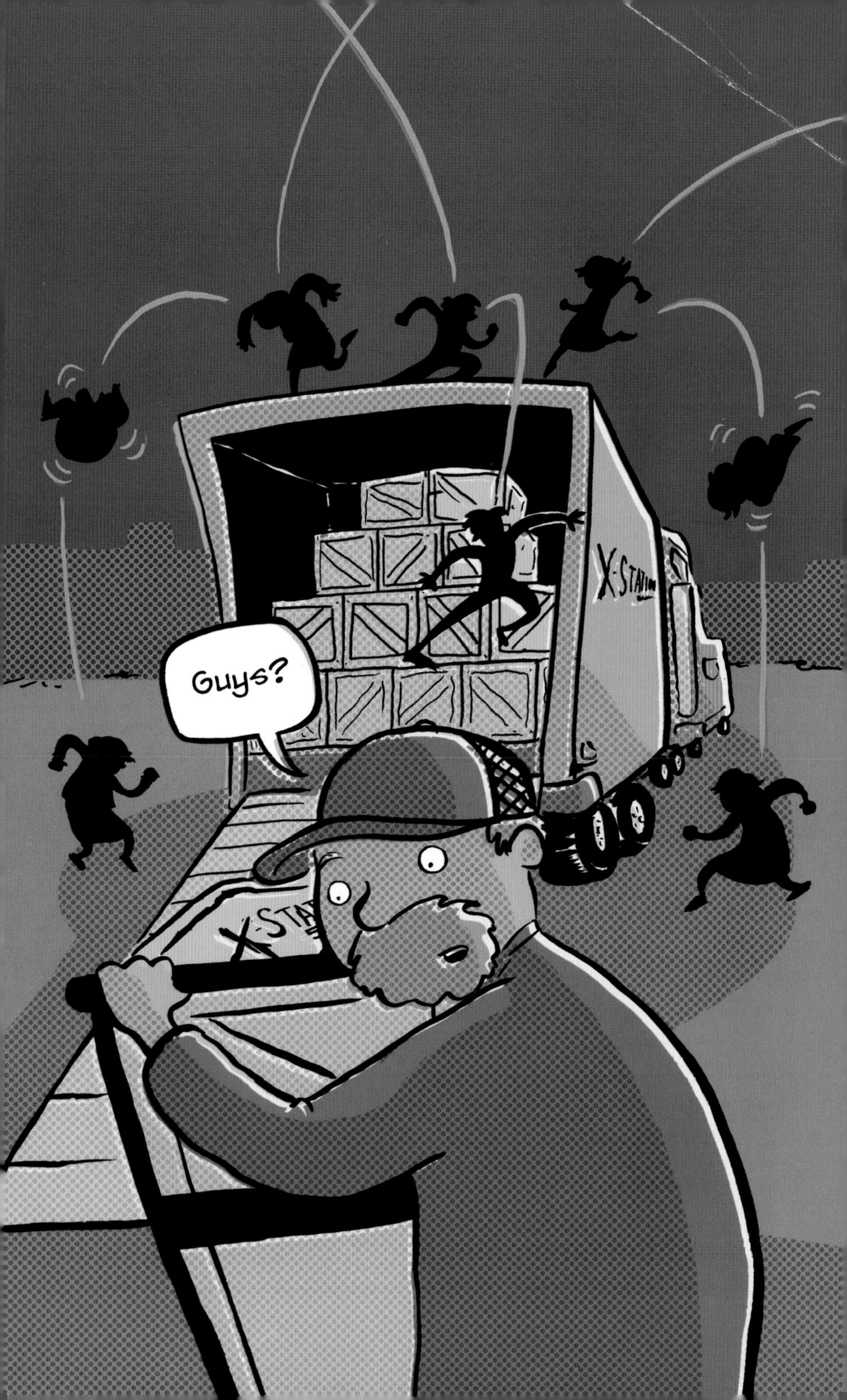
Guys?

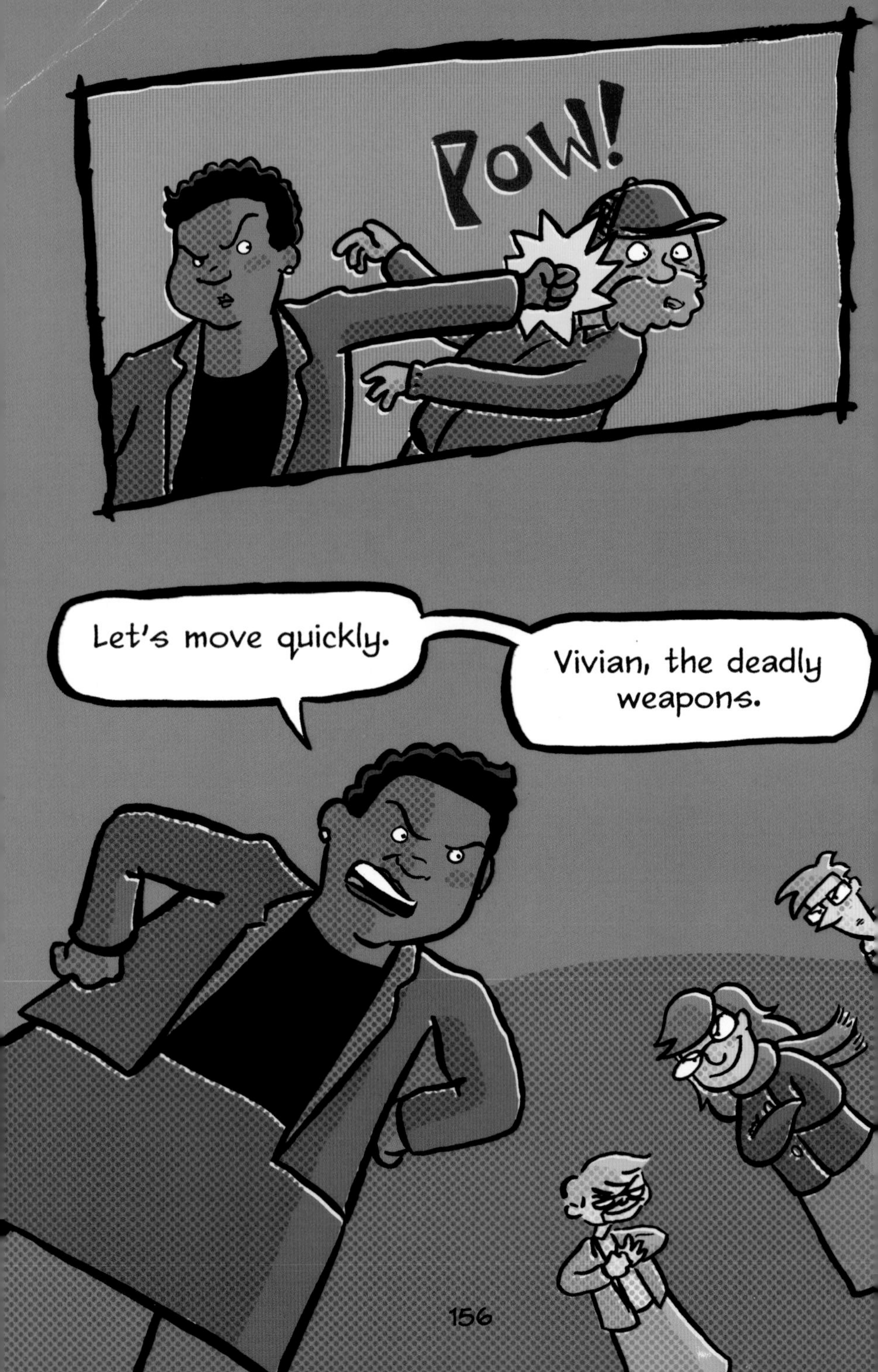
POW!
Let's move quickly.
Vivian, the deadly weapons.

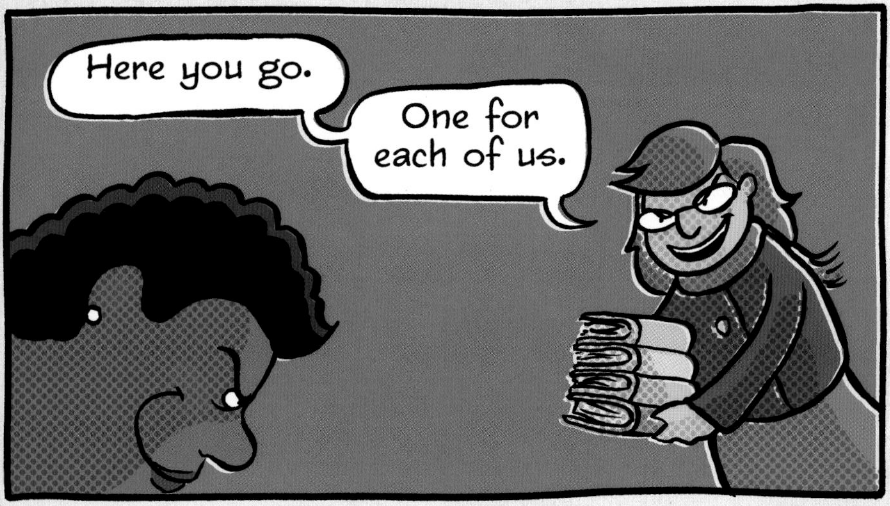
Here you go.
One for each of us.

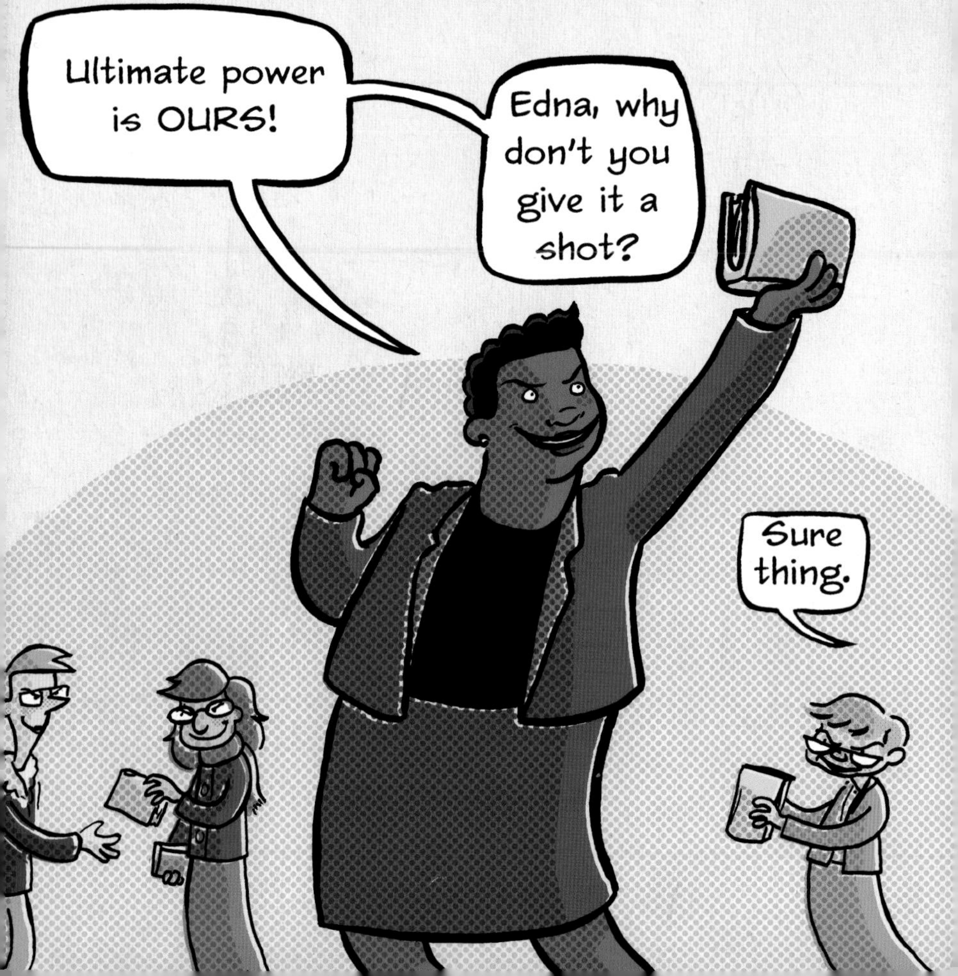
Ultimate power is OURS!
Edna, why don't you give it a shot?
Sure thing.

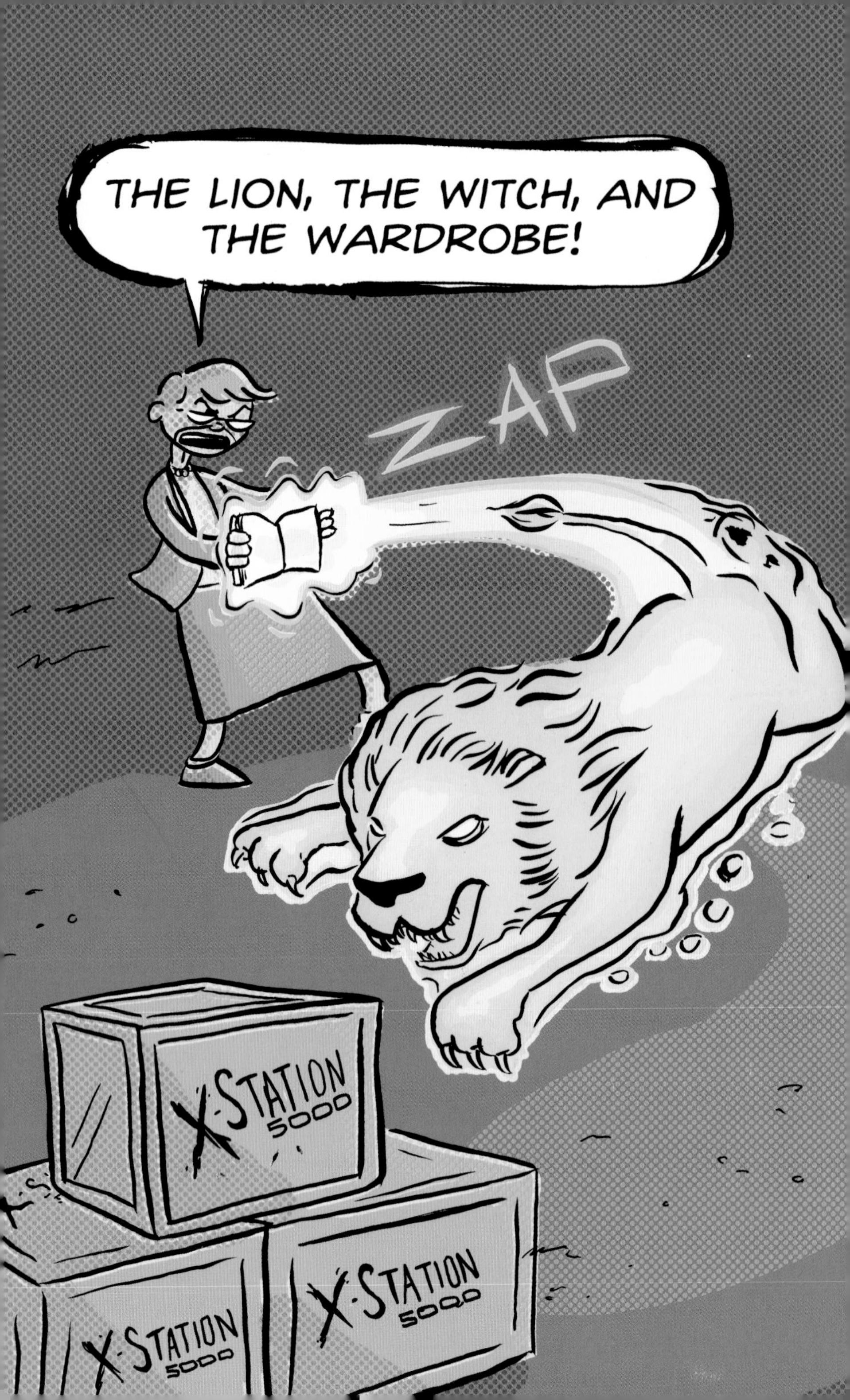
THE LION, THE WITCH, AND THE WARDROBE!
ZAP
X-STATION 5000
X-STATION 5000
X-STATION 5000

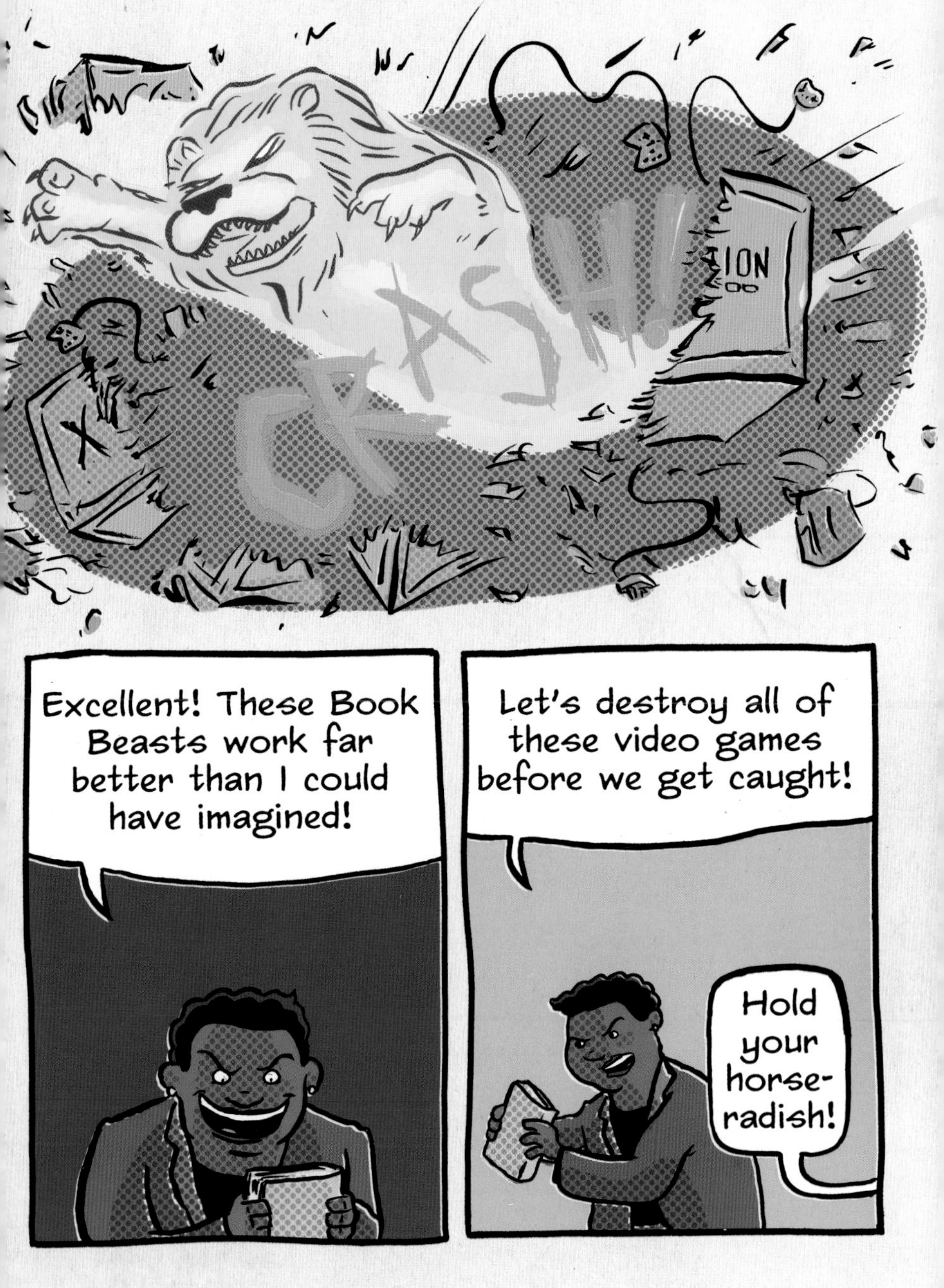
CRASH!!
ION
Excellent! These Book Beasts work far better than I could have imagined!
Let's destroy all of these video games before we get caught!
Hold your horse-radish!

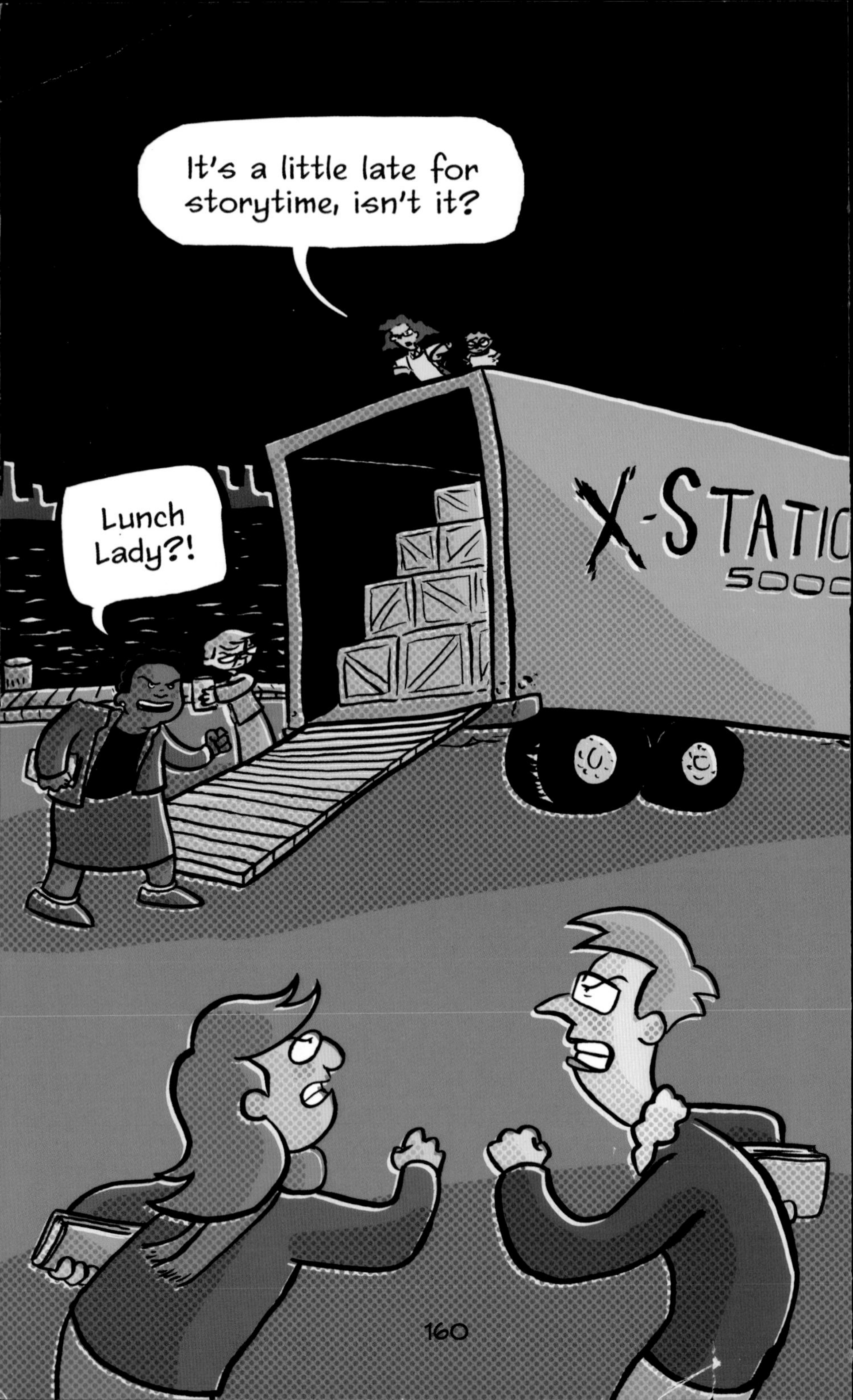
It's a little late for storytime, isn't it?
Lunch Lady?!
X-STATIO
5000

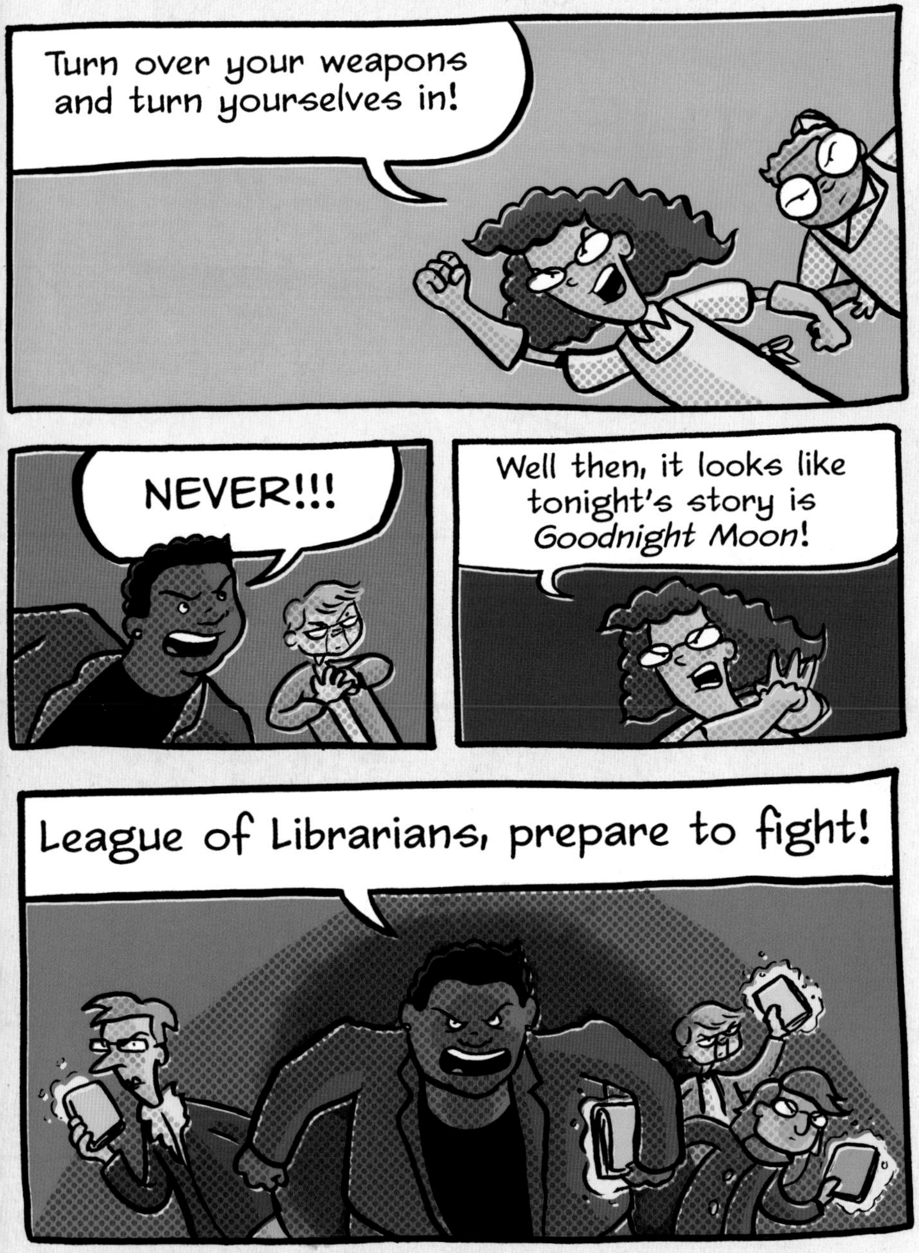
Turn over your weapons and turn yourselves in!
NEVER!!!
Well then, it looks like tonight's story is *Goodnight Moon*!
League of Librarians, prepare to fight!

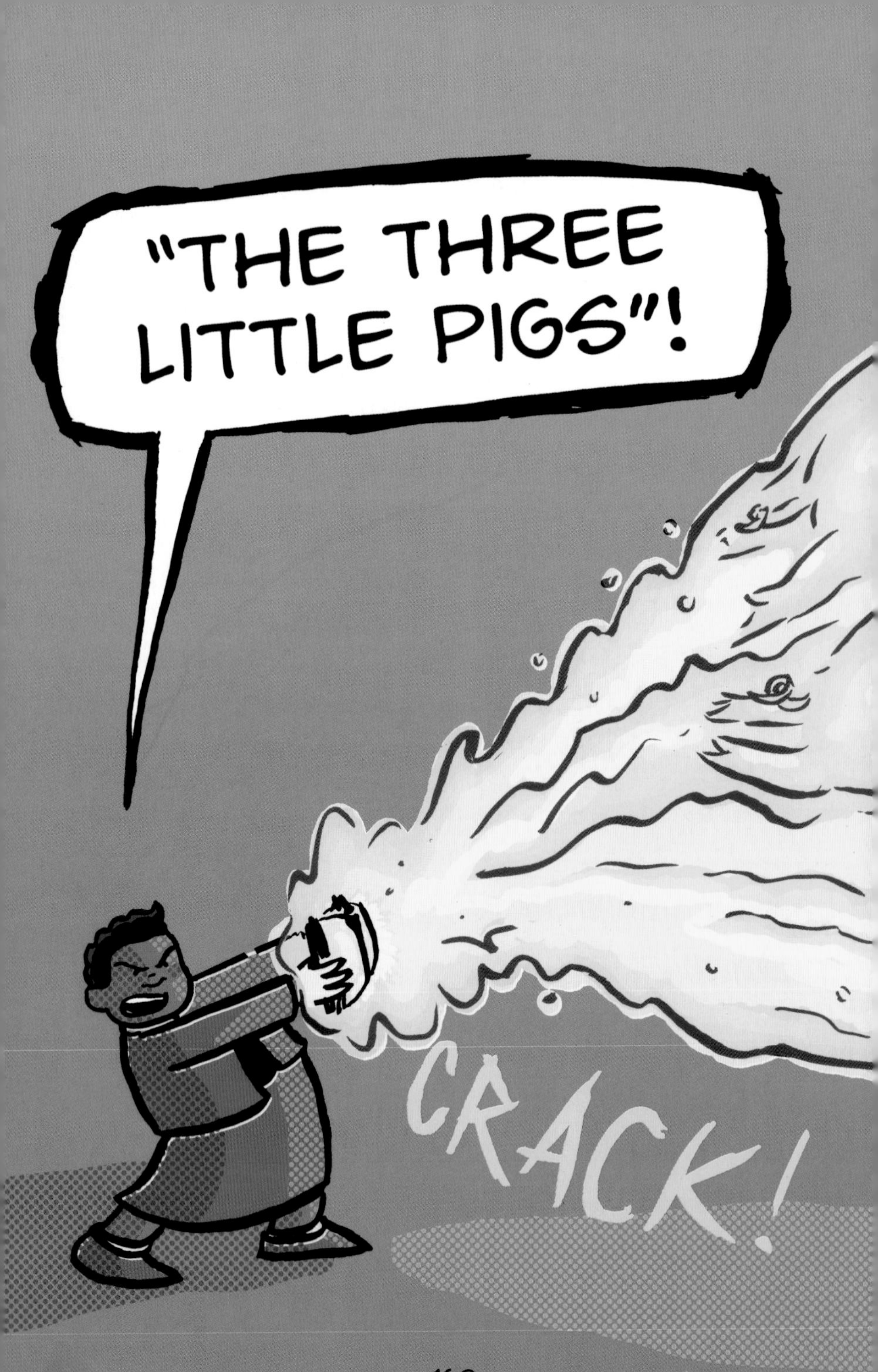
"THE THREE LITTLE PIGS"!
CRACK!

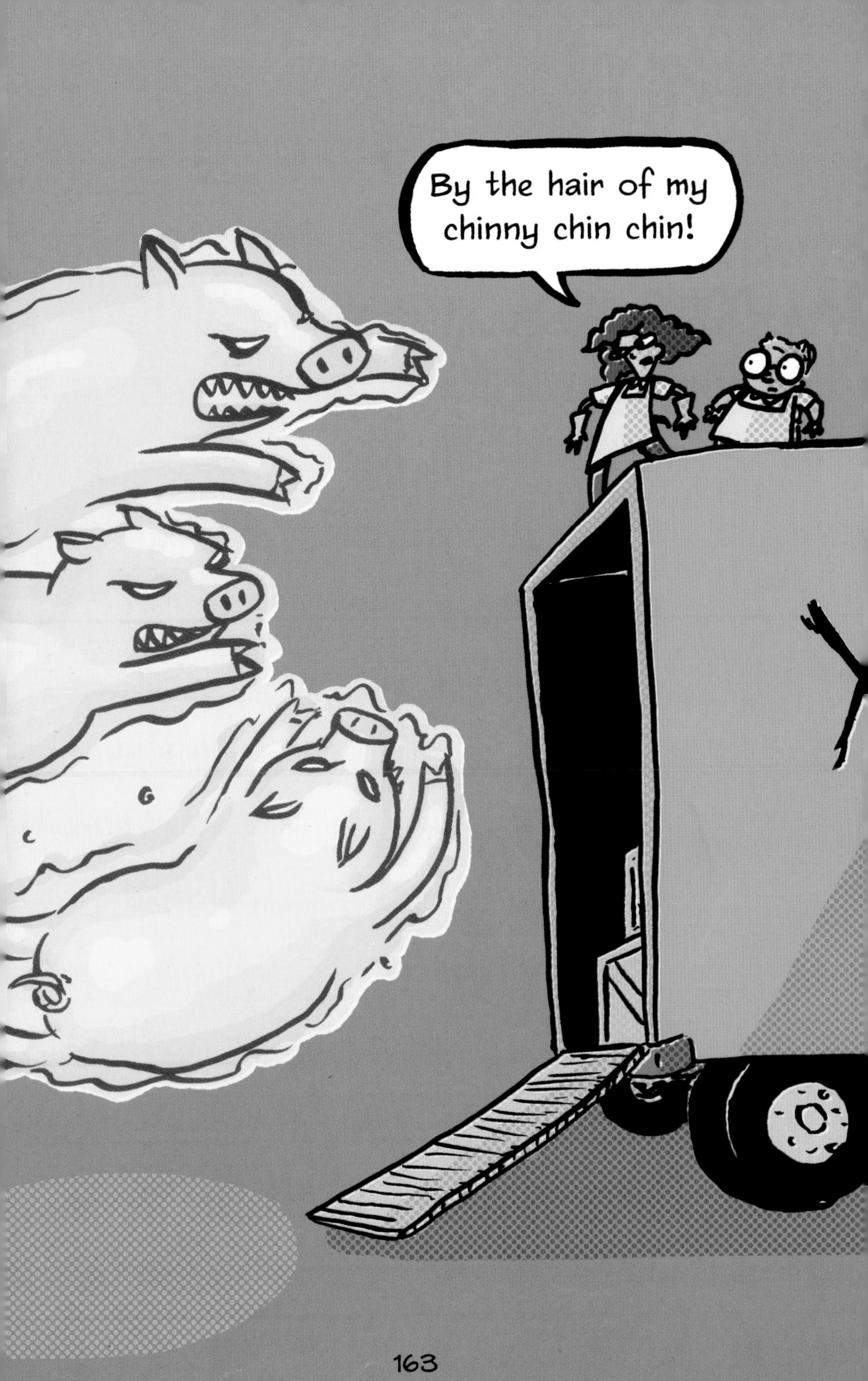
By the hair of my chinny chin chin!

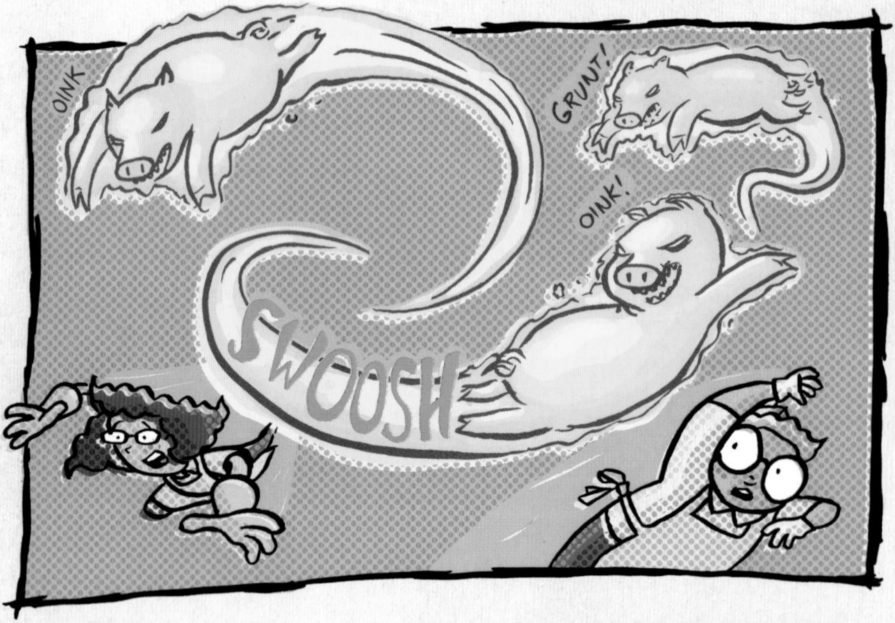
OINK
GRUNT!
OINK!
SWOOSH

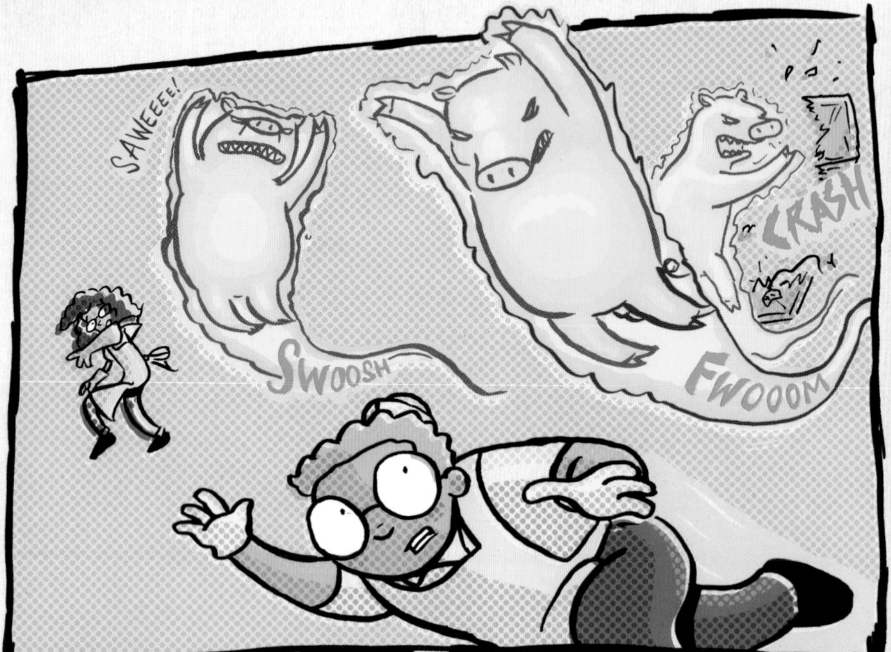
SAWEEEEE!
CRASH
SWOOSH
FWOOOM

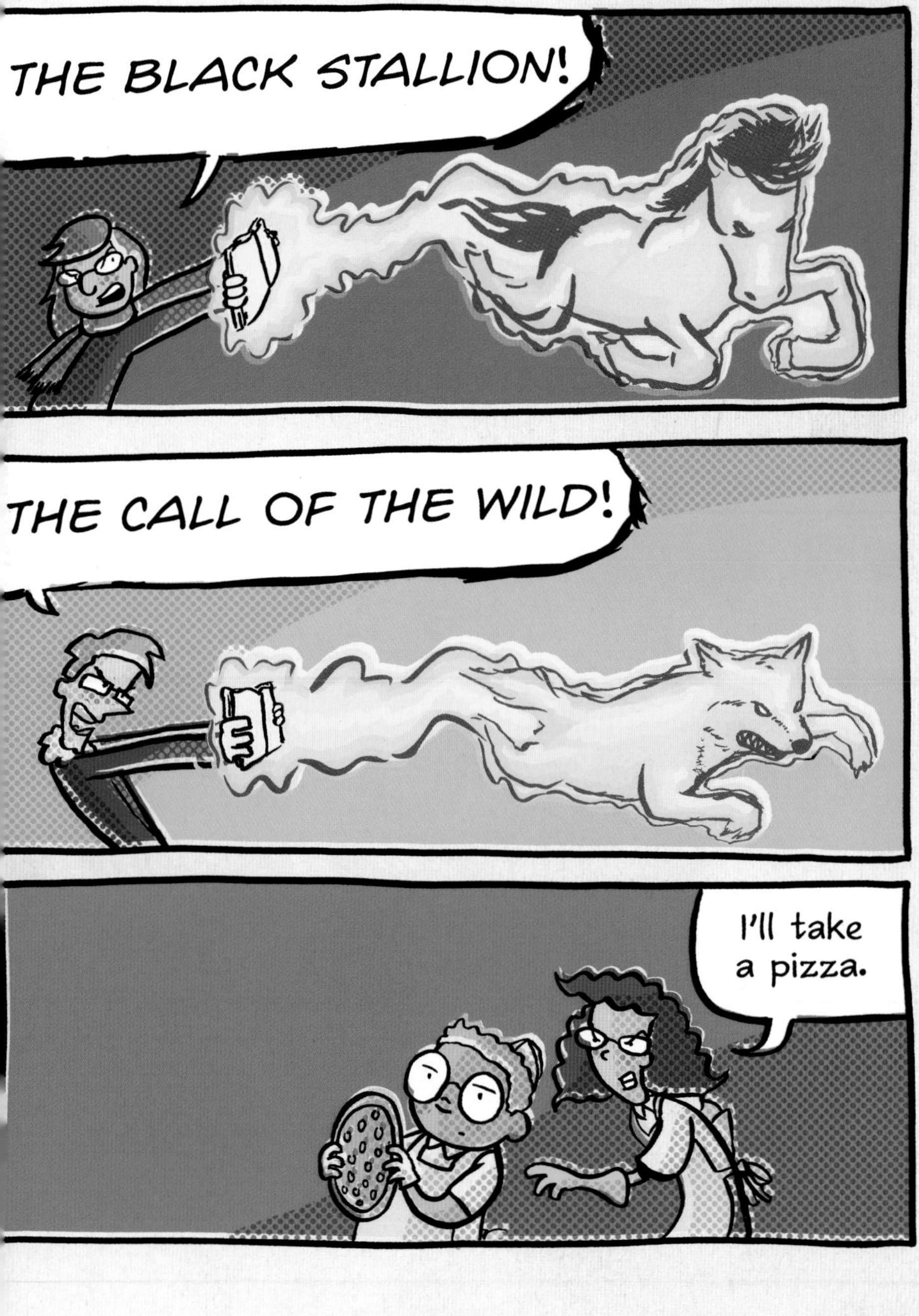
THE BLACK STALLION!
THE CALL OF THE WILD!
I'll take a pizza.

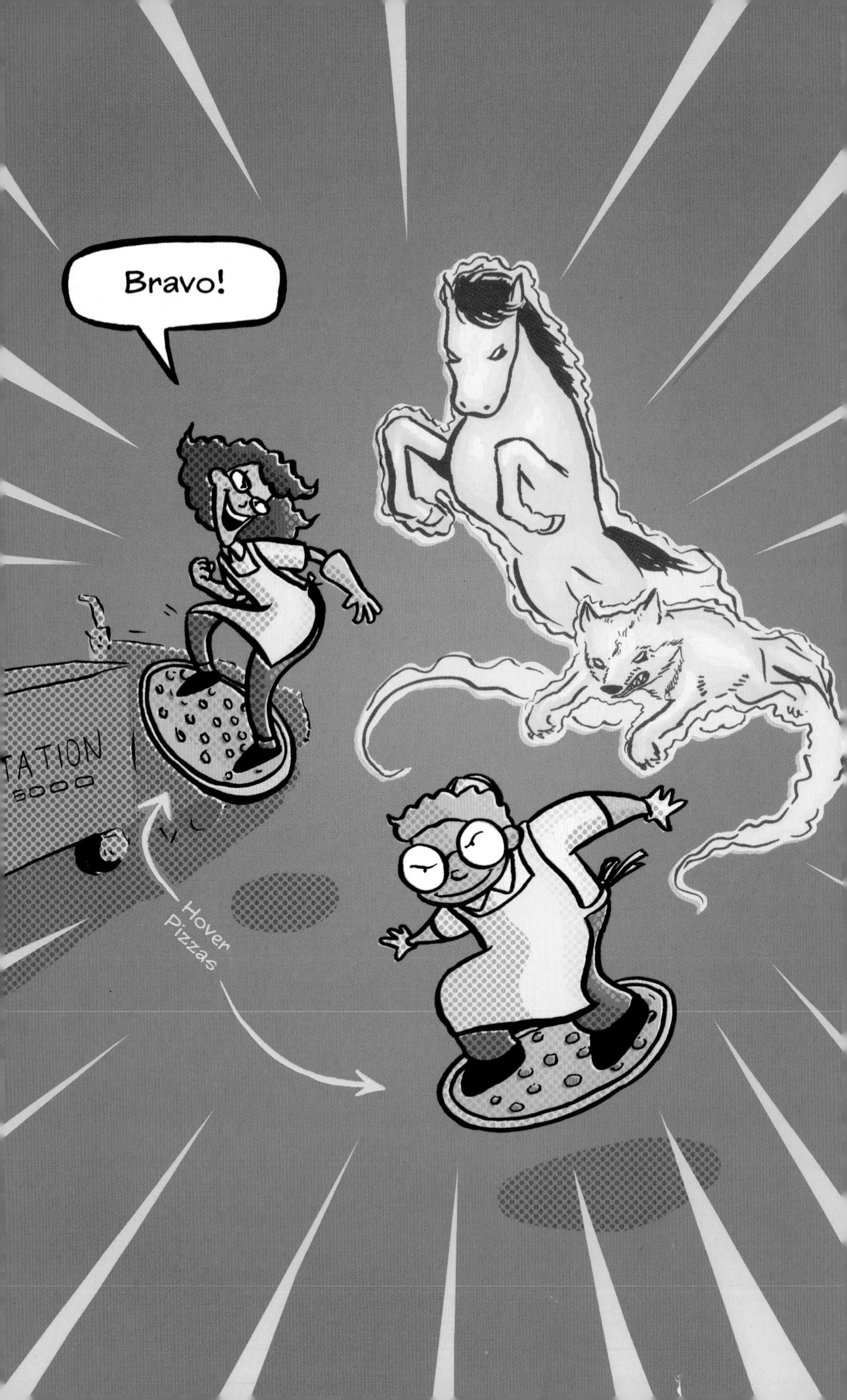
Bravo!
TATION
5000
Hover Pizzas

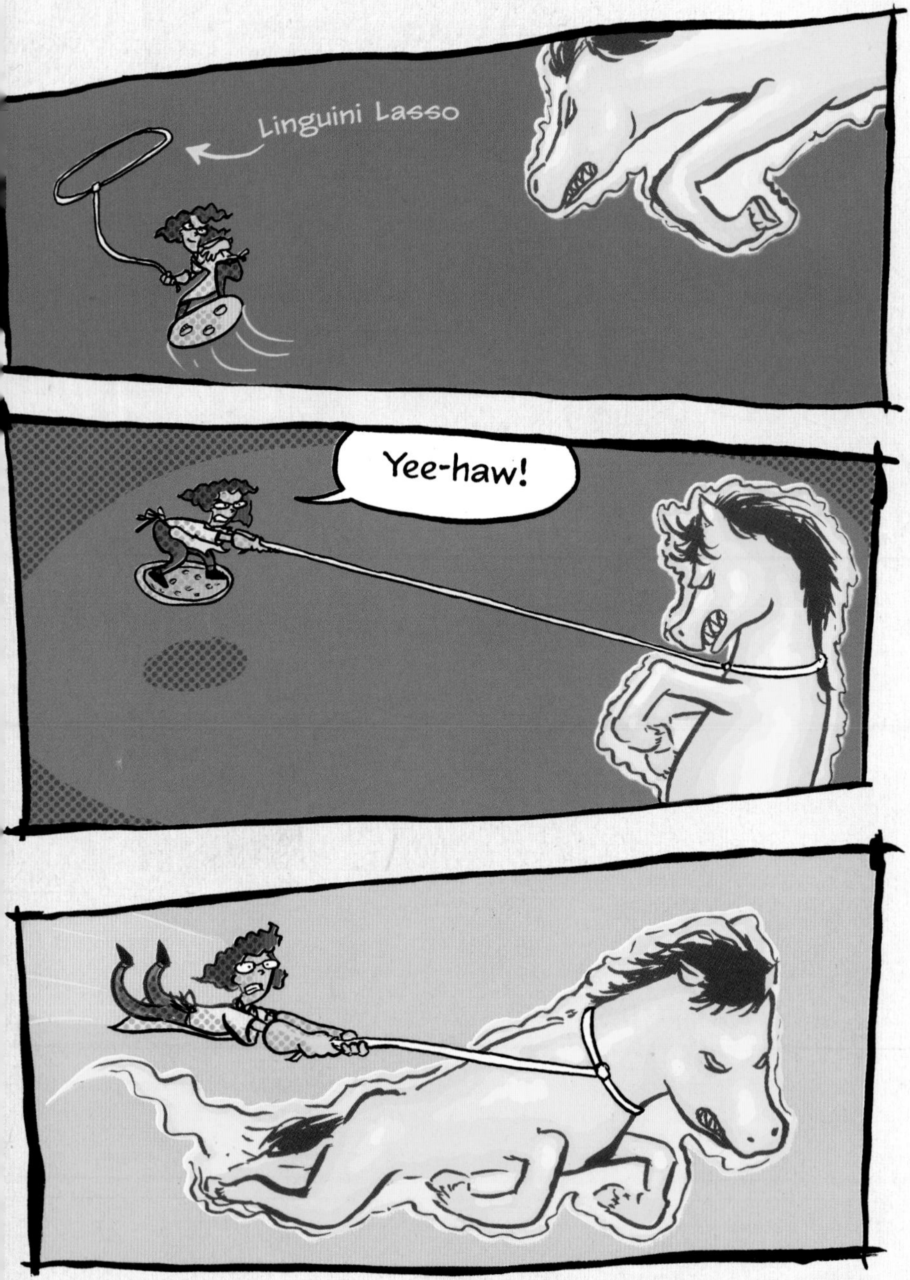
Linguini Lasso
Yee-haw!

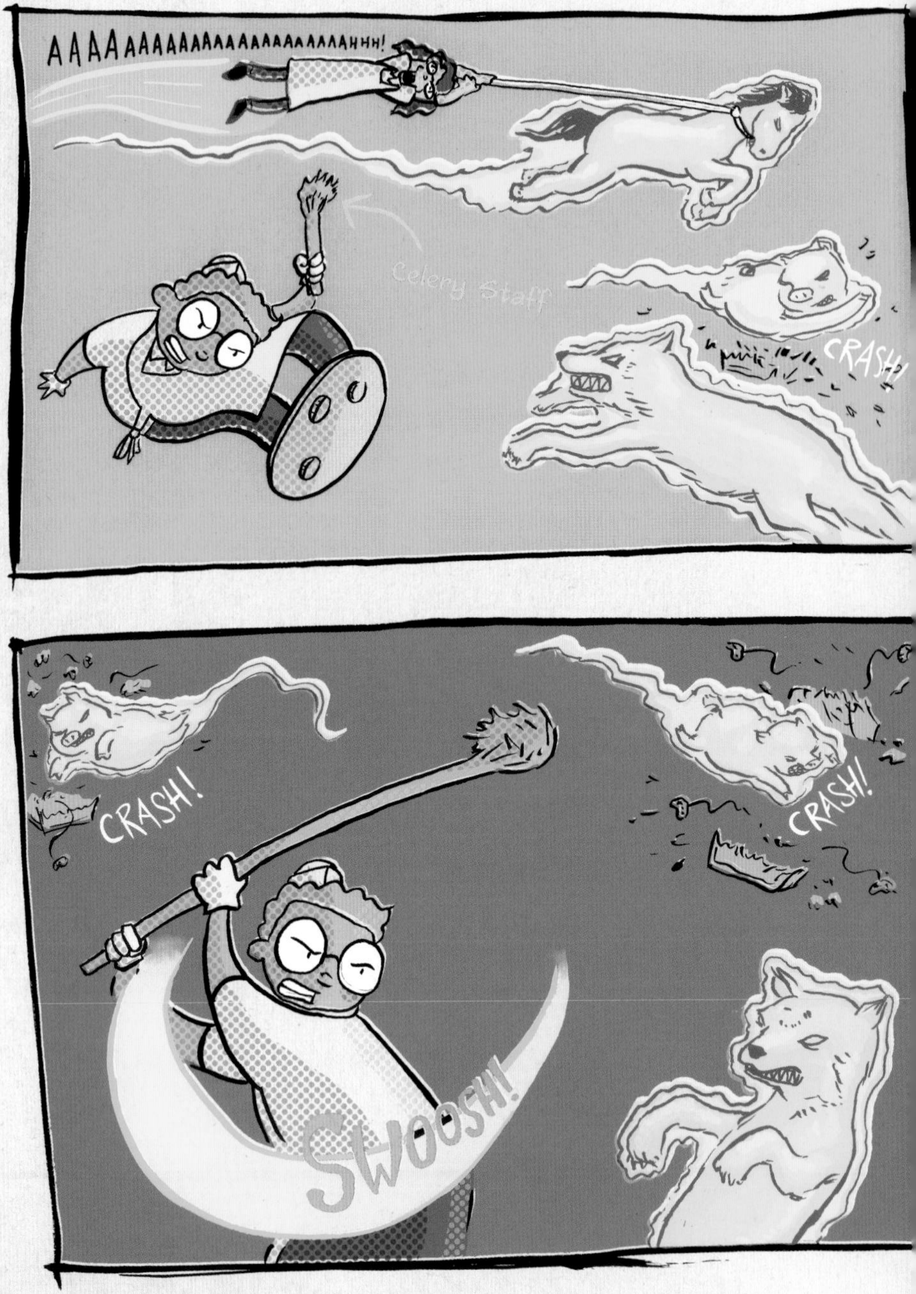
AAAAAAAAAAAAAAAAAAAAAAAAAAAHHH!
Celery Staff
CRASH!
CRASH!
CRASH!
SWOOSH!

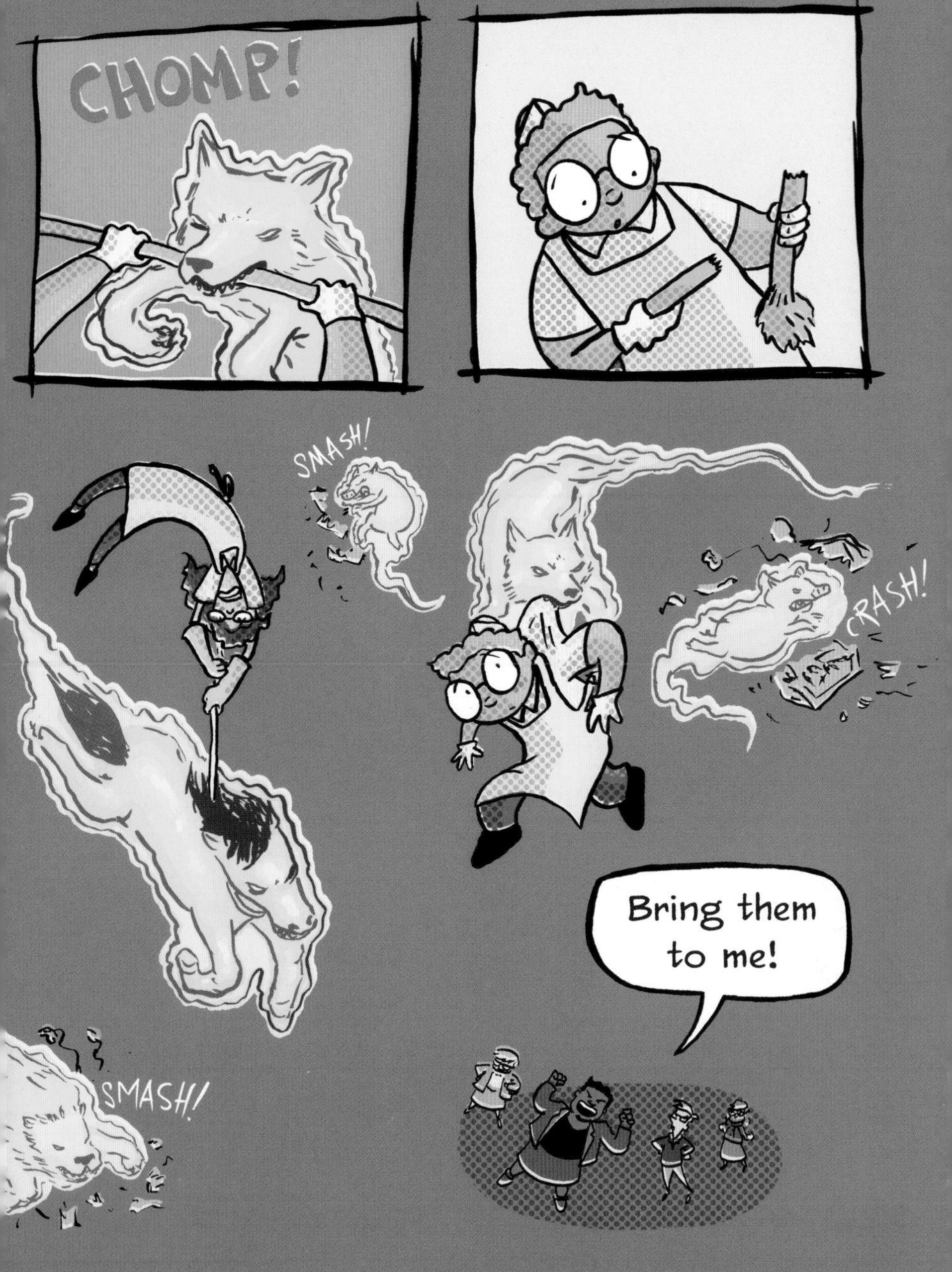
CHOMP!
SMASH!
CRASH!
Bring them to me!
SMASH!

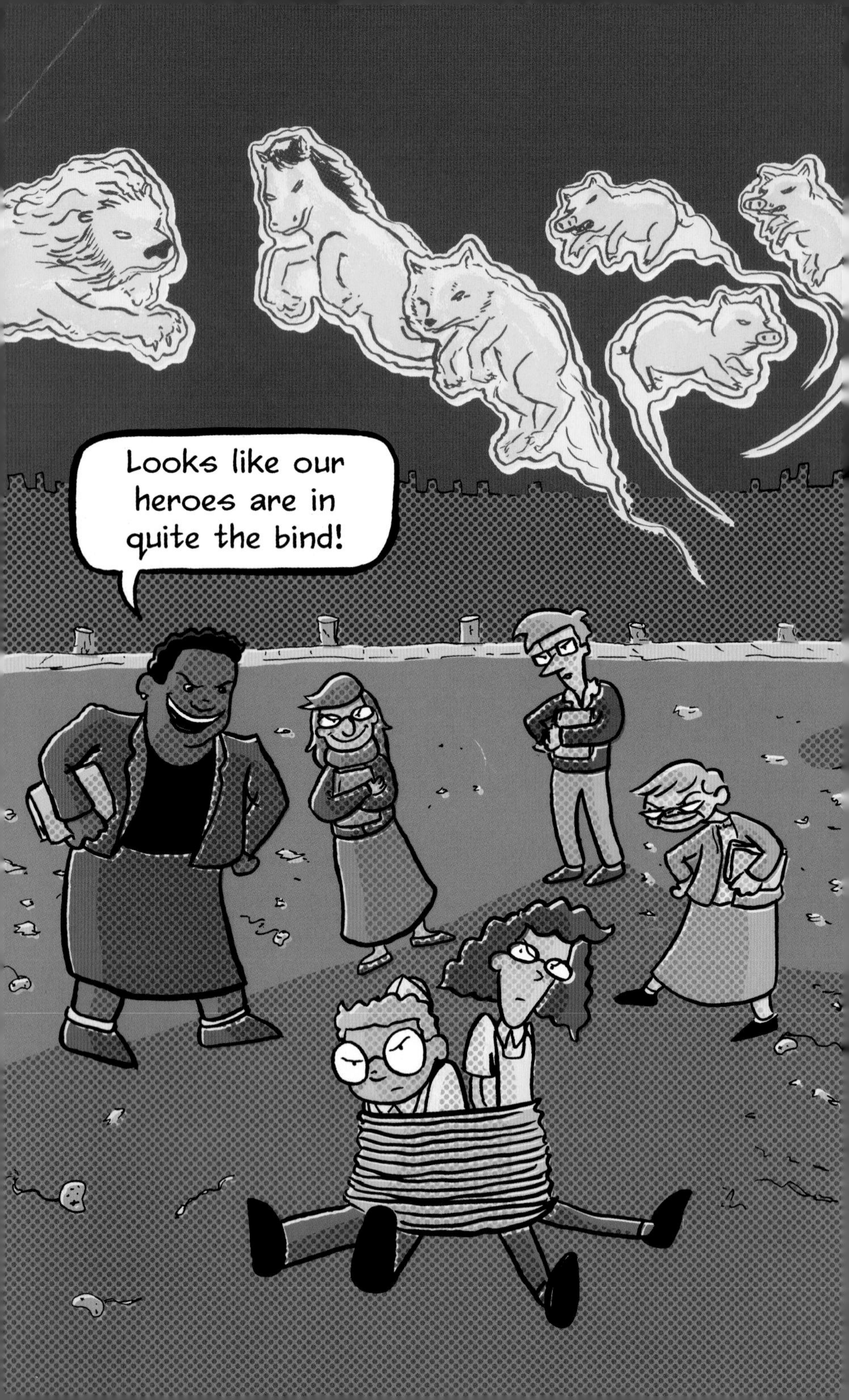
Looks like our heroes are in quite the bind!

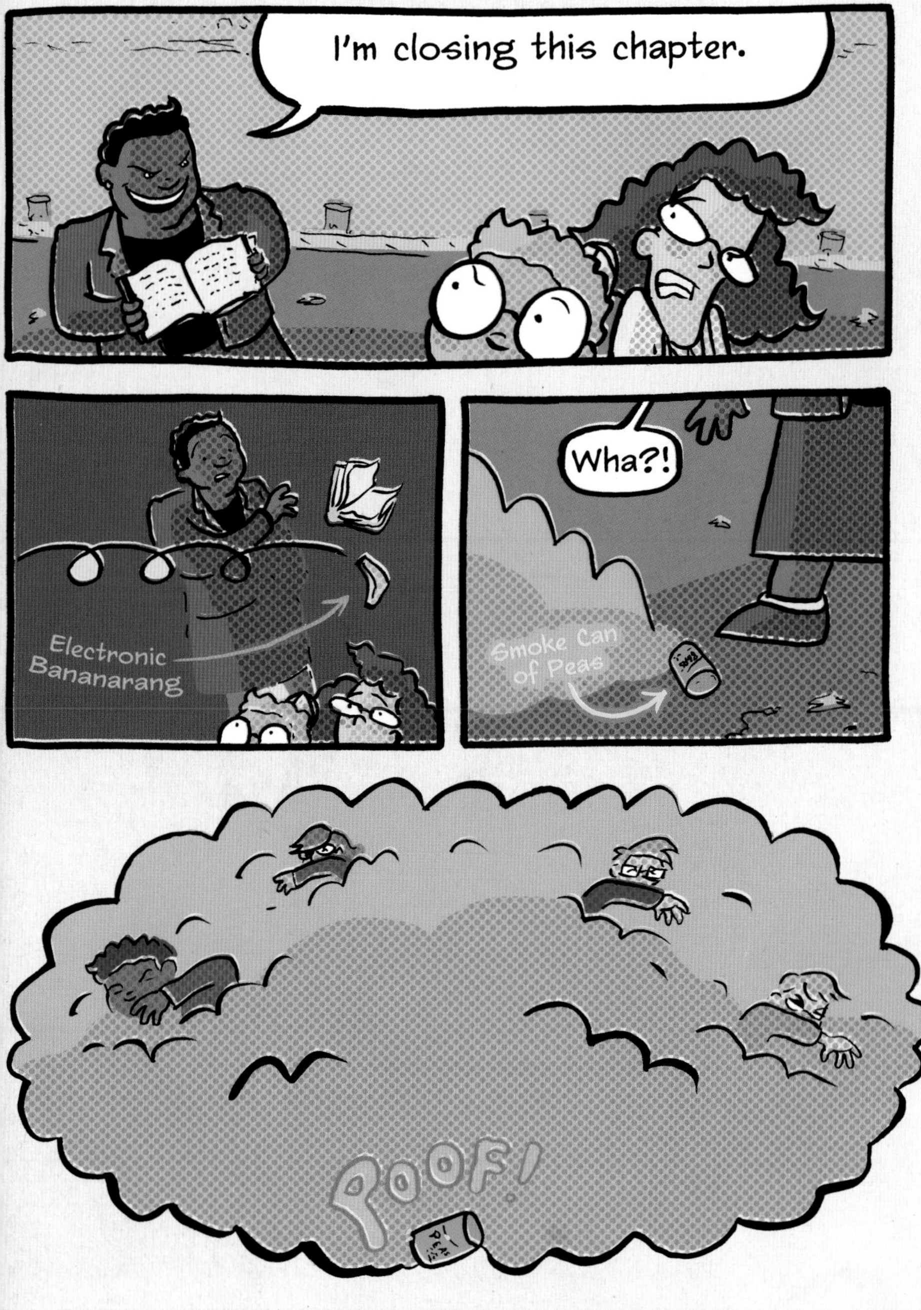
I'm closing this chapter.
Electronic Bananarang
Wha?!
Smoke Can of Peas
POOF!

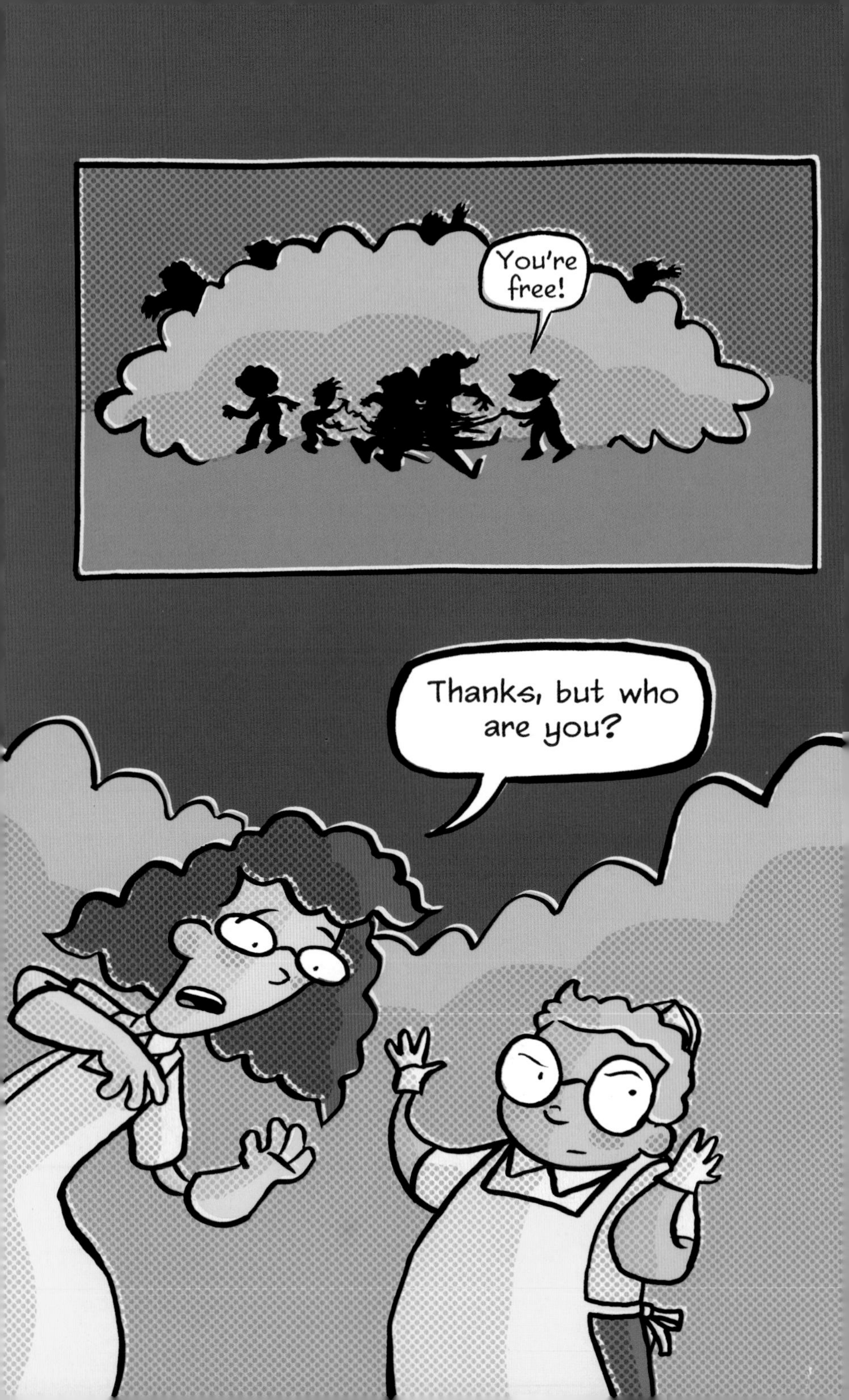
You're free!
Thanks, but who are you?

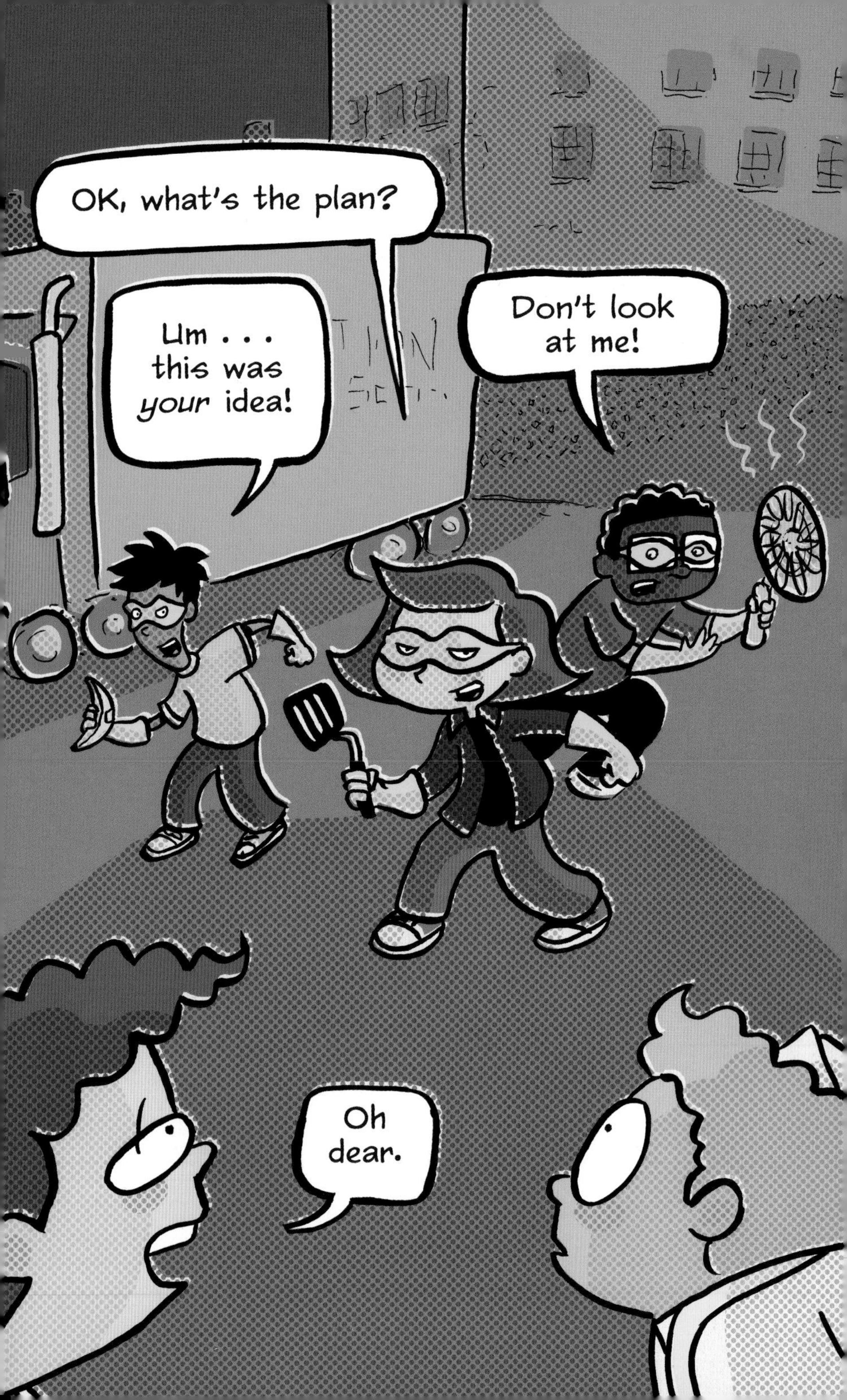
OK, what's the plan?
Um . . . this was *your* idea!
Don't look at me!
Oh dear.

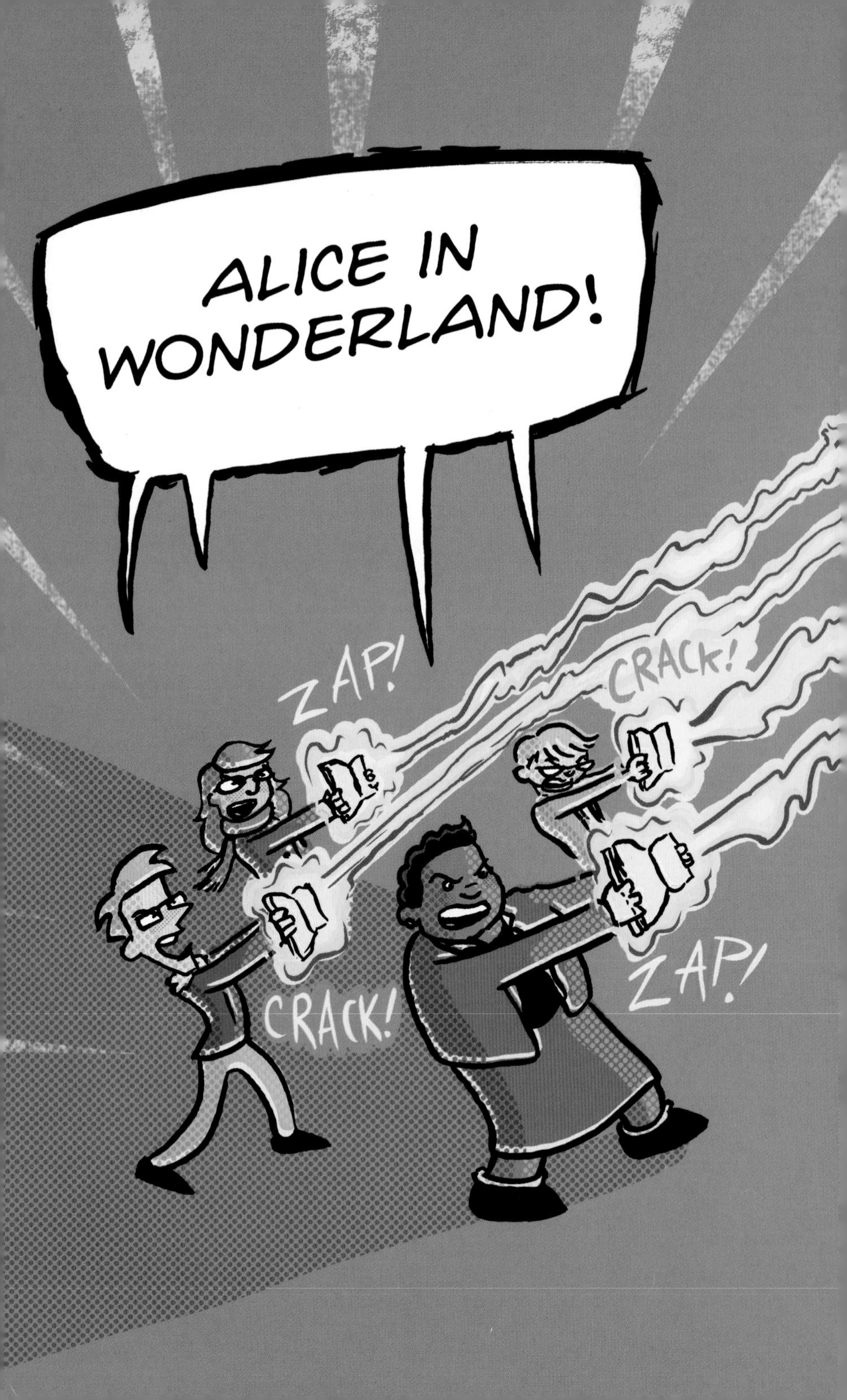
ALICE IN WONDERLAND!
ZAP!
CRACK!
ZAP!
CRACK!

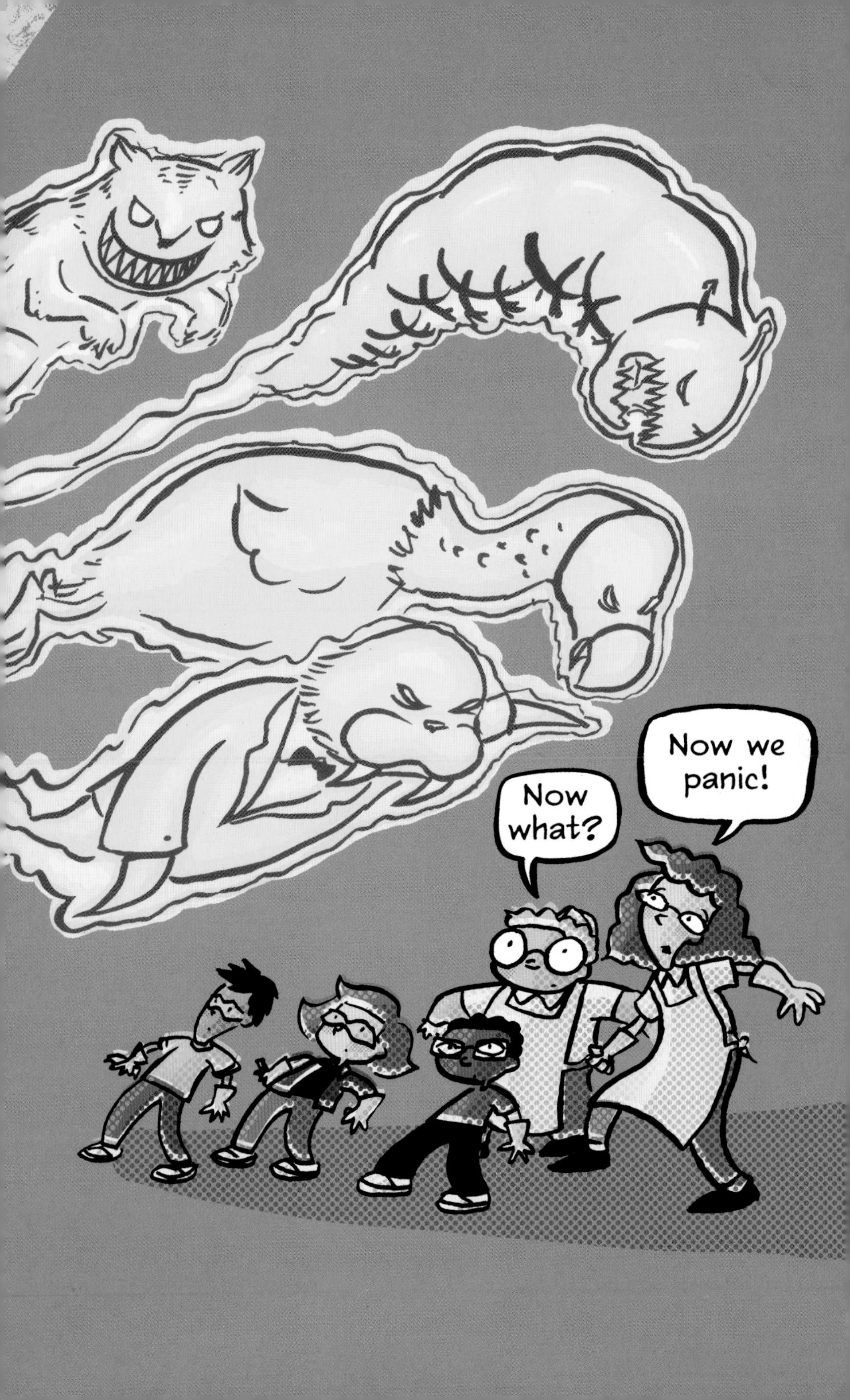
Now what?
Now we panic!

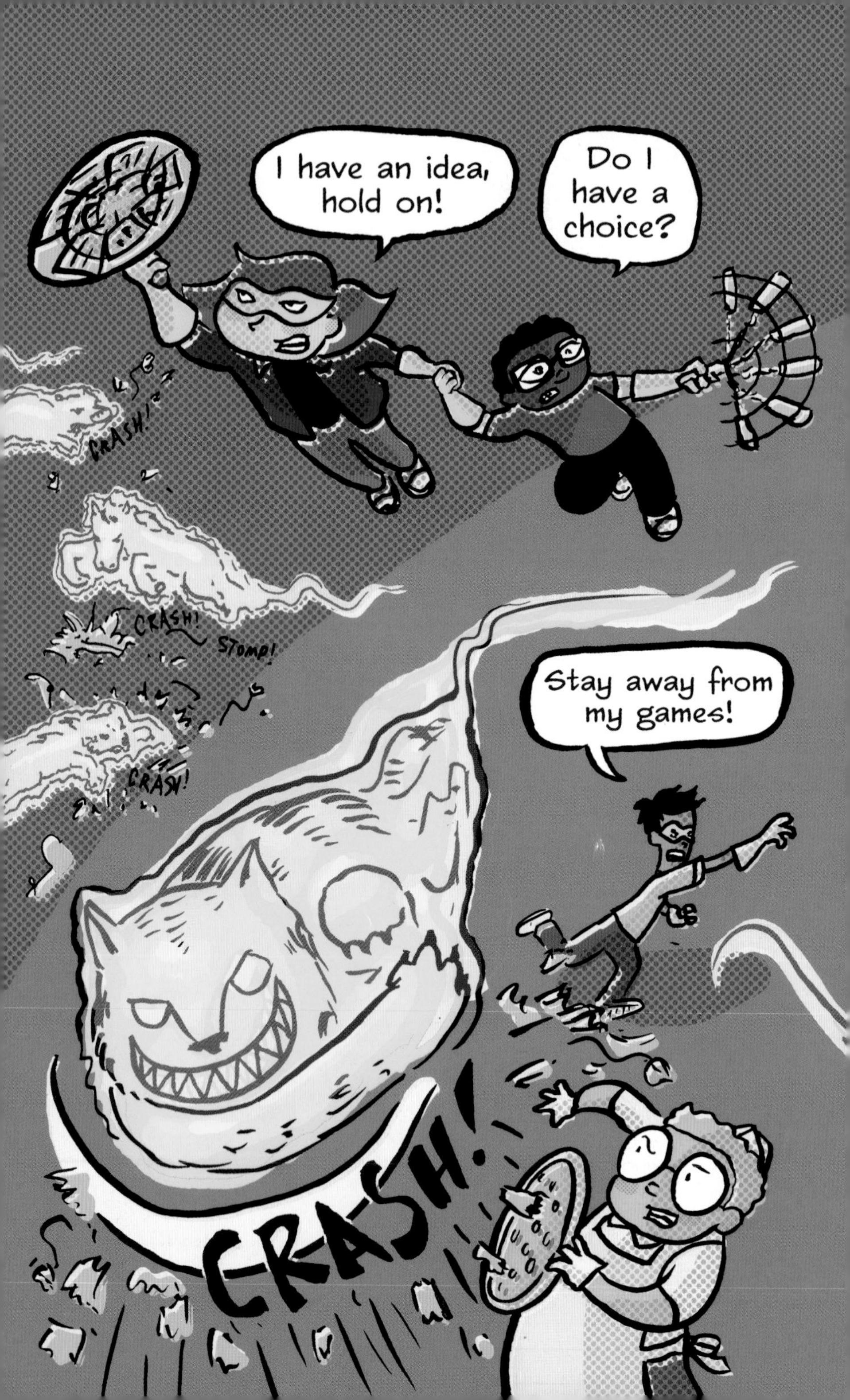
I have an idea, hold on!
Do I have a choice?
CRASH!
CRASH!
STOMP!
CRASH!
Stay away from my games!
CRASH!

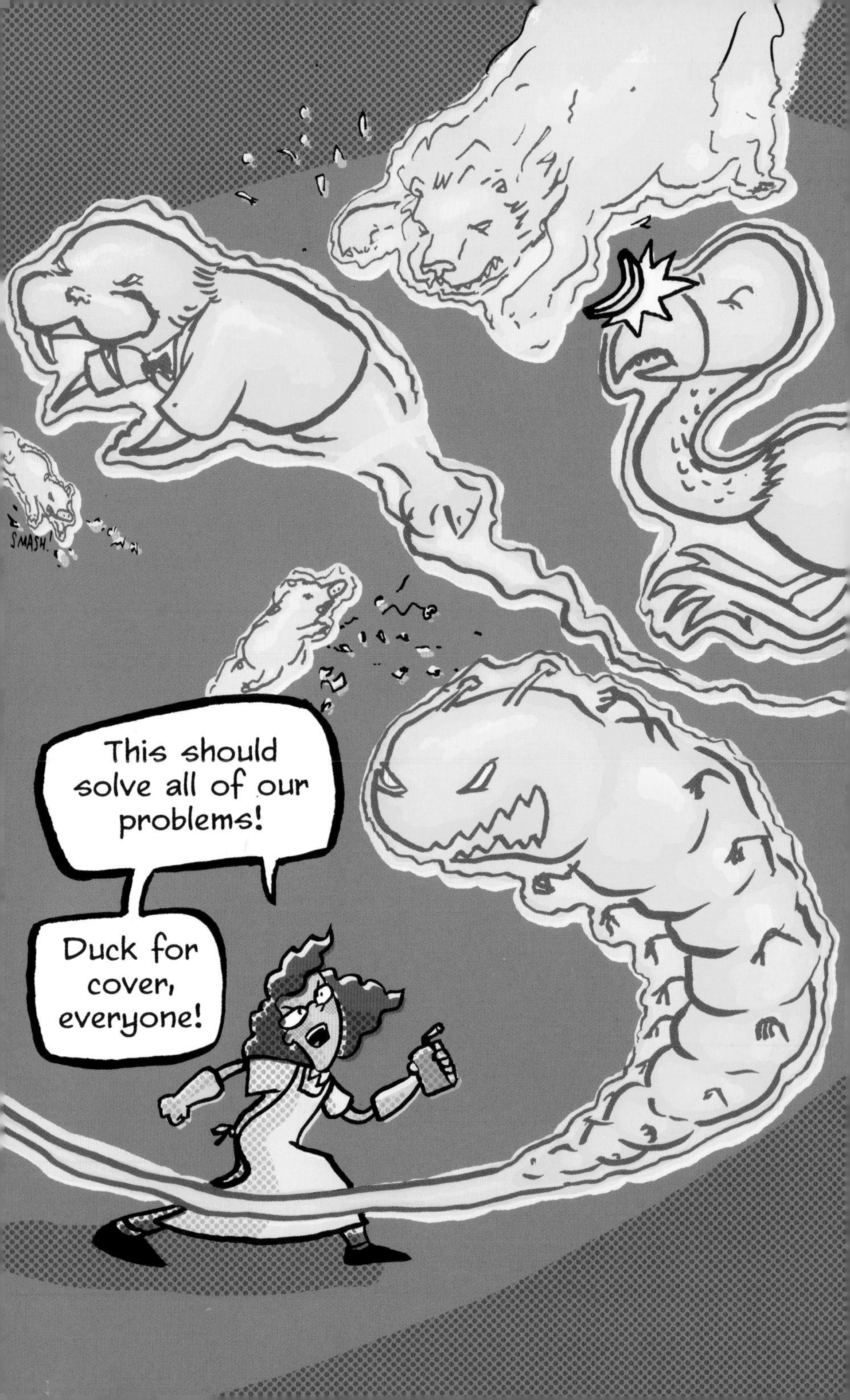
SMASH!
This should solve all of our problems!
Duck for cover, everyone!

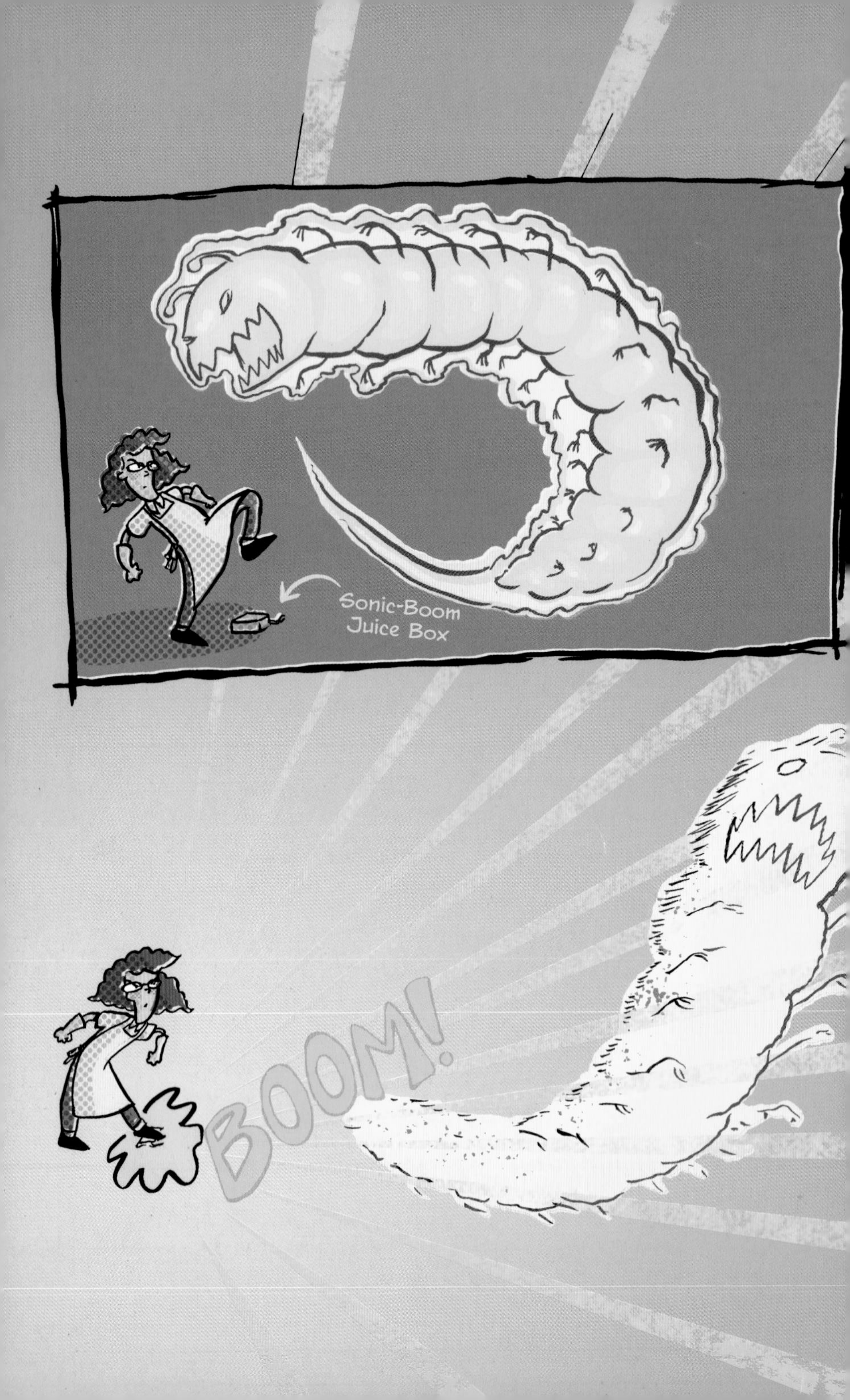
Sonic-Boom
Juice Box
BOOM!

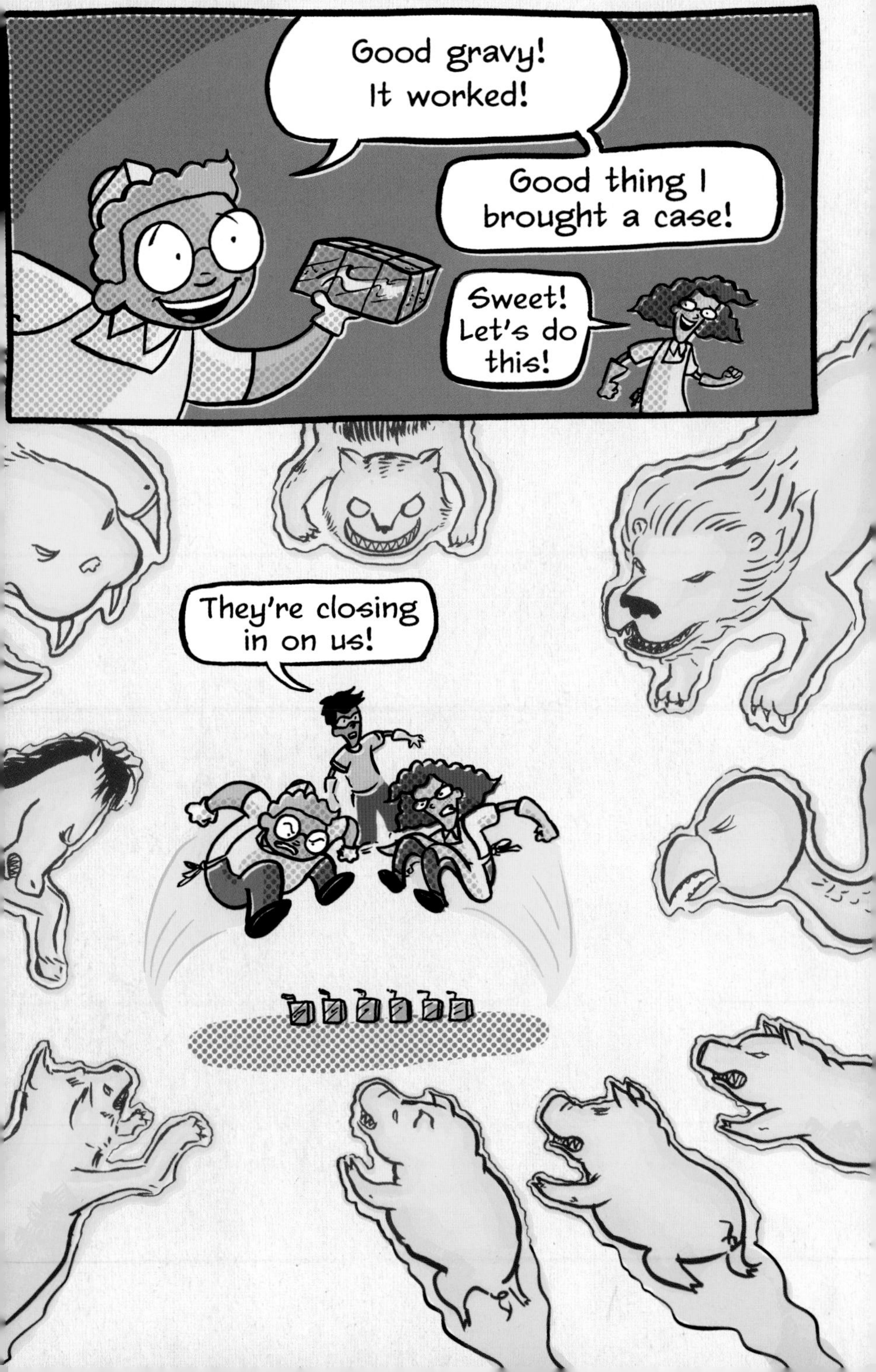
Good gravy! It worked!
Good thing I brought a case!
Sweet! Let's do this!
They're closing in on us!

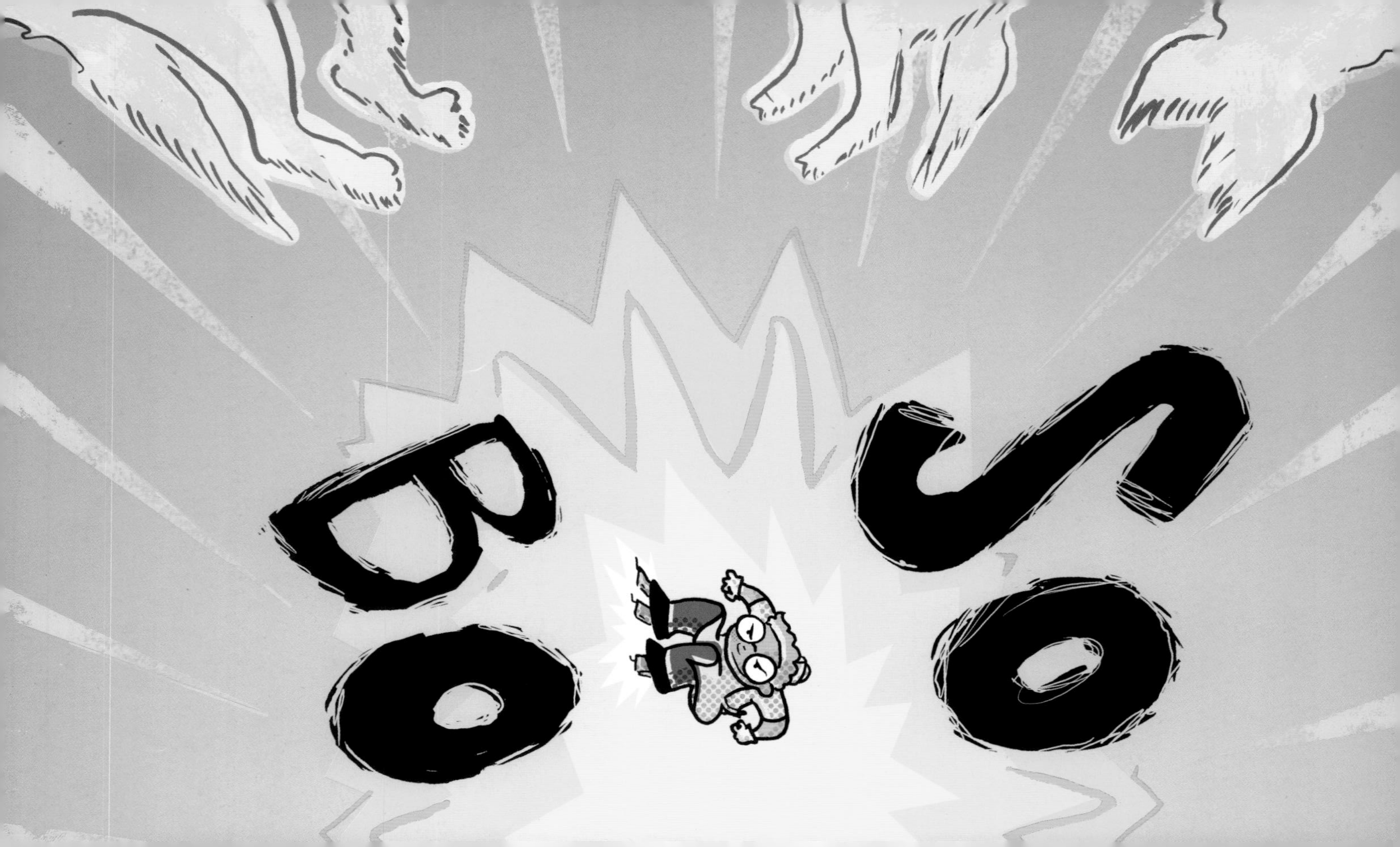
B O S O

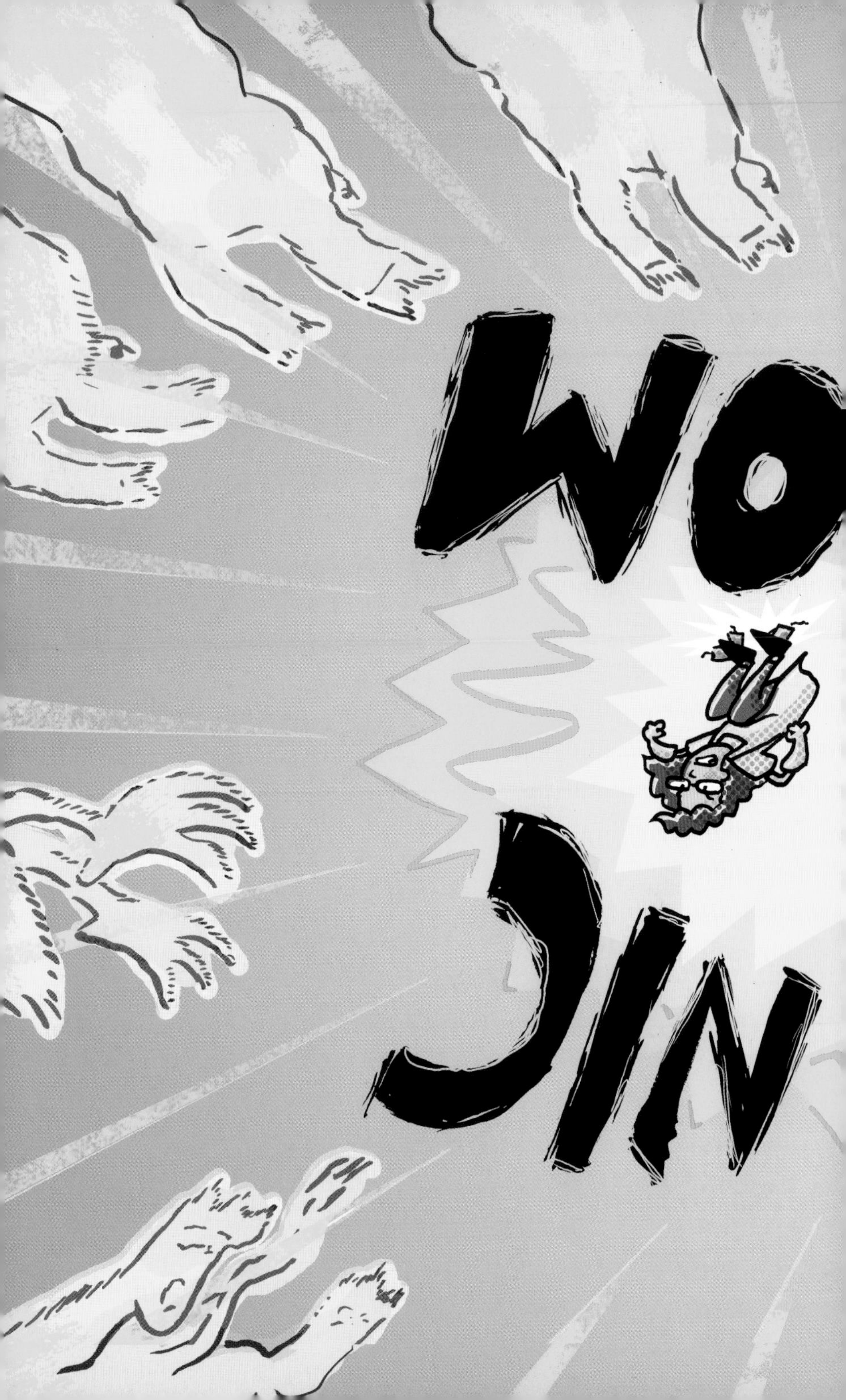
WO
JIN

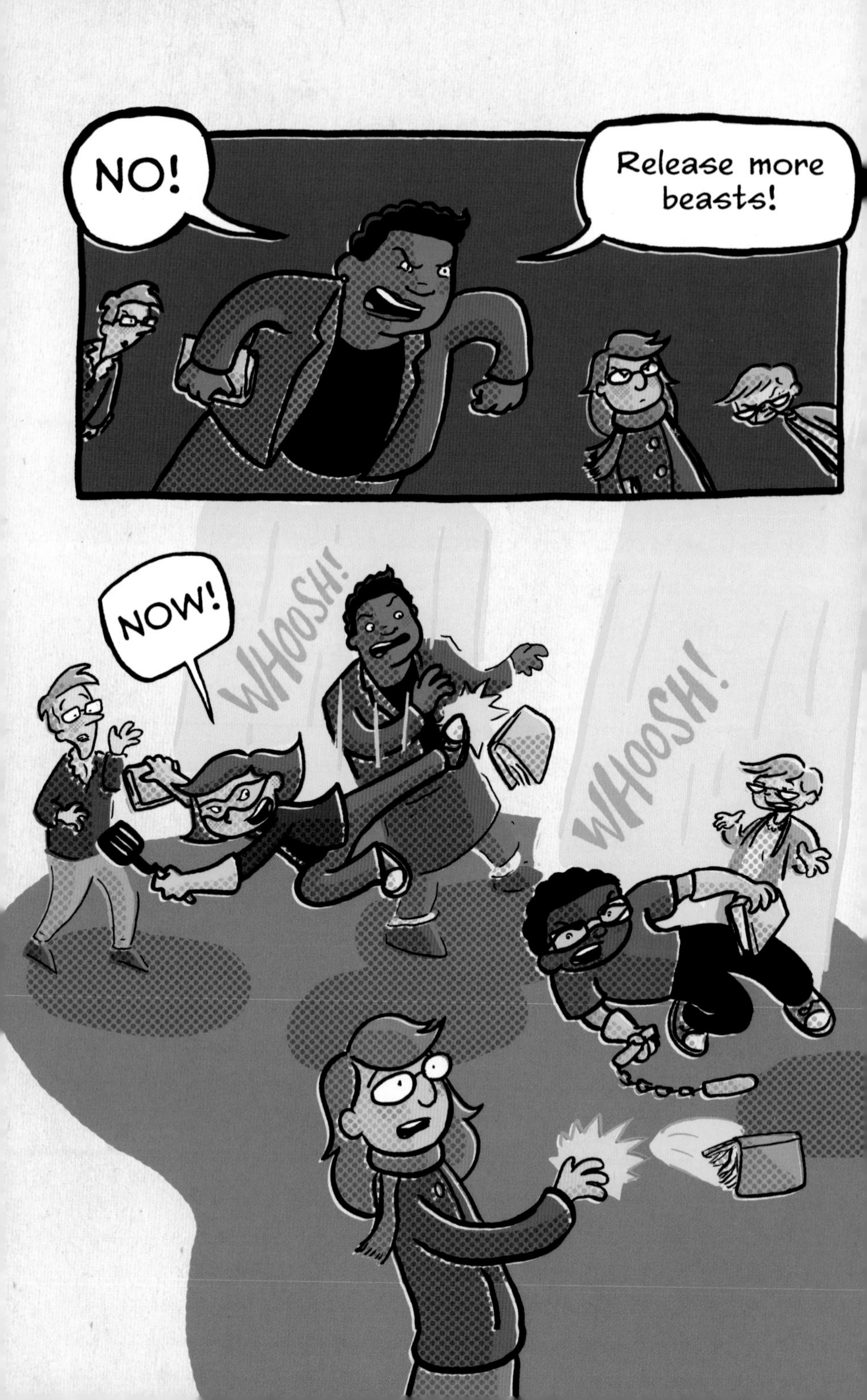
NO!
Release more beasts!
NOW!
WHOOSH!
WHOOSH!

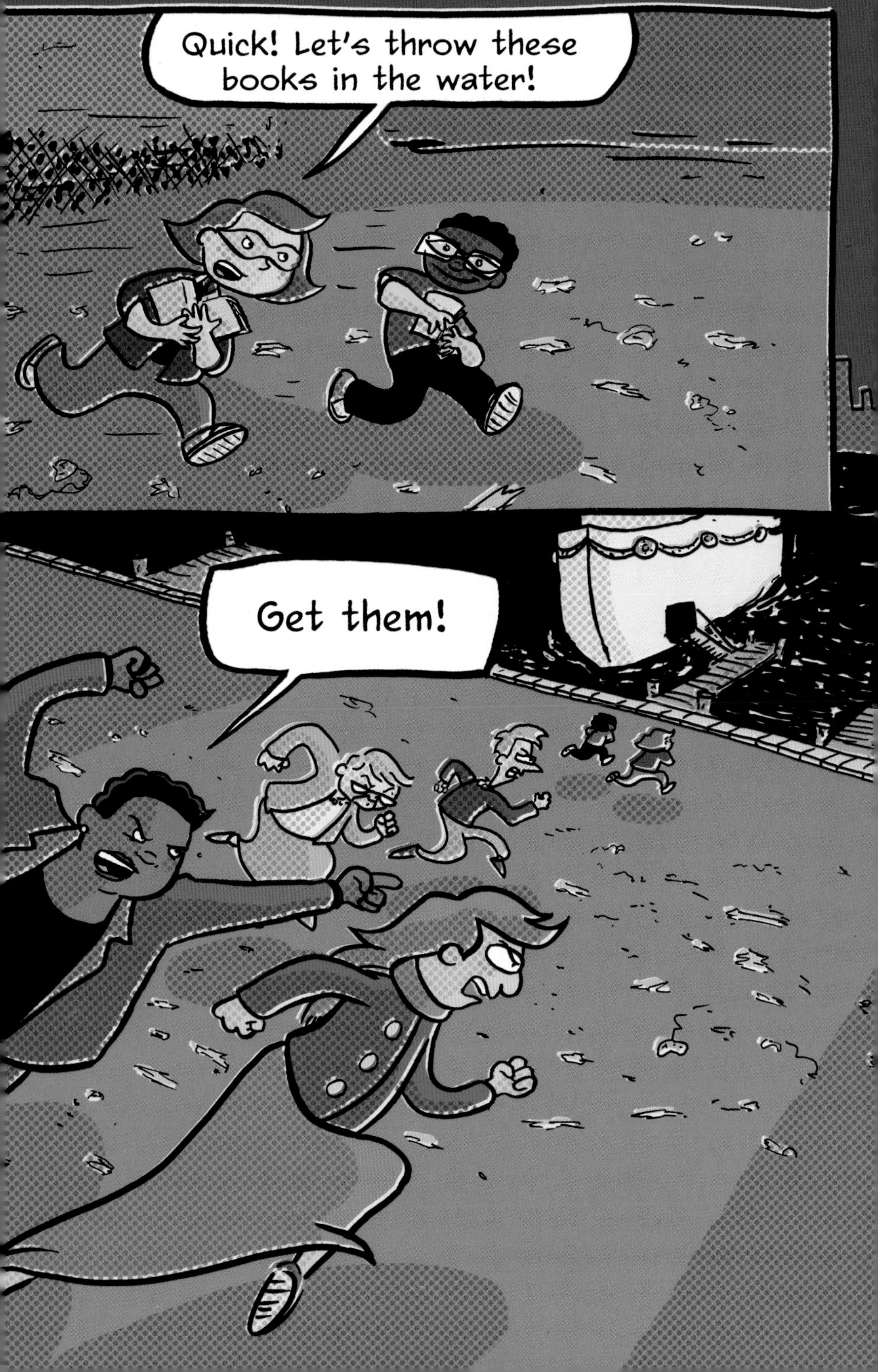
Quick! Let's throw these books in the water!
Get them!

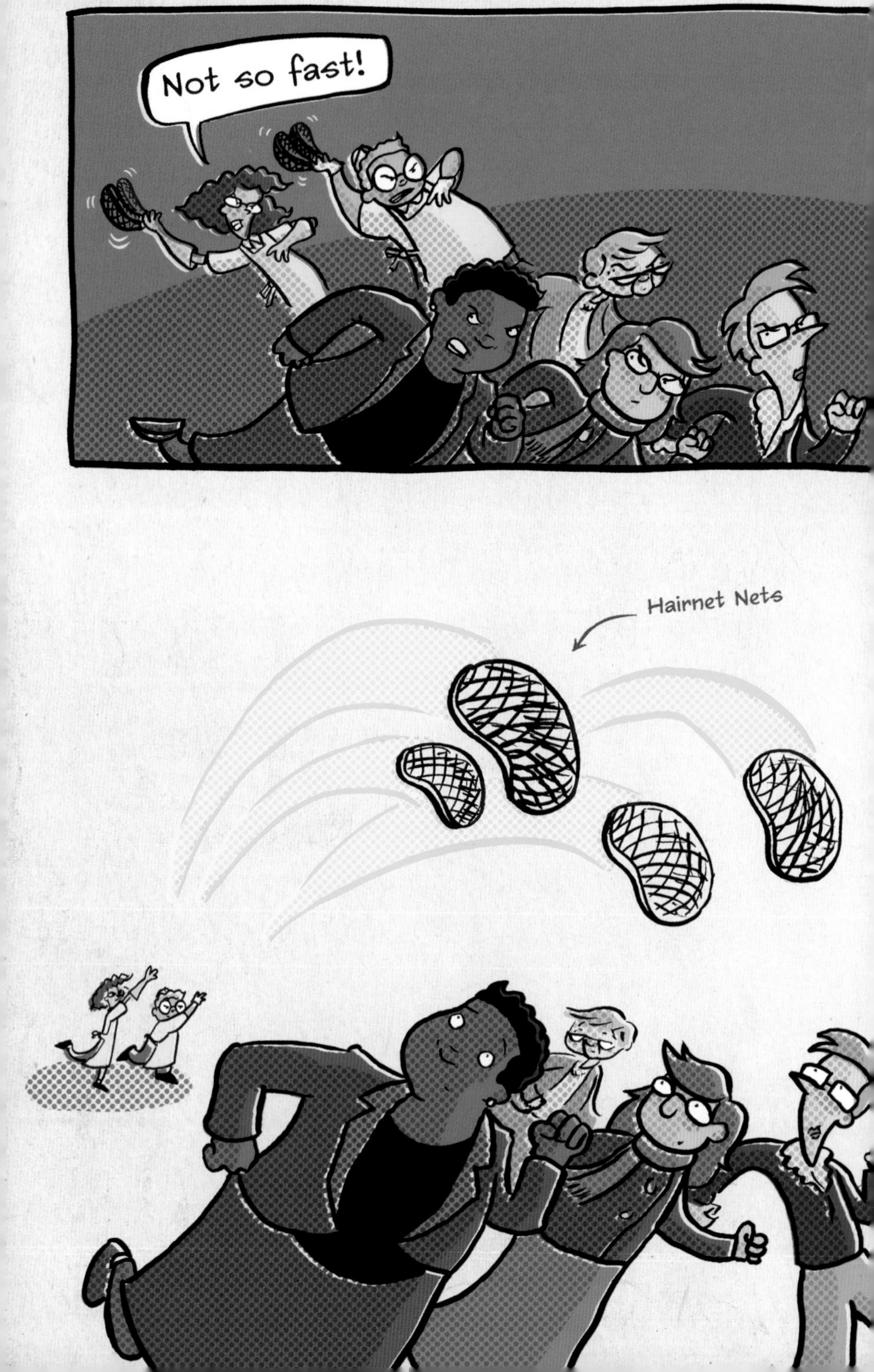
Not so fast!
Hairnet Nets

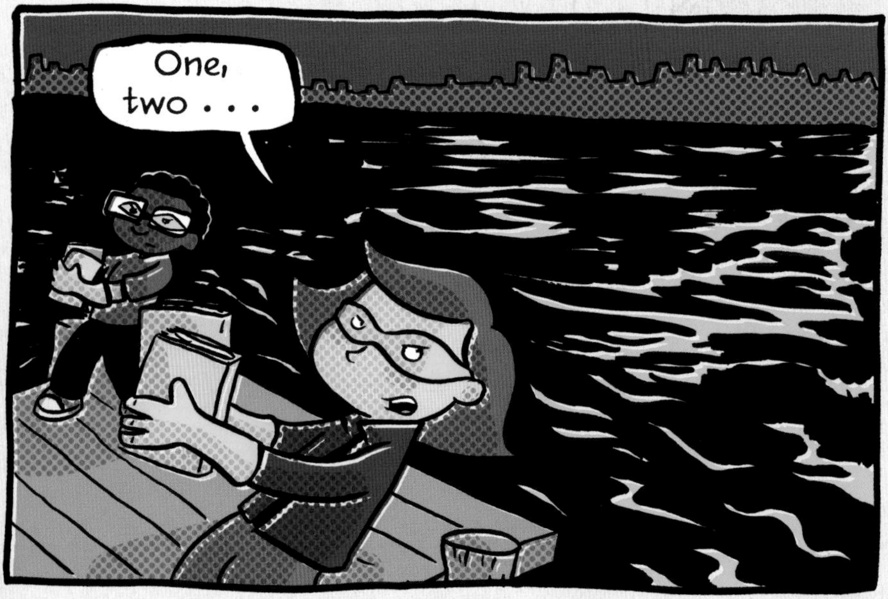
One, two . . .

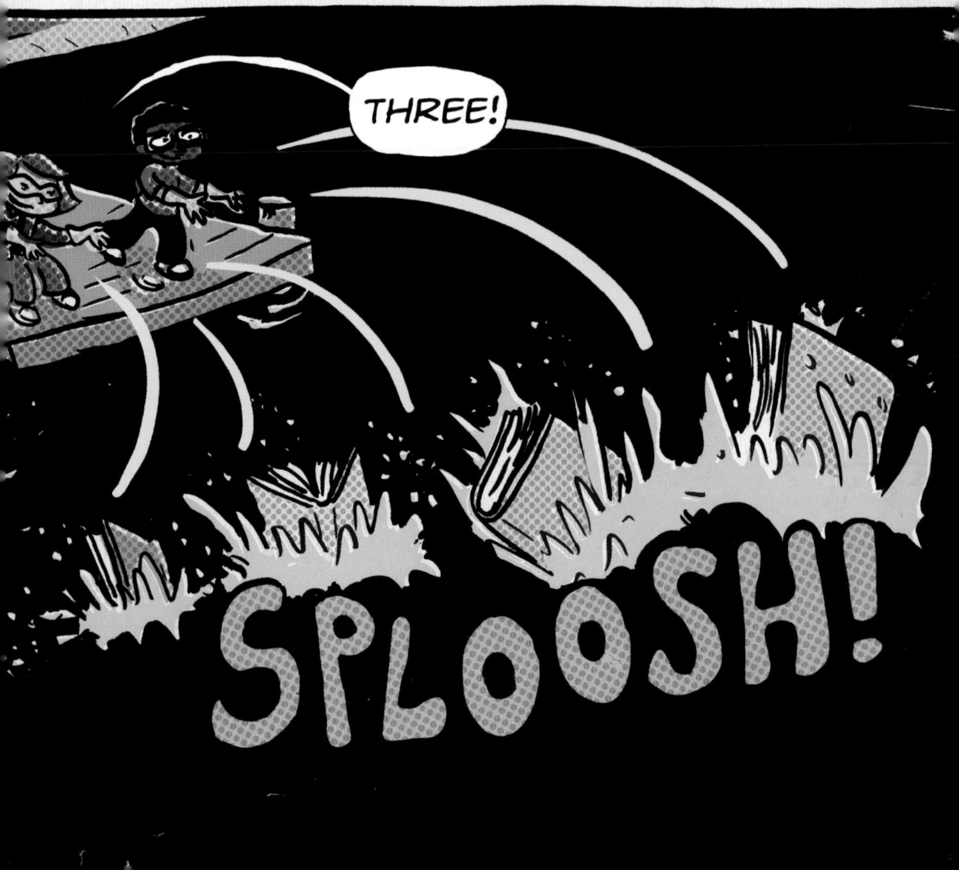
THREE!
SPLOOSH!

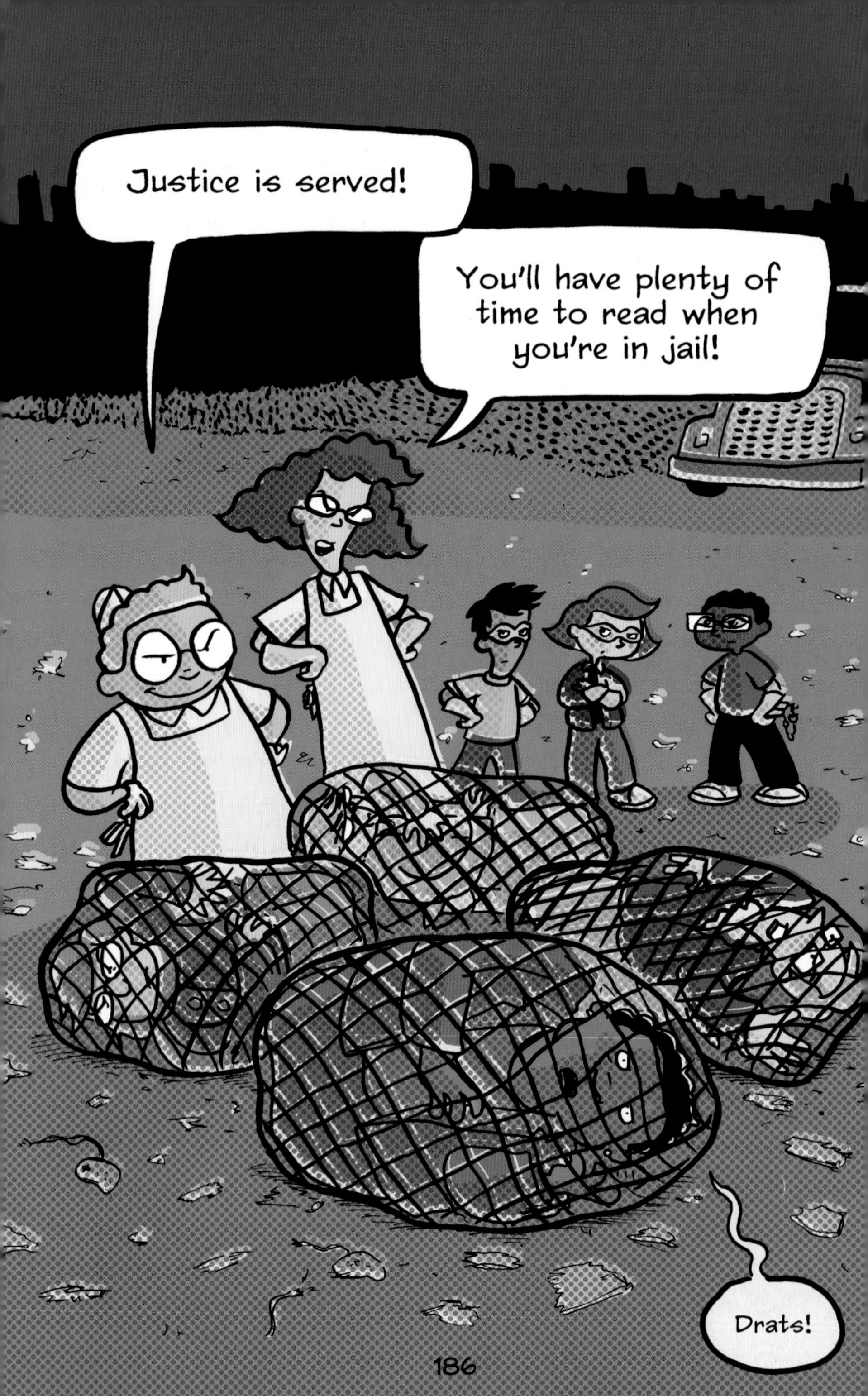
Justice is served!
You'll have plenty of time to read when you're in jail!
Drats!

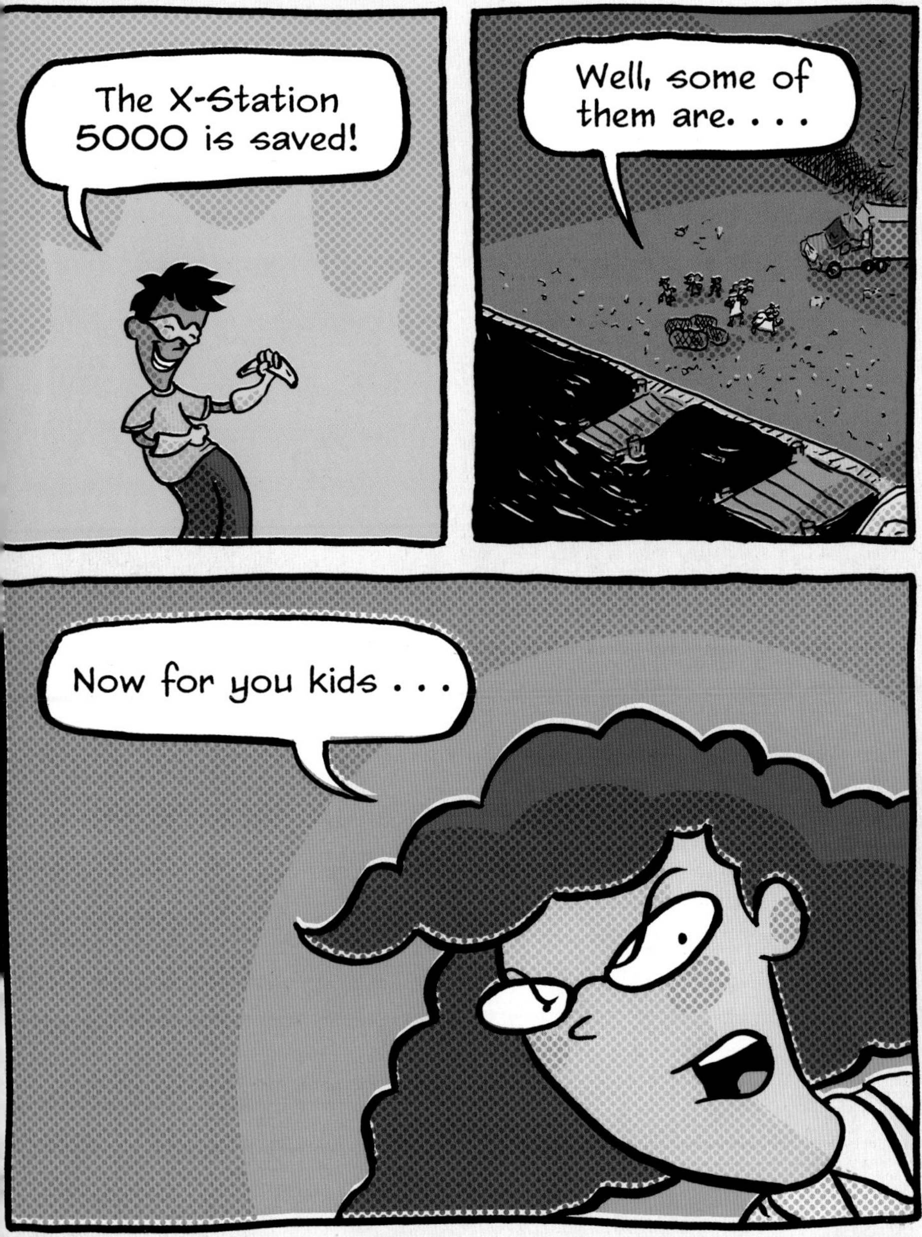
The X-Station 5000 is saved!
Well, some of them are. . . .
Now for you kids . . .

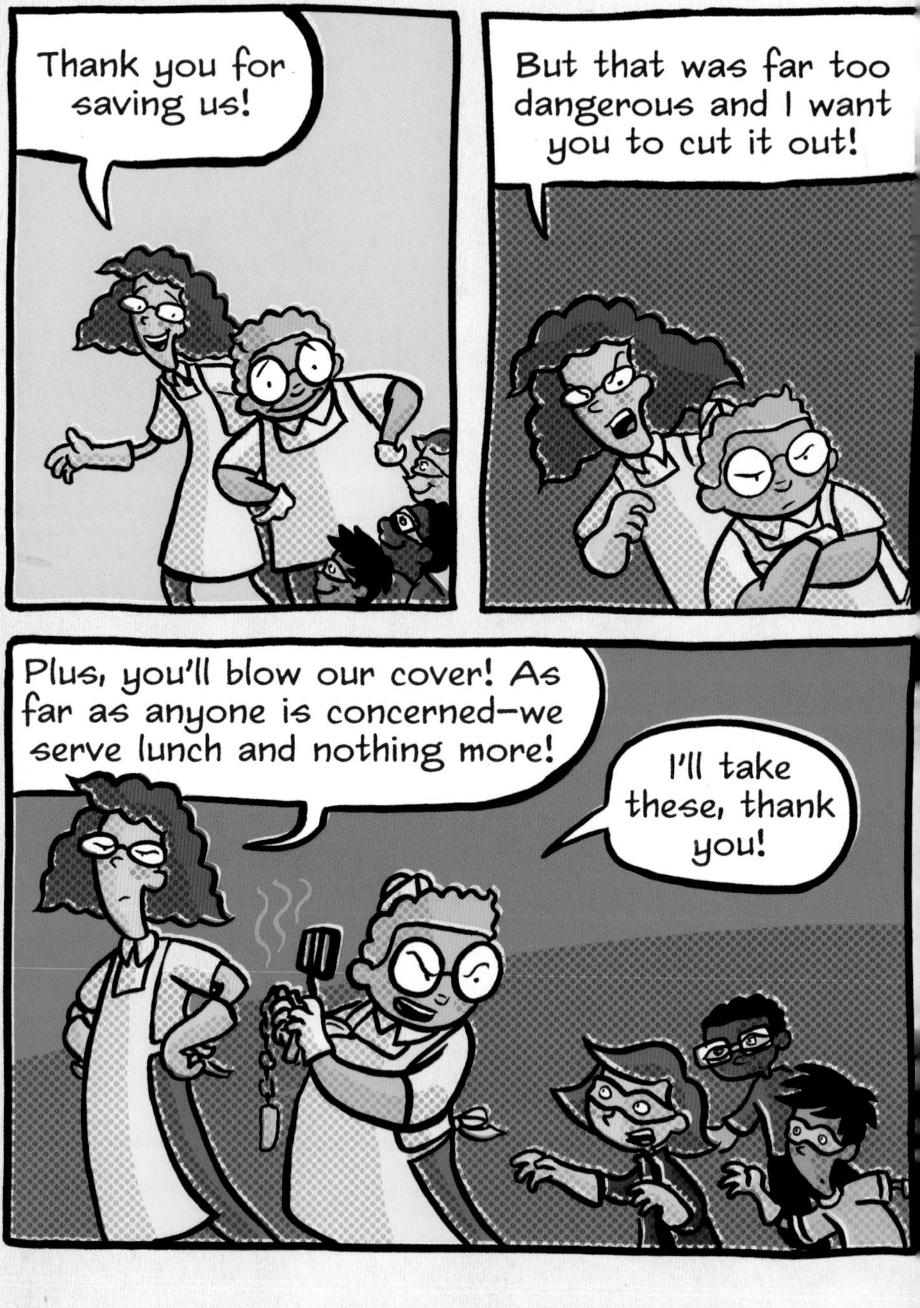
Thank you for saving us!
But that was far too dangerous and I want you to cut it out!
Plus, you'll blow our cover! As far as anyone is concerned—we serve lunch and nothing more!
I'll take these, thank you!

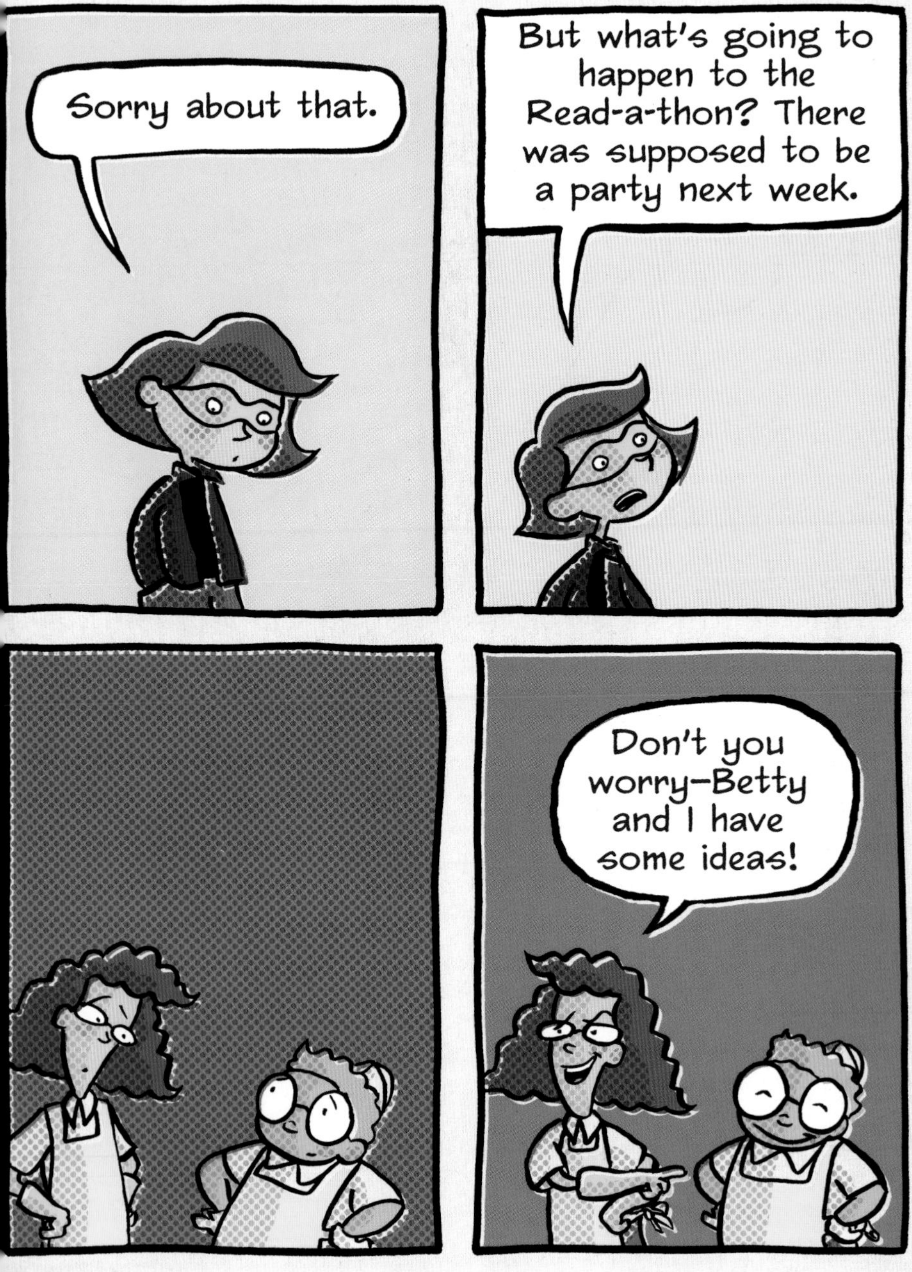
Sorry about that.
But what's going to happen to the Read-a-thon? There was supposed to be a party next week.
Don't you worry—Betty and I have some ideas!

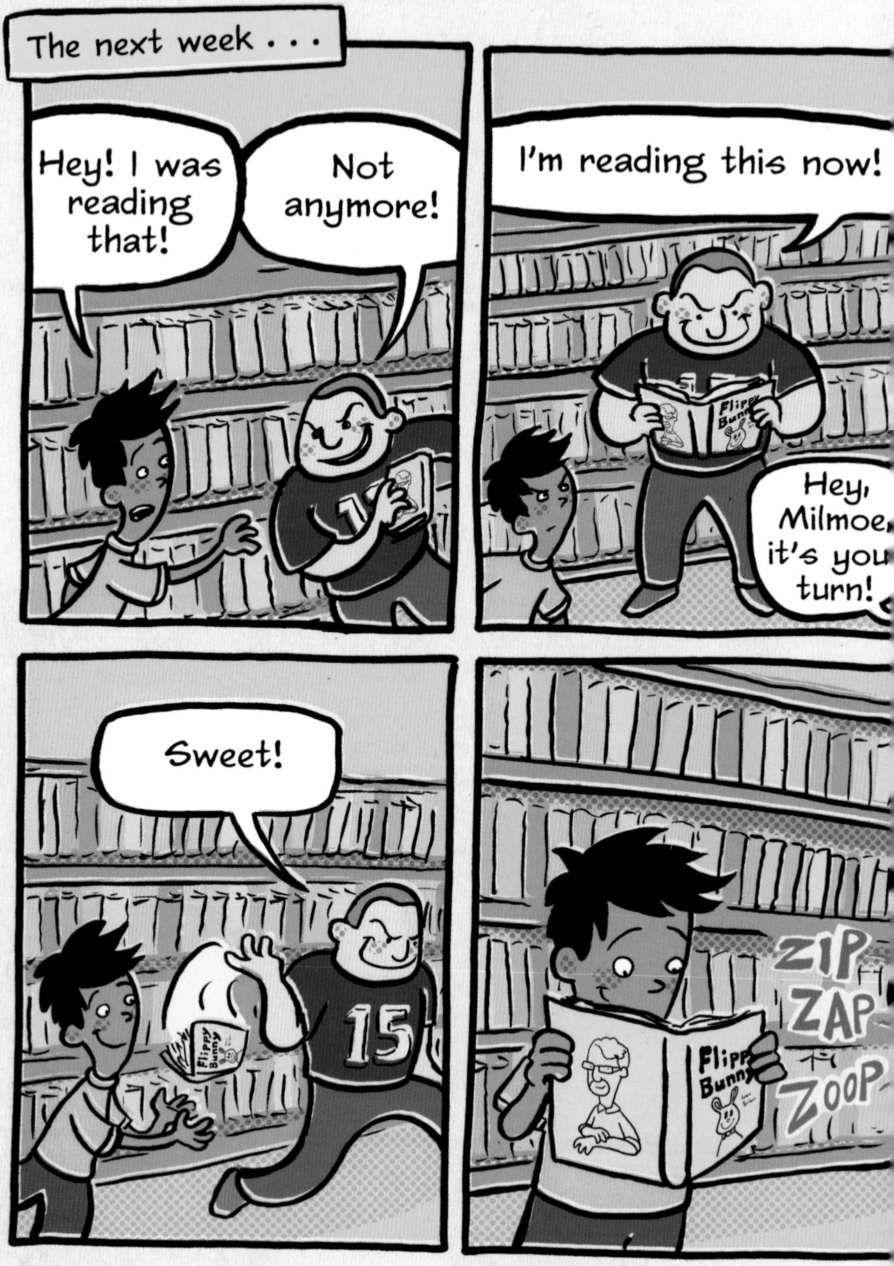
The next week . . .
Hey! I was reading that!
Not anymore!
I'm reading this now!
Hey, Milmoe, it's you turn!
Sweet!
Flippy Bunny
ZIP ZAP ZOOP

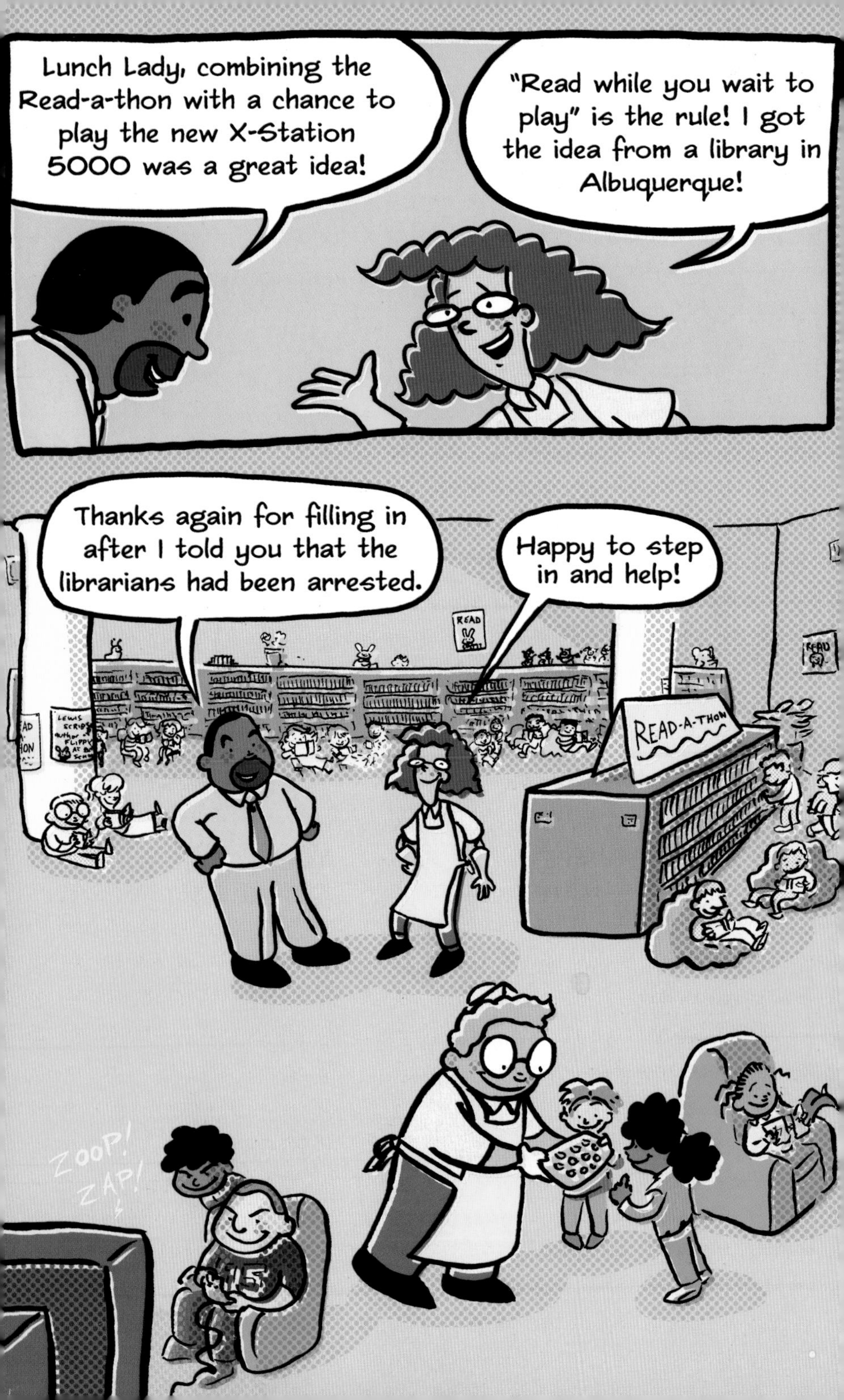
Lunch Lady, combining the Read-a-thon with a chance to play the new X-Station 5000 was a great idea!
"Read while you wait to play" is the rule! I got the idea from a library in Albuquerque!
Thanks again for filling in after I told you that the librarians had been arrested.
Happy to step in and help!
READ
READ-A-THON
ZOOP! ZAP!

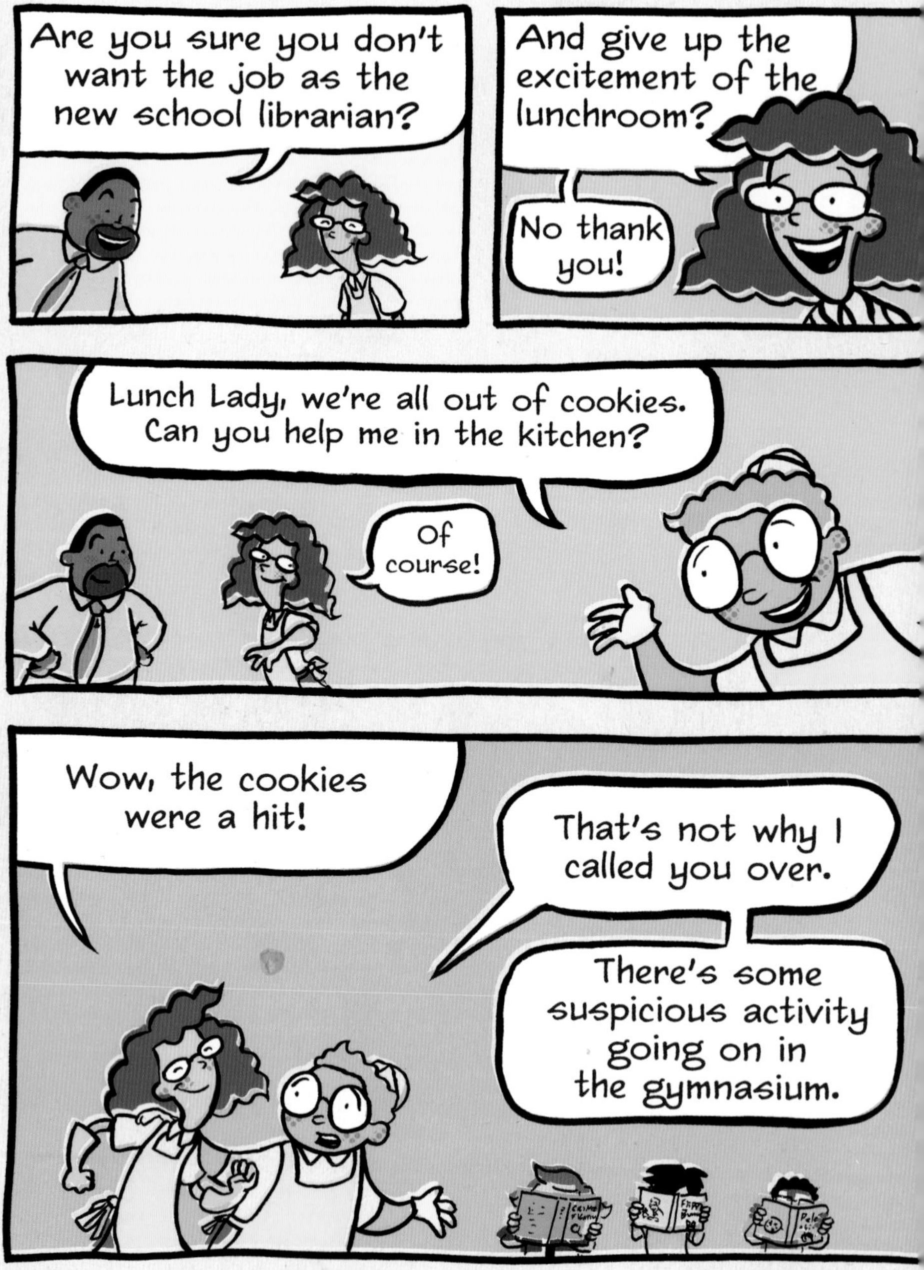
Are you sure you don't want the job as the new school librarian?
And give up the excitement of the lunchroom?
No thank you!
Lunch Lady, we're all out of cookies. Can you help me in the kitchen?
Of course!
Wow, the cookies were a hit!
That's not why I called you over.
There's some suspicious activity going on in the gymnasium.

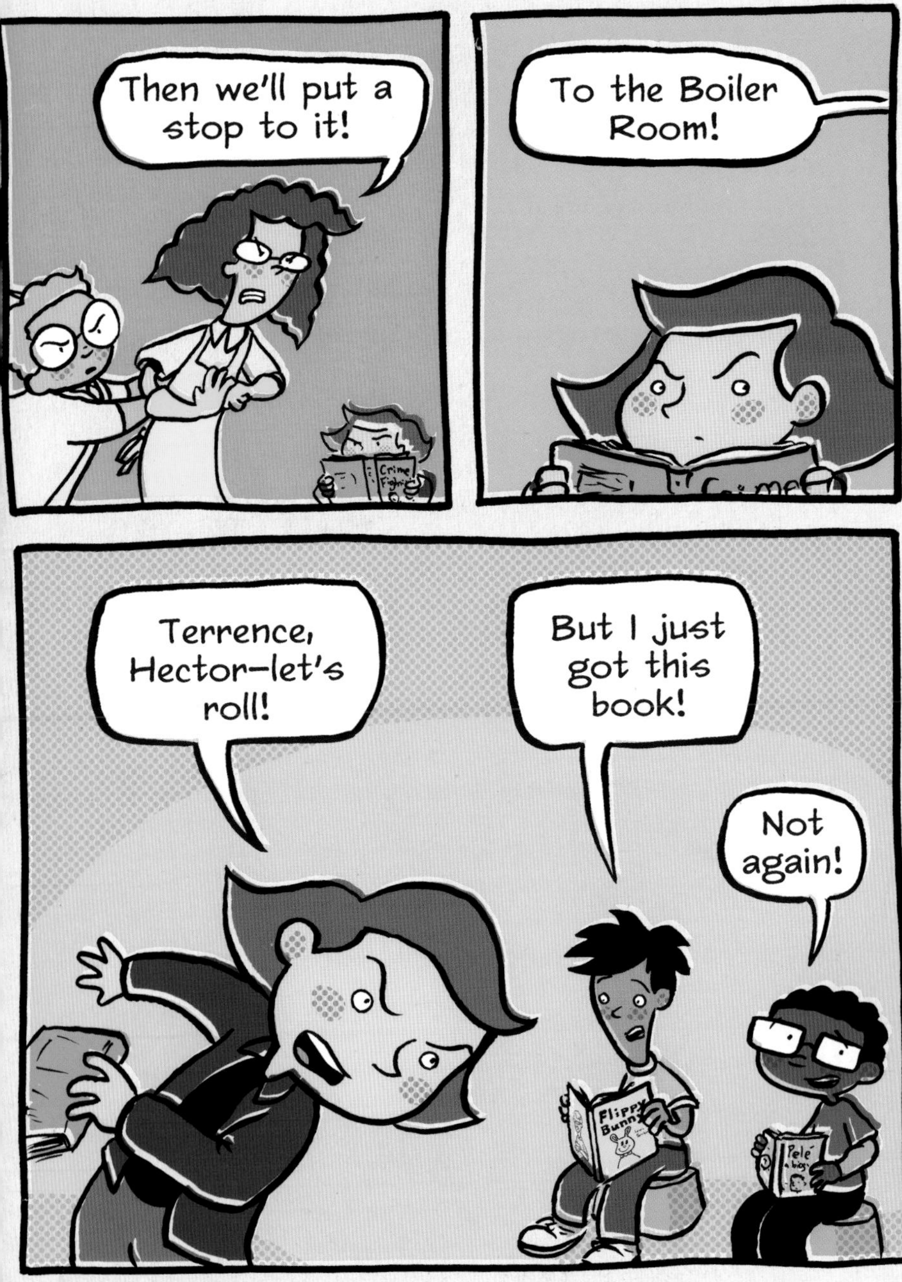
Then we'll put a stop to it!
To the Boiler Room!
Terrence, Hector—let's roll!
But I just got this book!
Not again!
Flippy Bunny
Pelé a bio

HOW A CHANCE ENCOUNTER AT THE LUNCH COUNTER LED TO *THE LUNCH LADY*

When my very first book, *Good Night, Monkey Boy,* was published in 2001, I returned to Gates Lane Elementary, the school I attended as a kid in Worcester, Massachusetts, to talk to the students about writing and illustrating. While I was there, I ran into Jeanne, the beloved lunch lady who fed the students back when *I* was a student. She told me what she had been up to and about all of her grandchildren. I was startled. My lunch lady had a life outside of school?! She didn't live in the kitchen with the tater tots?! This got me to thinking: What would lunch ladies do when they weren't cooking lunch? It was a lightning-

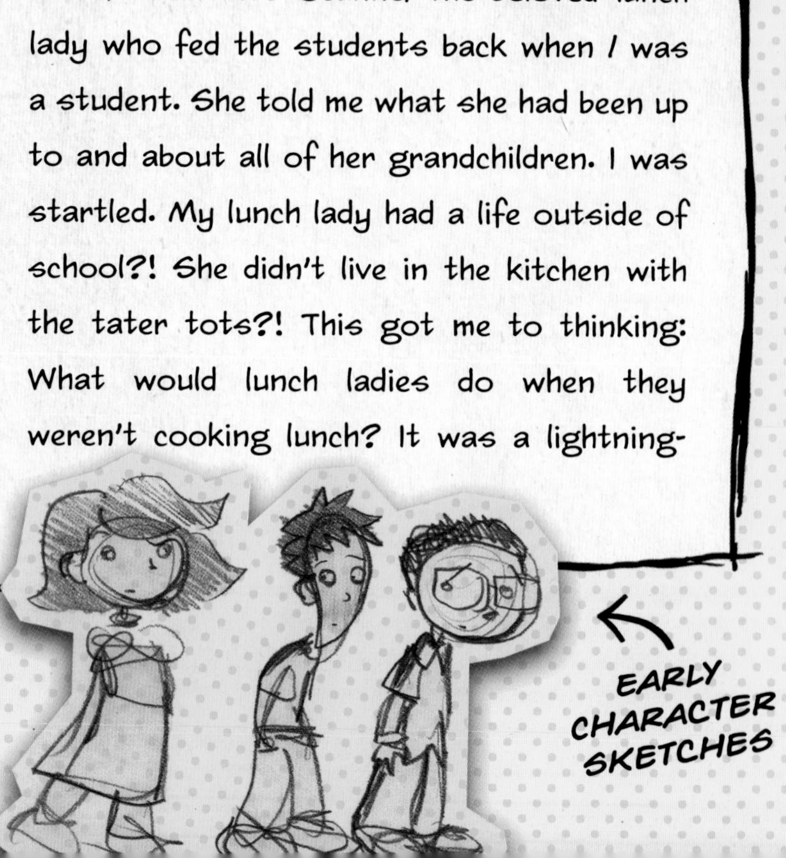
EARLY CHARACTER SKETCHES

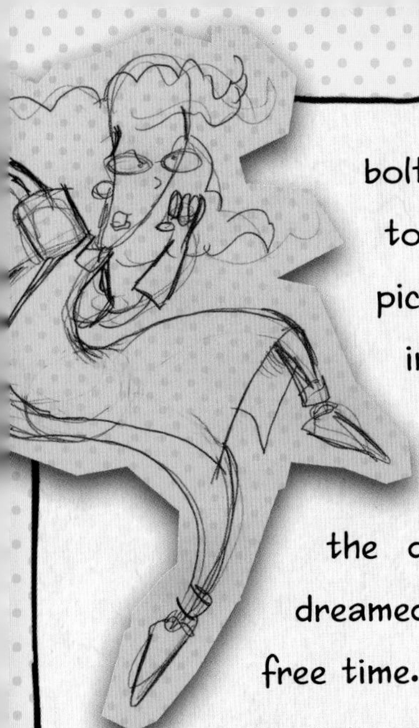

bolt moment that inspired me to sit down and write . . . a picture book. Yes, the first incarnation of Lunch Lady was a much shorter book, and it was more about the different activities the kids dreamed up for their lunch lady's free time. I became obsessed with that one concept, and the book took a very different turn. What if the mild-mannered lunch lady was secretly a crime-fighting spy? After a failed attempt at a Lunch Lady chapter book, I wrote a pitch for Lunch Lady as an animated cartoon, but then that didn't go anywhere either. Still, this creative process, which often travels along a zigzag path and not a straight line, helped me flesh out Lunch Lady's world. I invented all of the gadgets that she would use and realized she needed an assistant. And there most certainly should be some young characters for

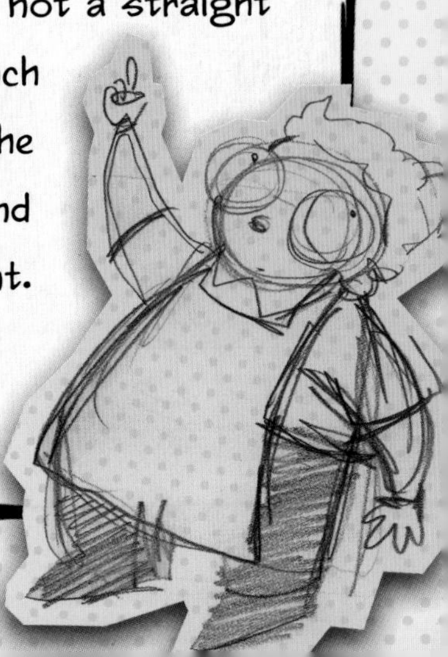

my readers to relate to. I was soon invited to be a part of an anthology where we were asked to make connections with the works we had written as kids. For this compilation, I reillustrated a comic that I drew as a kid. I fell back in love with comics, a format I had spent my entire childhood and adolescence working in. And I realized that this would be the ideal book format for my story about a crime-

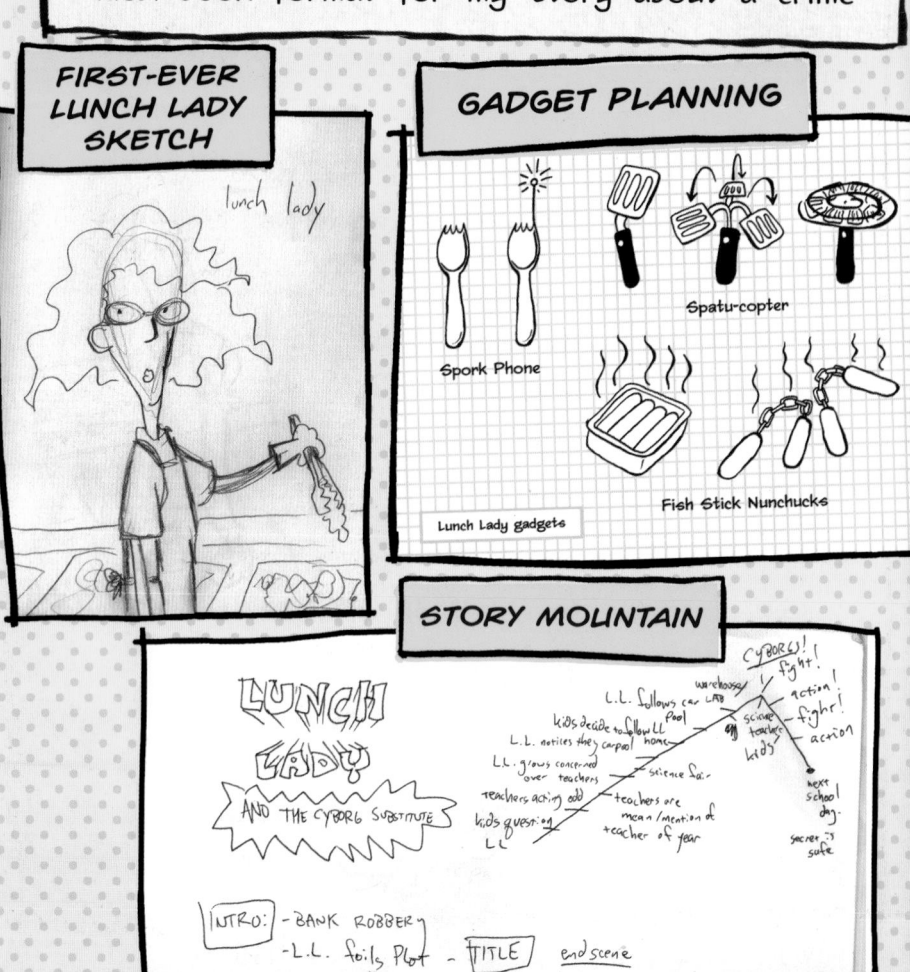

FIRST-EVER LUNCH LADY SKETCH

lunch lady

GADGET PLANNING

Spork Phone

Spatu-copter

Lunch Lady gadgets

Fish Stick Nunchucks

STORY MOUNTAIN

LUNCH LADY AND THE CYBORG SUBSTITUTE

CYBORG! fight!
warehouse
L.L. follows car LAB   action!
kids decide to follow LL pool   fight!
L.L. notices they carpool home   science   action
L.L. grows concerned   teacher
over teachers   science fair   kids
teachers acting odd   next
teachers are   school
kids question   mean / invention of   day
LL   teacher of year   secret is
                            safe

INTRO: - BANK ROBBERY
- L.L. foils plot - TITLE end scene

fighting cafeteria worker. I first submitted Lunch Lady as a graphic novel in 2005. But back then, graphic novels for young readers weren't quite a "thing" yet. Nonetheless, my editor, Michelle Frey, and the team at Knopf Books for Young Readers took this project of mine on, and the first two Lunch Lady books were published on July 28, 2009. Since then, I have traveled the country a dozen times over, visiting schools, libraries, and bookstores. And since I hung up the yellow gloves in 2014, a question that I get at least once a week is *When is the next Lunch Lady book coming out?* Well, LL #11 is on the horizon, but in the meantime, I am so thrilled to have revisited this world through the colorized omnibus edition of *Lunch Lady and the Cyborg Substitute* and *Lunch Lady and the League of Librarians*!

JARRETT J. KROSOCZKA is the *New York Times* bestselling author-illustrator behind dozens of books for young readers. These include the wildly popular Lunch Lady graphic novel series, select volumes of the Star Wars™: Jedi Academy series, the young adult memoir *Hey, Kiddo,* which was a National Book Award finalist, and picture-book favorites such as *Punk Farm.* Realizing that his books can inspire young readers beyond the page, Jarrett founded School Lunch Hero Day, a national campaign that celebrates school lunch staff. He lives in Western Massachusetts with his family . . . a crew that includes pugs Ralph and Frank and a French bulldog named Bella Carmella. Find out lots more about Jarrett and Lunch Lady—and check out some cool activities—at studiojjk.com.

UNTIL NEXT TIME . . .

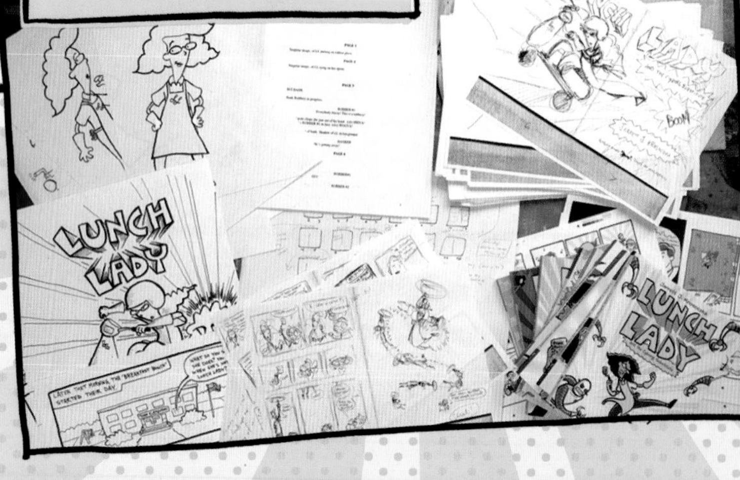
LUNCH LADY
LUNCH LADY
LUNCH LADY
BOOM